KU-008-062

THE RAT CATCHER

ALEXANDER TEREKHOV

Translated by Natalie Roy and B.T. Gall

ALMA BOOKS

"*Svetloyar is a small lake in the woods of the Nizhny Novgorod region. According to an old folk legend, the town of Kitezh resisted the invasion of Batu Khan by submerging itself under the lake. In the popular imagination, Kitezh has remained unchanged underwater, with all its houses, churches and people intact. And if you are pure of heart, you will get a message from Kitezh: you will see at the lake's bottom the church domes, and hear its bells ringing, but the sinners will see Kitezh as just woods and wasteland, and this will continue until the end of times, until the Second Coming.*"

From an old guide book

1

Two Toilets for Two Branches of Power

16 Days to D-Day – 27th August 1992, Early Morning

"Been slobbering into your pillow, have you?" I'd woken Oldie up with my telephone call. "You can get the money tomorrow and pay for the basement."

"So what's happened at those two flats?"

"The bloke who said his genitals were gnawed by rats... he's registered at a psychiatric clinic. I've got a certificate. At the other flat, the girl's bed creaked and she was telling her mother: 'Must be rats.' If only you'd seen her arse... you wouldn't have slept a wink."

Then I dropped off. Right there in the basement. The basement we had rented as an office, struggling as we were to make ends meet on small orders.

For millions of years brown and black rats teemed synanthropically in the rice paddies of China, blocked in by the Himalayas, deserts, jungles and ice, in the vile place from which they finally came to us, horde after horde.

As human beings migrated in search of gold, the glaciers melted away and opened up passes, and... with one bound the hordes broke out! They skirted round the Himalayas and headed north, to Korea and Manchuria, and pushed south, towards the allure of India. The East rolled over without even lifting its head up. The first creature to come and congratulate the Buddha on the New Year was a rat – and this rat was actually worshipped as a symbol of joy and prosperity!

Europe suffered grievously from the twelfth century onwards, and struggled to come to terms with the problem – after all, no rats were thought to have lived in Golden Hellas… But in fact black rats, the inhabitants of ships and garrets, had oppressed Ancient Egypt to such a degree that the killing of a cat, even if accidental, was punishable by death. As for our beloved Ancient Greece and Rome, they were saved by one thing – no mention of rats. They called them all "mice"… to think that we admired their cleanliness – idiots! But excavations have made clear precisely what kind of creature Aristotle was describing: "It is conceived and born from the dirt on board ship, it is engendered through the licking of salt." This was the creature that Diogenes upbraided for its carnal appetites, that Cicero blamed for chewing up his sandals.

The gods – including Apollo, the god of these "mice" – destroyed the Titans so totally that the giants lurched, fell over and the earth cracked. It was then that these creatures, the rats, came spouting out of the dark cracks – shlop, shlop, shlop.

And they surrounded the human race.

"The mountain has brought forth a mouse." What a devilish ploy: the most wretched piece of news is rinsed clean with a meaningless proverb, with no indication as to what the mountain and the mouse really are.

There are no windows in the basement. The darkness comes to an end when Oldie turns the light on. He pokes the key into the lock, picking up from the floor the sign that has fallen off the door: "RAT Co-op". I didn't get a good night's sleep. Oldie, the bastard… couldn't he have dragged himself along a little later?

* * *

Everybody gets his deserts. The bloke who brought the apples of paradise for his beloved ended up seeing claws sink into her fair white neck. So in the trail of their black relatives followed the brown rats – the triumphant victors! They strode along with the Arabs into the Gulf of Persia, across the Red Sea, while the Crusaders carried them further beyond Palestine, and together with pearls and spices the vessels of Venice delivered plague-riddled rats to Europe. In the fifteenth century the Church put a curse on them. But it was too late. The bones of a brown rat were dug up in the palace of the Shirvanshah in Baku.

The brown rats began to gnaw at old Russia. The convicts of the Solovki Monastery paid with their ears and noses for the free trade in Pskov and Novgorod, when the rats arrived with Peter the Great. In 1727 an earthquake in the Karakum Desert hurled a whole mass of brown rats at Astrakhan: the pincers were closing in.

In 1732 England got its retribution with a vessel from East India.

In 1753 Paris yielded, and seventeen years later the paupers were gobbling up rats during the Siege of Paris. The meat tasted like coypu.

In 1775 America capitulated.

In 1780, Germany.

When Russians arrived in the Aleutian Islands, the place was teeming with rats, so they called them the "Rat Islands".

In 1809 Switzerland fell.

Oldie walks around sneezing, the bastard. He sticks a carton of milk and a small loaf under my nose, and rummages about for something else in his bag. He's the boss, so he takes the table. I have a folding bed and sleep with my legs drawn up.

* * *

The rats moved on: they marked the end of the nineteenth century by taking Tyumen, Tobolsk, Yevpatoriya. The Russo-Japanese War rewarded them with Omsk and Tomsk, and by 1912 they had occupied the Trans-Siberian Railway.

The First World War kept rats, both black and brown, well fed with human flesh: Europe was vanquished. The Second World War glorified the rats' victories on the Volkhov Front and in besieged Leningrad: they warmed themselves in children's beds and inhabited the front lines of the defence. The evacuation carried them in all directions. In 1943 the brown rat entered Frunze by train.

"That's enough jerking your legs about," says Oldie, "enough sleeping. I've paid for the basement!"

I used to laugh in my cradle at my mother's funny words. Soviet Muslims learnt to eat pork: they received pig farms and everything else into the bargain. To the last pure places the rats were transported by goods trains, virgin-land labourers, along the Georgian Military Highway, in the Baltic hay conveyed to the Volga Region, Canadian wheat to Yakutia, potatoes from Northern Kazakhstan to Almaty. Everything.

From the fifteen-hundred-metre heights of the Carpathians to the submarines at Vladivostok – one word the world over: rats.

When a person devotes himself to one thing, he succeeds. But with this "one thing" he acquires something else. The "one thing" is of various kinds, but the end result is the same: it has ears and an icicle-like tail. I grew up when the rats were already in my home town.

* * *

I made a hole in the milk carton and nibbled at the loaf.

A grey-haired, thickset man in a business suit dropped in on us, scratching his neck as he walked, and fished a classifieds newspaper out of his jacket.

"Look, here's…"

It was me who'd put the ad in:

Annihilation of Rats in any Region of the Earth

Unparalleled opportunity. Prices lower than the international competition. We have rid the Vendôme Islands, Thüringen and the public toilets in Geneva (three hundred sitting places!) of rats. Laureate of the Swedish Academy – the "RAT Co-op"!

How to get there: Medvedkovo Underground Station, then bus No. 661 to the Municipal Vocational School stop. Cross over and go along the concrete wall to the gap. Cross to the motor depot of the flour mill. Ask for the building of the Society for the Blind. It's the first entrance in the basement, sixth door to the left. Tel. 431-60-31, from 10 p.m. to midnight. Ask for Vladimir or Larisa.

"That's all correct," said Oldie. "Draw up a chair."

The man's eyes fell on the vests and socks spread out over the radiator, and he looked at my swollen face.

Oldie introduced himself: "Master of Sciences, and senior scientific-research fellow at the Zoopsychological Laboratory of Moscow University. And this is a graduate student of the Severtsev Institute of Evolutionary Morphology."

On hearing these unknown words the fellow took a seat and said in plain terms: "You can make a fortune, my friend."

"We could – if we've got time," I responded. "We got back

11

yesterday from Stockholm. Next week, Lisbon. We neck a beer, and we're on the move again." I got up. "What kind of building is it? You're not paying in foreign currency, by any chance?"

The fellow spread a map out over the table. Oldie rested his elbows on it, scenting loot.

"Svetloyar Town – formerly known as Yagoda – in the Tambov Region. I'm the big cheese, the Mayor." He scratched his knee. "There's a hotel there, The Don, twenty-five storeys, with a cinema-concert hall – that'll be your job."

"The Don?" repeated Oldie.

"We've renamed the hotel. In honour of a certain event... You see, on the twelfth of September we're having a ceremonial unveiling of the source of the River Don."

Oldie ran his finger over the map.

"So that's where it is?"

The fellow sighed deeply, his low forehead wrinkling.

"This is not for the press, absolutely not. But there's an idea knocking about in Moscow of linking us to the 'Golden Ring', where they take foreign tourists: an old town where the Don starts, the struggle for liberty, a historic river and all that kind of stuff. We didn't even know about this project – we're not that old... a new build from Stalin's time. But our deputy to the Supreme Soviet is on the Committee for Culture. And he's arranged this whole thing. It'd be good to have foreigners around: we've got this distillery. So we've got on with it. The problem is, not even scientists know where the real source is – three different regions are quarrelling over it... We're laying a pipe to the Don – *that* will be the source... We got burial mounds from the Ukraine, from the Black Sea region... demonstration digs, swords collected from museums..."

"What about the name?"

"We've invited some historians, and we're feeding the idea to the press that Yagoda wasn't named after Stalin's executioner after all, but was founded by Prince Yury Dolgoruky, on the spot where a nun he knew lived, or in a place where the yagé plant grew."

"You've got yagé plants there?" I said, amused.

The fellow gave a further sigh.

"We're transplanting them, from the Tropics. That's my job. Our deputy overdid it a bit, he declared at the Ministry of Culture that we're unveiling this source, and inaugurating the festival, the town's thousandth anniversary, which just happens to coincide with the visit of the UN Secretary General. So now this Asian fellow is coming. And our own President. The television will be there too and... they'll have my blood. The rat situation is just awful – it's a meat-processing plant, you understand. We need this hall. Your job will be only the hotel's banquet hall. Will you do it?" He scratched his cheek, and we exchanged glances. "My name's Ivan Trofimovich. I won't be watching the pennies."

He touched his briefcase, and I sidled off for glasses.

"Well, in that case there's very little time left. So, well then... for this rush job, plus the hall, basement, loft, communication passageways, lawns, every storey and lifts..." Ivan Trofimovich opened the vodka bottle, Oldie totted up figures on a paper napkin, and I blurted out: "Sixteen thousand four hundred US dollars. Plus board and lodging."

Everybody was stunned. All three of us froze and listened to the prolonged rumbling in my belly. It was time to sleep, and we hadn't eaten yet.

"No. Far too expensive." The chap got up and mumbled through colourless lips. "I'll go to the State Health Service."

"You can try." I pushed Oldie's hand, which jerked to erase a zero from the declared figure. "They'll say: 'We don't have enough staff or poison.' You won't clean up a building like that in two

13

weeks, not for any money. You'll just lose another day. And then we won't be able to take up the job any more. If you're itching from rat-borne ticks, it's obvious that in your town you must have tularaemia and leptospirosis. Just imagine if some idiot writes to the State Health Inspector, or straight to the President?"

I rinsed my mouth with some milk.

Oldie took the scowling Mayor by the arm.

"Ivan Trofimovich," he whispered under the man's hat, as if addressing a child, "who's gonna help you? Nobody's gonna help you. You'll get mixed up with a bunch of con men, you'll sign a contract for 98% rat extermination. They'll show you five dead ones and off they'll go. And the rest of the population? It'll still be there. In another month they'll be jumping all over your jacket. But we can *really* exterminate them – get them down to virtually zero. We're the best in the country – ask anybody. They'll whack up a bust of you in your neighbourhood."

"There's one already." And the fellow crumpled.

We drained our glasses.

"If you like," exclaimed Oldie, "we'll clean the whole town out. Within three months! What if the UN guy wants to visit your bathhouse?!"

"They don't bathe, I reckon. They sent me his picture – looks like a gypsy. The town is to be cleaned by the locals, with folk remedies. We've got this new cooperative, 'Rat King' – that's the name."

I burst out laughing: "And why can't *they* sort the hotel out?"

Oldie, handing a glass over to the chap, shoved his elbow into my nose.

The Mayor of Svetloyar answered firmly:

"They won't take on the hotel. Nobody will. Before you, I went round to see everybody, both the private cooperatives and state institutions. Everybody refused. A dead end."

"Why?" I asked cautiously.

"My friend – it's a real mess. We've got used to the rats, they've become established. We just scatter some sausages in our basements and they stay down there. Everyone feeds his own rats in his own house. But in the hotel – they actually tumble down from the ceiling. And run into chinks in the wall. Even by day. Right onto the table. Even onto your head. It's happened to me – on my head." He took off his hat. "A baby rat. Right there." His eyes glittered tearfully. "We don't need them reduced to your 'virtual zero'. Let them run around. As long as they don't come falling down on just that one day!"

"Do they fall from the upper storey?" Oldie wanted to make sure.

"There *are* no more storeys above the banquet hall!"

"Do they get onto the roof from the basement?"

"There aren't any in the basement either. The hotel's the cleanest place in the town. They only fall from the ceiling. And you're trying to fleece me for treating each floor?"

"We'll find them on every floor if they're falling down. You're simply not seeing them," snarled Oldie, and he winked at me – but I was lost in thought.

Oldie poked around in the table for blank contract forms, and on his lips swelled the golden word "advance". Meanwhile, with a light heart I went out into the yard and lay down on a bench under the apple tree with a white-washed trunk. Admiring the iron-plated door of the "Used Glassware" establishment I breathed in the last of August – summer was over.

"I'm telling you; they're only to the south of Lenin Street. Where the authorities live, and where the office buildings are. Why don't they go north, into people's houses?" Ivan Trofimovich stood over my head in front of the road as if praying.

"That's typical. Pallas – there was a scientist of that name – journeyed around Russia in the eighteenth century, and also

15

remarked that in Siberian towns rats were only to be found on the south side of the main road. They don't like crossing roads."

"No, I don't think it's so simple. They want to get at me. What d'you think? In the evenings I'm afraid. I don't go out alone. My wife cooks up meat with onions and puts it down in the entrance at night-times, so they won't go up the stairs to our door. I say to my wife, let's go downstairs at night, look down the hatch at them feasting... Revolting."

"Sound like they are having a good time," I yawned and sat up.

He flattened his grey hair, evenly combed back, and muttered:

"Have you heard, perhaps, that there's some kind of rat disease?"

"My old granny told me so."

"Well?"

"Well what? She said that if you kill a rat – well then, you'll die. You'll wither up. But that's just... Don't think about it. A man doesn't die of diseases."

"Of what then?"

"He dies of death."

Ivan Trofimovich tipped his hat and headed off with heavy steps. Look at the car waiting for him! And a chauffeur holding the door open. He glanced around:

"And what's the cure? Didn't your grandmother say?"

"Herbs. Blackcurrant, celandine... especially the 'dog's tongue'. Alternatively, you should fall in love."

"Fall in love?"

"That's right. But seriously. And go right through with it. *Can* you go right through with it?"

Ivan Trofimovich blushed.

"Sometimes." Then he shouted from the car: "What about alcohol?"

"No. Absolutely not! They're drawn to it!"

Oldie was lying with his cheek on a wad of green money and shouting down the telephone:

"No! I'm not drunk! Larisa, we're going away!"

Oldie touched the sugar-white curtains, and clicked the light on – it worked! He leapt up on his soft bunk and bitterly acknowledged:

"I've never travelled first class before. Write on my grave: 'He never travelled first class'."

He produced a paper bag smelling of sausage out of his holdall.

I was moved and asked: "And when they bury me – please bang into the marble: 'He died without having his fill of cherry compote'."

Oldie got embarrassed and drew the compote out – there's a married man for you... The train steamed ahead. I glanced out into the corridor. By one toilet the gloomy Ivan Trofimovich was waiting his turn. By the other, at the opposite end, stood a balding, lanky character with bluish cheeks. Other passengers were stuffing themselves or rustling their bed sheets.

Down the carriage, a female attendant was forcing her way sideways; she was wearing a man's shirt with shoulder straps, which scarcely contained her ample bosom as she thrust it into each compartment in turn, like the giant eyes of a blind fish.

"Come and sit with us, Tanechka," I whispered, as my nose bumped into the middle of her shirt. "We love women in uniform. And we love them in black skirts. Beautiful legs remind us of an interesting book – you want to dive in straight away, and see what happens next!"

Tanya laughed, glanced at her knees, as big as Oldie's head, and took a bite out of our cucumber.

"Let me do your pocket up. We're travelling down to your area. We're rat exterminators. We're going to save the source of Russian freedom from rats."

"A-ha! So you're the ones charging us millions! You're fine fellows, but... what do we need you for? There's no money to finish building the bathhouse. Our bosses locked horns over you. They won't even have a cup of tea together. I've even had to open both toilets for them. They refused to use the same one. The Mayor's on the left, the Governor's on the right. So I'll have to wash both toilets."

I leant out into the corridor again. The blue-cheeked character must be the Governor. Two strongly built toadies were reading documents to him.

By now the train was travelling through the night. I pulled the leather blind down on the moon, which resembled a fish scale polished to a silver scintillation by the dishevelled strips of forest flicking by.

"We'll be happy in this town. We'll rest and have a high old time," Oldie said with a smile. "There's a meat-processing factory there. At meat factories they have sausage departments. We'll have all sorts of sausages: hunter's and Brunswick and liverwurst. My God, how long I have lived! How much I remember! At dawn we'll go to the river. Why do you say 'Forget it!'? Let's be young. I've got so many miles on my clock, yet I've never flown in a plane. This is my first time in a sleeping compartment. But I've travelled in a refrigerator car, in the post-and-luggage carriage, in the kitchen of the restaurant car, in the gap between carriages, on the luggage rack, under a table, on the floor, in a toilet... and in the attendant's compartment!"

Oldie prattled on while I followed his good example and went... to the attendant's compartment. Tanya was filling out a form to write off a bloodstained sheet, but within five minutes was roaring with laughter and dropping tears over the paper; then I moved to close the door so that no passengers would stick their snouts in, and remarked that it was hot, wasn't it, as I set to work on the various buttons and the zip – which was, as I expected, on the right-hand side... This explains why, three hours later, I was the one heating up the carriage stove with coal, holding the little yellow flag to give the signal for departure, and shoving in with a knee to the chest some hefty lad with a bandaged-up eye. At the Zhdanka station a crowd of relatives had lifted him three times onto the upper step with a sack of potatoes, supplicating in chorus: "Please, sonny-boy!"

Another sonny-boy, with a forehead as wide as a bus, was moping on the platform – there were no places – rubbing away cold from his pudgy elbows. I nudged him lightly:

"Third compartment. There's room. Off you go."

Then I returned, took my shoes off – and really let rip!

2

Un-Russian Victor

15 Days to D-Day

Oldie was chastely tucked up under the sheet, his astonished eyes fixed on the boy I'd done a favour to.

"Calm down, it's not me. This is Vic, a boy from Svetloyar, the town we're going to," I explained. "He's just finished at the Ryazan Medical Institute. He's going home for a break. And here's tea. At least one of you bastards could say thank you."

"Thanks." Vic's voice was so booming that it sounded impolite.

"Now, this is what I've found out. There's a governor, a Democrat, his name's Shestakov. He was a vet, but then was sacked, allegedly for telling the truth. He drank. The locals, the 'Rat King' co-op, are kind of his lapdogs. It bugs him that they can't sort this ceiling out... He begrudges us the money. He doesn't like Ivan Trofimovich. He doesn't like Muscovites. He wants to go to Moscow."

They sipped tea and, with customary morning doziness, turned their noses towards the window – beyond, low whitened fences alternated with yellow structures with the words "Gents" and "Ladies" in red, one-storey stations, small barns covered in chicken feathers, fallen apples on grey roofs – and all this was then replaced by orchards, pathways, crossroads with tumbledown, rusted ploughs and jumping crows; from time to time a creek dived under the railroad and fishing rods stuck from under the willows, with a heavy flotilla of geese sailing past.

"Oldie," I said, suppressing an exhausted yawn, "those pig-headed fools keep saying there are rats in the ceiling. The basement's clear. Of course, I know, that's impossible. But doesn't this ceiling bother you at all?"

"Sonny," smirked Oldie, "Son-ny!"

"Well, just look," and I fixed my eyes on the boy.

"What's your patronymic?"

"Alexeyevich." I hate clodhoppers with smooth fizzogs without bruises, pimples, moles, birthmarks or bristles. A well-groomed boy he was. A bit on the flabby side, tow-haired, with a thin nose, handsome. He'd already washed, combed his hair and splashed scent around.

He opened a packet of cigarettes. "Help yourselves."

To my regretful "No thanks" Oldie drew eight of them out with two fingers and said, after the young man left:

"He's been reading all morning. Interesting chap. If he wasn't reading, he'd be talking. He rolled up the bedding, paid for it, and didn't lie down again. He'd only glance out of the window to make out the station names. His eyes aren't thoughtful at all. Why did you latch on to him? People like that frighten me."

"Hey, is anybody there?" But in the corridor I only saw emptiness, and so I rushed to knock at the toilet with a stentorian:

"Can you hear? Is anybody there?"

I repeated it three times, banging with my fists.

The bolt clattered guiltily, and out of the toilet stepped Governor Shestakov, biting his lip; behind him emerged the two toadies, one holding a jacket, the other a razor.

The Governor removed his teeth from his lips and his cheeks quivered, as if he were sucking his mother's breast:

"How dare you! You whelp! You money-grubber!"

* * *

"Your target is sticking out over there," Ivan Trofimovich said, pointing out the hotel. I didn't even turn round, I was going to sleep.

"We'd rather stay some distance away from work; you've got to understand us… rats are vengeful…" Oldie was trying to give him a fright.

They dropped us off at a sanatorium for pregnant women on a round hill, where a ward was hastily cleared for us. The pregnant women packed up their belongings, trundled out the bedsteads and carried their bellies away. Ivan Trofimovich said: "There's a toilet across the corridor, the carpenter will put up a hook tomorrow, in the meantime you can attach a belt to the handle and keep the door closed that way." He whispered something to the policeman, who had arrived on a motorcycle that sputtered obscenely, and pointed out our windows to him. I collapsed on an uncovered mattress, gazing at the button labelled: "Nurse". I wish there had been a button for getting Oldie out of the ward. What the hell was I doing here? And I dropped off.

What was that? Oldie had raised the head of the bed with a screeching lever, so I woke up and did likewise. We were lying with our feet towards the window, like pregnant women resting, warming our bellies with our hands and looking down from the hill, laid out before us in the setting sun, the wind waving the washed-out curtains and treating us to the warm scent of this unknown land.

The town had oozed into my life, blending with my drowsiness, and was tormenting me with its pitiful buildings to the left and right of the main street and its stark contrast with the rosy light of the sky.

Further from the centre, the town became more reticent. On the outskirts bald roofs stuck out in rows and pairs, with thinly spaced hairs of aerials. The five-storey blocks from Nikita Krushchev's time lay like loaves of bread, grubby-white, speckled with green buildings with white seams showing between the panels. Hidden behind their shoulders were constructions with paunchy little balconies put up by German prisoners of war, and barrack-like buildings constructed by our red-faced war veterans – with lopsided black sheds in the yards and swings whirling somebody's little dress without creaking, like poplar down.

Further off, gardens branched away, with dovecotes sticking up. And the rest was workshops with chimneys in iron belts and smoke.

But nearer to its heart, the square, the town grew denser and taller, abandoning its pitiful provincial bearing. The first buildings of the Communist five-year plans resembled stone letters spelling out an incantation, before turning into the mould of a dead face – a broken mask with falling-off paint and plaster. But now – as the sun streamed down and the wind stirred up the shadows on the roadsides – the mask melted, releasing a fleshy, living grimace turned up to the sky, a sick glittering of the eyes, a delirious whispering which emerged from, but did not leave, the parched idol's lips.

The high-rise blocks, girdled with ascending tiers, swelled high into the air, decreasing in diameter; they pushed upwards with glassed-in staircases, lift shafts with dark carriages like roving blood clots, concrete balconies and round spaceship windows – each bearing a slogan beneath its roof such as "War Gives Birth to Heroes". They competed with the rough-hewn mass of the hotel, which appeared to be panelled with gratings and planted into the flat roof of the conference hall.

The long blocks came to an unwilling halt, with their roofs descending in steps; they pushed into the sky blunt towers with rectangular pillars covered with weblike glass tents, unfurling the upper storeys in a spiral, as if hoping to hurl their extremity – the gaunt spires – higher into the blue skies, where other buildings raised their stars, emblems and stone figures with arms thrown aloft. Tools of indeterminate use pressed close. Round the square, brightly coloured little kids were roaming under supervision.

Some people were draining the last drops of kvas from a yellow barrel into cheerful beer mugs, serving off-duty elderly women in ink-coloured overalls – others were transplanting flower seedlings into the flower beds, turning away from the fountain sprays driven by the wind.

The black flower beds gleamed with well-watered soil, thick clumps of flowers stretched out in pink and violet furrows, curling into circles, dispersing and reuniting in a diamond shape around the blossoming white and flame-coloured bushes. Wherever you looked, could be seen the crowns of maple trees, the bushy wigs of poplars, milksops of young chestnut saplings, rowan trees, lilacs and bowed hawthorns. A water tower protruded out of a birch grove.

"This is the kind of town where you could meet my old granny," declared Oldie. "Or me. As a young man."

"Or where you could have your face smashed in."

"I'll let my beard grow here. Can you see over there – butterflies? A paradise."

"You said the same when we were working in Lyublino. But there they stole two rat traps from us – remember? There are only basements for us. As far as I'm concerned, I don't intend to spend my time in a paradise full of predatory rodents. They must have a separate paradise. And then, we can't stay in the same paradise with them, since we're the ones who'll have done them in."

"We'll make money here. It's a food-growing area, and rich. We'll clean out the factories by the winter, and in February chill out in Egypt."

"In Egypt you've got the rats of Alexandria – they're thirteen inches long. Italy is better. Or Spain. There, they only crop up once in a while."

"As soon as we've got some money, we'll rent an office on the Yaroslavl Road. We'll take on more people, have a uniform made – so it'll look great. You'll be head of the trapping operations, I'll be chief of the scientific department. You'll finish your dissertation on the garden fly. Or on ants. You'll forget what a dead rat smells like."

"I'll never forget. I'll have my own secretary."

The head doctor in a tall, barmaid-like cap rolled in a small table with a telephone. Mooring it precisely next to Oldie, she explained:

"They'll phone you any time now."

The pregnant women, sitting on the veranda in a circle, were sorting out buckwheat and singing in subdued voices:

For mine own self I am not sad:
For my green green garden I am sad…

"Look at that nice girl…"

Oldie tugged at my sleeve with such force that I missed a step and nearly fell face first into the rubbish bin.

"Hey mate," I woke up the crop-haired driver of the official car. "Who broke your rear lights? Siddown, I'm just joking. Where are you taking us?"

The driver took offence.

"To Timbuktu, mate. To headquarters, where else?"

Oldie pointed out the strip of paper pasted on lopsidedly: "Car on official duty".

"Who do you drive normally?"

The driver looked at me in his mirror, and mumbled the names of various people he'd had to convey.

"You need a Land Rover as an official car," Oldie said with an ingratiating tone. "It's a pity to waste a car like this. It's all shiny. It's got camel-wool seat covers."

The man, smiling, drove into the school sports ground, crammed full of cars and trucks, and explained:

"It's my own, guv, that's why it's shining. Everybody's been mobilized, even people with drink-driving convictions. Like a general call-up to military service, it is. Till the thirteenth. That's why I'm here driving my own car. There, they're waiting for you."

Under the signboard "Secondary School No. 18", comrades in suits were tramping around, and a six-foot-six red-headed police officer was already shouting at us:

"You from the health unit? Where're your work clothes? Go straight to the premises. There's a meeting at eighteen hundred hours. Where are your poisons? Or are you going to strangle them with your bare hands?"

They gave us the once-over.

"Where's the Mayor?"

"What's the Mayor got to do with you? He's got his own business. You're under my jurisdiction. I'm Lieutenant Colonel Baranov."

"We're hungry."

The police officer led us himself.

"In the basement café the food's decent. I'll tell them it's on us. Have some food, then straight to the meeting. You'll introduce yourselves. Here it is."

A waiter sidled up, and I told him:

"We're simple folk and eat simply. Fish soup with goose giblets. Skilly with sheep's brains. Cured fish fillet, chicken breasts. Pig's head in meat jelly will be all right. But it's got to be with horseradish sauce and garlic. I also love pies with young hare-meat filling. That'll be all."

The waiter gulped and glanced at Baranov. He ordered:

"Just give them what you have. It's not Moscow here."

I bent down and scratched a fresh mark into the gnawed chair leg with my nail. I rose and walked up and down the wall. A well-stocked vault, varnished boards, lattices, stained-glass windows depicting bunches of dark-blue grapes on vines, some kind of music. I leant on the bar counter so that I was nose to nose with a stressed-out barmaid:

"Do they pester you a lot?"

"Who?"

"The rats. We've come to poison them."

"Oh, a lot. Once I brought my cat from home. But what a cat I've got – up flies a gnat and he covers his face with his paws, he's terrified. They're worse than the fellers these days."

"Cats won't save you. In the Uzbekistan Restaurant they had thirty-eight cats, but the rats just kept on eating straight from the frying pans on the stove."

"Same here... What are you after, guys? Champagne? Do you know how much it costs? Here you are... But just what are you looking at?"

Just what? From under a radiator, for the second time now, a baby rat was peering out, its ears twitching, its vibrissae touching the cords dangling down from a sausage.

"Let me find out a bit more." I stamped my feet. And went behind the counter.

I slid apart the trays full of cakes, swept the rubbish from under the radiator and examined it. I walked through the scullery into the kitchen and climbed down into the cellar; two worried-looking girls followed me.

"Have you noticed? We've put iron panelling on all the doors."

"Rats, dear girls, don't like going through a door. Sometimes it's open, sometimes it's closed – it's sort of unreliable. Rats love their own passageways. Just look – they've gnawed a hole behind the door frame. There's one at each door."

The bolts creaked, the hinges screeched.

"Didn't you have enough of it in Moscow? Disgusting!… We'd better stay here, right Valya?"

What if they lock me up down there and never find me? Three steps welded together from thick metal rods rested on white dust. I was in my element. Shelves, pipes, central heating. And this here? It was water. I stooped down into the corners. I glanced from the lower shelf to the upper one. Crates of sour cream were all bristling with ripped foil. Pathways of sour cream spread around. The beasties had been having a high old time.

Flour, cabbage and – what's this? – rice. Tinned food. A cold store. Meat. It was turned off – the refrigeration was broken. There wasn't a single sack left intact.

In the middle of the floor some idiot had dumped two traps dating back to pre-revolutionary days. A rat, sonny, moves in the shadows. You should've put it under the pipes. I went down on my knees – and nearly died when I sensed with my hair something moving above my head. On the pipes.

I'd forgotten to look on top of the pipes.

Mustn't move a muscle. So as not to scare them. I dared not even cover my neck with my palm. It was the kind of work I like, but I hate to work when they are watching me. And I hate it when our eyes meet – they understand everything. But it's my fault now. What if the girls begin to bawl?

I was sitting with my back gone cold. I moved a trap on the floor (the hell they'll touch it now) and, as if by accident, struck the pipe with it. Over my head there was a scrabbling of many feet which rolled down into a corner and, judging from the noise, moved onto some cardboard – then on they went further off into the depths. I straightened up. For a minute I simply stood motionless.

I found the girls in a box room with a red pennant. Instead of the expected package of food rarities I saw a pudgy-faced chap dressed like a sportsman. It wasn't like old times any more!

"Well?" the girls giggled cautiously.

"Honestly, you've got to close up, girls. Even the flour is full of rat's urine. You need to lay bait, cement their burrows up. Insulate cables. Refloor the place. A complete overhaul and refurbishment. Asphalt the yard. I've not seen the rubbish bins yet. But, of course, I can carry on like this if you like – you've got a fine rat farm here. Most likely you're itching all over."

Everybody laughed. Not a trace of sadness. I showed them a brown lump in crumpled foil.

"What's this?" I asked.

"We've never seen it before. You must've brought it with you. We don't know."

"But I do know. This is chocolate, guys. I'll tell you where it's from. You squeeze out chocolate from a mould onto the 'Pigeon's Milk' cake, right? There's always some left over. It can be saved and melted down into chocolate bars. It's done all the time, no need to blush about it. I understand you're in a hurry to steal, but why poke it into every hole? Get an iron box made, and save it in there. So, look. It's been gnawed. A rat – that's a hundred and fifty diseases. It's OK feeding people with leftovers. But that's until the first child falls sick. Then instead of chocolate you'll be floating timber down some river in the north."

The sportsman gazed at me with a vacant stare and, turning to the women, said with an insolent tone:

"Just you wait. We live in the same town."

Oldie was sitting with his gob full smiling at the people dancing.

"Did you introduce yourself? From now on – it's whatever God sends."

I tore a piece of bread off the loaf and attacked the fish soup. As we were leaving I made a cone out of a paper napkin and poured broken chocolate into it from the dish. I love the stuff...

The briefing was taking place in the school gym, behind school desks.

On the floor lay a huge sketch of the city. A colonel in field uniform was pulling over it a caravan of toy cars representing the guests' procession. The red-haired Baranov was reading:

"Mokrousov Street takes sixteen seconds. They'll be greeted by one-hundred and seventy-six people. Twenty-four on balconies. Sixteen from the windows. Nine holding up posters, forty-six flags. The clothes will come from the reserve stock of the civil defence."

"OK," said the Governor, and descended from the volleyball referee's stand.

When you gorge yourself, your throat feels on fire. I took a seat by the mineral water, beside a bespectacled, baldish old buffer, his skin stretched tightly over the skull. He didn't even turn his head, but sat staring at the Governor.

Governor Shestakov was towering up beneath the flags of Russia and the United Nations, leaning his fists on the oak table crammed with telephones and flashing walkie-talkies. He paused while I opened a bottle of mineral water with my teeth.

"Time. Time is running out," Shestakov hissed, as soon as

I'd had my fill and wiped my lips. "There's a lot to do. But not enough people. We're expecting three police squads from the regional authorities. The reservists have been called up. If there's any trouble, the local administration has allocated three more battalions. They're training in the Kryukov Forest. But if we don't want to mess up that day, we need a whole division, and tanks. What shall we do? We'll manage. Our military garrison is ready for action. Isn't that so, Comrade Gontar?"

"Yes, ready for action," responded the Colonel rising.

"On the fourth of the month we'll commence Operation 'Clear Field'." Shestakov watched the telephones and his cheeks quivered. "All unauthorized persons will be deported from Svetloyar. On the sixth it's Operation 'Clear Sky': the residents of the town centre and the streets along the guests' entry and exit routes will be conveyed to countryside schools. That's the responsibility of Baranov and his police. I'm overseeing the situation. We won't allow any nonsense. Such as foolish attempts to communicate with the President. Or even ask him a question. I'd ask you not to write anything down."

Everybody looked round cautiously. Especially at Oldie, who was biting into a piece of chocolate on a window sill. And at the door where two plainclothes were on duty with gun cartridges poking out from beneath their jackets.

"From our own side, the nearest to the guests will be comrade Klinsky's people" – the Governor indicated a puny official with a black head of hair so sleek it seemed to be wet, the only man without a tie and wearing headphones. "The town's been almost totally ruined," the Governor continued. "This is the result of the Mayor's mismanagement. The evacuated populace have to be paid for a two-day loss of earnings and meals. They have to be guarded – just in case. There's no need to explain anything to the populace! Otherwise they will all turn against us. There are two delicate points, which are giving me a headache. First, to enact the role of the populace along the routes and at the centre of celebrations by the 'Source of the Don' monument, we need people looking like townsfolk. The emcees calculated it has to be around ten thousand. A television crew will be there. As far as the men are concerned, it's easy: we'll dress up soldiers and cadets. The theatre could help with the hairdos. We've got a few children. We'll allocate two kindergartens, with our own children in the first rows." Shestakov drew a deep sigh. "But women are a problem. Where do we get so many women? Our own women won't be enough. They'd only cover the first rows. But the ones at the back? Fifty heads could be taken from the workshop for the blind, they could be put in pairs with soldiers at some distance acting as guides. The ballet dancers will have time to change after their concert, they're not from here, so we can use them. But the bulk will have to come from the corrective-labour institutions. Here and back by special trains. Five hundred female jailbirds. How to explain their procession from the station and back under guard? We can make them appear as a cross-country run of the soldiers' mothers. In the square they should be distributed among officers in a ratio of three to one. Keeping an eye on them in the crush would be difficult. Other considerations: should we take their shoes off? Or link them by chains from the shoulder joints? We'll decide later. We can get together an operative contingent from the actors of the drama theatre and from veterans of the law-enforcement bodies – somewhere around a hundred people. They'll be stowed in two vans marked 'Television' and will follow the guests' movements in case they're needed..." Shestakov covered his cheeks with his palms and continued in a low voice: "In the event that the guests want to chat with the common folk, they're being trained to say the right things. This is the worst-case scenario, do you understand? I personally think it's highly unlikely. I'm the one in charge of the whole show! But I do want to stress that everybody must be able to smile and come out with greetings. The celebration, with the dinner, should take up an hour and forty minutes. But the people accompanying them will arrive earlier, so we need to keep celebrations going for six hours running. I know it's really tough. But, as they say, this is really make or break for us. Our life is being decided for ever, for centuries, comrades. Let's face this with dignity – the question will be considered, at governmental level, as to the inclusion of Svetloyar in the 'Golden Ring' and in the inventory of monuments of national value. This, comrades, means hard-currency flow, which will sort out, as you know, all our troubles. There'll be something to remember us by."

The listeners stirred and began to clap.

"And here's the second critical point." Shestakov shot an eloquent glance in our direction – and I realized what that "critical point" was. "Rats, comrades, are in themselves revolting. They gnaw away at everything. That's why they're called rodents. That's the kind of legacy we've got from the past decades, but during recent years it's also down to the Mayor's bungling administration. Rats bite dogs. The citizens fear for their children. At my initiative, the extermination co-op 'Rat King' was set up. It'll use folk remedies to clear rats from the area of the festivities. In one night, before the guests' arrival. Free of charge."

At this even the guards at the door clapped. My elderly neighbour whipped his hands together so vehemently that his glasses slithered down his nose. Oldie gazed sourly at the map.

"But the banquet hall of the Don Hotel… you know its peculiar feature… some people here… have experienced it themselves. A key venue… We had to go to the capital. Ivan Trofimovich selected these people. They charge a lot and we've got to cough up. Well, they're a private firm. We're cornered. But we are entitled to expect results. It's impossible, even for a moment... out of the question..." I kept a sharp eye on the Governor – he had turned white. "Not even in a bad dream... Just imagine. At the height of the festivities. On the table. Or on the floor. On top of somebody. Or even droppings – which are everywhere there. No! Simply no! I'm giving this warning in front of everybody. Let our highly paid professionals take note!"

The assembly turned towards us. I smiled. They couldn't stand my stare. Oldie was fidgeting morosely.

"Colonel Gontar will explain the order of events."

"Be advised that at oh-six-hundred hours the headquarters will move on to an operational footing in the school. Sleeping places will be laid down in the teachers' staff room and the head teacher's office. The canteen will be in the library. The WC remains where it is. Army ranks will be observed. The school year will begin on the ground floor – just two classes. The external guards will be queuing for kvas and sitting in the 'School Breakfasts' van. Passes are to be shown to the sentry with a kid's pram. The commanding officers will inform you of the pram's colour. Dismissed!"

Everybody stood up, kicking at the basketballs rolling all over the place. I winked at my neighbour. "Well?"

"So you're the ones who are robbing us blind?"

"Yes. What are you in all this?"

"In all this I'm a captain. Captain Stepan Ivanovich Larionov."

"Captain, this place is like a madhouse."

Larionov winced sadly.

"Well I'm not a shrink. I'm the senior architect."

He left, and Oldie sat in his chair. It was ages since I'd stayed at school till dusk. It was like being at a dance, but without a single girl around. A night amongst the pregnant women. At least pregnant women have some advantages. I asked aloud:

"Oldie, why have we come here?"

The red-haired Baranov was standing by the shower room while Klinsky and Colonel Gontar eavesdropped on the exchange of vile abuse carried over to us across the hiss of water.

"I'll wipe you out, you vulture!"

"I'll wipe you out myself if you so much as open your trap! You'll go back to castrating cows!"

"I'm the one running the show!"

"Here's what you're running!"

The puny Klinsky took us quietly by the elbows and led us away for a short walk: "They're both hot-tempered and take things to heart…" He screwed up his eyes, as if peering deep into us. "You must understand the burden… This is the provinces. Nobody has ever visited us. Only Prince Dolgoruky, as historians just discovered. They're calling us."

The Governor and the Mayor sat wrapped up in sheets on the benches, turning their steamed-up faces in opposite directions.

"Any questions to Baranov," Shestakov barked at us. "We need just one thing from you: for the banquet hall to be ready from eleven in the morning to five in the afternoon on the twelfth of the month. You'll get your money on completion."

"Could you introduce us to your 'Rat King'?" asked Oldie.

"What for?"

"So's I can look at their certificates."

"No. Leave them alone. Let my boys get on with their work."

"Look, I didn't want to stick my nose in front of everybody, but all your promises concerning rats are just misleading and dangerous."

"Watch your mouth!"

"According to your map, your boys' area of operations is about twelve kilometres. You know what that means? Because of your negligence, over an area like that you might find thirty thousand rats – even forty. Thousands of holes. In order to reduce the rat population by one half, you'd need hundreds of rat catchers, imported chemicals, and four months of hard work! And you say one night! Nonsense! We – and we're the best in Russia – undertake to clear one hotel in two weeks, and that's just about enough time. Perhaps you want to burn the town down? Or drop a neutron bomb on it?"

"Oh yes – you've nosed out your rivals, haven't you – ha-ha-ha," Shestakov suddenly went off into fits of laughter. "Russia's not Moscow, we've got people capable of running things down here as well! What have they hired you for? For a hotel. Don't interfere in what's not your business. My boys are not promising to exterminate them, but just to edge them out for one night…"

"His boys, his boys…" put in Oldie in an unpleasantly patronizing tone. "I'm telling you again: it's impossible! Anywhere! Not even in Moscow! Not even in America! And all the less so in your lousy town! And he goes on about his boys… Ivan Trofimovich, with that one… well, there's no talking sense into that one! You don't even want us to meet your windbags. Just you remember, barbarous people work in a barbarous way. I suspect your boys have brought in piles of unpatented rubbish like the Chinese 'Good Cat' stuff with its nerve-paralysing gas. It's deadly for humans! Or maybe they're spreading out swift-action poisons in food establishments. You're not going to get by without funerals. You'll come running to us for help. I'll tell you in good time: we won't help! Then let that one and his 'boys' sort it out then! Keep well!"

Behind closed doors Oldie was dictating to Baranov with a dry tone of voice:

"For tomorrow. Helpers – don't have to be professionals. Passes to all establishments. A car on round-the-clock call where we're staying. A map of the sewage system."

"Can't get you any maps," Klinsky said, coming up. "Everything's been organized so daftly that the sewers are considered off-limits. It's the same with the cabling. It's worse than getting a visa to America… It'll take ages to get permission from Moscow."

I realized what the little dark-headed official's job was.

Baranov galloped up and down between the cars.

"Here's yours."

We piled into the familiar "duty car". Baranov instructed the driver:

"Stay with these lieutenants. To the pregnant women's sanatorium now. You'll sleep in the car. Keep in touch with me. And you lieutenants, wipe them out good and proper. Not just any which way. Last time at the dinner on Police Day one dropped right into my salad bowl."

"I'll come with you," said the Mayor, thrusting himself into the front seat. "Off you drive, Konstantin."

Konstantin took the wheel, not suspecting what the coming days had in store for him.

Oldie burst out: "Ivan Trofimovich, why…"

"Don't ask me. They don't tell me anything: who, why… They eat me alive because I'm not one of them 'Democrats'. I thought I'd be able to hold out till the festivities, but now I can see they've got no patience. It's important to them who's going to do the greeting. I can't fight with them, can I? I've earned my pension. Don't get cross with them, just do what you've got to do, take your money and get out as soon as possible."

I felt depressed by the murky night, barely diluted by the lights. Oldie was muttering that he was a reserve captain, that when rats were being edged out of Moscow for the Olympic Games, the KGB hadn't let him into the sewage system either, nor into the three-storey basements of the General Secretary's residence in Kutuzovsky, and all his efforts had gone to rack and ruin.

"Shall I drop you off too?" the driver turned to the Mayor once we'd reached the sanatorium.

"No, it's only about two hundred yards from here."

He stood there with his stooping shoulders as if he'd forgotten all about us.

I offered him a torch.

"No thanks. Then I could see them. My house is over there."

And he strode forwards with a swift pace, straight down the middle of the road, waving his arms vigorously. He lifted his knees high, as if squelching through water.

Konstantin handed Oldie a paper bag.

"Some geezers came from the meat-processing plant. They said, give the exterminators a gift sample. It's Svetloyar ham. I've never tasted none myself."

"Mmmm…" Oldie sniffed it, screwed up his eyes and hurried to the duty nurse for a knife, while I went to the toilet. They'd nailed up a hook to keep it closed – good for a carpenter! One minute later a strange sound shook me from counting the layers of rust on the sides of the bathtub.

I looked into the ward. Oldie was standing rigid between the beds, arms spread wide. He was gazing down beneath his feet at the wet floor.

"Did you remember to leave a piece for me or not?" I asked.

Oldie lifted his crumpled face and threw up again. He moved further back from the puddle spreading out on the floor. I could then see the table. There, from the choice cut of ham there protruded the blackened tail and back paws of a baked rat.

3

Remembrances of a Blue Rat

14 Days to D-Day

At five in the morning the foggy breath of autumn had already arrived – none of that blank lightness of June when you're not expecting anything to happen. A corpulent watchman at the meat-packing factory, in a black overcoat, was yawning away into his green mittens. He was sitting on the steps of a wooden ladder set against a stack of concrete blocks by the gates, as if he'd painted it and was now allowing it to dry.

"Give the chap a honk." said Oldie, tugging at Konstantin, and as a terrible honking blared out, he gave me a shake. "Don't fall asleep." Then he shouted to the watchman: "Hey, granddad! Is this the sausage section? What've you got shoved in your gloves? Hiding gold rings, are you, or what? You're scared to open your mouth – is that all made of gold as well?"

I glanced at the close-cropped, chubby-cheeked lad on the back seat. I could've been lying there.

"I'm Victor – d'you remember me? You gave up your berth to me in the train. I came home and they'd slipped a call-up notice under the door. They shaved my hair straight away. Civil-defence training, they said, for a month. You'll be a special messenger, they said – but I haven't a clue what this is all about. They're going to give me a uniform tomorrow. They'll dress you up too. You're the lieutenants, aren't you? Do you remember me?"

"I'm not letting you in," the watchman droned, his grey moustache showing in the window.

"Who's asking you? Let's get out, Kon, let's find out where that ham has come from." Oldie pushed the bundle a bit further away from him.

The old codger unsuccessfully tried to pull the lever of the siren and then fumbled in the grass for the whistle he'd dropped. I could have done with some sleep, but Victor was in the way.

"So you're scientists, are you? Do you start so early every day? Perhaps you'll let me spend some nights at home? At least every other night? I'm about to get married, you see."

We got out. All around, red-brick workshops with dirty windows. Behind the concrete fence with its barbed wire on top was a sandy slope with tufts of grass, dusty bushes, scraps of paper and posts, leading to a low-lying area gleaming with water. I walked round the concrete blocks – no reek of carrion there – and sat down on the rim of a black tyre filled with earth for planting flowers, stretching out my legs.

The boy came over too.

"Are you angry with me for some reason? Is it because I disappeared on the train? My fiancée was travelling in another carriage. I want things to be clear between us straight away… That's important to me. Colonel Gontar said: 'If you are lousy at your job, I'll send you off to Kamchatka to pull the aeroplane tails out of the mud.' So you tell me how to do things right."

"I'm just bored."

"Help! Alarm!" the old man bellowed at last from the checkpoint. "They've broken into the premises!" And he had a coughing fit.

"Come here, old geezer. I'll give you a drink."

"We haven't got any with us." Vic whispered. He should have done his stint in Kamchatka. His girlfriend would stop answering after the third letter. That was my advice. He ran off to the car.

I nodded to the old man, who had come in a flash.

"Why make a racket like a cattle breeder? Didn't you find your whistle?"

He kept a resentful silence but accepted a glassful. I didn't drink any. It's immoral to toast the "beginning" of a job – we'll have a little drink "on completion".

"Perhaps it ended up in the ham by accident?" Victor pushed the cork into the bottle.

The young chap had no idea how sausages were made, how many mincing machines and graters the meat passes through, how the sausage is encased, what screeching sounds these machines make in the morning when they're running on empty.

In an ordinary meat plant, there are four rats to every square metre. Huddled close. The males bite away at each other. They live in the cold stores, inside frozen carcasses, and build nests out of tendons. We eat the rats' leftovers. After our two-week disinfestation of the Bolkhovsky Meat Factory I couldn't eat meat for a whole year. There are always bits of rat in the sausages, though all minced up: fur, claws, bone, skin. Not whole rats though. But there's no difference: we imagine it. And that's what makes me different from a brown rat: I can imagine things. And how does a dying old man differ from a dying young man? He imagines he's seen life.

The old man disappeared. The ladder creaked as he climbed onto the concrete blocks. Vic has a well-fed face. He shaves without cutting himself. He's engaged.

"Hey, granddad, is it time? When do the rats come out?"

"I'm not keeping a log of their times. It should be soon." He couldn't restrain himself. "Get up here immediately! Why the hell are you hanging around down there?"

Vic bit his lip and looked at me.

"You get up. If you're disgusted, turn away."

"And you?"

"I'll stay here. They follow the scent on the path they've beaten. They don't care about me. They just go their way to drink."

"And that's just what my dog thought," announced the watchman from above. "You know what you are sitting on? You think it's a flower bed? No, you're sitting on a grave! You should have heard how he wailed. I lay on this block with my head shoved underneath my overcoat. The manager drove up, and there was nobody to open the gates. I lay there till dinner time, and I'm still coughing. Only the buckle from its collar was left, and a skeleton without any hind paws. The hind paws were never found."

With three creaks Vic went up the ladder. He reproached the watchman:

"What, didn't you have a gun? And you didn't come down? Even a stick... If you'd only stamped your feet, you'd have scattered them. And you let your dog..."

"You fool! I can see you've never had a rat leap up your shirt. If you kill a rat, you won't be living long. The town Mayor, Ivan Trofimovich, skewered a tiny rat with a ski pole in the kitchen. For a couple of months he's been in a daze. Cancer's eating away at him. And he's a strong man, nobody could out-drink him or out-sweat him in the bathhouse. There's not a single girl in the office he didn't paw."

I heard Oldie bickering with a man called Grisha, from the sausage plant – they clambered up onto the concrete blocks and had a drink there. Grisha kept swearing on his mother's life that he didn't know the chaps who had come the day before: it was market day and lots of people had turned up. They had given him a bottle of vodka and asked him to roll a rat into the ham – a gift for someone's mother-in-law. Oldie hissed: "You would sell your own mother for a little vodka…" They fell silent.

"I'm taking the ladder away," the watchman whispered with a hoarse voice.

The sky began to get brighter and stretch out overhead. I closed my eyes – the stench of carrion filled our nostrils. It was a long time since I had dozed off alfresco – I could catch cold. I stuck my fingers in my ears: I didn't want to hear the whistling which would start the whole shebang.

I touched the grass. What kind of grass was it? Some kind of sage? Clover? Or perhaps scurvy grass? Pennycress. Or pellitory.

Oldie cleared his throat and said:

"Amazing colours! I can see some white ones. Yellow ones. I can't see their undersides though. Here are some red snouts. Look at that couple over there. The last time I saw a light-blue rat was at the Kiev vegetable depot in 1978. We were going berserk: we couldn't pin it down – was it a brown rat or a black rat? We measured the ear. It reached to the corner of the eye. But its skull was like that of a brown rat. Oh well, in socialist times I could've collected material for a doctoral thesis on this rubbish heap. Come here and have a look!"

"Get lost!"

We didn't manage to drive away for another hour. The watchman and Grisha, who had a big, crowlike beak, were getting the last out of our bottle. Oldie went to have a look behind the concrete blocks: Vic and the driver were throwing up there, kneeling on all fours opposite each other.

"Don't take it to heart, guys. Just pretend it's a grey blanket." He squinted at me. "And why are you sulking?"

I was hungry. Grisha ran to fetch some sausage. Buses were bringing in the first shift. The watchman came by some bread. Vic stepped out from the back of the concrete blocks, like a lynx wounded in its behind, blinking repeatedly as if he'd been splashed in the face. Grisha pointed his big nose at me:

"Can they eat a human being alive?"

"Hardly ever. Not counting babies and the wounded, scientists know of only one instance: in Scotland a drunk man was eaten to death in a mineshaft."

"How did one of our people end up in Scotland?"

"He wasn't one of ours. He was a local, a Scot. Also in Moscow, after the war, there was this case of a janitor gnawed to death – but not everybody believes it. In fact, rats can chomp off bits of flesh without any ceremony. The soft parts: cheeks, nose, ears. And something else as well."

The watchman and Grisha laughed in chorus. Vic stepped aside and stuck his head in the bushes. "Are we going to spend the night here?"

Breakfast – which was served on the sanatorium balcony by female orderlies with violet veins on their swollen legs – consisted of a cabbage-and-carrot salad with sour-apple slices, a warm heap of rolls covered with slivers of mincemeat and a bowl of pickles – from which I fished out now a cucumber, now a burst tomato – plus an earthen jug of cool compote. I drank down the juice and enquired about the fruit that was supposed to be at the bottom. They oopsed and brought some. Oldie waited for fifteen minutes while I spat out prune stones and stuffed pear after pear into my mouth, holding the stalk between my fingers. Then I hiccupped and drew a deep breath.

"Vic, please report the meat factory's gift to the police. Or to your colonel. To whoever appointed you to us," Oldie requested.

"Oldie hasn't expressed himself clearly." I got up from the chair. "Report to those who didn't send us this baked rat. Not only to whoever you ought to report to. But also to whoever didn't send it. We can still make a rat catcher of you. An exemplary health protector." I raised my right eyebrow and, unsticking my lips, spat out a prune stone, aiming at a pregnant woman with a blond ponytail warming her belly on a bench beneath a fir tree. She laughed so loud that a nurse emerged from the porch and led her off into the shade.

Vic frowned and went off to put the lamps and a packed lunch in a bag, while we came down the hill along the path to the gates, which was lined with larch trees.

"Everything's fine, Oldie." I stroked my swollen belly. "But I miss female company."

Just then female company appeared.

"Excuse me, are you looking for something? Can I help you?"

I raised my eyes: a waist as thin as a wasp's, bare shoulders, large, dark lips with irregular edges, hair the colour of wet sand, eyes which you long to close with your mouth.

"Girls like you can't help me any more, my dear."

Stomping and jangling – you'd better not smash these lamps, man! – Vic overtook us, shouting as he ran:

"These are my commanders. Rat catchers from Moscow. This is my fiancée."

"I've got serious intentions," I said. "I am not suggesting marriage."

Her eyebrows, thick by the bridge of her nose, almost disappeared towards the temples. She was serious and unsmiling, which made her lips protrude even more. My belly ached. Of course. An idea flashed in my mind: she was engaged, but she'd end up falling in love with me.

"The girl doesn't know what a deadly danger is hanging over her," Oldie affirmed sympathetically.

Only Vic laughed – she didn't even blink. She was carrying a jug of kvas, which she held out to her boyfriend. As he shoved his face into the jug like a suckling piglet, I threw my hand forwards and touched her nose. She didn't scream, but only recoiled, belatedly throwing up her arms.

"Just a security measure. It's impossible to fall in love with a girl if on first acquaintance you've grabbed her by the nose. Although grabbing her behind's more reliable."

"What are you..." The young man was about to punch my face. "You... you... who do you think I am? If it wasn't for the recruitment office... well, you know!... In Moscow you can do as you like. But here, if you try to touch..." Once again he clenched his fists. "Even just a word, just one word... then I... you won't get out of here!"

"I'm really sorry, Victor," said Oldie, alarmed. "My friend is a bit deranged and has been prone to dark moods. Not long ago he buried his wife." Oldie was trying to pour oil on troubled waters with his tear-jerking inventions. "If your... relation... refrains from visiting us during work hours, he won't be tempted to... And you won't be sent to hard labour for the murder of a Ph.D. graduate – a biologist. Anyway, he will promptly apologize."

"Yes, I beg your pardon. All the more so as this will save only me. She won't be saved."

The lovebirds ran off, with the jug of kvas rocking between them. We old jades trailed along behind, across the square. The hotel stuck out opposite the sanatorium, cut off at the back by the boulevard from the southern, rat-infested area of the town. The patterned tower – similar to party headquarters in Soviet Asian Republics in former times and only partially enlivened by arches and columns supporting the awning of the Conference Hall – was our target.

Builders' cradles hung down from the surrounding houses, and female workers were slapping plaster over the pockmarks on the walls. Some guys shouted as they moved sheets of iron on the roofs. Others were carefully offloading ashlar blocks from three lorries by hand. A couple of masons were cladding the broken shell of the nearby bus shelter. Women in overalls were still messing around in the flower beds, as the water-carrier was signalling to them. My heart was thumping – if I'd opened my mouth, you'd have heard a raucous ticking.

"Close your mouth. Everybody's looking." Oldie stood up. I did the same.

By the hotel, police jeeps were huddling together. An officer bellowed at some soldiers sitting on the benches, and they got up, adjusting their belts and throwing away their cigarettes.

From the entrance, people with white overalls sprang out, pointing at us – is it them? The civilians turned towards us – the two love-birds were already there, and they looked in our direction too.

Above their heads, I saw some people peering out of a shop window – a grand lady stood in front, with fair curly hair and brightly painted lips, as sturdy as a bottle. I smiled and waved to her, hugging myself as if to say how much I could love. The people around her stirred and said something in the ear of the fair-headed statue. She didn't even switch the weight of her bulk from one foot to another.

One yellow-and-blue police car started off, then another, their lights flashing as they skirted us at a sluggish pace. They parked by the shop on the corner, which revealed a pile of scarves, bags, and dresses – and all around a host of wrinkled faces, so many that some were sitting on the trees – all staring at us. My heart was beating harder and harder.

Half a dozen cops were twirling their arms around in front of the crowd, as if they were driving geese. The crowd had made way? No? We couldn't see. But they were clearly gazing at our unshaven faces (Oldie was growing a beard, I was just too lazy), at Oldie's outfit, similar in colour to a school uniform, with iron buttons and worn out at the knees, sagging over rubber boots (Oldie always worked in high boots), at his shirt with one side of the collar outside and the other under the jacket, at his wrinkly Caucasian nose and his greying locks – at my sweater full of holes (courtesy of the barbed wire on the fence of a poultry farm in Lyublino), at my stinking work trousers with pockets all over and beach-style plimsolls over grubby socks. The summer was coming to an end… a time to stop and a time to start.

"Comrades, disperse!" a megaphone wheezed with the drawl of a slight echo, as a third car rolled up to the crowd. "As for the rats, apply to the local health units!"

From the hotel they were waving to us: "Quick! Get in!"

"Comrades, don't press around! Who told you this? Nobody's come from Moscow. Now! Three steps – back!"

They took us by the arms and dragged us into the hotel. It was empty, and the floor was being washed. On the upper floors some machines were sanding the parquet, producing a howling noise. In a bare cloakroom crammed with hooks hung army overcoats and gasmasks.

"The rats are a real plague for our people," said the architect Larionov with an apologetic tone. I recognized him by his spectacles: his bald pate was covered by an officer's cap. "I've been appointed deputy."

He was pushed aside by two women in white overalls from the health service, a terrifyingly ugly mother and her spinster daughter with identically protruding eyes. Their overalls crackled as if they were made of tarpaulin.

"I studied with Professor Odinets and Dr Melkova, while Vladimir Stepanovich was the best and favourite student of Mark Kunashev," I said, satisfying their curiosity.

The mother was dumbfounded: she didn't know that my specialization was garden flies. Her daughter prattled on about what she had learnt the day before – the Gero trap and zoocoumarin. I picked up on that:

"There's no hurry, girls. We'll come to that in due course. Meanwhile, find out what we can get for bait: flour, sausage, pear syrup, valerian. Until then, you're free. Go shopping if you like." I pointed towards the shop window with the imposing lady.

"That's a bank," pointed out the girl, growing redder and redder. Oh, a bank.

"Oldie... I mean Vladimir Stepanovich... I'll take Captain Larionov, so that Vic won't lay hands on me. And since I have no wellies, you'll take care of the sewers."

Larionov, the warrant officer and twenty privates were standing in a circle over a map.

"Where's the canteen?"

"There isn't one. It was planned, but the budget was cut and they never finished it. There's a café on the tenth floor: they've got eggs, sour cream," Larionov said. "They don't cook here."

"We've already eaten," put in the warrant officer. OK, fine.

I deployed the privates round the hotel, assigning each one of them to their area. "Search slowly, under every step, don't miss any cracks, pay attention to the wooden parts – chips of wood, scratches – especially joints, corners, outlets of pipes, door frames, anything – is that clear? – holes the size of a small coin or more – mark them off with chalk and call me. Go!"

I positioned myself on the nearest bench on the boulevard, looking, in between yawns, now at the bank window, now at Larionov, who was eager to help me.

"Er, yes, as a matter of fact, they really fall down from the ceiling. To tell you the truth – I'm no expert..."

They bellowed: "Here!" They shouted: "There! Comrade Lieutenant!"

After an hour and a half, all that we had found was four decent-sized holes. I could say with confidence that two of them were rat lairs – though they were blocked up with old junk – burrows from a couple of years ago. Only in one spot, on a low window frame, was there something like a gnaw mark, but even that must have occurred before this summer.

Any health doctor who has learnt the rudiments of rat extermination from the *Manual for Assessing the Degree of Rat Infestation* might have been happy to declare the hotel "free from rodents" and sidle off to down some beer in a bar not totally free from rodents, but I was obliged to say in a wheezing voice:

"Next: the rubbish-collection room."

Some geezer was painting the door of the garbage room. Behind the door, the rubbish chute was buried in such a mountain of paper and food scraps that the reception tank couldn't even be seen. Greasy, dense rivulets of rubbish trickled into the basement. There was a reek of fish tails and an acidic smell of milk. How could you sniff out a rat in here…

The privates brought in a spade. I banged it with all my strength on the chute, in the hope of hearing a scrabbling commotion shooting away overhead. No. Damn!

I sent a private to trundle up and down in the lift to see on what floor the rubbish chute was blocked up.

Out of frustration, I ordered the others: "Clear out those two corners."

And of course, there wasn't a trace of anything there.

If rats are falling from the ceiling in this hotel, then in a dump of a town like this, on opening up a rubbish-collection room, you should see millions – millions! – of rats' tails! They should be sitting in clusters on the pipes, afraid of nothing!

The private returned: the rubbish chute was totally blocked

on the eleventh floor. There were also a few jams above. What a lovely town!

"And who are you?" I asked the painter.

"I'm the superintendent."

From his face I gathered that this was the first day in his working life that he had not knocked back 200 ml of vodka before his midday meal.

"Take us into the basement."

"It's dark in there... the bulbs are burnt out, and these days..."

I pulled off the high boots from a smiling private and, without inhaling, without looking down so as not to come across some wet cat's ribs, I clambered over the stinking mountain and slithered into the black entrails of the basement. The others came squelching after me.

I let one private go ahead with the light. On the eighth step I stumbled into him: what was in front of him? I stooped down in the yellow triangle of light – there was no floor, just a smooth, gleaming blackness and clouds of insects dazzled by the light. I remained silent for a moment:

"What kind of shithole is this?"

"Water. They were testing the fire system and flooded out the basement. Three years ago – and it still hasn't dried out."

The best thing now was to give up. The knuckleheads came trampling after, breathing down my neck.

"The lights. Turn them all on the water. Are there any dry spots?" Two: in the middle and in a corner. "Carry me over – don't stand there gawping!"

They carried me as orderlies do: two of them, hands coupled to form a seat. Larionov and the whimpering warrant officer were carried on backs. The first dry spot turned out to be a tangle of hoses from the discarded fire system. I leapt down onto the second: earth, glass fibre and debris. The warrant officer's bearer went under into some kind of pit, hurling his commander headlong into the waters and bringing his whimpering to a halt. They splashed in the murky pool like a couple of behemoths, and as they looked for their service caps the officer promised: "I'll have you diving down until your demob day!"

I got down to work. The others held up their lamps and rolled up their puttees.

Slim chance the rats would go swimming across to the garbage heap to eat. Not a single burrow. That's the kind of day it was – getting worse and worse. No rats' "tables", no latrines. At the pipes' inlets the plasterwork was undamaged, and the dust on the pipes showed no trace of footmarks. In such dimness you can't have a proper look.

"Hey, mister – the bulbs are burnt out, you say – but where are the bulb-holders? Wasn't it you who came here with a boat and unscrewed them all? Moron."

Larionov intervened: "Don't flare up. That's the way it is down here…"

"Like it is everywhere. I'm sure they've been begging for this Swiss fire-prevention system for five years. Then they tested it and left it here to go to rack and ruin until the water goes away. But it's three years now that the water hasn't dried up – the floor's made of concrete. You're an architect? Fetch the spade and uncover this bit here for me… careful…" I knocked over a bucket with holes in it, which covered the only burrow we had found. Its sides had slid down, so it was uninhabited. I just wanted to let off steam.

The privates were digging. Larionov had the timid look of a botany professor gazing up an old elephant's backside. I waited on top of a bent piece of iron, catching cold, then sloshed along the wall, where it was shallow, and fumbled my way in the dim light along hillocks of broken bricks and sand, until I landed on some concrete blocks. From these blocks I looked over the partition: water everywhere. I didn't like this search at all. I had the feeling we wouldn't find anything.

It was slippery. Behind some blocks the light revealed a large overcoat, its buttons glinting.

"We've dug it up, comrade lieutenant."

They'd dug for nothing, like digging into a grave – the solid burrow, containing two nests, had long been uninhabited. In one nest – the upper one – there was paper gnawed to bits. From the bottom one, what I collected with my gloved hand and laid out on the spade under the light was bones, hamster skin, a copper rod, two skulls of house mice, a piece of string, grape seeds and tomato peel, as well as remains of eaten human faeces. That meant a family of rats had eked out a meagre living here.

"Fill up the hole, everyone to the entrance!"

The paint reeked. I massaged the small of my back – too much stooping down. Those who were wet dried themselves out. To be on the safe side, I sent the rest out onto the boulevard to look for burrows. We had been searching the basement in vain, and we ended up finding burrows in the street beneath a maple tree – thirty-two of them.

I walked round the hotel again. There were no pipes or cables providing a route from the adjacent loft. The superintendent had finished painting the door and looked much more sober now.

I squatted by the painted door. A cable outlet had been sawn off in the corner above the threshold. The cable swung loose: it fitted snugly into the hole. With room to spare. I rubbed my finger over the slot: yes. It was uneven. Dented. Jagged. By how much? About seven centimetres. A rat run. I lay down: there was a spider's web across the hole. The web dampened my joy. So it turns out it hasn't been used for ages.

"Why don't you take a break?" Klinsky laughingly stretched out his boyish hand. "The Governor is itching to check things out. I'll tell you a couple of things. One from my heart and one relevant to what's going on. From my heart: don't get angry at our masquerades – the boys go a bit too far, but essentially they're worried about the town. They don't know how to do things... It couldn't be any other way with them. We're still learning. I'm an amateur myself. I've been in the State Security Service for three years now. Before that, by the way, I taught chemistry and biology in a school. I earned a little bit extra on the side as an insurance agent. Without a car as well, you know. I got used to shanks' pony."

We hadn't found the main thing – the location of the rodents. And I hadn't had a good night's sleep either.

"And as to the other thing, Shestakov is going to pester me every day. That clever clogs wanted me – haha – to appoint someone to keep an eye on you. That's his way: everybody keeps an eye on everybody else, to be on the safe side. Let's agree – I'll leave you alone, I'll lie to him: things are bubbling up nicely. When you're through, you'll call me in. I have great trust in you. Not in our 'Rat King'."

"What kind of people are they?"

"Don't know. I've never had anything to do with rats, that's for sure! Come to see me – we don't often have visitors who're educated. I live on the north side of the town. So I've not gone over to the wealthy side. Because of the rats, of course, but I've got used to my neighbours too – I live in a communal flat, they're like my own relatives now. If you have time we can go to the Kryukov Forest, see the burial mounds – the digs are amazing! If you have any problems with Baranov... to tell the truth, he should be called Bananov. If anything happens report it to me."

A thought suddenly occurred to me:

"Listen, isn't there a bomb shelter beneath the hotel? Or something of that sort? Or special communication lines? I need to know."

Klinsky's brows knitted. He frowned.

"I'll have a think. Good luck."

No point. Rats need to eat and drink, build nests — what use is an underground bunker to them? Although in this kind of shelter they do keep water and grub.

I checked on the privates on the boulevard and dismissed them. Thanks. Idiots, all of them. I found out where the nearest rubbish skips were — too far away.

The matron in a white overall came rushing up.

"Are we beginning a systematic hunt, then?"

Watch out they don't hunt *you*, you dim-witted cow.

Oldie, the fool, was standing in the middle of the hall. His soldiers were carrying out the chairs stacked up in rows. He was staring in perplexity at the high ceiling. Judging from the air, they'd still not penetrated the sewerage. Judging from the general atmosphere of dejection, the inspection of the four storeys and the storerooms had been utterly disappointing — so I wasn't alone.

"You look like a pterodactyl," I whispered, then added a bit louder: "It was worth travelling five hundred kilometres — I've never seen you with a more puzzled face."

"Just imagine… It's clear of rats everywhere. And yet…" he pointed at the bluish-faced Vic holding a plastic bag with two little rats, one crushed to a pulp and the other still twitching — with each jerk crumpling Vic's face even more. "Before my very eyes…"

I craned my neck: well, an ordinary ceiling. Fissures creeping out from the lights, not too noticeable.

"Open up the floor," I barked.

With the lift operator I sniffed around the entire lift shaft, and on the twenty-fourth floor – the last one – I scraped out from the grooves under the doors some rat droppings. But once again, obviously last year's.

On the roof – what was the point? – I sat down on the tarred ventilation inlet. I closed my eyes when it blew in my face – otherwise I looked over the houses, beyond the road to the left of a grain lift, and saw a forest on the far side of a yellow field.

"Is it so bad?" said the elderly Larionov in a sympathetic tone. He was talking about the hotel. "You guessed right: it took ages to build it. Mokrousov, the original architect, didn't stay to see it finished. While he was still around, they put up the skeleton, the general plan, but he wasn't here when they decorated it. He disappeared without trace. Seven years already. I think he went away. You know, old people lose their memory, he may've ended up in a railway station – may've wandered into a carriage and forgotten his name or address. Although we don't have too many trains here. Only two local ones. In the summer, five through trains at the most. His absence was only noticed later, there was nobody to ask after him. He lived on his own. Imagine, an honoured architect of the Soviet Union perishing with no name in some kind of old folks' home. In fact, Mokrousov had designed the hotel a bit differently: on the roof there should have been some connecting semi-circular turrets. The façade was supposed to have chipped-out angles and be covered with crushed granite. Above the entrances there should have been a gold relief against a kind of flame-coloured background. Like on a flag. It said 'Russian Arms'. Anyway, the concept has been preserved: glory is represented by the storeys rising high, and democracy by a conference hall in the form of an amphitheatre. Democracy and glory. Actually, it was to be the crown of his career. I was with him all my life. Just what kind of architect am I... one who's appointed to any old thing! Beneath the hotel there – just typical – rat territory. I glanced at a pre-war plan: the abattoirs of the meat plant used to be there."

Home now. The lift let me out. Directly to the sanatorium. I didn't turn round to face the powerful heels swiftly trying to catch up with me.

"But where's Vic?"

"In a deep arsehole. Just like the rest of us."

I tortured myself for five minutes in the ward: sleep straight away or ask for some porridge in the kitchen? I had no strength to press the question further in either direction. I guess I could sleep on it – and I switched off.

4

The Suspended Village

13 Days to D-Day

I groped my way to the kitchen, poured some water into my palms and quenched my thirst. As I sneezed, I pried my gluey eyes open to discover it was 6 a.m. and Special Messenger Victor was there.

"Having any trouble getting to sleep? I can show you how to do it. The main thing is to lie down correctly."

Vic was clutching at a mop. He was sitting on a stool in the middle of the kitchen, his back hunched, his half-shut eyes staring somewhere under the iron cupboards.

"Seeing rats in every hole? The bedsteads are too low, uh? Curly tails everywhere?" I sidled away yawning. "They won't let you sleep. You might as well stick that mop up your bum – a rat, my friend, can bear a blow straight to its skull and still get at your throat. And you shouldn't be sitting with your back to the ventilation shaft: any baby rat can jump on your neck from there... Sleep well."

Someone's singing. I cock my ears: the pregnant women are singing somewhere in the garden. So I am not asleep. On the window sill is a pigeon with a fluffy old neck. I pinch my chin wondering whether to have a shave or not. Summer is waning away with its first bonfires wafting smoke over us, its dry, fresh

61

winds, its colours, its wet roads and clacking heels. It feels as if there is a new life ahead, which you can see only if you are quick enough. I dreamt about the love of my life. I was languishing at a tram stop and my heart was aching from this certainty: she did exist and was about to come. Even now that I'm awake, it still aches. How easily can my ageing body be deceived by a stranger's call... Not a stranger – it is she who's calling... who's coming.

As I lie down, the pain starts oozing out of my mind, like the scent on her blouse... you've hit on it, but each time it takes more time to catch it, and it gets fainter and fainter. And when you find it, you freeze as if pricked by something sharp – you know that it's that very scent... you know that soon it will fade away, and that even her clothes will only smell of the wardrobe. It's been a long time since I've had a dream. It's because yesterday I saw that girl. That pure, beautiful girl must have stayed on my mind... this is why I dreamt of one like her. Dreams are merciful things... and they're all earthly, they can all be explained. I'll go and have a shave.

The idiots had cut up the watermelon from top to bottom – the juice had trickled out. They should have sliced it in narrow strips crosswise. I polished off the third chunk, chewing the white seeds and spitting the brown, glossy ones onto my plate.

"Thanks a lot for the watermelon, Ivan Trofimovich."

The Mayor nodded, his cheeks quivering. The war council was completed by Larionov – who reeked like a hairdressing salon – the warrant officer and Vic, who was picking at his fingernails.

"We won't report to you every day," Oldie began. "We'll deliver our report when we get our money. Tell your people not to follow us around. I go down the sewers and there are three people hanging about there, for God's sake!"

"They're repair men," Larionov put in.

"What, in calfskin jackboots? Look, we've got nothing to hide. And you won't be able to copy our extermination methods – should we have to resort to them."

Larionov scratched his brow in perplexity.

"Well, I'll report this… it's not me who makes decisions."

"Now to the point: we haven't found any rat colonies in the hotel. On the basis of any known method of investigation, the establishment is not populated with synanthropic rodents."

"So what's falling down, if it's not rodents?" the Mayor reeled.

"That we can't deny. And we know the agreement: on the twelfth there mustn't be any rats falling down from the ceiling. But… Ivan Trofimovich, I must confess that tomorrow we might give up. As a last resort, consider plastering the entire ceiling. It's high up, it's a huge space, and I don't know whether it'll help or not. Since we haven't figured out yet where they're coming from, I simply cannot promise they won't start falling from the walls, flying out of your sleeves, or whatever. I don't know. But it's possible that tomorrow morning I'll have no other suggestions to give you. Now leave us."

Chairs scraped. Ivan Trofimovich shifted his knees: he couldn't just get up and go. He cast a wretched look at all the people in the room, which I dodged by dashing out onto the balcony – far from the watermelon, unfortunately.

Some junior nurses were chasing the smoking soldiers with their brooms from beneath the larch trees. The soldiers ran away submissively along the path to the gates, and after them raced the warrant officer, shrieking, "Where're you off to? Who gave you the order?" while Larionov shuffled along in their tracks trying to tighten his belt – which was too large for him – and fingering the holes in the strap.

"Stepan Ivanych – where are you shambling off to? Come back, quick! Well, maybe not that fast. Smell the flowers first. Don't hurry to come back."

I sat down and rested my head snugly between the pot-bellied columns of the balcony balustrade, without looking at the Mayor when he turned his lifeless back and walked off. Peace. I jumped as the balcony door slammed.

"You're not having anything else to eat?" Vic's girlfriend was togged up in a doctor's coat – unrecognizable. "Shall I clear the table?"

I nodded at her polite words. She said she had decided to take care of our food. She was on vacation and had time to be closer to Vic – that way she didn't have to worry about what he was eating. Well, great. I nodded and turned round: through the gaps between the columns, the Mayor was looking straight at me from below. He waited until I made eye contact and blurted out:

"Now you understand? It's not enough for them that I go. They want to crush me body and soul. I'm not expecting anything from you now."

The girl sank her clean little fists into her pockets, moving her feet a bit further apart.

"Are you comfortable sitting like that?... Fine. Listen, I need to talk to you."

"Maybe later?"

"Am I intruding in your thoughts?"

"I'm waiting for you to stand in the light. To see whether you're wearing a skirt or not."

She thought for a bit and then, button after button, she undid her coat, which smelt of the laundry.

I screwed up my eyes and laid my hands on the cool stone behind my back.

Vic's girlfriend was wiping the table. When she bent her head, her hair flowed over her cheeks and covered her lips. I would now be seeing her every day, and every day my heart would be pierced by

64

that blunt pain of the dream. She'd be looking after our food... It was like those autumn days in school, full of trepidation: you'd come in, and in the class there would be a new girl, alone, with nobody to sit next to yet. I kept following her with my eyes, not aware of where I was looking. You can't take your eyes off a girl like that – and if they ask you what her legs are like, or her breasts, you'll be at a loss: her every movement could attract a crowd. And how generous she was... she shifted the chairs, shook the towel, put it on the radiator to dry... just being herself in the room where I was.

"Damn it! Could you pay me some attention too?" Oldie burst out. "How long do I have to wait?"

"Just you wait until I lock you up in an almshouse! With all your drivel you're helping the Mayor to his grave! Stepan Ivanych, what kind of ceiling is it?"

"I will tell you!" Oldie waved his fist at Larionov's opening mouth. "It's a suspended ceiling. Do you remember in 1989 that high-rise block near the Kazakhstan Cinema House? Something like that. One hundred metres by sixty. Twenty-two metres from the floor! From the main ceiling – thirty centimetres. The main ceiling is solid: the damp-proofing is not damaged. The roof's in a fairly good state. We combed through the loft – it's clear of rodents."

"And the light fittings?"

"The entire wiring is in the loft, in full view, and it's sealed. Now – where do the rats on the suspended ceiling come from? It hangs on iron pins, half a metre's distance from each wall. They are blind walls – no pipes, no cables. The original plan did not provide for people accessing the suspended ceiling. And they expect me to believe that rats keep dropping from there? What do I think? Nothing. I've got only one observation to make: the rats are seen only when they hit the floor. Nobody has ever seen where they tumble out from. You raise your head and – a-ha! – cracks in the ceiling! So that's where they must be coming from... Well, who knows what games the locals are playing... I surely don't. Some disgruntled citizen may be bringing along some rats and flinging them from offstage."

"Sorry, but... for two years in a row?" hissed Larionov.

"Think about it, Oldie," I added, "it's mostly baby rats. If there's a whole herd of them on the ceiling, obviously the young ones make false steps more often – it all fits in."

"Yes it does," Oldie nodded sourly, "but it's also much easier to trap baby rats for throwing. I suggested straight away that the hotel might have some hidden recesses, for government communication systems for example. Though why should the government want to be linked with this dump? Or maybe they bricked over some inner cavities and forgot about them. But I doubt I'd have overlooked them during my inspection. If I have, it's time for me to go and sell lemonade in the street."

"If they can't get onto the ceiling, we must assume they're living on it."

"Living on it? On blocks one inch thick? And do they make their nests out of their own excrement? And feed on excrement? And what do they drink?"

"Well, goodbye for now," rang out the voice of Vic's girlfriend. "See you at the evening meal. Don't have a quarrel."

I turned to Larionov.

"What is it, a bare suspended unit? Any construction debris?"

"There's a layer of loose haydite, as there should be."

"And they've buried themselves in haydite!"

"Don't fly off the handle. This is really bizarre: there's a teeming rat colony, and right in the middle of it you've got a rat-free hotel – except for the ceiling! Why's that? There's lots of free space around. If any disinfestation has been carried out in the hotel over the past two years – then it could be explained by migration, by a rare case of embedded settlement, like in Volgograd, where they hid on the fifteenth floor…"

Larionov wiped his misted spectacles. I levelled my finger at Oldie's hooked nose.

"I'll tell you why! The hotel *seems* to belong to the rat-infested area. But in actual fact it's cut off from the south side by the boulevard – a broad street with no restaurants or rubbish heaps. So it's like an island. Therefore it's not replenished by the neighbouring rat families. Why a local family would settle in the ceiling is anybody's guess. They might have been living there since time immemorial, when the abattoirs were here. Or perhaps they settled in the construction site when materials were brought in or while communication lines were laid – and they created a passage, which I found by the door of the rubbish-collection room. Maybe they had settled in the basement, but when it was flooded they shot upstairs along the rubbish chute. So we've got all we need: nests on the suspended ceiling, food in the rubbish chute… and to drink they go down through the chute to the basement, or else there's a pipe trickling somewhere. The only problem, then, is to find this passage between the ceiling and the rubbish chute. It should be between the ceiling and the wall on the chute side. They can easily leap across to the suspended ceiling – the distance is only half a metre."

"Excuse me. Do you need me?" Vic peered into our room.

"I can't stand young people. They're way too much like me. But my hat off to you, Victor. Even here in the provinces you've got to be very brave – almost mad – to marry a beauty like that. Today on the balcony she showed me how her coat unbuttoned. True."

Larionov rushed to intercept Victor's hands.

"Vic, you know who's saying this and why… Don't sink to his level."

"Oldie, take the boy with you, measure the height of the ceiling in relation to the rubbish chute and clear the chute for one storey up and one down. See how sound it is. I'll be with the architect in the hall. Stepan Ivanych, first of all we need two pairs of binoculars, and second, keep your mouth shut."

In the hall, two soldiers were sticking their bayonets into a piece of plywood.

"Who are these guys?"

"The guards."

"Get the hell out of here!"

The architect raced in with the binoculars, which still smelt of the kit store and had white numbers on their cases.

"The lights. Turn 'em all on. Which wall is closest to the rubbish chute? Get the binoculars and move from that corner to meet me – we're looking for holes in the wall. Right at the top, opposite the suspensions. Or higher. Any damage to the plaster, damp patches, stains…"

We spent an hour walking with our heads turned upwards.

I massaged my neck with my fingers. Larionov, tapping his glasses against his binoculars, groaned.

"There's a reflection. On my side the wall's clear." He spat into his handkerchief and wiped his glasses, peering at me blindly. "What about you?"

"One crack. There."

We stared up like astrologers.

"Yes," Larionov confirmed. "But it's hair-thin."

"Look higher up along it. It's scratched open, see? It's reddish. As if the plaster's been flaked off and a brick's sticking out. A red brick in the wall?"

"It was red bricks they laid."

"That crack – it gradually moves down and to the right. And continues to go down and to the right – what does it mean?"

"Faulty plastering. Or the wall's damp."

"That's not what I mean. The crack follows the line of the brickwork. The drunken bricklayers must have laid the wall any old how: there must be gaps, a passage, in the brickwork. Now sit or lie down – whatever's most comfortable – and don't take your eyeballs off that bit of brick you can see."

Larionov took a seat. He looked and looked – and finally declared with a hoarse voice:

"What is it exactly that we are expecting?"

"If a rat leaps from the crack onto the suspended ceiling, it means they've got their little village there. We'll all lie belly up."

"And how long are we going to sit here?"

I sat down beside him and thought: "Yes, how long are we going to sit here? The rat pack have a flexible routine – they eat when humans are asleep, when there's no noise from footsteps. But that's only if they haven't proliferated too much. If they've managed to stuff themselves in one shift. Otherwise they have to come out in broad daylight."

I smirked at the ceiling: "Can you see me, green-eyes?"

It would be better to wait till the morning. But some knuckle-head may dash to have a drink right now. Or some auntie rat may jump from the ceiling to escape the lust of a dominant male. I put out the light, leaving only the security lighting. To give the impression that humans were asleep.

"Can't see much." Larionov said with a worried tone.

The pack will come streaming out, you'll see. Then I had an idea.

"Stepan Ivanych, dash off to Oldie. Tell him to smoke into the rubbish chute – he knows how to do it. And then run back here again."

I stared through the binoculars: the brickwork was no longer visible, only a streak of grey light between the wall and the suspended ceiling: when they come, you'll see a few ripples up there. It would be bad if only one darted across – you'd wear yourself out wondering if you'd imagined it. We'd have to stay here till morning. Here's the architect rushing back in. I took the binoculars from my eyes and stroked my eyelids, which had been rubbed sore – ah, it was Vic.

"Where should I look?" he blurted out.

"There, see where I'm pointing? There's a crack, along that one to the ceiling – if there's a passage, it must be there. Don't stare at the wall: lie down and look at the strip between the wall and the ceiling; the rats will jump across it. Make sure they don't fall down on your face. How's Oldie doing?"

"Vladimir Stepanovich's asked me to inform you that the metal rings of the rubbish chute have been displaced on all sides: there are lots of chinks…"

"Don't shout…"

"We can't clear it out," he whispered. "Vladimir Stepanovich sent Larionov to look for a smokescreen. I wanted to ask you: what would happen if you or someone else were to tread on a rat path over there, at the meat-processing plant?"

"But who would do that? Their water path is clearly visible, so just step two paces away and you're OK. Unless some foolish young rats start jumping all over your trousers. It's another matter if they're migrating…"

"You've seen this?"

"No, I haven't. Count Alexei Mokrousov in the nineteenth century saw it. He left an account of how a whole pack emerged from a blazing country estate – the cats leapt on the fences and men climbed up the fir trees. But how many of them could there have been in one estate? About a thousand. The threat is not in their number but in their cohesion. For us, in times of trouble, it's every man for himself, but rats press together tight, the dominant males at the head followed by scouts from subordinate ranks. They lead the older females in the middle, the frail and the blind, and the rat king – if they have one – while other subordinate males close the ranks on the edges and the rear. Then it can be dangerous – you should prick up your ears."

"For what?"

"For the rats – they talk among themselves. They cough. They hiss if you've driven them under a radiator with a mop. They snort when they fight over females. The most disgusting sound is the screech when a trap breaks their spine – as if they're screaming 'Mummy!'… Last year on the Arbat in Moscow we were disinfesting a building site, and the excavator bucket all at once turned up three nests – the mothers went leaping around out of the bucket, and the baby rats – as tiny as a walnut, and all covered in down – how they screamed! I can't bear that sound. That's why I tend to work with poisons. There's also that whistling noise they make. Count Mokrousov observed: before migration, the alpha male, the dominant rat, whistles. And not softly either. If you hear that whistle, run for your life."

"What if I don't?"

"They won't eat you up! I've been fighting them for so many years and I heard of just one death: the janitor they bit to death after the War. In the morning he was sweeping at the high-rise block in Vosstanie Square and an old rat was nibbling at the corner of a rubbish skip. They were made of wood then, Oldie says. He threatened it with a broom – the beastie squealed, and they came jumping all over the janitor. People say they even came leaping from the trees. He rolled like a barrel. People were yelling, the fire brigade came, but only took away his bones. But that was after the War. Just imagine in those days: two thousand people attacked by rats every year. People kept hen houses in the yards, grain, water. Ninety-five per cent of the houses were infested with rats. At the Central Department Store before the opening each morning they released a pack of fox terriers into the building. They brought back twenty-five tails each. There you are. Oldie doesn't believe in the dead janitor story, though. He doesn't trust Count Mokrousov either. He respects him as a man, but not as a scientist. The Count was an amateur, and an eccentric..."

I glanced sideways at Victor: he looked like a corpse, his eyes entrenched behind his funereal binoculars.

"Don't get too impressed," I added. "That's just zoopsychology. We're rat catchers – exterminators. A rather narrow specialist field. Oldie goes in for public catering and residential buildings – my forte is factories and warehouses. As for open territories – rice fields, pipe routes – we're not so confident. In Russia there are practically no specialists on open territories – that line of research has never been properly funded, no local school has been created. In the last century you could trap them and poison them, and do zoopsychology into the bargain. Now you're lucky if you remember how many scales a brown rat has on its tail – about two hundred, I think... The ear is one third the size of the head. I'm gonna find someone to relieve you of your duties. What?"

"I wanted to ask..." The words were sticking in his throat. "You, personally, have you ever been tempted?"

"How d'you mean?"

"To go in... when they're moving. To go among them. Did you hear what I said? Are you here?"

"Funny... Mokrousov came up with the idea that a rat never dies by itself. When it's fed up with its predatory life, it gives itself up to a cat. But the cat's no fool. It plays with it and then abandons it, however bored it might be. The Count predicted many things about the extermination of rats, but often made

72

some stupid mistakes. He wrote that a rat lives seven years. But in fact it's only two winters. If you see any rats, shout 'Hurray!'"

On the porch I bumped into his girlfriend – what a sweet scent! She shook me firmly by the shoulder.

"Why did you tell him that? About the balcony… That I…"

"I don't want any bond between us. What's this perfume you're wearing?" I hurried down the boulevard – she didn't fall behind.

"Let's talk."

"Later, miss."

"Right now!"

As she grabbed me by the collar, the shirt cut into my throat. I jerked an elbow free, but she didn't let go.

"I said now. I promise I'll never take notice of you again. I don't like having to ask you. Just this once, please. Help us, please."

"We are beyond help."

"I mean Vic and me. Vic's so sensitive and impressionable – this job isn't for him… He tells me such horrible… haunting stories. He's watching his step. He's got a different way of walking now… he's scared… he's a different person!"

"That's the way it is at first. Buy him a rat. A white one."

"I'm worried that Vic might become like Ivan Trofimovich," she mumbled, with a vacant stare, "torturing himself just like that… you didn't know Ivan Trofimovich before, and all the people who… he's a wreck now. Please, help if you can – help him too. Distract him somehow… He's very dear to me, he was a friend of my dad. I'm used to Ivan Trofimovich always being around."

"Who gives a damn?"

"I'll do anything for you. I'll give you money. I'll scrape together as much as you ask. Help them – do it for me. Perhaps you want some medicines from Moscow?"

"No. Even if I could have a go with you... even then, I'd say no. Live on your own. You're prettier from a distance. And you're nicer when dressed."

She wasn't listening. She just stood there with a stiffening face.

The bank was guarded by a grey-haired police sergeant. A woman was taking round plates with cakes and turned to look at the hissing samovar. I took a good look round – no fair, curly hair, no solidly built stunner. I poked in at the "Reception" window.

"Where's my love?"

"That I wouldn't know." The woman at first frowned at my mangy clothes, but on a second look she said: "You are one of the rat catchers, eh? You could have changed your clothes. This is a public place. In Moscow you wouldn't come in dressed like that..."

Behind a door reading "No entrance" meandered a corridor with toilet doors. The policeman tagged along, eager for a chat, so I just looked around as I went along. I found my lady ensconced behind a door with the sign: "Manager of the Svetloyar Branch of the Savings Bank of the Russian Federation, Alla Ivanovna Denisova. Meeting times..."

She was gazing at the window sill – from which peered red, white and violet flowers – and biting into a juicy apple. As I skirted the table and moved close to her, she turned around on her chair.

"Sorry, I've only just managed to get free." I cast a sideways glance at the policeman. "You are eating in your workplace, scattering crusts of bread over your desk... The corridor's going all green. You can stick your foot in the cracks of your door frame. Look, it's totally worn out by rat ticks..."

The policeman shuffled away to his post. I put my hand on her shoulder.

"The rat ticks, Alla Ivanovna, are weeny little insects. And they create tiny passages. Even when they leave, you'll still itch for a couple of weeks."

"Let go."

"Perhaps we can meet? And go all the way?"

She rose, throwing my hands off.

"Come on, dear – go and find yourself a girl."

"Shall we meet up, then?"

"Sure, sure. Now let me pass."

"Then let's meet up soon – like now."

She retreated into a corner, grinning and pulling wry faces, trying not to burst out laughing. She heard footsteps behind the door and placed a chair in front of her, to bar my way, then shoved me away as I tried to grab at her skirt.

"This is not the place. What is it they say? 'If you let all and sundry have their way, the bedstead will break straight away.'" She threw her purse, lipstick and keys into her handbag. "You're no spring chicken, but you still like playing around. What do I need you for? We don't have any rats here, we're on the northern side... What's your driver's name? Is it Konstantin?"

"I don't remember. What about the driver?"

"He's my husband. Drive carefully, don't make him smash up the car. Off you go."

"You'll be calling me soon. And bawling about the rats."

"How do you know that?"

People were crowding at the entrances. I hung around behind them: somebody was kicking up a fuss about tinned meat and mattresses. I turned to a woman with a white headscarf.

"What's going on, miss?"

The old woman waved one of her withered hands, clutching her grandson with the other.

"They've put up notices. They're going to take us all out into the countryside." She shouted into the crowd: "For how long? What's written up there?"

"Three whole days plus travelling time. There's no dates."

"How d'you mean no dates?" someone said in the crowd. "It's written here... where is it?... Here we go – departure by decree."

"Granny, what about our puppy?" the boy whined.

"I can't even get out to buy bread every day," muttered the old woman as she moved away. "I get this thumping in my temples. And now they want us to go into the woods... so much walking!" And to her grandson: "Why should your old granny drag you along?"

The boy stared at the funny faces I was pulling.

Out on the boulevard, the patrols weren't letting people through. I was identified by an officer and ran in among the empty benches. A young man perched on the fence like a sickly crow.

"Why are you sitting there? Have you given up your post or what?"

Vic slunk down to the ground and gazed at me with a vacant stare as he brushed his backside.

"There's no need any more."

"W-what?"

"It's all clear now. They were there. Came leaping out."

"Really?" I laughed out loud and clapped my hands. "Great! Did you see them?"

He nodded his pale-faced head and climbed back up onto the fence, pointing at a lanky fellow.

"He's been waiting for you."

I looked more closely: Governor Shestakov was staring back at me, holding on to a bench as if it were about to slide away from beneath him.

"Well?" he croaked. "Nothing?"

"We've found them. And tomorrow we'll wipe them out. Everything's fine. Come what may."

Shestakov heaved a loud sigh, then rubbed the bridge of his nose, got up and wobbled off to a vehicle surrounded by his people.

"You said: 'Come what may'," he rasped. "If I understand correctly – this means that on 12th September, from eleven to five, no rats are going to drop down?"

"That's correct. For the agreed fee. Come what may, everything will be fine."

I pushed my way through the fire engines surrounding the smoking rubbish-collection room. Oldie was in the hall, where the soldiers were collecting the rats which had dropped in their flight.

The pack had been feeding in the rubbish chute when Oldie started the smoke from below. In the crush they pushed one another down the narrow passageway, and then, stunned by the smoke, they hurled themselves towards the suspended ceiling, forcing the older rats and the baby rats through the cracks. I stirred up the heap of carrion, which was teeming with tails. The largest rat was about twenty-five ounces. A pregnant female.

Oldie was in the company of Grisha, the chap from the meat factory who had brought us the little ham "snack", and the drunk superintendent.

"What else?... Comrades, gather up the fallen rats in a sack and take them in our car to the laboratory before they've cooled down, so that they can be examined for parasites. And you," said Oldie, trying to steady up the teetering superintendent, "what do you do when a bulb on the suspended ceiling burns out?"

"We put up our turret... that's a kind of tower."

"So we don't need to rack our brains," Oldie exclaimed. "We'll put up this turret of yours, and dismantle – one, two… the six panels opposite the crack. They won't be jumping six metres. We'll fill the crack with concrete. They'll have nowhere to go, no food, no water. We'll work around the edges of the suspended ceiling for three days with strong poisons. And we'll finish off with anticoagulants, just to be on the safe side. There'll be none left! What are you smiling at, young man?"

"Let's go and eat now."

As we crossed the square at a brisk pace, Oldie issued orders for the following day and lectured away, while I conjured up rosy visions of what could happen in the bank. A chirpy Larionov minced along for a while, but then dropped behind to have a rest.

"Ah… Can't keep up with you! I've got used to taking my time. After all those years with Mokrousov… He had an artificial leg, he'd lost his left foot."

When we went to the bathroom to wash our hands, we found three thuggish-looking guys with grim faces and a chap in a yellow jumper waiting for us… Their hands looked pretty coarse….

"Hello, young ladies," was my greeting.

The nearest thug landed a punch on Oldie's chin. Oldie plumped backwards onto his behind, clasped his beard with a groan and rolled onto his side, drawing his knees up to his belly.

"Well done! Who's the boss? You, probably? Can I give him a good battering too?"

Two thugs lurched towards me with a threatening look – the third, who was standing with his back to me, struck me in the teeth with his elbow as he swung round. A completely unremarkable bunch of people they were, stinking of cheap cologne. I sat down by the wall, licking my numbing lips – the bastards, here they go again, all together, one by one! I clenched my fists so hard that my nails drew blood, and was unable to unclench them.

But the thugs surrounded Oldie.

"Something you ate in the café didn't agree with you? You liked our little sausage though, didn't you? We'll settle the score with you soon." And spitting in Oldie's beard they disappeared.

An hour passed. I took off the ice pack and sat dejectedly by the mirror. My lip wasn't bleeding, but had swollen up like an inflatable mattress.

"You look like a camel," was Oldie's comment. He was lying on his back, opening his mouth every two seconds, struggling to believe that his jaw was still intact.

Outside, Klinsky bellowed down the rank of soldiers, his voice slipping into a shriek:

"You've got to hunt them down! You have tried?! Shut up. You've slept or eaten, maybe! I'll teach you... you'll remember! Feeling sick? I sent you on a task – not to puke all over the fence! Don't blink at me! How could they get through? Who let them in? You? Or you? Didn't you see them from the car? Who do you report to? And you? Can't you move your arse a bit faster? You'll move it fast enough to collect your pension! Dear chaps, my throat's sore from screaming. And I'll make you howl if I see just one non-pregnant bastard without a pass! I'll kill you!"

He came in and spread his arms.

"Idiots! It's my fault. But I can... they're looking for those scumbags."

Showing great sympathy, he leant over Oldie, who asked without raising his head from the pillow:

"We'd really appreciate if you could call off your search. We can hardly remember what they look like – we wouldn't recognize them. And we certainly don't want to see them again. It's also possible that we didn't show enough respect towards them..."

"I understand... It's OK. You are only thinking about one thing now: the railway station, the train to Moscow. Of course. You'll get nowhere with these oafs. They're supposed to be on duty and off they go for beer. Oh, damn it! Don't go! Your presence is vital – you know it yourself. Damn the President, damn the 'Golden Ring'… it's not for that. It's for something else. Look, I'll give you my example: I've travelled everywhere, but I was born here. Why did I travel? I was searching! A man is not perfectly rounded – he's got rough edges, he's like a cogwheel. And I rushed around looking for a town suitable for me, just as rough round the edges as me. And with cogs matching with mine. Couldn't find one. Then I realized that there's no such town. If you're not completely pig-headed, you should adapt your hometown to your cogs. What you see is filthy rubbish dumps, louts mucking around to make an impression so as to get a warm berth and a spoonful of food… Yes, that's true. But what else do you see? People should raise their heads! They can clear away the filth… celebrate. If we just dig under our feet – there's our native history! The burial mounds of our forebears – not just some barren spot. You see how many there are! And if just one rat falls on the floor, everything will go pear-shaped… If we fail, that will stand for ever as a blot on our name: we'll sink in the mire. Everything's turned out so badly. At dinner Ivan Trofimovich handed in his resignation… you were put in my charge from Baranov, and now this assault. Is it a question of money? We can sort out the money, we'll scrape it together. Well, boys?"

"Ten per cent more," Oldie said with an indifferent tone.

Klinsky embraced him like a son and hugged me like a brother, then dashed away in his wailing car.

"Oldie, for the prestige of our company it would be very appropriate if one of us had his throat cut at work. And I already know who. Where's the lamp?"

Oldie prised his aching eyes open.

* * *

"Where to, guv?"

Konstantin was spreading out a blanket in the car. "Drive home to get some sleep. Go to your wife. Just get a tanker of water organized for me by five in the morning, for our disinfestation procedures. It can be service water."

I wanted to take a breather, but foul stenches were wafting over from the meat-processing plant. The wind clambered through the trees, breaking off the dry branches with its light feet – and also blew on my swollen lip, as the blood pounded inside. Cockerels cried out on the balconies above the cars, above the cooling grass that lured the leaves to the ground. The streets lay in the grasp of an electrical cobweb that chased the night away. A man was rocking a pram back and forth, chanting a song. I smiled at him. Bending over the pram, he said:

"There's a bloke leaving the block. Not sure who he is. We'll follow him."

I crossed the street. Without going in, I gave a kick to the entrance door – run, rats, run! I rang the bell.

Ivan Trofimovich peered out, wincing.

"Ah. It's OK. Come on in. Let's go into my study... My wife's resting. Vera, don't get up, it's a colleague. You think I can't make tea?... I wasn't doing anything – I'm retired now. Just sitting around, waiting..."

"What for?"

"Well – for anybody to come." He sat down on the covered sofa without leaning back. Behind his back lay his pressed ceremonial dress all a-glitter with decorations. "It's for tomorrow," he explained. "We're having a little celebration. All in all, I've planned things on a modest scale – with no cameras. So that they don't have to come from the regional centre. One of our artists keeps pestering me: 'I want to paint a portrait for the museum!' There's already an entire wall of my photographs there. Well, let's hope they don't overdo it – at least people will have a good memory of me. And it's all in their eyes. My father was a hod carrier on a building site – an outstanding worker and then a front-line soldier. My mother was a raker – also an outstanding worker. I remember the wall of our room in the workers' hostels was covered with quotations. When I was only sixteen, I became the head of the collective farm, the one here, the 'Lake Farm', on the way to the Kryukov forest. And on and on it went: the building of this town, the draining of the lake, the construction of the large cattle-breeding farm by our Komsomol. You might be interested to know that when they chose—"

"No, I am not."

There was an agonizing pause. Ivan Trofimovich added under his breath:

"Er… now I'll do a bit of fishing. Up until now I couldn't fish, because the lake had been drained, but now… now that I'm retired I'll travel a long way away… well, I've got a car, so I'll also be able to see my grandchildren, if I keep my health! Let's go and have some tea. Won't you?"

"How are you feeling?"

He gazed at the polished floor. Twice he tried to say something, then only mumbled:

"A sense of weakness…"

"When I came, there were some lights burning in the basement. Do you turn them on every night?"

"As a matter of fact, they're on round the clock… Well, it's not me who decided that – it was the tenants' committee. It's to frighten the rats away. There's a flat for those on duty, but…"

"But you've got the keys to the basement?"

"Yes, in fact, I've got them…"

"Let's go."

A shaft of light piercing the darkness through a peephole soon guided me to the exit. Ivan Trofimovich still remained seated. I waited for a couple of minutes before whispering down the corridor:

"Are you a man or what?"

5

Gandhi and the Breast-feeding Girl

12 Days to D-Day

He was kitted out as if he was going fishing: waterproof coat, high boots, he was leaning on a ski stick without a plastic ring. Most likely it was the one he'd nailed the baby rat with. I snatched the stick from his hand and hurled it into the grass.

"Ivan Trofimovich, they are just the most common order of mammals. The brown rat is up to ten inches in length. The tail is shorter than the body. A pair of chisel-like incisor teeth, bevelled backwards – look me in the eyes! – a large number of scales on the tail. Stocky legs. A head with no neck. An awkward body. A rather long tongue. Yellow-brown fur, with a darker back. Yellowish-white abdomen. Abdomen and back have different colours. The hair, if you pull it out, is variegated: the base is grey, it's black at the top, and a yellow band in the middle. Don't look down!" I shoved him on the shoulder. "Are you deaf?"

I blurted out these words without stopping, raising my voice to drown out the heavy ringing sounds which are part and parcel of my work. We were surrounded by avalanches of scratched-out plaster, scrabbled piles of rubbish and spluttering water pipes. Sudden sprints in the matted grass under the maple trees, feet scarpering in the tangled grass. I could already single out noises – snorts, squeaky skirmishes – were they the sounds of the night, or was it all in my head? A gust of wind! Oh, damn it! Now the leaves were rustling behind his back. He didn't understand. The leaves, dragged along by the wind, were scratching the asphalt with their dry brown claws, stiff with cold.

"It's the leaves!" I turned him round to look at the leaves, his back to the building, the rubbish skip and the grass. "Go on, die, if that's what you want! But let me tell you something: your fear is imaginary... Yes, the rat is a predator, but to whom? It bites small household animals – although... I don't even remember any instances of that. Rats don't attack people! They're simple animals. Can I at least drive that into your head?! Like pigeons. With one difference: they're afraid of man. They come out only when people are asleep. Are you afraid of pigeons? So why of rats? You find them disgusting? Just don't look at them! That's just ignorance: the tolerance threshold in your head is zilch! It doesn't go further than synanthropic rodents. In life one has to go beyond that. Psychologists say that if a child is properly brought up, there should be no difference for him between a rat and a squirrel. Like in Guinea. Eighty per cent of people there eat rats with relish. They hunt them for food. Lots of free meat. And our countrymen ate them during the siege! Look at it this way and your life will change! You put a couple of traps in the basement, and in the morning – straight into the frying pan! As for their fur – they make such nice mittens..."

"Stop it!" Ivan Trofimovich implored.

"But why? You eat pork, don't you? And what sort of crap doesn't a pig eat? But a rat only eats top-notch stuff! Grain, milk, sour cream, smoked sausage... unless it's been poisoned – in which case it gets disoriented and crawls out by day to die under your feet... You can see one like that straight away: it staggers about, its movements are uncertain. But even then it doesn't bite. Unless you kick it in the side or stretch your hand out to grab it by the back of the neck. That's the one that makes you shiver."

I drew a long breath, and drowned out the sounds of the night with my sniffing, spitting and loud yawning – then I had a look at him: was it working? His face seemed to soften a bit, his shoulders had relaxed. He said with more assurance in his voice:

"I've seen a big one. Like a tomcat."

"Pull the other one! It's the darkness that makes them look bigger. Oldie's been killing them for twenty years – he's heard so many stories like that… but he has not found a single one bigger than the palm of his hand at the end of a job! Sure, there are fourteen-inch-long ones. But where? On the Vendôme Islands. People just lie. We tell lies ourselves. Without some embellishments, we'd be embarrassed to tell people what we really do. But now there's only the two of us – why should I lie to you? There was a photo in an Italian magazine. A bloke was holding a rat by its tail. Its torso almost a metre long. But we could see it wasn't an ordinary rat… it was a muskrat."

Was he ready? I scrutinized him – then ordered:

"The keys. Cheers. I'm off to have a look around. Can you wait here by yourself?"

As he mulled something over, he gave me a nod.

"Stand under the light. Be careful over there, towards the trees, that's where they have their summer nests. If you feel nervous – clap your hands. And keep moving around – they've got bad eyes, in poor lighting they might not notice stationary objects."

I went to the basement, jingling the keys, and from there I said:

"Ivan Trofimovich?"

"What?"

"Relax. Don't mope. You're not a small household animal."

I flashed the lamp on the threshold and the door frame – all OK. I unlocked the door and pulled it open, holding it up a bit so that there would be no scraping.

The stone steps, their edges sprinkled with slaked lime, led downwards to a whitewashed wall bearing a graffiti sketch of an amorous coupling. To the right of the wall extended a tunnel with a trampled earth floor. To the left was a rusty door bolted shut. The tin plating at the bottom had been torn to shreds. There were scraps of paper and potato peel scattered around. An empty tin. A-ha. What was that down there on the right?

A communal corridor branched off to the right and left – were these storerooms? Don't think so. These were the authorities' lodgings – they wouldn't store potatoes here. And they'd keep bikes and skis in their loggias.

The corners of the first step were undamaged, and unsoiled by excrement. I groped my way over each step, keeping an eye on the rusty door. It was getting cold. The building was full of chinks – draughts licked the back of my neck. I had stepped in some water on the floor – my trainers squeaked. The steps were in good condition. I walked on my heels – they squeaked. On my toes – ditto. The final step. I squatted down and there was a terrible squeak – the blood rushed into my head. What a fool: it wasn't the shoes squeaking – it was the beasties: but where?

The door?! Not there. From the right? A few squeaks – maybe just one? But – there you go! – now I can hear a whole pack. The time's right. After midnight. They're close. Surely not round the corner? Don't think the burrows are behind the door. It has numbers daubed on it – must be some switchboard room. Looks like one of their "tables": they gorged themselves here and filed off their teeth on the tin plating. Two millimetres a day – "otherwise the teeth grow too long, and the rats die from a locked-open jaw", in the words of Tkachuk, head of the Moscow Health Service. He was no good at disinfesting residential properties: his dissertation was on the Turkestan rat, which he really knew inside out – he loved field research in hot climates with willing female assistants. After the Olympics he booted Oldie out, just for breathing a word about doctored rat-infestation figures.

The floor had been freshly trampled. Their main pathways, marked out by scent trails, ran along the wall. Beneath the lowest step was a hole, an opening in the hard soil, two and a half inches wide. I let out a groan: it would be the work of an amateur to leave an open burrow behind my back. This was the time when they milled around. The first one out would go round my back and, with its beating little heart and the stench of death in its nostrils, would hush the squeaking and scrabbling inside the cracks – they would all sit still, unleashing a torrent of horror throughout the basement. They'd freeze in mortal fear – an intruder! Better go easy with the old man waiting outside.

Barely touching the ground I raced outside.

"Ivan Trofimovich, come here. Well? Any attacks?"

He answered loudly:

"No."

"Don't shout."

"Only two in the grass, playing like kittens. There was a scratching noise in the rubbish bin, but I didn't see anything."

"So?..."

"Nothing. I'm telling you – they won't come out."

"What I'm asking is, do they still make you tremble?"

"I can cope. You know, I hadn't tried standing by myself before. I felt uneasy. But now it seems to be OK. My hands were sweating, though." He shook his hands and smirked. I felt a pang in my stomach – he was about to go off the rails.

"Let's move quietly. Do as I do, all right?" I sensed his hesitation. "What are you afraid of now?"

"I'm ready. I can cope." He stopped short and drew a wheezing breath.

I shook my fist at the two blokes who were smoking by a distant entrance, helped the retired Mayor into the basement and closed the door.

First of all I asked for a handkerchief and, unfolding it on my palm so as not to burn my fingers, unscrewed the bulb over the door.

The sudden eclipse didn't send them scurrying off to their burrows.

"Can you hear their characteristic tut-tutting?"

Ivan Trofimovich froze, on the verge of tears, his cheeks white as lime. So the pack's playing around under another bulb. Let's move on. So the hole under the step was uninhabited. It's certainly inconvenient for them with people going up and down. Had they begun to dig it and then abandoned it? They wouldn't have a toilet and a table beside an inhabited hole. Although…

We went down. I pointed to the right:

"What's that?"

His lips trembled – it was the corridor. Certainly not a ladies' bathhouse… Did it go all the way across? Fork off? Stretch to the end of a section? He was shaking: he'd never been down there. Not once since they moved in. Very helpful. What if the burrow – mmm… about twelve metres long, maybe with three nests and two maternity chambers – was inhabited? Then a rat would jump straight in front of us and… Let's focus now. Where next?

I groped for the empty tin, found it, and rammed it with my heel into the hole beneath the lower step. That's it. I peered round the corner: the corridor ran through the whole building. Light bulbs scattered here and there. I don't like corridors like that, where you're in full view. There are pipes suspended high up. To left and right – too bad. No rat seems to be leaning over or running around. That's on the left. On the right I can't say as yet. Listen. Damn, he's puffing like a steam engine. I looked around: he was gulping hard, his skull protruding from his grey-haired head – perhaps I shouldn't… Shall I stay here? No, let's go and have a word with him:

"Ivan Trofimovich, we're in control here! I'll show you how they play. Then we'll stamp our feet and they'll disappear. A demonstration. To consolidate the lesson."

He was somehow apathetic. Should I repeat myself? I stepped out into the corridor and went straight to the wall: the pipes to the right were clean on the outside. Straight along – ten metres – there was a broad opening in the wall, about three metres wide, with light behind it. Was that their playground – where they stretch their legs?

I didn't take my eyes off the corner nearest us – here the wall and the light ended, and that's where the vermin would emerge. It'd dash out in the dark, feeling the wall with its whiskers, and bump into my toe. Touching the wall with my back, I headed for the opening, beckoning Ivan Trofimovich. I caught sight of the rat too late. You can't keep an eye on everything. It shuffled down the middle of the corridor straight towards us. Why didn't it turn into the opening? What the hell did it want with us? I pressed Ivan Trofimovich's shoulder – he still didn't see it: "What?" It stopped short, and stood sideways on. By the wall. Damn, surely it couldn't stand sideways onto a bare wall. Who was it showing its indignation to by standing like that, sideways? There must be another one sitting there. It was dark – I couldn't see.

Ivan Trofimovich shuddered as I, with an unpleasant feeling of confusion, gazed around in succession at the pipes, the opening and the corridor. That's it: more beasts were gliding down the corridor: an adult and two baby rats. I scratched my head – would the whole pack rain down now? I touched the lamp switch. They strutted right to our feet, running apart and coming back together. Could they be heading for that burrow?

Here we go. They slowed down near the opening, huddled closer, looked in – yes, in there – watchful little creatures.

Here now: the older ones now slithered along like a grey ribbon, three of them – where had these three come from? The baby rats swept along behind. Odd – they all started bouncing back... I distinctly heard a rasping sound: "Tak-tak!" Must be something trickling down, like gravel. Where were they jumping off to?

And they broke loose in a good old rumpus: rustling noises echoed along the walls, from every corner! To be on the safe side, I rustled my feet on the floor, hunching up in expectation of some sharp-clawed creature stealing along the pipes overhead, or little ones dropping on my neck in a very foul mood. Rule number one: work while they're asleep. On their territory, yes, but not in their presence. The green-eyed beasts should not see their exterminator. And he shouldn't have to mind his every step.

We bided our time, then sidled to the opening in the wall. I lit the lamp, and cast a smudge of light along the corridor to keep them away. Now it's our turn.

A corner. I grabbed Ivan Trofimovich by the collar and sat him down in front, like a dog, gesturing to him to keep his trap shut. I poked my head round the corner... There was a kind of pit, an iron staircase. Some bales, debris. The rats had not run away – they were there! I gave Ivan Trofimovich a little nudge – look!

A space opened in front of us, six square metres in size, about seven feet below the corridor level. The wall slabs showed lots of cracks. The insulation material in the bales was all torn to pieces. The rats were leaping on the rubble, among jars and bottles... There was a concrete floor... surface nests? Maybe I shouldn't...

I looked down the corridor. Ivan Trofimovich stared at the rats' playground as if it were a vision of hell, his face aglow with a purple sheen.

We peered out of the dark corridor. The lamp illuminating the pit had dazzled the rats. They were wandering around... too many for an ordinary pack. On the pipe, the older rats were warming themselves in clusters, while the subordinate ones stood with their black tails hanging down. The younger rats were sitting around in groups. Amidst the brick debris, a trio of large subdominants or females were gnawing an old rag – no, not a rag... what were they eating? Looked like a baby rat. They were all very nervous.

One of the females is not so skittish after all – she's being groomed by her son, or her lover, who's jerking his head and croaking hoarsely as he raises himself on his hind paw to reach her back.

They're nervous – but why? One of them is stirring, they all stretch their tails and cock their ears forwards... A neighbour's shifting place – sideways on to him... He's baring his teeth... vicious. Too many of them? Is it the intrusion into their marked territories that makes them angry? Maybe. But what else? Hunger? Are they so numerous that there isn't enough food? It's not typical for a house basement. For Svetloyar it's probably normal.

But the weird thing was... I couldn't see a dominant male. Who was the centre of activities? Was it that huge male over there, humping a female beneath a pipe? What an enormous specimen. The female didn't snarl. But would the other three be gorging themselves if there were a dominant male around? The rat gave up on the female and scuttled away... In fact, he growled at those coming near him. Then he sat down and cleaned himself. A baby rat next to him paid no attention. How could tyrannical dominance be identified? Not easy. But I could recognize the lowest subordinate straight away.

The subordinate was sticking out between the bales, only rarely raising its head in the direction of the eating trio. It was easy to spot – its colouring was unusual: a ginger "cowl" over a downcast snout. It threw furtive glances around, without looking up. The trio dispersed in a rush, leaving tiny fragments on the "table".

The baby rats grouped closer beneath the lamp and began to play. Five of them shot past, huddled together, jostling each other and tumbling down in a heap. I calmed down and relaxed. They were nipping each other's tails, jumping on each other's backs… Suddenly they stopped playing – they scarpered away and sat down in the corners. Had they sensed our presence? Ivan Trofimovich could not take it any more.

The lowest subordinate scraped its way out of its chink, reeling. As if its left hind paw was aching. If it still had one. Its fur was mangy and showed bald patches. It moved forwards, the fool, dragging its hindquarters – scrabbling on all fours. It was trying to get lower down.

The subordinate threaded its way through the pack as if among hostile humans in broad daylight; it crawled, stopped, looked around, then crawled again, stopped, looked around – where was it going? Where would the invalid head to? I shuddered to think. Could it really be heading for the feeding centre? I was really annoyed: in the presence of a dominant a subordinate couldn't possibly approach the leftovers. Was there no dominant here? Or maybe he's not showing up because of our intrusion?

Having finally satisfied the female, the huge rat took himself off, crawled over his squeaking companion and shoved himself into the hole. He twisted and helped himself with his forepaws, his tail spinning around. Then he leapt off and raced excitedly among the other rats, who were lying low. He thrust himself into the burrow again and began to spin round. Ivan Trofimovich turned his ashen face towards me. The huge rat was prancing around like a dominant male. Was it him then?

The entire pack froze. The lowest subordinate, huddling on the floor, crept up to the abandoned "table". Then it dropped flat, moving its vibrissae over the bricks.

"This is it," I declared.

Ivan Trofimovich forced himself forwards with his eyes closed. I'd really like to give him a good kicking now!

It was as if a shadow had dropped over the pit. It was dreadful.

I shook my numbed hands.

"Open your eyes!" I whispered.

And then the real dominant appeared.

A reddish, raging creature sprang from a top crack and dived among the heart-rending screeches of the scrambling rats. I hid behind the wall. The leader, hitting the ground, couldn't keep his balance: he fell on his side, onto the fleeing baby rats, but an instant later, pawing into the ground, he reached the burrow in one big leap and, taming everyone with a brief roar, thrust himself into the side of the squealing, hoglike male, which disappeared through the rubble like a stone into the abyss. The leader whirled around the space scented with his urine, biting, shoving, turning over, while from the pipes, bales and chinks the other rats leapt and darted about, shooting off into their burrows and disappearing from sight. The lowest subordinate also attempted a lame and blind retreat to its little hole – but ran straight into the path of the leader. Snout to snout. The ginger-cowled rat ran for dear life, but then froze stiff as it bumped against the brickwork. Spreading its surrendered paws – one crooked, lame, twisted to one side – it revealed its belly. I kept blinking absent-mindedly as the leader, with calm, thrust his teeth into that whitish stomach, just as a tired animal dips its bloodstained jaws into longed-for, ice-cold water. A shriek shot upwards, piercing the air, then it dissolved into a long rumble and snapped, turning into a hollow, weary, almost relaxed moan. I pulled Ivan Trofimovich back into the corridor. Then, the usual scene: as the leader twisted and turned, a few toadies joined him and stuck their impatient snouts into the fleshy pulp.

Between their tails protruded the upturned head of the lowest subordinate, with glistening eyes and a good-natured face, slightly twisted to one side. It was as if they were tickling it and it was gaping. I turned away.

I waited a bit, then with my foot I found a piece of plaster and flung it behind the wall. I cast a questioning look at Ivan Trofimovich. He went and screwed in the bulb, and on catching sight of his watch sighed.

"Goodness me! My wife must be on the phone looking for me by now. Seen how I frightened them, eh? They scrambled away like cockroaches!" He grinned. "I just showed my face and... look at the result... Let me see that insulating material. I never had time for anything... The kitchen in winter's like an ice-house – last year my grandson got pneumonia – and here's plenty of insulating material... You're not in the mood, are you? Are you tired?"

Yes. He went down the stairs into the pit, counted the bales of insulating material, climbed on top of them and stamped on the brick rubble.

"We'll organize a day of voluntary work! There's so much space here: it could be a gym! We could grow mushrooms. I've never had time for anything... but now..."

He went off to comfort his wife, and got out a bottle to comfort me, then we sat on a bench. Ivan Trofimovich was all smiles, and got up and stomped on the grass pretending to tread on the beasts' tails, to show them who's the boss. Suddenly he grabbed me by the lapel and mumbled:

"Thanks, son... I'm alive..." He started crying, so that the whole street could hear, then he said, sobbing, "The state I was in, I had no strength left at all."

A cropped head popped up from the bushes.

"Comrade Lieutenant, need any help?"

At that, Ivan Trofimovich improvised a Cossack dance and called me to join him, while his wife, wiping her eyes, whispered: "Do come in. Why in the street?" I smiled and screwed up my eyes so as not to burst into tears. It was the last day of August, the last day of summer.

I plodded along, stiff as a board. Better not to rush: I could scare my sleep away. All was deserted, as if I'd got out from somebody's sleepless bed onto an early-morning bus, before the metro opens, among silent summer cottagers and factory workers. There's a fine large water tanker. Ten cubic metres. The driver was asleep at the wheel. Let's get going, mate...

"The café. In the basement near the school, you know it?"

He woke fully and asked: "That one there?"

"Yeah. Do you see that ventilation duct into the basement? Go and pour water down it."

"Well, you're not from here, boss, and that caff's run by important people."

"This is an order. Disinfestation measures. Let me write up your assignment. You can write the time yourself. Go and pour... do you want me to unplug your ears?"

I walked on – across the square some geezers in black overalls were pushing a trolley with a builders' hoisting cradle – this, apparently, was the "turret" they'd been talking about.

They growled an imprecation at me, gave up pushing and started arguing about how high it would lift.

In the sanatorium the worn-out waitress groaned, stifling a yawn:

"You going to eat?"

No. Oldie – his brow moist with sweat – was totting up in a notebook the outlay on poisons for the mother-and-daughter couple of the health unit. He lifted up his bearded face.

"Here's my orders. Since we're carrying out extermination operations on the rodents' territory, we'll work with zinc phosphide mixed with oatmeal. In bags of a hundred grams each. They don't have any monofluorides. In forty-eight hours we'll apply some Ratindan in a concentration of five parts to a thousand."

It would do. I pulled off my sweater, my shirt and my trousers. Oldie vanished, and so did the ladies in overalls. Then the warrant officer turned up.

"Should I make paper cones from newspapers?"

"Absolutely not. They mustn't smell of ink…" I swirled the quilt around me and turned to the wall. Damn, I have not drawn the blinds. Let's see…

I had a dreamless sleep. It was time to get up and wash. A voice from the loudspeaker croaked: "One, two, three, testing." The blinds' rings rattled – probably the wind. Must think of something nice – dinner, women, football on TV – and get up. I pulled back the blinds. They got stuck. I pulled harder – and a rat came tumbling down on my arm!

"Bastard!" I jerked my arm wildly, and managed to shake off the tenacious weight. It leapt behind the bedstead, touching my shoulder with its tail. I hurled myself onto the floor, ripping off the quilt and kicking the bed. Dirty little fucker…

"What's the matter with you?" Oldie rushed in.

"He's tame!" Vic blabbered, behind him. "It was me who brought him in, from the Pioneer Palace. It's a male. It's called Gandhi. Gandhi… Gandhi… it's crawled under the bed."

"For Christ's sake! Get it out of here! Couldn't you find a better place, you fool… you idiot!"

"What's wrong with you?"

I cooled down in the bath, and my heart resumed its normal beating. What bastards, the lot of them – I don't know…

They were waiting to have lunch on the balcony, and fell silent when I came out. No sight of Vic's girlfriend. There was cold kvas soup, potato wedges, chicken, tomatoes, little cucumbers, round-headed leeks, cherry compote and some rolls. I shot round a swift glance.

"Why've you put your Gandhi into a jar?... Let him run around, no?"

"That's just for fun..." Vic said apologetically. "It's interesting to observe him. I know so much now thanks to you."

I told them about the previous night. The rolls turned out to be with fish filling. And the kvas could have done with some ice.

"Yes, well... you know what you were saying about the dominant and the subordinate..." said Larionov, who was no longer enjoying his food. "This subordinate... what is it? Is it like that by nature?"

"The social life of rodents has not been sufficiently researched," Oldie admitted. "But there's no predestination. At the training ground I separated a dominant rat from its pack. And it wasn't always replaced by a subdominant. Sometimes it was replaced by a subordinate rat. So stratification is purely contingent. Chance. One day a rat takes an ordinary step and it suddenly produces exceptional consequences. And the rat is crushed. For instance, a chap is going over a bridge, takes a step, and the bridge collapses from old age. Yet it was just an ordinary step. Don't you agree?"

"No. The chap is aware that the bridge has collapsed."

"Nonsense! In short, there's no such thing as predestination. In open biotopes it's freer – you can observe, more or less, a situation of equality. Hierarchy and oppression occur in a state of overcrowding. Lack of space..."

The scientist and the architect set off to spread the paper bags of poisoned bait on the dismantled edges of the suspended ceiling. I polished off a roll. As he cleared away the plates, Vic still tried to advance his knowledge:

"What's the rat king? Is it a dominant male?"

"No, that's a number of rats whose tails are knotted together, in a ball. The largest ever observed was thirty-two."

"How do they knot together?"

"In the nest. The newborns weave their tails together. Their tails are soft, cartilaginous, easily wounded. Pus... blood... filth. Mange. And the tails grow into each other. I've never seen it myself. Only the Americans once observed it in one of their training grounds. However, it turned out there were rats of various ages in the cluster. So the devil only knows... The king dies in the burrow. We pick up corpses on the surface – so we've never seen one."

"But what does it eat?"

"It's fed by the pack. In general, rats don't store up food. If they're hard up, they eat their elders, excrement, their babies. But they do feed the king. That's where the wild tales come from that in the middle of a tangle sits an enormous rat – the king – and, all around, his chariot. In actual fact their tails have grown together in the dirt. They pull in all directions and can't move from the spot. But the neighbours feed them... If you hang around with us they'll gobble you up... Go to Moscow, visit the Kremlin..."

Gandhi was gnawing at the gristle on some chicken bones. I'd got used to it now.

"If you are nice, it'll be fawning all over you. If you frown, it'll bare its teeth. That's what my instructor said, Master of Science Toshchilin, who used to kill brown rats in Kstovo, in the Gorky Region, and beat the extermination record in the Volgograd Region in the '60s. I wonder if he's still around."

"And there's no other type of rat king?"

"Oh yes – your fellow townsmen! The Rat King co-op! They've promised to clean up the town in one night! And your bosses fell for it. I've got no time now, but I'll show those idiots one day…"

"You think they can't do it? It's impossible?"

"That's two separate things. Of course they're lying. As for it being impossible… why? When you kill rats, it's not a question of time. I am never bothered about time. The scale of the extermination only depends on how deeply you delve into the living matter. There's a formula proposed by classical authors such as Davies and Christian: extermination is achieved by cutting off the resources of the local environment… What that means is: here's Svetloyar, the former Yagoda. You want to wipe out the town's rats? Cut off the resources of the town. You can poison one. Or a pack. Or a colony. Or aim for total extermination. It simply depends on the scale. On whether you can do things in a big way."

Vic stopped and asked for clarification:

"Kill, you mean?"

"Delve deep into the living matter. That's more important. You have to understand that the town is a whole complex. It includes its past and it includes you. So, go and bury yourself too. I'm sure those idiots have no guts. I'll go for a stroll."

"There must be some other kind of rat king," he persisted.

Sure. A village. A town like yours.

By the gates a steamroller was backing up over fresh asphalt and a tar burner was smoking. Some labourers leant on their rakes. On catching sight of me, they shoved their bottle behind a lamppost.

Around the square, the cordon officers – in full uniform – were dying of boredom, and were teaching the Alsatians to lie down and sit. I headed across the square towards the bank.

On a wooden crate in the middle of the square, an officer wearing a service cap was testing a megaphone. People herded beneath him. A portly clergyman with a bucket-like black hat and a round badge on a chain beneath his grey beard was clomping along to join them. Keeping a respectful distance and carrying an icon, a censer, a cross and a standard, some rubicund lay brothers in gold-and-blue surplices minced behind him.

"Stage one!" was heard through the megaphone. "Fags out! Who's spitting on the ground? Sviridov – the guests, who's going to be the guests?!"

"Comrade Lieutenant, comr—" A paunchy warrant officer with sweaty brows, looking like a lightweight wrestler, scooted up to me. "Only a minute. Please…" He seized my wrist with his damp hand and dragged me over. "Here's a guest, Comrade Colonel. Same size."

The garrison commander Gontar examined me from the crate.

"He'll do. For now."

He smoothed out a sheet of paper. The captain clambered onto the crate and held the megaphone to the Colonel's mouth with both hands.

"Stage zero. Comrades, dress rehearsal. Remember: confidentiality, responsibility. Our aim: make sure who follows whom. Finalize the general picture. Right then, to your starting positions. One run-through and we're done. Sviridov, who's guest number two?"

The crowd stirred and formed into ranks, revealing a chalk inscription – "RED CARPET" – at the foot of the crate.

"This way, please." The warrant officer prodded me towards the crate. "You're still in the car. Now who else… Comrade Colonel, I can be guest number two myself!" He slipped in and wiped the sweat from his brow.

"Ten-shun! Listen. 'September the twelfth. Twelve hundred hours. The sun has gilded...' Right, I'm not reading all of that. Right then, the President and the Secretary... of the United Nations... out of the car... they've arrived!"

The warrant officer led me two steps forwards and stopped. We were at our designated spot.

"Ours is on the left. The other's on the right. Who's not paying attention? Remember who's where. Just a reminder: their secretary is an Arab. That's a kind of a gypsy. Orchestra!" Colonel Gontar waved his cap and on the boulevard they started beating a drum. "The blessing, the blessing... what're we waiting for? Start moving before the music stops, so they don't have time to look around."

The warrant officer moved aside and twisted his face into a sanctimonious grimace. The priest advanced, wrapped in something that looked like a waterproof cape, a cloth of gold embroidered with pearls, covered in blue and scarlet flowers with six petals. Sumptuous reflections glowed in the faces of the meek subordinates. The priest waved incense over the crowd, and intoned a prayer in a basso voice, throwing glances at me. The crowd bowed and crossed themselves with broad, sweeping gestures. I stood up straight and lowered my head with the rest. The warrant officer put his hands on his hips in a haughty gesture, as if to say: I don't understand.

"Now comes the blessing. Kiss his hand," Gontar hissed.

The priest handed the censer to a lay brother, then took my hand and kissed it respectfully.

"Kravchuk! What the hell..." the Colonel swore in exasperation. "Get that goat's beard of yours out of there! Who's the bishop? You're the bishop! You do the blessing, and he does the kissing! He holds his palms out, and you stick your bloody hand on top! He kisses it, and you make the sign of the cross over the back of his head! Stop tugging at your beard! Is it too hot? Sviridov, we can do it without the beard today."

"What if he won't kiss it?" enquired the "bishop" in a malevolent tone.

"He will. It'll be a clean, perfumed hand... He'll also be told what to do. If he hesitates, then cross his fat face and move on. What do you mean, where to? What about guest number two? You've got to bless the gypsy! Girl, bring up the bread!"

Suddenly there was music from horns and a psaltery, and a shapely girl with a face as red as a traffic cop's came over with a bouncy step, holding an empty chased-metal tray.

"The girl says: 'Pray taste of our bread.' Hold it out, and don't straighten up: let him get a good look down the front of your dress! Don't look down. If he smiles, give him a wink. Once. With your right eye. He takes a bite and chews it. Then he passes the bread to the gypsy. Then the girl, without straightening up, takes a present out of her bosom. Then she says: 'Dear sir, I have sat up through the night waiting for you, and I've embroidered the shorts.' Sho-orts? Is that right? Sviridov!"

"That's right, Comrade Colonel. That's what it says in the book."

"In the book! Sviridov – a clever dick, are you? See that you don't end up in the cooler! Who's going to read your book! The shorts my arse! What's he going to think – that we are pushing a loose woman on him? Anybody here from the museum?"

"Yes, Comrade Colonel," someone shouted from the crowd. "It should be 'the shirt'."

"All right then. Come on, girl."

"My dear sir, I have sat up through the night waiting for you and I've embroidered this shirt." The girl ran her tongue over her lips and thrust a hand into her bulging bosom.

The Colonel rapped out his approval:

"Good girl, good girl... I wish everybody did as well. 'Then the girl runs off, the hem of her skirt rises so that her underwear can be glimpsed...' It doesn't say what colour, but it should. Sviridov, see that they embroider her phone number and name on the shorts or whatever! Cossacks, let's have the Cossacks!"

Two policemen on light-brown horses rode over from the boulevard and around the crowd, whooping as they went.

"'Out runs a girl feeding...' Where's the feeding girl?"

"Here!" A gymnast in white trainers stepped forwards, about twelve years of age, totally flat-chested and with sharply pointed elbows.

Gontar pushed the megaphone away from his lips and hissed:

"Sviridov. Haven't we got a more bosomy candidate?"

"She's the district champion."

"But how's she supposed to feed... Oops, sorry, I see... 'Out runs a girl feeding... pigeons!' All right then, she feeds them, turns a somersault, does a cartwheel. Then a thousand pigeons, representing the age of the city, go flying up in the air. The veil falls from the 'Source of the Don' monument, and a stream of water lifts up an effigy of Ilya Muromets holding the flags of Russia and the United Nations. Then the orchestra. Exultant citizens press the guards against guest number one – don't get him confused with the Negro! – and a woman with a blind child breaks through. Right, quick march!"

The crowd pushed forwards, and a woman with a worn-out face lifted a boy in a blue T-shirt up above the swaying shoulders of the bodyguards, wailing mournfully:

"Lay your hands on him, O Saviour. Forgive me if my faith is not strong enough... I beg you..."

The child stared upwards with an expression of pain, as though an invisible hand were pressed across the bridge of his nose, and kicked his legs so hard his sandals flew off.

"That way they'll crush the woman," Sviridov hissed.

In a sort of daze, I tapped my hand against the child's reddish forehead. He jerked his head and bawled out:

"I can see. Mummy, I can see! The sun and the grass and our beloved city. Who is this good man?"

"He is your saviour," said the mother with a sob, pressing the child to her and caressing him. "I can hardly believe this... We shall pray for him..."

"Then she is pushed aside," Gontar read slowly. "Hold him good and close so he doesn't get photographed. The head doctor certifies it as a case of healing. An ambulance takes him away. On the corner of Sadovaya and Mokrousov Streets, the midget gets out and the child gets in, and you go to your flat and wait for journalists. An old woman tumbles out of the crowd. All right, Larisa Yurievna, let's see you tumble, please."

A woman with her face caked in powder, wearing a velvet jacket and silvery silk trousers, crept under the cordon. She spread out a newspaper at my feet and knelt down heavily on it, supporting herself on the extended elbow of the stooping Sviridov. She thrust a fat hand covered in rings and bracelets into my face.

"The guest attempts to raise her to her feet."

"Oh please, let me be, I am older than you, and you must hear what I have to say." The woman gave a feeble smile and adjusted an imaginary headscarf. "I never thought I'd see the face of an angel, but now I have I can die in peace. When I tell the people in the village, they won't believe me, they'll say I'm a liar. Hear now the one thing I must say. You are our hope: make our land bountiful, pay no heed to fallen women, turn away from taverns, curb despotism, dry the tears from people's eyes. Do not forget you are Russian. Remember your roots. If you ignore the earth, the earth will not forgive you. Do not give way to vain pride, do not be ashamed to repent, do not seek foreign lands and do not

106

be ashamed of your own. We have waited for you so long." The woman sniffed, and her tall hairdo swayed to and fro in its net. She held out a post-office envelope containing a sprinkling of sand. "A charm to guard you, earth I gathered from the burial mounds of the Kryukov Forest – it will save you in the dark hour of night."

"The old woman is carried away," Gontar prompted. "Tears. Get on with it quickly, Larisa Yurievna. The guest breathes in the smell of the earth. Song: 'O Russian land, beyond the hills afar…' Is that right? Isn't it 'so fair' rather than 'afar'?"

"A fart?" suggested the captain, holding the megaphone.

"Five days' close detention in the cooler! Sniff that earth! Is that the way to sniff? They're not offering you shit on a shovel! Watch this, I'll show you how to sniff your own native earth!" The Colonel jumped off the crate, took the envelope from me and stuck his nose into it. He took a deep lungful, screwing up his eyes in ecstasy, then he suddenly grunted and barked out: "Sviridov, where did you get this?"

"I did as you ordered… I got sand," Sviridov said in a startled voice. "I got it from the sandbox, in the yard… Let me have a sniff."

"At the double! Take down all the dog owners' names, sieve all that sand, find out which animal shat in it and take it to the vet's. Put the mangy cur down! And do it now! Now for everybody: in three days' time full dress rehearsal. Learn your lines. First company, right turn! Second company, left turn! At the double. On the command 'at the double', elbows bent at ninety degrees, trunk inclined forwards with the weight balanced on the right foot. Quick march!"

Warrant officer Sviridov slouched off about his business at top speed, holding the envelope up to his nose and then keeping it away from himself at arm's length. I finally recovered my wits.

Everything had gone so smoothly that my mind was carried away and I didn't have time to laugh or even think...

When I reached the bank, it was closed, so I left. Before twilight I wandered around, hoping to find a suburb with front gardens, piles of birch wood, chicken fluff in the grass and bucketfuls of apples "for sale" along the road. Instead, there was one barrack after another, people smoking by the entrances, ironing school uniforms and eating suppers with no shirts on, kids touching the bayonets of the army patrols, crows' droppings flopped on the road. On the other side of the road, concrete fences drooped forwards, with sagging barbed wire on rusty pegs. I ended up at the bus station, where I bought some sunflower seeds – large but not ripe – from an old woman, and where I shook off the hand of a gypsy woman who was offering to tell my fortune:

"You nice young fellow – there's a ghost after you..."

"Get lost!"

A horde of gypsy women was trailing along the trading booths, barefoot in the velvety dust, avoiding just the small window where the stout police chief Baranov held sway among a bunch of incensed Caucasian market traders. Two women with heavy make-up were sobbing.

I offered some sunflower seeds to one of the drivers, who was following the riot from his bus.

"What's going on there?"

"Someone nicked some silver spoons from a stall. One woman says: 'I didn't take 'em.' Another says: 'Me neither.' They work in shifts. The stall keepers, those Negros, are furious – ready to kill."

"Which stall is it?"

"That one over there."

Circling the stall, I called out:

"Hey mate, get this stall lifted by a crane. It's probably a rat that's done the pinching. Must be there in their nest."

Baranov gave me the look you give to a naive child and turned to the shopkeepers, who'd all fallen silent.

"I forgot to tell you," I added from behind his ginger-haired nape, licking my swollen lip. "We searched the hotel basement – there's a kind of overcoat there, where the blocks are piled up. Looks like a man…"

As I continued walking, the town came to an abrupt end, without fading into the countryside. Behind a motor depot extended a field littered with blackened lorry skeletons. A bit further off, the railway embankment stretched on. I settled myself on the skull of a deceased car, examining the first stars and the crows on the clipped poplars. As I rummaged in my pocket to fish the last sunflower seeds, I spotted an odd-looking painter. He had placed his box under the fence and was daubing away in the dark. But the gnats were eating me alive, and I couldn't stay there any longer. The painter was turning his back on me, but my guess was right:

"Comrade Klinsky?"

"Fed up with walking?"

He folded up his box. "Not many people around – I tagged along behind you. So that no rogue would touch you. Shall we be on first-name terms?"

"Sure. Let's have a look at what you've painted."

"To hell with that! Landscapes are not my forte! People are more my thing. I've got some sketches with me. This is the First Architect Mokrousov. A local… he's dead now. I've painted him from the waist up, so as not to show his wooden leg. And do you know who this is? Ilya Muromets. The legendary protector of Svetloyar. He rode to Kiev through the impassable land of Viatko. And he built himself a cabin on the lakeshore. That's the lake Ivan Trofimovich drained after the war. The mighty warrior bathed in the lake and our girls kept an eye on him. So the prince asked them: 'What's he like?' And they said: 'His complexion's fair, his face is bright.' Hence the name Svetloyar – fair and bright! In Kiev they didn't believe that Ilya had taken a direct route. They said his eyes had failed him…"

"What's he got on his trousers?"

"Stripes – like you get on uniforms. The old song says: 'That old Cossack, Ilya Muromets…'" We walked back in silence. Klinsky drew a deep sigh without lifting his small black-haired head, giving out a whiff of alcohol. He stifled his yawns and had his eyes fixed on the ground.

"Anything wrong?"

"We won't let anything go wrong! It will be business as usual. A letter's come. They want to assassinate the President." He stopped. "It's not you who wrote it, is it? Only joking. And you wouldn't have any idea who it was? Maybe you've heard something? Joking again," he said with a sardonic sneer. "They want to assassinate him. In Svetloyar… In this town, if you sneeze your wife knows straight away who's said 'bless you'. Cut down on your walking. With all those rats – you've seen it yourself. Especially at the meat-processing plant. Kids get bitten. It'll be packed with people – unfounded hopes, aspirations set too high. I haven't got enough staff to protect you. If you want to relax, visit the archaeological sites in the Kryukov Forest."

Oldie was asleep. Larionov and Vic were having tea with the buffet attendant.

"Tomorrow we'll take away the first corpses," the architect announced. "We've ordered your return tickets."

Klinsky immediately added:

"See that you have a big enough purse. Wh-at a me-ss..." he complained, barely visible on the stairs in the warm deep-blue night. "They'd organized a send-off for Ivan Trofimovich in the café, but the basement got flooded – there were rats all over the guests, all over me... even on Ivan Trofimovich's necktie. They wanted to give him an award, but the old chap ended up in the hospital. He was blue in the face. The police are turning the café upside down, but what's the point? It's hopeless, our life. And my son's going to school tomorrow. Do you hear that, rat catchers? I'm relying on you!"

"He had too much to drink," Larionov said in a soft tone. "You didn't know what happened to Ivan Trofimovich? It must be surprising even for you."

I shrugged my shoulders.

"No. I can well imagine it. Basements flooded with subterranean waters or melting snow are a very bad thing for rodents."

Drowsiness crept over me, and we went our separate ways.

6

The Russian Troy, or The Thirty-three Jets

11 Days to D-Day

"Lieutenant. Come here."

I hesitated by the gates, peering out: who's that?

In a black old banger Baranov was waiting – alone. A newspaper glimmered white on the seat. There was also bread, cucumbers and a bottle.

"Get in. Hate to drink by myself. You're a star! They lifted up the kiosk – the spoons were in the rats' burrow. There's your friend from the hotel basement."

I looked across. By the hotel, nose to nose, shone a police jeep and a blue van with a red cross. Police and civilians crowded in between them. A man in white overalls was bending over a black oilcloth bundle which looked like a wrapped-up Christmas tree.

"An old man. Probably a tramp doing odd jobs round the market. The body falls apart in your hands. One leg is missing up to the knee." Baranov gave his ginger forelocks a tousle. "Such bad timing. There are no signs of violence – I'll hush up the case… Otherwise the regional authorities will kick up a fuss. They're just waiting to give us a hard time before this visit. It's a vipers' nest as it is. We've had a send-off for Ivan Trofimovich… There's a real man for you! Forty-five years of hard work. Since he was eleven, on a collective farm. Five medals – a hero! He was beaming like a young boy, and he started dancing. And just as the music began, the rats started jumping all over – up his tie to his throat. It's not for nothing that he's gone off the rails over them. Those nasty creatures have done him in. What a life!" He suppressed a tear. "What will he have died for? Are you going already?"

Out of boredom I trudged towards the single lit-up entrance, where the ambulances were parked. I hung about a bit. A woman orderly shooed me off: "Get lost! Just you wait, I'll call the police. Don't wait for Verka, she's gone to bed. Not looking for her? Well, I'm going to bed. Here's the phone and the police are just round the corner. That face of yours, it's not from round here, is it?"

It was cold sitting around – too long till dawn. A cat was dozing against a shaggy broom, screwing up its eyes at me – should I shoo it away? I walked towards the birch trees to find a bench, but had to sit on the grass.

The children's swings had the black sheen of a gallows: a weeping noise from that direction. I knew right away who it was. Goodnight.

"Sorry." Vic's girlfriend turned her face into her headscarf. "We've pestered you enough. This is a small town – you go out and meet everyone. His window's over there."

I didn't look.

"Go and see him… I met him in the morning… he was on his way to the barber's, with all his medals on. He waved his hand to me like this: I'm alive, I'm alive. He was laughing. I'm coming to you out of desperation. You nearly succeeded. Vic is all right now. But Ivan Trofimovich needs you!"

I yawned. Sod him.

"He keeps saying there's something he hasn't properly under-stood… It's a weird illness – a nervous breakdown. Now he's…"

"Stop it. What's the point…"

"He said: 'I'm gonna die, I know it – and you'll have to come to terms with it too.' Well, I'm trying. But I don't seem to be affected. I can't apply it to myself. I don't know if I'm scared of rats or not. What about you?"

"Well, they're so harmless, really. They dangle their tails from the pipes. You pull on one, and it falls down belly up. They annoy me when I get tired…"

"Crowds are what annoy me. You can't be alone anywhere."

She stood up. I wanted to get a good view of her backside. But she didn't leave.

"You've not even asked me what my name is."

"That's so boring. You're a beautiful girl, with beautiful legs and other beautiful things. 'Vic's girlfriend' fits you fine. That makes you a mystery. Heaven knows who you are. Off with you. Well, I'd better see you off."

Another night shift!

She walked close to me, touching me with her shoulder, not allowing me to lag behind and get a view from behind. Fancy walking along with such a looker in the backstreets of Svetloyar!

"Any healthy person is afraid. That's our nature. When a man is walking, a shadow crawls behind him. The shadow comes closer and closer. The ancients feared storms and lightning. Those who came after them, sea serpents, dragons and mermaids – human-like creatures. Later on, their own creations terrified them – windmills, abandoned wells, graveyards. Later still, they feared human beings: robbers, vampires, enemy invasions. The shadow got real close: what was there to be scared of? Skeletons. Death. As for rats, they're another step closer, towards the essence… Towards the human in you. You

ought to be afraid. But not terrified. 'Afraid' is a childish word. You're afraid it'll rain, afraid of being chased, caught, beaten. 'I'm afraid' can't lead to death, can it? No, that's something different. The presence of a master. A stupor such as when you are looking at your beloved's backside. You sense a force which can do anything! That's not frightening, that's deadly... when nine girls turn you on and then suddenly you tremble in front of the tenth... there's honey and cherry blossom in her eyes. Everybody, deep in their heart, you too, right there, if you'll excuse me..."

"Hey, don't touch me like that!"

"...have an untightened screw. Some people fall for it, like Ivan Trofimovich... the screwdriver gets into the groove and the screw is screwed in. And your heart is skewered. That's similar to rat-killing. Have you ever thought why it's rats and not something else? Why now? Why here? The Greeks never noticed them... it was a Golden Age. The thirteenth century: Europe is invaded by rats and we are invaded by the Tatars. It's unscientific. In simple terms, people look on things the same way as science does. Science says: that's a dog – and people don't argue. And only on one thing their opinions diverge – on rats! Suddenly, from the thousands of rodents, people focused their attention on one particular sort, called them 'rats', and developed a fear of them. Nonsense! To develop a fear of something that doesn't exist! Science can't differentiate rats. Where do they start, where do they end? What's their minimum and maximum length? What kind of scales do they have on their tails, exactly? Why is a mouse not a rat? Or a hamster? Or a shrew? Basically, they're all the same. Who precisely stumbled on them? Who invented them? Like a first

love is ruined by the other side of the coin: behind the façade you suddenly see the seamy side. At first you're happy and you are flying high. And when you start falling, you can't land on either side. You bump onto a post. Between the eyes. And between the legs...

"Is this the entrance to your block? Someone's getting into the basement with lights. Well, are your parents away in the country? Aren't you afraid to be on your own? How about a cup of tea?"

"I was meaning to ask you... When you first saw me, why did you say that... well, that I'd fall in love with you?"

I stared at the illuminated windows of the basement. What was this all about? From behind a bench emerged the ugly face of a soldier.

"Why don't you go home, Comrade Lieutenant, it's already late."

Vic's girlfriend roused herself.

"Yes. Thank you very much. Now off you go."

"I'm going in. Let's hope they have broad window sills down there. Let's have a look at what kind of public-minded individuals are rummaging around your building..."

"Come on, look at the time." The ugly soldier took me by the sleeve. "Reveille's at six in the morning... you've got to get some rest. Don't wear yourself out like that..." There was an anxious expression on his red-haired, coarse-nosed, freckled face.

I see: he didn't want to let me in. Vic's girlfriend quickly entered the building. The soldier, stumbling, knocked against my back with his shoulder.

"I haven't even had my lunch or my dinner," he complained as he followed me. "I've just been sitting there in the bushes, and didn't move from there. Believe me, Comrade Lieutenant, I haven't even had time to take a leak!"

"Thanks for reminding me!" I pushed forwards into the lilac bushes and unzipped my trousers.

The soldier raced behind the lime trees, emitted an avid hissing moan, harrumphed, and then suddenly let out a piercing shriek:

"Ha-a-alt!"

But I'd already covered a fair bit of ground. I made it just in time: two soldiers were locking up the basement, without putting down the canvas sack they were carrying. They stared at me as if they were my own little kids.

"Hello, mates…" I kicked the sack, which squirmed and screeched in response, and I tugged out of their submissive hands a gadget only too familiar to me. "A rat trap! Made by the Shakhovskoy Factory." And I bellowed: "Who gave the order?!"

"Gubin."

"Who the hell is Gubin? Where can I find him?"

"We don't know. They asked us to catch a few live rats and deliver them to HQ. To this Gubin. And you kick up a fuss. Go to HQ and sort it out with them."

"The Rat King?"

The soldiers looked at me as if I were an idiot. I turned round as the other soldier approached.

"Man, you look like a sprinkler system," I said, staring at his trousers. "Next time, you should do it running backwards." And I walked off, smiling the rest of the way.

The ward was lit up. An attendant was angrily sweeping away fragments of glass into a dustpan. Through the smashed window the night air blew in. Oldie looked dejected.

"The brick came with a letter."

On the calendar page for 11th September of the current year somebody had clearly inscribed "For the café" and had added a cross. Beneath the windows, flashing lights spun silently. Police officers were running around behind their Alsatian dogs, holding on to their caps. I switched off the lamp.

"I've had a bit of a think about this," Oldie said in a soft tone. "Perhaps you shouldn't be hanging around with this girl?"

The draught had made it an even better place to sleep.

"Oldie, why the hell are they catching live rats?"

"Who cares? We'll do what we have to do and then go."

So it's 1st September: the kids are lugging their satchels, the school tannoy shouts: "Where are the boys with the chalk?" and scraggly-legged young girls shuffle about in fashionable shoes – two paces forwards, four back – while the wind whips their hair up. It's still warm.

Oldie gives an order, and from the ranks emerges the last in the line, a puny chap. Come, come here, walk normally, you're not on parade, take off your cap. Arms forwards. Larionov fits rubber gloves on the soldier's hands, as if he were a little kid, and fixes a gauze mask on his mouth.

"They'll lift you up." The soldier kept a watchful eye on Oldie's palms. "First you'll pick up the dead rodents from the edges of the suspended ceiling. Just throw them down one by one. Those you can reach by hand. Then pull yourself up and worm your way onto that suspension – it should be easy for you, you are of a small build. Get hold of the rodents like this – by the jugular vertebrae. Have you got that? It's possible some of them will still be showing signs of life. You may find them in a sitting position, trying to get up on their hind legs – don't be scared. Their sense of balance is impaired. They are getting stiff. They won't bite. What's your name, please?"

"Shorty," somebody prompted from the chortling ranks.

The soldier whispered only for Oldie to hear:

"Pavel."

"Be careful, Pavel, there's plenty of time. Pick them up with your right hand, and with your left hold on to the iron rods – there's lots of them up there. OK. Attention! Is the hoisting tower ready?"

The tower carried the soldier up to the suspended ceiling, from which six sections had been removed to cut off the rats from the passage in the wall. The soldier, clutching at the handrail of the circular platform, stared down at the floor covered with tarpaulin, at his hushed colleagues, at the nurses, at Gontar and Baranov, at the upturned face of the Governor, and he touched his nose through the white gauze. He raised his arm – that'll do.

"You'll get extra leave!" bellowed Gontar.

The soldier grabbed a dark lump from the edge, took aim and dropped it, waiting for a squelching noise, which resounded throughout the entire hall. All those present bent their heads and then stared upwards as if bewitched. I hastened out, smirking at Larionov:

"The stronghold is destroyed!"

Outside, I ran straight into the driver.

"Comrade Lieutenant, Klinsky ordered that you go to the Kryukov Forest, to the gravediggers. 'There's fewer people, more air,' he said. If you dig your heels in, we'll have to drag you away by force, he said."

We'd hardly left and I already felt quieter inside – I felt knackered.

"Konstantin!" I blurted out. "How's your missus? Do you go to the bathhouse together? Do you get all hot and bothered?"

"Well, we… yeah…"

"And who gets more 'hot and bothered'? You or your wife?"

"Well, basically… so to speak… both of us…"

The road ran alongside railway tracks and factories, then

stretched like a grey canvas through a copse, past hills, gullies, green fields, threading together the trackmen's huts at level crossings, petrol stations, farmsteads; the sun illuminated the damp woods right through to the ground. Then tree trunks became darker, fir trees appeared, maple saplings spread out their golden scarves over the grass. We rolled along through blasts of rain, until in front of us a hare shot past, its sturdy rump jumping behind its ears. I dozed off straight away, and in my dream made advances to Vic's girlfriend, who didn't put up much resistance, poor thing...

"That thing over there is for water, it's brought in by a water-carrier. It'll warm up during the day. Below are partitions, they wash there..."

"What?"

"That's a water tank up there in the camp."

The spidery waves of the oak trees clustered densely ahead, interspersed with fir trees and hazel groves. That was the Kryukov Forest – but where was the camp?

I climbed out, thrusting aside thistles and various grasses, and at the third step I fell down a slope, knocking my back onto the ground. Shit! Konstantin grabbed at my collar and stopped me from tumbling down any further. I rubbed my throbbing temples – bloody hell! – and kicked my heels, trying to find a firm foothold.

"You idiot!" Konstantin grunted. "Watch your step!" And he pulled me out.

Invisibly in the grass, the earth came to an abrupt end, breaking into a sheer drop across a broad sweep of the land, where tents were lined up, people's backs glistened and the earth smoked as it flew up from shovels. A black water tank stuck out, like an enormous egg from which a steam engine was about to hatch. I looked across at the opposite bank: there it was – then grass again, not too far straight ahead.

Konstantin was brushing his dirty sleeve and mumbling reproaches:

"Dipstick. Serves you right…" Then he said: "You see how the tents are arranged? It's the architect's idea. Ancient Roman cities were like that, he says."

"Is it a quarry, or what?"

"They say there was a lake here. They drained it when they were looking for somewhere to build the meat-processing plant. The land itself is no good: it keeps subsiding. But other people say the lake wasn't here. One old fellow shows you one spot and another a different one. My granddad says that in the times of some tsar or other they used to quarry clay here. They wanted to build a stove for the Tsar that would keep the whole town warm. They put up the stove, but there was no draught, so they made a church out of it. God knows if it's true. They've sent these people from the poultry factory to do the digging. Let's go. Here's a lad with a tommy gun – guarding the path."

The sentry was waving a twig at the flies. When he saw me, he moved to the side of the path.

I stopped.

"Can I pass?"

The soldier chuckled:

"I don't give a damn. Come along if you want."

I descended into that grave-like abyss, mostly at a run. The bare clay was curled by the baking heat into brown scabs. Along the path bristled an ailing web of grass, with patches of dried-out moss here and there. The spread-out tents grew plump in the middle, bursting belligerently at their sides. The Roman city began right at the end of the path.

"You brought anything to smoke?" called out another guard.

He was annoyed when I replied: "Where's your boss?"

"The boss is with his gangsters."

"Oh, OK. Where's the director then?"

"He is where the problems are."

"I hope you rot here till retirement age."

There was a strong reek of chlorine, which two chaps were sprinkling into an open four-holed latrine.

I got to the mess room along the main street. A female cook with bronzed shoulders gave up peeling potatoes and seized hold of me.

"Here you are! Let's go in here, shall we? You are an expert in this sort of thing, aren't you?" She led me into a tent: "They'll be back soon. You don't mind if they're old or young ones, do you?"

"Well, it depends…"

"Could you make do on a camp bed? I'll lie like this – it's not too low for you, is it?"

"Well, it depends…" I repeated like a cracked record. Well I never…

"Come on… before someone arrives. My period's a bit late." She fiddled around under her apron.

"Lay off it!" came the bark from the window.

A thickset, sweaty fellow burst in exclaiming:

"Here you are! Great! Warrant Officer Sviridov, commandant of the digs."

"I was in that rehearsal with you…"

"Sure. You wouldn't even recognize your father." He said, shoving the cook out: "He is not a women's doctor!"

"Then let me go to town!" she wailed.

"Why did you stop working?" Sviridov bellowed outside. "He's a pub-lic hea-lth doc-tor. That's lower than a vet! He does not cure, he just exterminates. Team leaders, bring your people to heel – the man's come all the way from Moscow… Shame on you!"

123

He came back into the tent – not alone, but with a short-sighted lady wearing a sunhat and shorts.

"May I introduce my deputy for... what's the name..."

"Archaeology."

"That's it! Due to the unhygienic conditions of the site, Comrade Doctor... sub-standard water has caused an outbreak of the runs – I mean evacuation of fluids from the intestines. People simply refuse to hold it back and evacuate wherever they are. In dozens of separate streams – not counting the small calls of nature. It's impossible to sit anywhere. This is a restricted area. To prevent unauthorized departures from the site, we're imposing a curfew. But we can't enforce it – they go running off to evacuate. I've authorized shooting them with blank cartridges, but you can't scare them enough: they crawl away on all fours. I tried to appeal to their conscience – after all, astronauts hold it in for eighteen months or more, and nothing drops down on our heads here, and these people can't toughen themselves up for two weeks. Listen, could you have a look at this here now – right there in my side there's a pinching pain whenever I wave my arm." Sviridov pulled up his shirt. "Yelena, you'll come after me."

"I don't cure, really. I only kill."

"Is that right? You're not kidding? That's a shame... So let's go and have a look at the treasures. We've dug up a pile of relics. Yelena!"

"What!"

"Don't be scared – it's me, Sviridov. Dozing off? Lie down and take a nap. Well now – bed, rest, pillow. Understand?"

"Sure."

The tents lay on a patch of level ground, behind which the pits of the excavation works stretched deep and wide. A whole army of diggers were bending and straightening up all around, carving out terraces and steps. The huge quarry looked like a circus. On the strip of land at the bottom, an iron contraption and a wheeled engine speckled with gas oil stuck out.

"It's a drill," Sviridov said, smacking his lips. "You can't bring in an excavator here, but I had an idea…"

"Why did you choose such an inconvenient spot?"

"I've not been quite fair on the people here, they're angels… There's a couple of professors, a few history students, and the rest come from the poultry factory. Everything's done by hand, with care. The relics are fragile: if you hit 'em with a shovel, they are gone for ever. New finds every day. And what finds they are! That's a placard that tells you what they've found today. In the evening the professors tell us so many stories about each pot… and we end up with people taking this information back home to their little kids. It's like a people's university. They think Communists built this town in the virgin countryside. But it's not like that – we've been unearthing our roots. But let's not reveal any of this yet." He grasped my shoulder. "We'll make it known to the entire country. To the world! Three Germans dug up one town and became famous. But what are those three people compared to two hundred and fifty-two of the common Russian folk and a guards company reinforced with machine guns!? Let me whisper a secret into your ear. We haven't just dug up one town here. We've dug up everything. You understand? Climb down… I have to run… just one minute. My insides are leaking – evacuation of fluids…"

And he bounced away like a ball: down the wooden stairs, and from terrace to terrace. I went down: the labourers slowed down and turned to look at me…

The sun oozed down right over my head. The bucket-shaped bottom of the quarry provided no shelter on any side, but the tightly packed, moist clay breathed a cellar-like chill. Behind the drill there lay a deserted pool of water, smooth as glass, the size of

125

a tip-up lorry – ice-cold. I dipped my fingers in. I couldn't spot a spring, which would have thrown out watery ripples and bubbles. It looked as if the rain had created that waist-deep pool. I had an unpleasant feeling. What if I could never leave that place? I was alone and couldn't move – something was bearing down on me. I finally managed to clamber out.

The archaeologist Yelena spread an old piece of cloth over the highest ledge and sprawled out on it to get a tan, covering her glasses with a hat.

Sviridov intercepted me on the second stairway and took me for a walk.

"But why is all this so valuable? Russians built their towns carelessly. What's the point of building, if tomorrow you are invaded, burnt down or driven out? That's why they always built in open spaces, on plains. And the whole country kept moving around, the boundaries of our homeland became blurred. Add to this the proverbially poor Russian memory: nobody remembers who their ancestors were. And as a result there's a lack of faith, and no one believes that the soul goes to Heaven. How about you?"

"I don't believe in that."

"And that'll be the end of you... They're all scattered around: the house is here, the yard's over there, the cesspit's in the neighbour's yagé bushes. Scythians, Kiev, Vladimir, Moscow and beyond. But we are coming to the rescue of Russia. We've found the spring of life. Right here," Sviridov jabbed with a finger at the ground. "It turns out Russians have always lived here! It's the eternal city. Rome! Even better. Svetloyar is the only town that has never moved. I swear to God, we've unearthed the whole of history throughout the ages. From Neolithic times... These terraces go throughout the ages, one on top of another."

"Like graves."

"You people had no idea about this." The warrant officer waved his arms: "When we spread the news, the town will stand tall. Russia won't drift around any more. Our internal exile will be over. We'll start building! Russia will stay here. It'll be like a big wedding. They wandered away from the Don, but its source will return us to our origins. The President knows this, I'm sure, and he's coming to announce it. It's got nothing to do with money and local prosperity: it's the end of our enslavement. We'll return Russia to herself, resurrect her…"

"Listen… what's your name?"

"Warrant Officer Sviridov."

"No, I mean your first name."

"What – mine?" the officer blinked and touched his shirt pocket. "I'm Fyodor… Fedka."

"Fyodor…" I looked around: the workmen were sitting to one side taking turns to smoke. "Listen – Ivan Trofimovich told me everything."

"Everything?"

"That you're not digging for real. That, in actual fact, there's nothing here…"

"What?… Where have you…"

"What's the point of putting on an act in front of me? You're bringing the stuff in from somewhere else."

"Us bringing it in?!" screeched Sviridov, cupping his cheeks with his palms. "Ivan Trofimovich must have gone off his head! And how could you? Look… these people… just look at them. They've been digging here. How can you say… Do you mean that I… that they…" He pushed through the weather-beaten labourers. They stepped aside, spitting, scraping off their shovels one against another, while the women squatted on their gloves, looking at me from below, scowling through their burnt brows.

"Open your eyes wide! All right, we won't go any deeper:

127

Neolithic – that's the black layer, the layer that displays the first signs of culture. They've unearthed ceramics, fragments of pottery and a kind of bone dagger. They've dug three excavation shafts… Who's done a good job today? You, Prokhorov?"

"Yes, me. I dig the whole day, and nothing," responded a big-nosed fellow.

"Then?"

"Then – I hear… something clattering, but only me…"

"And there was the point of a javelin and, what's more, the remains of fingers stuck to it! Just look over there, there's Lusatian burial plots… Fifteen centuries before Christ. The ashes were put in a pot, the pot went into the pit, with a bit of clothing and food next to it… and the same in the rest of the area. And do you know what's beneath your shoes? The ancient Viatichians! You're a Russian, but do you know who the Viatichians were? But here anybody can tell you. In a second. Kostromin, can you tell the Lieutenant about the Viatichians!"

A close-cropped chap stopped picking at an old corn on his palm and said:

"It comes from the word 'vento' – the ancient nickname for the Slavs. It's written in the chronicles: Viatko settled with his kindred upon the River Otsa, and from him was that place named…"

"And they buried…"

"Up to the twelfth century they buried their dead in earthenware containers – small vessels on pillars – at road crossings. They loved freedom: they were the last ones to be annexed. People travelling between Kiev and Murom made a wide detour through the Smolensk territory so as not to lose their life in the woods of the Viatichian land. And the essence of Ilya Muromets's exploit is that he went straight through that land, not around. The Viatichians were educated by Kuksha, a monk from Kiev, and they paid a tribute to the Khazars longer than the rest."

"That's enough. Good men, good men. He's a blacksmith's assistant, but he's learnt his stuff quick enough. And you bear it in mind too. We've unearthed an ancient settlement. Here's a little promontory – from over there it's fortified by a rampart, and from over here by a ditch. The street is narrow – just three metres wide, and to the left and right are half-buried dwellings." Sviridov jumped down into a pit marked out by pegs, with me behind. "The remains of wooden execution blocks – touch them! Walls... The corner where you are now was a stone stove. Touch this here. What's this?"

"A board."

"A wooden grain holder! And there's never any rats around here. In my quest for knowledge, I've personally sifted through two mounds." Sviridov counted on his fingers: "Large horned cattle, pigs, horses, dogs, beavers, elk, bears, martens, boars, foxes, hares, badgers, birds, fish and one specimen of the northern deer. There's a mountain of bones – but rats? No!" Sviridov flung open a vast plywood box. "Sickles, grindstones for crushing grain, a honeycomb cutter, spikes. See the labels: who found what and where. In those ages there was no gold yet, and hardly any silver. But who'd imagine we'd dig up a big goblet made from horn and set in silver – wow! See these historical treasures! But we've come across even better stuff: filigree, beads, coins, dirhams. But you can see it with your own eyes. As if I need to justify myself..." Sviridov resentfully slammed the box shut, and stroked his belly. "I have to run. Have a look yourself."

I ran through the finds in the box, one by one. Along the shoulders of an earthenware jar fragment ran a pattern like a braided cord. A chap was sitting nearby, inscribing a label in decorative lettering: "Found by Y. Kostromin, 2nd August this year."

"Moulded pottery," explained Kostromin, observing my puzzlement. "They didn't have potters then. It's a simple design:

129

indentations and notches are made with a shard." He climbed down to where I was. "Let me warn you, while we're alone: don't believe everything the warrant officer says!"

"Oh yes? I think I've alr—"

"Yes, he's picked up a few bits of information... but he gets confused. He was telling you about this stone stove. But in reality, it's clay."

I waited for more, but he smiled in silence and then added:

"We're already all like Moscow Professors here! Lessons on artefacts! After the army I'll become an archaeologist."

Lying right across the path, Yelena Fyodorovna was basking in the sun like a turtle, knees pressed together – should I step over her? I broke off a blade of grass, dry as a bone, and thrust it under the lady's hat, making a tickling motion.

Cr-r-runch! In my hand remained only the tip of it. I glanced beneath the hat. The archaeologist was staring at me, chewing the chomped-off blade of grass:

"Who's that?"

"I'm the public-health doctor, Yelena Fyodorovna. I arrived today."

"A doctor. Which one?"

"Me. Right here. Who else would I be talking about? I'm the rat catcher from Moscow."

"Who?"

"I'm from Moscow. There are two of us in all, but the other chap, my colleague, he's stayed behind, in Svetloyar."

"Who?"

"My colleague! He's a doctor as well. A fellow doctor. I'd better go..."

"And who am I?"

"What? Oh you – who are you? You're Yelena Fyodorovna." I raised my voice: "A female archaeologist."

She sat up and haughtily spat the grass out.

"I'm a postdoctoral research fellow... I've got students. Must have dozed off... Seen our finds?"

I squeezed her wrist – she unexpectedly smiled.

"Yelena Fyodorovna, I'm a bit confused, perhaps you can..."

"Have you inspected the site? The town itself begins higher up: the trading quarters outside the city wall, the citadel and a wharf. A wharf means – water. Twelfth century. Thirteenth century. My favourite period. If you want to relax – pick up a shovel. I am dying for a shovel. But I can't. My expert supervision is required. So far, we've got four archaeologists. In November we expect an entire archaeological team. We've unearthed the very essence of Russia. One more layer. They'll all come together. Without exaggerating, this is one of the most important strata: this is where Russia came from. Start digging yourself. Newcomers are always lucky."

"Yelena Fyodorovna!"

"Yes? I'm listening, dear comrade, thanks. Thanks very much, all the very best."

"Yeah, nice chatting with you, damn, but... over there, the last circle, at the very bottom of this circus: what's that down there?"

"In simple terms – that's the Neolithic part. It's the first settlement – it's already been looked through. Now the other finds will be in the town, in the higher layers."

"Why the hell do you need a drill then?"

"Drill? We don't need a drill."

"What's that sticking out over there, then? A dog's tail?"

She wiped her glasses with the brim of her hat and gazed intently at my forefinger.

"Just look down at the bottom. Just look!"

"Oh, yes – a drill. That's Sviridov's whim. There's no material evidence at that depth. He wants to find grain. That's the trouble with all those lucky neophytes – they are dreamers. An excavation is like a tree: there's a trunk, and then branches spread out from it... He thought: well, at the very bottom there must be grain. He wants to get hold of grain."

"Why?"

"To transplant it into new soil. But down there the subsoil's dead. I know that." She slipped her hand from my fingers and concluded in boredom: "I know just how dead it is. But you... don't just run off. Often what seems to be bad is just common sense. You come and go. But people have to live here on a permanent basis." She finished off with a vigorous voice, brushing her firm, bare legs, and I thought...

"Now you... Oh, don't be worried..."

But I had jumped like hell at the crackle of machine-gun fire.

"They're just calling us for lunch. Time for plates, Mr Public Health Doctor." And she laughed.

I almost gave her a smack on her backside.

We all ate the same food in equal portions. I joined the second shift, so that people wouldn't breathe down my neck. Conscript Kostromin poured some piping-hot cabbage soup with traces of meat. I wolfed it down with a chunk of black bread, followed by two platefuls of millet porridge with buttery lumps – and topped it all off with a sweetish drink handed out in beer mugs.

Then, with sleepy eyes, I looked at Kostromin, who handed me another mugful of stewed fruit and a tiny dollop of butter. I spread it with a tablespoon over a crust of bread – and it was only after that, when the dishwashers' cauldrons had started steaming and the queues for the toilets had thinned out, that I sat in the shade, overcome by gloom. I glutted myself on black bread again. I knew it would give me heartburn and wouldn't let me sleep... I woke up in the same foul mood. It's always like that when you sleep after lunch. I freshened up at the washstand and headed "into town" across the toilet area...

Autumn overwhelmed me in that pit. Like the previous autumn... Was it in the kitchen of the restaurant Uzbekistan? And also No. 17 on Volgograd Prospekt – one of the worst hotbeds of rat infestation in Moscow. The building was circular – on the ground floor there was a "Sausage" shop, a baby-food centre, a canteen and a butcher with only one counter that served customers – the others bore the notice "out of order". I saw what was going on straight away: they were scared to come near them. Yes, that autumn we disinfested that butcher until the client ran out of money. So what? But there was something else. Not only that.

When I left the camp behind (a track consisting of two boards, like the stripes on a general's trousers, led to the stairway), I glanced around in the hope of picking up a spade tossed away during the sleepy after-lunch hour. Far off, where the sky met the pit, a water-carrier was rolling along. A few soldiers spread out fire hoses. The vehicle backed up towards them and, with a soundless banging of the door, discharged a woman in a white dress – so she's come.

The woman walked down the path as the soldiers gave way, their eyes glued to that apparition – but I was heading "into town", and sighing at every step – what was the matter with me? – I couldn't keep my heart at bay.

The "town" was lavishly decorated, like an Easter egg – clearly they had decked it out to impress the guests. On both sides lay wide slopes with the remains of the ancient settlement. Opposite the camp, they converged into a square, where the citadel had been unearthed. Explicatory panels cropped up everywhere.

I checked out the decomposed wooden piles on which the wharf had once rested. From this wharf a roadway made of logs led up to a humpbacked embankment, where the town gates had once been. Some men were rolling out a swathe of insulating film over a hovel that was in better repair than the rest. Through the entrance I could see the mouth of a stove, remains of cooking utensils, sleeping benches, a rounded scythe and a sickle-shaped poleaxe, as well as a table and stools in the near corner.

In the centre, on a soot-blackened copper-smelting kiln, the "skeleton of a young girl" was displayed in a glazed box, its joints fastened together by copper wire. Rings with pointed blades – the seven-bladed temple rings adorned with patriarchal crosses – were sewn up with coarse threads to the temples of the skull. A further clarification was added: "Rarity".

I went out onto the street, and recognized the chap who was nailing down the insulating film with upholstery nails: it was Prokhorov. He spoke to me straight away:

"Have you seen the girl? I stuck my spade in and – cr-r-ack… She was also wearing, just there, around the neck, some beads on a strand of horse hair – thirty-five of them! And some twisty silver thing. A kind of pendant. But they've taken them all into the citadel for safekeeping. If they manage to get the President to come to the excavation, they'll give them to him as a present, so he can keep them in the State Treasury in the Kremlin. But… you know, I think…" he leant towards me, "it would make sense if he dug them up himself. Let's give him a spade of honour with a bow on the haft. Let him dig a sod for the sake of history. At the designated spot. He digs in a span or two… and there's a casket! He'll be delighted, and we'll all be honoured…"

"He won't fall for it. It's too much. He'll take offence."

"He'll believe it all right! He knows the Russian land like his local pub, like the back of his hand. He knows that our land is rich in buried treasures. I can see it for myself here. Every day we dig out something. You even get tired…"

* * *

I kept turning round – much too often, to my shame – towards the tents to see the new arrival. Could it really be her? What if she's looking? What if she came to me? Not likely. But... On the other hand...

Along the ridge of the embankment protruded wall fragments connected crosswise. By the gates they were mending the foundation of the tower. I leapt over the wall. Some men were sifting the grey soil using netting from a bedstead, others were lifting from the pit pieces of a brick plinth, fragments of white stone, pink and bluish slabs – it was the foundation of a cathedral. I removed three bricks, then took a spade from the nearest pair of hands – have a rest, pal. Where should I start? Little by little among the pegs? I swung the spade back and thrust the steel into the clay.

I straightened up.

"Had enough already, eh?" an idling chap grunted.

"Got a chopper? There's a root or something down there."

The fellow came bounding up.

"What kind of root can there be down here, at this depth? Call the 'cheologists – must be a find! Oi, Ivan, go and get Yelena Fyodorovna! Well, my friend, we've earned a glass of vodka each for this. It's a deal – we dug together – yeah? And we are gonna drink together, yeah? They're running over here!"

A quarryful of academics and enthusiasts bunched round, landing like cats, on all fours. They received Yelena Fyodorovna into their midst and directed her to the heart of events, while Sviridov shouted down from the top:

"Is it a treasure? Holy bones? Ah, you lucky finder!"

Dust flew up over our heads. Brooms, fingers, scoops and dustpans could be glimpsed, as the woman's hat kept surfacing and dipping.

"Byzantine brocade ribbon. Horizontal burial, at ground level. The deceased is in a hollowed-out trough, wrapped in birch bark. On his back. There are flint arrows. It suggests he's a sorcerer, or somebody of high birth."

"A prince?" burst out Sviridov, crashing into the raucous crowd.

"Position of the corpse: north-east orientation. Male. Spiked helmet. In his right hand a sword of the Carolingian type, its blade almost a metre long, with a groove in it. Over seventy years of age. Excellent condition. Hair remains at the temples. In his left hand... an almond stone. Two copper signet rings..."

My co-discoverer and I were pressed into the clay.

"A twisted copper bracelet. An icon-holder. Two halves of a copper button in the region of the stomach. Comrades: a trader's seal with the stamp of a town on the Rhine! Like in western relics from the thirteenth century!"

The crowd pushed, pressing my back into the hard soil. I gasped for air. Above our necks, above our shoulders and backs, above the pit, like a white flame appeared Vic's girlfriend with her hands clasped in front of her – lower than for praying, closer than for diving. She was bending over, her hair covering her face. I saw that she was rubbing her palms as if to warm them, but much slower, and that she wasn't looking at her hands at all. What she was looking at were the heads that filled up the pit, like seeds in a sunflower. It looked as though she was husking ears of corn and sowing grain, watching the kernels fall down like snow – a little to the left, a little to the right. And then she shook her hands, as if throwing off the remaining husks and chaff.

The crowd pressed harder. I tried to wriggle free, but toppled right over my co-discoverer, who was spitting clay and wailing at every push: "Shi-i-it!"

"Comrades, make space! This is important! The corpse has no

left foot. More precisely – it's been sawn off with a tool, and these cuts, of the correct form and abrasion, clearly indicate that what we have uncovered here is the earliest example in history of amputation and application of a prosthetic appliance. Which all goes to affirm the superiority of the ancient Russian healers and medical specialists!"

"Then it's a bottle each," chipped in my co-discoverer, and collapsed under my feet. They let down ropes to lift up the coffin. Above the pit everything had been cleared up.

Sviridov embraced me.

"You, my friend, are now an Honorary Citizen of Svetloyar, the source of the Russian land," and he turned round. My sharer in good fortune was tugging at his sleeve: "I'll remember this!"

It didn't get dark all at once – the inky hues mixed with the haze bit by bit. The radio seemed to be chewing, without being able to swallow, an opera in the Belorussian language about a Polish student who'd gone off to Italy – the whole camp was thundering with it. I took refuge in the citadel, dangling my legs into the trenches. The view was good, but there were lots of gnats. I swirled around some rings and beads in the flat-bottomed box; I picked up bronze pins shaped like birch leaves, cloak clasps the size of a girl's hand. From the camp, smoke stretched out. The radio died down – it was time to sleep.

Vic's girlfriend, lingering over every step, was going down into the heart of the digs, wrapped up in a black cloak, peering round and waving her hand in front of her face... gnats! She didn't want to be alone. But there was no one around. Then the steps resounded more resolutely – down at the bottom.

Panting from exhaustion but still sober, Sviridov found me – his eyes popping out of his puffed-up, babyish face at every breath as he spoke:

"Let's go to the bonfire. It's time to sleep. What a great day! Just look at how you hit it. They've opened up three burial mounds. Actually, one was empty."

"How come?"

"Well, some must have fallen by the wayside. A soldier, a traveller. So they make an empty mound for him, to remember him."

"Comrade Sviridov," I blurted out on the stairway, "just when will you start drilling to find grain?"

"So Yelena's been blathering?" and he spat. "Silly cow! I want to drill a hole to put up a mast. We'll stretch out lines from the mast, fix a tent, and the artists will paint motifs on it. We won't cover the whole site, just the citadel. It's my secret dream, I've kept it from everybody, and now out of revenge she's invented this story about the grain – bitch. Hmm – huh… mm, yes, well… Look over there – talk of the devil! Where is she coming from?…"

Vic's girlfriend showed us a bowl containing capsules and packages.

"I've washed Ivan Trofimovich's medicines in the holy water in that pond. It's amazing what straws you clutch at," she said, shivering. "The water was co-old!"

"Ah, aha, aha, yes… Well, Comrade Doctor, old women say the lake water was holy. They didn't even cut the oak trees around it. And, incidentally, they didn't bathe in it. Who knows if that pool is what remains of the lake, or," Sviridov continued in a whisper, "if people just peed into a hole. But if you want to take a bath, there's a full water tank over there; it's warmed up during the day, so go ahead, people must be asleep by now, if you want to wash or do a bit of laundry."

The sentinels had gathered by the fire. Sviridov shooed them off, and only Prokhorov remained, tipsy. He clambered around the bonfire, showing me with gestures that wherever he sat smoke was hitting him in the face; then the warrant officer sent him away to his tent and the smoke rose in a pillar.

Vic's girlfriend stared at me from across the flames, took off her cloak, dried her hands at the fire as if stretching them out to me – palms up. When I tore myself from her gaze, her hands clenched.

The bonfire – little more than a few logs and flames – engulfed everything. I sighed, but didn't yawn. If you doze off during the day, your brain is completely befuddled by the evening.

"You're so funny when you're embarrassed."

Sviridov picked at his ears with both hands.

"Don't get too excited." She got up and waited a bit, put her hands behind her head, and let down her hair, while the flames were licking her dress, casting bluish, meandering, solid shadows and turning it pink and gold.

She glanced inside a tent and swiftly walked away, clasping a white object to her breast.

"How about a wash?" Sviridov hissed. "Let's go. We'll keep guard." He wiped his smoke-filled eyes. "Our washing cabin's got no bolts. But everybody's already asleep. I'll make sure they're all asleep. I need to lay my head down – I'm tired. You have a sit by the fire. Or else go, if you feel like taking a stroll. There's nothing here that can catch fire. Every night we leave it like this…" And he vanished, bellowing into the depth of the night: "Oi, Ryaboshapka! Where's the road? Eh? Then keep looking in that direction – understand?"

7

Wanted: a Viatichian with a Broken Arm

10 Days to D-Day

Everything settled down quickly – the flames, the wind from the grass and the earth. Boots were drying out – hordes of them, like army ranks, in groups, as loving couples, as quarrelling couples – all worn out. The shovels were resting. A bed was waiting for me alongside others. Yes, I'd leave now – nothing would come of it. Clouds of insects twirled in the translucent smoke hanging over the heat. The moon was about to appear in some form or other: egglike or shaped as a wood shaving – was it a new moon, a crescent? It's over now – it's past summertime. Not quite over yet: the earth is still warm. Ready to go, but not gone yet.

Smoke whipped into my face. I got up to avoid the fumes, and it looked as if I was heading… stop staring in that direction. And it's stupid to tell yourself. Almost like you said it aloud, in fact worse. You feel like a total fool.

I was tormented by this kind of feeling. Just like ages ago. I thought it'd never be like that again. Because fate gives you only one chance. Or rather, you can succeed only once. Later on, you can walk on water as long as you like, but all you can do then is wring out your trousers in the nettles, mumble out with chattering teeth "e-ver-y-thing we-nt fi-ne" and receive a grateful slap on your wet backside.

I sighed. It all comes down to this: that you can't sleep. On the other hand, you may sit wide awake, but then the moment you lie down your eyelids stick together. Even after lunch. How many times have you turned up late, and promised: I won't ever gorge myself again, I won't fall asleep. And you still can't restrain yourself – all that bread and sausage... you lie down, you start thinking some kind of nonsense – and you're asleep.

My place in the tent consisted of a mattress and a soldier's blanket on a camp bed.

It was chilly, and I hadn't had any supper. If it were hot or after a tasty meal it'd be... Or if she'd led me by the hand... Aha. There's a squeaking noise, and the smell of tobacco, but no gnats. It'd be nice to have a shave, if there's actually some warm water left. It's not too late yet... But somehow... one thing and another...

Larionov drove up with the rations at some unearthly hour of the morning, when it was still dark, but Sviridov had already been pestering the cooks and stretching his chest muscles... I told him I was leaving. This was discussed in whispered tones, and Sviridov wrote me a leave permit for the "exit of one person with empty pockets". We drove off. I yawned, relaxing on the back seat.

"Stepan Ivanovich, why are you down? I didn't sleep the whole night – it's me who should be out of sorts."

"Yesterday evening we removed more rats from the ceiling. It's... getting on my nerves. They kept falling down during the night. The soldiers had to finish them off with shovels. Should they still be falling like that? Eh?"

"Of course! Their guts must be burning – they're running around like hell. Rotten deal. No water, no way out, and not the usual food. There's new food, but they die in agony from it. And there's nothing to feed the baby rats, so they eat them. In general, to avoid the agony at their feeding places, the use of strong poisons is not recommended. In this case, they've got nowhere to go. It's only for two days. Then we'll lay out anticoagulants."

Larionov turned round with a hostile expression.

"What for?"

"Basically, they'll stop eating, so we'll change the bait and put out drinks – beer or pear squash. Or tomatoes. The anticoagulants are not so perceptible: they'll crawl about in their system for a couple of days – then their blood will cease to coagulate and they'll croak from internal haemorrhaging. And there'll be no direct link with their feeding places."

"And then... will they stop falling down?"

"On the contrary. Their insides will be on fire – a blinding pain. All the better for us – fewer corpses to take down – and the effectiveness of our measures will become apparent. In a week's time we'll have wiped them out. Hey, why are you turning your face away from me?"

"We're being followed." Konstantin informed us. "They are not overtaking us. And they are not falling behind."

Behind us was a Moskvich two-seater van commonly known as "boot" or "pie".

"There's two men there."

Larionov searched under the seat and drew out a green helmet.

"Where's the gun, Konstantin?"

"Isn't it there? My kid was playing with it. My wife must have taken it. They'll get it from me today. At lunch I'll show them what for."

Stepan Ivanovich stuck the helmet over his glasses and blinked ahead malevolently.

"Konstantin," I said. "You know where our beautiful girl lives?"

"Well... I know the block. I took Vic there once."

"Let's drive past."

"Well then – to Lenin Prospect." He turned off, and the "boot" followed. "Over there, that's her block!"

Yes, there it was, four brick storeys high – a heart-warming sight... but I didn't know which were her windows... And I bumped my head against the car window.

"Are you mad?"

Konstantin was swerving here and there.

"What the hell are you doing? Stop!"

"No need," Larionov blurted out.

"Stop this minute, damn!"

Aha – that's why we were swerving round! At first it looked as if there were squashed beetroots on the asphalt. But on closer inspection I made out a black tail in the bloody liquid – it was a rat. In the middle of the main road. I see.

I see. A male. I placed my hand next to it – about seven inches long. Tail the same. Ear ripped off – long ago. In a fight. On the right forepaw two missing phalanges. The snout facing north. Could have been twisted by a blow. Or run over at full speed. Or maybe some boys had thrown it on the road.

The "boot" also parked alongside.

There and then I saw a second rat, almost next to it, a wet pulp with furry wisps. The direction could only be gathered by the tail: northwards. Damn. Any more? Yes, two. First one, likewise in shreds. The second one... the second one had had its back paws sliced off, but had crawled and died here, with its disfigured snout stuck into the kerb. The north-side kerb. Into the freshly fallen leaves. Fresh carrion, dying all at the same time. Last night. I beckoned over to the architect, who had turned into a half-crazed wreck on seeing those road decorations.

"Over there, you said, you haven't got any rats?"

"No. Not in the north side of town. Why do you ask?"

"Do lots of people drive around here at night?"

"They carry white beet to the sugar factory. But you can't say there's much traffic. Why?"

On the northern side some windows, already showing signs of activity, were flooded with a yellow light that enlivened the exotic flowers and bushes on the curtains, as well as the tenants inside. The corpses indicated a systematic movement – they all headed in one direction. But this number of corpses in such a small area... a whole pack must have been on the move. Four crushed. Little traffic. Instinctive caution. The first time they've ventured to cross the main road. Only a flood could have urged them. Terrible.

If you multiply the number of gestation cycles by the number of survivors in each brood... in three months both sides of town would be equally rat-infested. All right. They'll all live. The worst days would be today and tomorrow, while they're burrowing in. The pack will go berserk without a nest. Fear will make them roam in entrance halls, attack dogs, clutch at trousers and bite children's hands. And in less than half an hour people will be setting off for work, to schools and nurseries... going shopping...

"My fr-end, my fr-end, pl-ees. Could you com' 'ere." From the "boot" a Caucasian man was waving, while another was unlocking the back doors.

Larionov pointed to himself – me?

"No. Don't go!" he whispered, grabbing at me.

"Some time or other I'll have to anyway."

Meeting my hand with both his hands, the Caucasian said in a confidential tone: "It's from elders, you not offend them?"

In the "boot" there was a dish with a large bunch of grapes that looked like a brain, little bags of walnuts, persimmons, prunes and a small jar of dried apricots. I pinched off a grape and spat out the pips. The two men observed me with a glum expression from under their beards.

"Very fine it is, yes, on a morning like this, we see such a gr-eat big man."

They moved and I sat down. They weren't that old. They smelt of tobacco.

"A nice fine meeting this, yes? You've found the silver belonging to some good people. What problems you have? You're dressed so…"

"It'll do."

"Gut lad! Gold glitters everywhere! There's one thing we can't find. You know what. Very precious. Find it, fr-end. We give you two days. We'll repay. Off you go. Guut lad."

His companion squeezed my hand.

"You no find where is – you took it yourself. You die."

And he went to lock up the back doors. I nodded to the driver thoughtfully:

"Problems?"

He shook his unshaven face.

"Are you from the café? You're with them?"

He denied it again.

"That's a shame. It would be a lot more convenient if you were all together. Explain to your people: I'm a public-health doctor. I kill rats. Their silver – it was pure chance. I knew from experience that rats love little things like pencils and coins. And beneath the kiosk there was a burrow, you get it? I'm not going to look for anything. If you kick up a fuss, I'll hand you over to the police."

The other man handed me a sack of gifts from the market.

"Two days."

"I explained everything to your driver."

"He no understand Russian."

And off they drove.

We removed more corpses from the ceiling. For the following day we prepared anticoagulants from the substances we'd brought with us – but we were in low spirits. Two flocks of soldiers were hurried past the hotel – the police cars went howling by. Larionov had disappeared, summoned to headquarters.

"Just look at that," Oldie said.

Across the square, a traffic-police motorcycle led a procession of watering machines – soldiers were standing on the footboards, with a red-crossed ambulance in the rear. Our hands were itching: why didn't they call us? What was that clanking over there? Some soldiers were offloading iron panels on the grass from a lorry. They were piling them in heaps and tying them up with wire. A big woman covered in a downy shawl was washing a porch and wringing out a rag.

"Comrade Lieutenant, get back into the building!"

I glanced at her boots and kicked the wash bucket.

"Why did the rats escape, Oldie? It's from the same house where those damned 'Rat Kings' were mucking around."

"I'll have to look at the place."

"The bastards… they'll spoil everything and then come running to us. They'll drag us away from our tables."

They wouldn't let us out for lunch and brought pots of cabbage soup to the hotel and pilaf with green tomatoes, which looked and tasted like elk dung – but also two jars of cherry compote.

Oldie curled up in an armchair for a nap, and I spat the cherry stones into his boots. Vic was spinning some yarns while I just ate and spat out…

"They say you've dug something up over there?"

Yeah… And she's come back.

* * *

"Can't sleep?" Klinsky said, when he came towards the evening. "Get ready." He turned to Oldie. "You too."

He twittered away like some little bird.

"Did you like it? Why didn't you stay? My dream is to dig up the fortress. In limestone. Four and five metres thick at the base. With seven towers: the Gate Tower, the Provisions Tower, the Alarm Tower and so on. Can't remember the rest at the moment. Each tower has three tiers. Battle passageways and entrances, loopholes with funnel openings. I still haven't decided whether to set them out irregularly, with corners, or in a square… Mustn't forget the hiding place with a water well."

"Do you want to sit out a siege?"

"Me? Why? Maybe our ancestors. We'll go on the attack!… Incidentally, here's what I found in the *Short Course of the Communist Party of the Soviet Union*: 'Fortresses are easiest to take from within.'"

By the school little girls were jumping over a skipping rope. The boys were battering each other with satchels.

"They can't come up with anything," Klinsky complained. "If I don't suggest an idea, they'll spend the whole holidays like that – skipping ropes and satchels. There are so many other traditional games, no? Come along with me."

"They haven't found any manuscripts yet, have they?"

"We'll find 'em. Soon."

I didn't give in.

"And do these notorious manuscripts say anything about your celebrated town?"

"Well… they will. Up until now the manuscripts have not been interpreted correctly. We need an angle to make them fit. Don't forget, this is just the beginning. We can go a long way from here..." He gazed at me with intensity. "You can't imagine how high we set our aim."

On the Governor's table they laid out plates, cups and jugs. We ate in a group, informally, in our shirtsleeves.

"Hello! Give it to me."

Larionov drew a curtain over the town's map and gave the Governor a sheet of paper.

"Today, in the town district of... in short, two blocks down Lenin Prospekt and three down Mokrousov Street... the presence of rodents has been reported. In the northern side, you know. Until now, the Lord had spared us. This has caused popular unrest and even police insubordination. I'm in charge of the situation. Anyway... The population links this disaster with your work. That's the first point. And, as you say, some criminal individuals must have been trailing on your heels. Which is the second point. Our police, of course... we'll bring them into line... You've got to understand and forgive us... you're not alone: there are many other concerns. Therefore, to protect you, we're detaining you until the end of your assignment under house arrest. You will go from your place of residence... straight to work. And nowhere else. And back. Is that all right? You think you'll manage? For that kind of money, I think I'd manage too!" He burst out laughing – and that was that. Larionov, covering his eyes, also chuckled, as he turned his salad over with a fork. "Do you want to say anything?"

"We sympathize with your misfortune," Oldie began, with an air of importance. "This migration of rodents is highly uncommon. I trust this is in no way connected with the actions of any of your subordinates – that would be a criminal offence... But what can we do to help you? I'll be very honest with you: it's impossible to make the rats go back. And they can't be exterminated either. But, if you make a separate agreement with us, we'll take care of the epidemiological situation without losing sight of our main task, and ensure your peace and quiet."

"But you're already too expensive as it is," Shestakov interrupted him, picking up his spoon.

"We're talking about a reasonable sum. Two thousand dollars."

"No way."

Baranov moved closer to us and, with his brows, nose and paunch, showed us the door. They practically pushed us out.

Larionov slipped out too, dangling his bald head.

"Barbarians." said Oldie, putting his seal on the proceedings. "We'd be happy to help for nothing."

Larionov stirred as if troubled by a sense of guilt, then glanced at me:

"Did you know what was going on this morning?"

"You wanted me to yell at the top of my voice?"

"I mean, in those houses…"

"If your people don't give a damn… Come on, Oldie. No point quibbling with them."

We reached the ground floor. The man on duty ordered us to wait.

Twenty minutes later, Baranov turned up on his own.

"Help me," he pleaded. "As a personal favour. I'll do you a good turn too."

Oldie's beard broke into a grin.

"You've got relatives in those houses?"

"No. Tomorrow's payday at all the workplaces. Cashiers will be here from the entire region and our bank's on strike."

I smiled. Baranov scowled.

"It's no laughing matter. People have been upset all day. Close to a nervous breakdown. One filthy bugger ran through the hall of the bank – the women refuse to go back to work, they're in hysterics. My people can't cope. You've got experience…"

He looked perplexed. There was someone behind my back. I turned round.

"Alla Ivanovna, here you are! What did I tell you?"

"How is it going?" Oldie muttered.

The woman was standing there like a bell. An enamel brooch restrained the collar of her blue dress, which seemed inclined to slide down from her ample shoulders. She was leaning on the table, bending a knee for her comfort, but not stooping – and all her solidity was marvellously visible, with two-headed bulges and receding slopes in the right places.

"Let's go," Alla Ivanovna said to Oldie. "I'm the bank manager."

"Hey, what the…" Oldie suddenly winced and groaned, having received an invisible kick on the ankle. "We usually use bait to kill rats – we'd need at least twenty-four hours. For you we'll do it by hand, as a rush job. That's my colleague's area of ex-per-tise…" He indicated me with disdain and, limping, led Baranov aside as if to discuss business.

"We'll go all the way?" I asked.

Alla Ivanovna screwed her eyes up sarcastically and nodded yes. Yes.

"So I won't have to ask twice."

"Yes."

Baranov ordered his people and Larionov to go with us, so that the incensed crowd didn't tear us to shreds.

At the bank, a group of spiteful old ladies and a number of cashiers were waiting.

"Anybody seen them?"

The policeman had seen one running in. One. Two office ladies saw one zipping by under the tables.

"It was black as a beetle," said a cashier, snivelling. "Like a kitten. Perhaps it was a kitten?" She caught my drift at once. "I'm not coming with you!"

"Lena, I think you should. They can't go alone – the keys are on the table, the safes are open, God knows…" and the manager gave her a hug.

Oldie and I wedged the door open and ordered the guard to ward people off. On the porch I explained to the cashier and to Larionov:

"Don't stand in the middle of the corridor. Leave the passage free. If it runs off – don't budge!"

Oldie and the cashier went into the bank hall. I sent Larionov off to the offices while I stomped along the corridor, banging on the doors, on the walls, on the cupboards.

"Didn't find any," Larionov reported.

Then the cashier's scream nearly burst my ears. She jumped!

My position was fairly good, but I had my back to the entrance. Larionov remained aside, and the guard – that idiot – ran in at the scream into the corridor!

"If you move, I'll kill you!" I hissed, in the one instant left to me. I wanted to lower my chin, to improve my view, but the rat was already coming. The guard gawped but stood motionless – good for him! I lowered my gaze – nothing. It was either too late, or it had slipped between my legs. Something rustled behind me! But no victorious squeal came from outside. Only the cashier was howling.

Oldie shut her up and peered into the corridor without making any noise.

"Are you all right?"

I sprang up like I'd been stung and grabbed hold of the half-dead Larionov.

"Did you twitch, old boy?"

"I moved my leg – it ran straight over my foot." He took off his glasses and rubbed the bridge of his nose. "It ran into the office, I think."

"So you closed your eyes too! Damn. Why are you staring at me now? Bring a table here!"

"A bunch of... incompetents." Oldie snorted.

"Shut up, will you!"

I blocked up the corridor with the upturned table, enclosing the area regained from the rat, and locked the remaining doors along the way to the exit. I searched for holes – there weren't any.

I handed the guard a mop.

"Sit on the table. If it comes out drive it this way. Architect, you too. Don't let it get near you. See it doesn't jump on you, damn!"

In fact, to find a rodent hiding in a house is a big problem indeed. I mean finding it quickly. And if you search for hours on end, you'll go off your head. In its lived-in area a rat gives itself away in three ways: grub, drink, hole – and, if you spot the burrow, the "feeding centre" and the "toilet", or at the very least some passageways, then you must be a complete idiot not to grab it by its tail within twenty-four hours. However, some burrows are only identifiable by experts.

For instance, in the flat of the late stage director *** on Tverskaya Street the local health unit gave up. There were rats everywhere, but not a single hole. A bit randomly, they sealed the kitchen, the bathroom and the toilet, caught a dozen or so in traps, but – the night comes and... sc-r-r-atch... tap tap...

We were tempted to work on that flat because they were paying in foreign currency.

Oldie's first guess was: a raised nest. Some twenty centimetres from the floor. The rat is guided by its ultrasonic hearing as it gnaws passages through hollows – that's easier, that's why the passages are branching out and the holes can end up anywhere. The state health-service staff, who poison rats in between shopping and collecting their grandchildren from school, search in the usual places: in the skirting or under the pipes.

Nothing came of it. All day we crawled around on all fours. With the help of neighbours we moved cupboards and chests – damn, nothing. Despite the foreign currency. We had to ask the family to spend some time at their country cottage. Overnight I lay flat on a dusty cupboard with *Disinfestation News* and a pocketful of sunflower seeds, a table lamp switched on – but turned to the wall and wrapped up in rags – while Oldie was doubled up on a kitchen sideboard. The kitchen was the most important place.

I was reading – and could hear the rats whenever they moved. My body would prompt me. So many times you doze off – bang! As if you'd slipped running, and nausea seizes your throat. Still no sound – yet you know... they're out there.

The first night – nothing. The second night – a spoon clattered in the kitchen. Oldie spotted a rat and scared it away, in order to follow its retreat path. It escaped into the corridor. But the corridor twisted round, and there were two more rooms. The following night we kept an eye on the corridor. At midnight, out they came. They fussed about, twittered in the dark, and we waited. Sssht! A black rivulet cautiously sneaked into the kitchen. From the toilet? Oldie slithered closer to the toilet door, and I clapped my hands. And so we found their passage.

From the toilet, rats were pushing through from under the door, though the gap there wasn't more than two fingers wide. I touched the bottom panel of the door – the board bristled with a little bit of wood fluff, while on my fingers stuck strands of rats' fur... It had been an oversight: we should have found that passage.

In the toilet itself they were coming out from the toilet bowl! Thanks to Oldie, who'd heard a splash, we found the water splashing in the mouth of the lavatory – you couldn't block up a pathway like that. I had read once that in post-war Germany they'd turned up and bitten in unexpected places, but in the Soviet Union there was only one case of rats emerging from a toilet bowl – in the former Königsberg, forty years back. We had not expected such resourcefulness right in the middle of Moscow.

We had to disinfest all the flats linked to the sewer pipe, though they'd only paid us for one.

You can guess the whereabouts of a settled rat, but when it takes refuge in a lived-in house as it escapes from death, it becomes unpredictable and completely irrational – and you start to feel uncomfortable too: you grope about and, somewhere close to your hand, its little heart palpitates and its beady eyes film, and a slight movement from you may cause it to jump at your neck like a little grey ball, with a heart-rending scream.

The room looked different now that we knew there was a rat inside.

We glanced around. There were three tables cluttered with papers. A shaky safe. A cupboard with faded curtains. Three shelves niched in the wall. Coathangers. Must have been sixteen square metres.

We began with the obvious places, though I knew it was pointless. Oldie inspected the curtains, recalling a three-month trip to a hotel used by Russian workers in the Vietnamese province of Quan Dong. I combed behind a radiator with a rolled-up newspaper, remembering my bad experience at the nursery on University Prospekt. There I had sniffed around a bedroom with two nannies for two hours, until it occurred to me to ask: why's that bit of old rag stuffed into the radiator?

We stacked the papers on the tables. From the window sill Oldie examined the cornice and tucked up the curtains, while I placed the chairs out in the middle, looking under each one. I drew the waste-paper baskets from under the tables, giving them a good kick first. I shook the rubbish out onto the floor, stuck the baskets inside one another and carried them to the window sill, banging them from below and from the sides.

Oldie was poking his beard along the walls – I rocked the safe and looked under it: nothing. I squatted in front of one of the tables. I wished we had someone to help. While two persons stuck their noses into the corners, the rat might slip across to an already inspected spot. Yet it was no use calling Larionov. I had faith in my cunning: the rat would make a noise in the spilt rubbish.

I pulled out the drawers, looked under the documents, tapped on them, and threw them on the floor. Oldie had failed to find any holes in the walls and was now going over the shelves. On the top one some rolled-up papers stuck out – a likely spot: I'd been casting sidelong looks at it myself. Oldie tossed the whole lot onto the floor, but some distance from himself and bit by bit – in case the rat would spring out.

The bottom drawer. I pulled gently, and jerked my hand back. Footwear. Women's boots and shoes. Cleaning cloths. My first thought was: there.

I don't know why. It just cropped up by itself. The boots were slightly puffed out. And a rat would fit in a shoe as well. Hey, Oldie – I reckon it's here! He swiftly made way through the papers and, when he reached the door, informed the guard:

"We'll knock it down. You strike it with your mop!"

Turning away and hunching my shoulders so as to bury my neck, I pulled out the drawer completely. Heavy. Yes?

Stretching out my arm to the limit, without wobbling, I carried my burden to the door and, without shaking it, threw it into the corridor – making sure that it didn't turn over. The guard started thrashing it with the mop: One! Two! He rummaged among the footwear and the rags – we stood waiting. No. Damn!

"Use your hands," I said to Larionov. "Lift the boots up, shake them out! If it's in there, its spine's already been broken."

Oldie, the bastard, sidled up himself and shook crumpled newspapers out of the boots – that's the way they keep footwear through the winter.

I went back and removed the other drawers. Then night fell. Oldie lit a lamp. In the livid light I grew tired and irritable. All this was monotonous, boring, deadening. I went through all the tables. Oldie had checked out the shelves and the cupboard – nothing. And it was a simple room – not much rubbish, no ledges, clothing, hats.

We stood up, and I felt a certain stiffness in the small of my back. I could have done with a bite. I lifted the edge of the table and dropped it with a crash. I did the same with the other two. Nothing.

"The rat's not here," was Oldie's conjecture. From the street they were peering through the windows and shouting: "How much longer?"

We'd run out of sensible things to do: now we moved about aimlessly. The window sill, the corners, the plaster, around the sockets, pipe outlets, the curtains again, under the safe – all empty. The tables, the rolls of paper, boxes, behind the cupboard, on the cupboard, the skirting boards – where else?

Oldie raised his head to the chandelier. I lay on the floor and stupidly looked under the safe. Could the old chap be mistaken? But that door – the nearest – was open.

"Oldie, what about behind the pipe under the ceiling?"

"I've looked there twice already!"

Stupidity is infectious. Oldie climbed up to have a look for the third time – from the top of the safe he removed a water decanter, a tray and a serviette, then he stepped from the window sill onto the safe and stuck his hand behind the pipe. He gestured to me: nothing.

"Is the safe closed?"

"You locked it yourself." Oldie knelt down on the safe and glanced behind it.

"Yes I did."

"And I did too."

"But the rat's here all the same."

Oldie agreed wearily:

"Yes. There she is."

I leant with my stomach on the safe and peered behind it, pressing my head to the wall.

"Almost at the bottom," Oldie let out.

"Yes, I can see it."

A huge black rat had wedged itself between the safe and the wall, like a trapped glove. The little bugger's head was pressed to the wall, and its upturned tail to the safe. That's why I couldn't see it from below.

"All right, Oldie, you're an old pro. Now get that mop. And put the light out. Stepan, where are you? Come here. Comrade policeman, stay in position, we're seeing it out of the building. Stepan, look: I'll stick the mop behind the safe and you poke in from the bottom, let's say with those posters – but crumple the ends so it doesn't slip through. So its only way out is through the door. Off you go!" I aimed and knocked the rat onto the floor. Larionov – again with closed eyes, the idiot – shoved the papers under the safe, and the rat, bristling all over, leapt towards the light, and in wavy bounds flew off along the wall into the gaping doorway, hardly touching the floor with its tail. The policeman stamped his feet, and a moment later the women outside cackled – it was over... We'd done it.

We searched and searched. No more rats. Soon there was nothing else for us to do. They asked us to continue, and we loitered around. I'd grown accustomed to running my hand over the wall. Look, leaves were falling. There were already so many of them on the window ledge. They were feebly knocking against the window. We had not eaten. People were coming back into the bank, taking their places. All of a sudden there were so many sounds that I felt like hiding.

"You knackered?" Larionov said. "My hands were shaking."

That wasn't as bad as two years before, when we had to comb a trade unit of sixty square metres. For four hours. There were two chairs, a large pot with a rubber plant and a still life hanging on the wall. After the refurbishment the place was still empty. It was known there was a rat inside. A sense of dejection overwhelmed us: there weren't many things there, nowhere to look. We were going mad: we stamped around with our boots, set fire to papers. Complete madness. A glittering varnished floor six metres by ten. Lilac-coloured walls. Smooth whitewashing, and this rubber plant. And the still life. People passing by the shop windows. It was winter. We were just pretending we were still looking: we crawled around, squatted down. Our knees were raw with rubbing, it was hot. We didn't find it.

The cleaning lady did. We were putting on our coats, ready to return the advance, and she was wiping the leaves of the rubber plant. The rat was hanging on the plant, clutching to the underside of a leaf – had been doing so for four entire hours. We killed it, of course.

"Never mind," Oldie drawled. "Soon we'll be home."

There we were now: two cheerful idiots in a room in disarray. Some people looked in. She'd come soon. There she was.

"You've torn the curtains. Why did you mess around with them?"

"Will you keep your promise now?"

"What promise? The rat's run into our basement. You get it, and then come and see me…"

"If you remember," Oldie observed, in an ingratiating tone, "our agreement was to evict it, not to kill it."

"I made no such agreement with you."

It turned out that directly from the porch the rat had leapt into the gaping basement window.

Alla Ivanovna guided us. Oldie went down, muttering in a sullen tone:

"You think I'm a greedy person. You should watch how little I eat. I'm not greedy. I'll give you a hundred dollars back in Moscow. And you'll get a much better one. Even a couple of sizes bigger."

Bending down, we pushed crates and cans to the left and right, while Alla Ivanovna jangled her keys. The last crate by the wall contained milk bottles. I stopped Oldie.

"Hold it."

"Well, what now?" He was already fed up.

"It's under this crate."

"If you say so," Oldie gave me a reproachful glance, and knocked the crate onto its side.

The rat stood still, not realizing it was out in the open. Suddenly it raised its snout sharply and hurled itself at the white feet of the bank manager! She dropped her keys, screamed as if we'd pinched her butt and leapt to the exit, holding up the hem of her skirt. Oldie jumped over the crate and ran along the wall, but the rat dived into a crack in the corner, its tail vanishing swiftly down a deep hole.

Alla Ivanovna kept glancing at Oldie and laughed nervously, covering her mouth with her hand. I hugged her and ran my lips over her cheek.

"I'll get it tomorrow."

"Don't lie to me. I'm a simple girl. And don't touch me like this... you know it's not easy for me..."

Oldie held his tongue.

I nibbled some warm bread, got hold of the crust and scraped fried potatoes out of the pan. I only lifted my fork to spear an oily chunk of sausage or to pick up some of the mixed salad. And I could eat no more than nine pork-meat dumplings, which I'd livened up with pickled cucumber. I don't like them like that. As a drink, they'd diluted some cherry jam with cold water – what, had they run out of stewed fruit? For dessert, there were a couple of stale sweets – chocolate ones, but only two.

"Look, Oldie, the soldiers are building something."

Oldie leant over the balcony. With one movement I swept up his sweets and said:

"Where's our cook?"

"Relaxing at home," Vic replied curtly from his bowl. "She's been with Ivan Trofimovich all day."

"Yes, you are right... Stepan, what are the soldiers up to so late at night?" asked Oldie.

"They're going to the infested area. To fill the holes with concrete, lay traps. Or at least calm people down. I can't tell you everything, but... common people are very agitated. They're not so well off over there, but never mind – at least we have no rats! Vic and I will carry out everything the health service tells us to do." He frowned, thrust his fingers under his glasses and pressed down on his eyes. It seemed he was on the verge of tears.

"And what about your 'Rat King', Comrade Gubin, with their folk remedies?"

"Something can be done with traps too," Oldie said

161

sympathetically. "I'll lie down for a while and then join you, to show how to lay them properly."

"You can't go out. But if you give us your advice…"

"Boys! Come here, all of you. Each one take your trap and show it to me."

Oldie was speaking from the balcony. "Does everybody understand the mechanism and the way it works? Does everybody understand the difference between baited trap and set-up trap? The bait is a slice of smoked sausage: you rub the trap with garlic, and your hands with oil. Place them firmly along a wall. Don't put them on pipes. The rat will prod unknown objects."

Vic noted it all down, while I whispered to Larionov:

"Don't leave the soldiers. Keep them under your control and supervision. Let them practise their skills. Especially Vic. Not less than an hour."

"It depends how soon we manage…"

"I put it in plain Russian: if you let him out before an hour's up, I'll put you down like a freak of nature!"

I went down to the gates and sat on a bench. The pregnant women had kitted themselves out in warm housecoats and were gathering leaves, giggling at my hiccups. The unit trickled out through the gates in a helter-skelter fashion. I caught the sleeve of the one bringing up the rear.

"Hold on. Show me the trap. The catch is faulty. Shout to them that you'll catch up with them."

"I'll be right with you! I'll catch up!"

"Go to Vladimir Stepanovich – the one on the balcony – he'll fix it. Run. Give me your jacket and cap – it's getting a bit cold! Go, quick!"

He skipped off and I slipped into the jacket, pulled over the cap, and trotted off after the unit, not getting too close and turning away from the guards.

When I reached the main street, I chucked the jacket into the nearest rubbish bin and went over to the building I knew so well. The soldiers on the other side broke into groups, one for each infested building.

After taking a good look around, I entered Vic's girlfriend's place, past a group of young boys and smokers.

"What's this?" She came racing down the steps to meet me. "Oh God – how did you find my flat? Have you been knocking on every door?..."

"You were looking out of the window, weren't you?"

"Oh well, come up..." She was wearing again a long white dress. She touched her lips and shifted her hair on her shoulders. She didn't know what to do. "Right now I'm with a neighbour..." she lied. "Just let me have... a couple of words... with her..."

"OK, I'll come up. I'll wait until she's gone. What's your flat number?"

She told me and ran off, her wide skirt waving behind. I breathed deeply and tried to relax. My voice was trembling. I felt like suffocating.

I noticed a burning smell – probably wafting in from a bonfire in the yard. Overhead, there was a slamming of doors. No words could be heard. They must have been different doors, although they sounded like just one. She pretended that she was seeing off a neighbour. I went up.

"Quick," she beckoned from the threshold of her fragrant, crepuscular, mysterious flat with its virginal settee, its mirror on a bedside table cluttered with perfumes, mascara, little pots, needle cases, money boxes, with a calendar and a sewing machine bought for future use...

"I just wanted to tell you... I really like you. You're a lovely girl…" There my voice cracked, and I instinctively took her hand, which was cold, passive and unresponsive. "I don't know how to do this kind of thing." I let go of her hand.

"Come on in! Thank you. But there's also a lot of bad things about me…"

"For example?"

"Well, I'm… not the domestic sort."

"That's not a problem."

"Come in! Someone might come out of their flat… Look at me… stop looking at the floor… This flat's high up: there aren't any rats here."

"I could do a monthly plan for your flat… Listen, I've got to have a quick look at the basement."

Now it was she who took my hand a squeezed for a brief moment – just once.

"Can't you do it later?"

"Later there won't be time…" You went up to ring them to come and get me, didn't you?…

I left her there and flew downstairs. The people on the benches outside were struck dumb when they saw me career through the doors and hurtle down to the basement. It was locked, so I got hold of the nearest old lady.

"Is there something burning in there? How long it's been smelling?" I fell on the ground and sniffed through a cat flap sawn into the door – yes. From the basement came a burning smell.

A bunch of local residents immediately came after me – all muscular young workers, close-cropped, in overalls.

I dashed to the back of the building, escaping from their spread arms and bursting through thorn bushes. In the dark, I bumped my knee against an iron fence post. I leapt over it, but was then knocked down by a blow in the face from a man who was ahead of the others. Without taking the hands off my face, I tripped him up, and then raced off, grimacing at every stride from the pain in my knee, heading towards the cars on the street. When I reached the asphalt, I slowed down and raised my hand as if to say, "Don't run over me!" The breeze carried a whiff of petrol and the smell of burning. Lorries hurtled by, transporting beetroots. Behind my back the locals kept shouting at me, vying with each other in their verbal abuse:

"It was you who let the rats loose on us! Plague-spreader! We'll sort you out!"

I sat in the middle of the street, faint with exhaustion. I prodded my poor knee – damn... not the best place to be in my state... I stopped groaning – my groans wouldn't arouse anyone, wouldn't touch anybody's heart and make them think: maybe he's in distress, maybe he needs... It's just that there was nobody now to... It'd pass. Somebody was shining a light, forcing my eyes on the ground. Then the light was switched off and I saw: "Ambulance". A doctor was shouting in a hoarse voice:

"Which arm's broken? Lift him up!"

In the car I slid from the stretcher and asked the anxious-looking Klinsky:

"Need a Viatichian with a broken arm?"

"You! You scum!" he blurted out. "Nosey sod! Shut up! Sonofabitch! Why did you go and pester her! What do you want with her? Shut the fuck up! You sneaked out of the gates this time, but you won't be able to jump over all of them! I won't be able to get you out of the next scrape, you understand?" The car sped along, wailing. He touched the driver and said calmly: "No need to go so fast. Straight to the sanatorium." And he roared afresh: "They'll bump you off! You flooded the café... and the old man... what's the old man done to you?"

He had a cup of tea at our place. A nurse bandaged up my knee and left. Klinsky looked up at Oldie.

"I propose an agreement. To you – freedom of movement. With the exception of the girl's house. Leave her alone."

"Fine." Oldie shrugged his shoulders and sighed.

"Meaning? You give me your word?"

"Sure – you've got our word."

"Today's what? The second of September. You need to sleep, and here's something to amuse you before you sleep." He ripped a page from his notebook and beckoned me over: "Sit down, and don't get into a huff. I've received another letter." He started drawing. "This is the square. This is Lenin Prospect, branching off from it. One, two – the sixth street on the right is Mokrousov Street. There's a fire station there, with a watchtower. I'll draw it here. According to this, just as the President and the bloke from the United Nations drive up to the fire station, a fire engine will drive out on a false alarm, pushing back the guards' vehicle protecting the left side. The President's buggy will be exposed to shooting." Klinsky tapped three times with his pencil. "They'll fire from the ground floor of the watchtower, from the latticed window. It's four metres away. Even an idiot couldn't miss the mark. They'll leave through the unguarded checkpoint, and a blue Niva will be waiting at the nearby junction. They'll drive out at the back of the column of celebrating people, behind the cordon. And off they go to the back of beyond, having received their money." Klinsky added nine zeroes to one side of his drawing. "Two snipers' rifles will be found a week later, without fingerprints, at the meat factory." He relaxed and summed up: "The bastards know that fire engines are deployed from the station for emergencies. And that you can't access the tower from the street – the gates are locked. This letter – somebody's written it. Do you understand? I'm going off to sleep, the time is approaching." He yawned and rose.

Oldie rose too.

166

"But… surely you're going to take measures?"

"Why? Because somebody's informed us with a detailed letter? Just remember, when they come I'll already be out of the picture. Other people will be in charge. They can do anything. Or so they think. But they don't have much of a hold of the town."

"This is an unusual letter, isn't it?"

"All the facts have been worked out. But according to the plan of the festivities, they don't intend to turn into this street. There's no procession past the tower. I will do nothing and say nothing to anybody. It's all plausible, but the main thing is…"

Oldie waited, and then could no longer restrain himself:

"What?"

Klinsky inclined his head slyly.

"There's no reason for it. There's no 'Why?' That's the way people do things here, and that's what I would have thought. But the route of the procession… Unless the higher authorities have some plans of their own …"

I looked at his drawing and shoved it in my pocket.

We didn't get to sleep for ages. My leg ached, and Oldie was chewing cud. Then he said to me:

"Don't get involved with them."

"So you know who 'they' are, do you? The town. The rats."

"It's obvious that they won't allow the inspection of the basement from where the rats escaped. What could they be burning in there? Perhaps it's just a coincidence. However much I think about it, I can't figure out what they are up to. But if they're hiding things, there's something shady about it. We've got to focus on what we were hired for, get paid and go. I'm asking you a personal favour: leave that girl alone. She, of course… but, well, generally speaking… you understand. There are girls like that in the lab here. Two of them. Go there."

"It's too late."

8

Count Mokrousov's Vengeance

9 Days to D-Day

The anticoagulants didn't increase the number of rat casualties dramatically – in the morning they removed a couple of dozen corpses from the suspended ceiling, plus four which had dropped during the night. Three more days to get the suspended ceiling down to a "virtual zero", and then we'd go.

At the health unit I chose a trap in good working order and rushed off to the bank. I'd had a shave, and was now wearing the smile of a young boy. With a cold whimper the wind was turning over the leaves on the road. At a slight touch the leaves were falling in clusters from the branches. The autumn, which had arrived so early, peered briefly from each lead-coloured puddle, soon to be covered by leaves. The pregnant women were singing on the veranda. In the distance the orchestra was rehearsing, and the soldiers were already stationed by each building, chalking numbers on the entrances and checking out anybody entering against a list. Over their shoulders people were pushing – "Here, that's me" – and the roads were still drying out: dry dust was still visible, and the day was still transparent under the unshaven cheek of the sky.

What do I know about you, my dear? In the pitch-dark basement of the bank, I was inspecting a hole by touch. During the night you scraped out four bucketfuls of earth with debris. You dug all night, chucking out lumps of soil with your back paws, then turned round and shoved with your snout. As you delved deeper, you carried out earth in your mouth, and now you're four metres from my hands. You're an adult female. That's good. A young rat has a brisker digestion: suppose we have to resort to poison, it could survive.

In the morning you marked your territory – your new glade. But you still haven't found your staple food – which would tell me what your favourite titbits are. If, say, it was sausage, you'd crave carbohydrates – and I'd bring you flour. If flour was your food and you lived in a grain elevator, I'd give you water to drink, with milk or sugar. If you had plenty of food concentrates, I'd pamper you with fried fish and croutons. I know everything you like. But there's not much time. One trap will be enough. You're unlucky: you'll run straight to me. One doesn't survive such an honour.

Death is easy to arrange. Let's say I place this dirty stick by your burrow. It's a new object. You're scared of it. You starve for a week but don't step across it. But I've left a passage for you, not the most convenient – that's important: a convenient passage will put you on your guard. The path is along a pipe. Then you'll go round the shaft of light projected on the wall from the window. And on your path I'll place a trap covered with a bit of dust. I'll bait it with a piece of black bread crust. Not smoked sausage, not pumpkin seeds. Not ground meat with fresh tomatoes – that's what the textbooks tell you. I know: even a cigarette end dipped in oil will kill you. Simple things kill. Before mealtime. The new surroundings make you excited. You're sure to go out.

Before the bank opened, I sat in the sun, looking at the sky from a bench: the wind was snow-fresh. Across the main street I could see her block of flats. Her windows. I looked at the other side: from the infested buildings a small delegation – the mother-and-daughter couple from the health unit, Vic and Larionov – was approaching, all looking glum.

"How is it going with the traps? What are the results?"

"Not too effective," the health officers acknowledged. "They're just not going into the traps. They won't touch the poison."

"Poison?"

The girl read from a document:

"Bactocoumarin? We've had it for three years."

"Wha-at! Ladies – have you really been using that? Bactocoumarin?!" My face flared up. "Now the two of you, well I never... Salmonella pathogens in a residential block! We don't even use that in warehouses, which are restricted to the public. Tomorrow your dogs will start dying, and the day after there'll be coffins in the street! Seal up the basements! Have preventives handy!" This amused Larionov. "But what about the traps? Not a single rat?"

"There was a tail in one, a paw in another – they must have gnawed them off."

The two women shuffled off to the red-crossed vehicle.

"I'll report this to HQ!" said Larionov, preparing to dash away.

I grabbed him by his sleeve.

"Hold on, will you? Over three years old... the bactocoumarin will have gone off ages ago. It doesn't last even a summer. It's delicate. OK, so maybe just a couple of kids will croak... only joking!"

I went and tried to help them. Traps can't work in one day. They have to be charged with bait but left open. The rats will try them out: today they'll eat from a few of them. Tomorrow, from others – and never from the first lot. When they get used to the traps, you can kill them. A clever rat won't get caught at all.

In Leningrad we'd been clearing the Hotel Moscow – its loft, rather. The rats had eaten the bait, but the trap was empty. Three days in a row. We lay in ambush: an old rat came out and gave a big shove to the trap from the rear – it clicked shut. The rat made a sound and its babies came running out to devour the bait. They went round all the traps like that. And they taught others. At the training ground we released into a pack a rat which knew how to open the cover of the feeding box. The entire pack picked up that skill! But they still forced the instructor to open it – if it shirked, they'd bite it. They thought that this new piece of knowledge was a con, and that the first to die would be the one who brought it. But they were all eating.

At the first entrance I spotted a rat that seemed to be poisoned.

I slowed down: those idiots couldn't understand why. They exchanged glances, and were too embarrassed to ask why I was stopping.

The rat was lying in the grass, by the side of the road, hunched up amidst the dried-out stalks. Above it, crows were cawing and moving around. I guessed it was the rat with a missing paw, the one that had escaped. I certainly didn't want to play around with bactocoumarin… The rat had crawled out to die – its snout was heavily sunk onto its breast, like a drunken sot. Just in time before a dog could catch it – or a crowd gather at a child's scream. How do we know which is the best place to die for it?

"You stand here." I ordered Vic. "Don't look at it – let it die…"

He cast a quick glance around.

"Don't let anybody come near."

"I'll kill it!" he said. He snatched a broom from a woman who was sitting down to have a rest, and rushed back. The rat saw the threat too late with its eyes blinded by the pain burning its insides. It backed up in three wobbly movements, getting stuck in the grass. After the first blow on the back, the rat hissed and rose on its teetering paws like a filthy witch and, before Vic hit it again, moved its paws in front of its face as if warding off the blow. I turned away and screwed up my eyes. There was one last choking shriek as Vic trampled on the rat. Its spine burst with a crack. Very loud. The crows started a round dance, waddling closer towards the middle...

I could have made a mistake. The rat could have sat there for another hour. Or bitten a child. If he'd hit it. I wonder how my trap is doing. I'll ask for an army jacket for myself. The cats are making strange noises... There's a good boy for you... what a bastard.

"What about you..." Larionov screamed into my back.

There was someone else sitting on my bench. An old man with an aquiline nose was scraping the mud from his shoes with a stick. His face had a purple tint, set off by grey whiskers and grey matted hair that could no longer hide an expanding bald patch... He flinched as a young boy banged his ball against the back of the bench. The old chap reeled forwards.

"Vot da-y..."

"Tomorrow."

He shuffled away, scolding the kid:

"That's e-nuff of that beat-ing! Ven a man's sat down – he needs his rest. Don't you know! It's time you had a good beating yourself!"

The boy went round the bench, balancing the ball on his foot, and suddenly sent it right in my face.

I seized the ball, resisting the temptation to run after him and give him a good thrashing.

"Catch!"

The kid caught the ball and beamed.

"They told me to tell you: you'll pay for the caff tomorrow."

* * *

I had lunch in the bank, wondering all the time if I'd manage to get off with Alla after the meal. There were other women around – she was pressing my hand under the table between her knees.

"What sort of food is this?… The eggs are off. God knows what they put in these meat rolls. And we pay good money for this." Suddenly she parted her knees and, leaning with her breasts on the table, greased her lips red in front of a powder case which swiftly misted over, chatting with her neighbours:

"Alla, has your mother-in-law moved out yet?"

"There's no balcony there. Life's better with a balcony. You can dry your knickers out."

She finally got rid of them all and pushed me away:

"Cheeky monkey. You should take up sport." She avoided me, slipping from my arms, and when I finally caught her she was puffing and snorting. She turned her face from me, accidentally touching my lips with hers. "Have you caught that rat? Go and catch it." And she stuck out her tongue.

My little darling had thrown earth over the trap.

You don't want to die? You know that the hunt is on, uh? Don't be rude, or I'll be offended. I'm pressed for time – that's why I take short cuts. OK, you repelled an open attack… but on the tenth night you should have taken the bread crust, no? I mean, after the required ceremonies.

I had brought fifteen traps – it was getting ridiculously deadly down there. In my salad days I got to know a young one. She was a gentle sort: that's why I got to know her. At a tram stop I met a trainee rat catcher carrying a parcel. I knew, of course, what was in it. This trainee told me that he'd found a young female rat by an overturned trap, without a scratch – but dead. He was sure the rat had grazed the trap, and that the trap had clanged shut. The rat must have died of fright – he thought – her heart must have failed her. The idiot was prattling on, and I was already looking around, because I guessed that the rat had just passed out. The young lady had already woken up inside the parcel. I didn't have time to move before she sprang out and, sneaking between our legs, whisked off into an alleyway.

I did find her in the end. She too didn't want to die. It was a long fight. I can't describe what it was like being with her all night, just by myself, while in the background autumn was passing away – yes, it was autumn then too. Like many others, she was brought down by loneliness. It's hard to be just the two of you: death and yourself. She resisted valiantly, she understood everything. I was always there. She didn't trust me. So… I introduced her to a friend. A timid one, who couldn't have killed a fly, but… alive, warm to be next to, who could rub your back… a handy friend. I had trained him beforehand. I had trained him to eat porridge. The right sort of porridge. He always approached that kind of porridge without fear. And she followed him. When she breathed her last, she crawled up to him and bit his tail.

And as for you… Oldie calls this method "a game of chess", but I call it "check-row planting". Take a look: the traps are placed in three rows, in terraces, forming a solid wall. There's no going round it. The rat simply has to go out and sharpen its teeth, lick the dew on the rusting pipes, look for food. She'll come out all right…

"Turn the light on. Is there a light in here?"

"No, no light," I mumbled, wincing. "Why? Who's that?"

I took a good look into the dark: Vic's girlfriend was shivering on the stairs.

"What are you doing?" she exclaimed, clasping her hands to her mouth. "What's that on your hands?"

"Flour. I'm sprinkling flour on the floor. To see the tracks, the pathway. How the rat gets to the trap. I'm catching one here – I'm hoping to catch it by tomorrow. What are you afraid of?" My own heart was pounding in my tightening chest.

"Well, I got scared. I come in, and you're sprinkling a white substance on the floor and whispering. I'll wait outside."

"What happened to you yesterday?" she asked, when I joined her outside. "The way you ran away…"

"I shouldn't be seeing you."

"We can sit here. Are you bored?"

"Tomorrow there'll be some fun."

"I can bring you some books. It seems to me… that you don't read a great deal."

"What do you mean? I do read. For instance, Melkova's *Synanthropic Rodents and their Elimination* or *Biology of the Brown Rat*, by Rylnikov. Accounts of rat extermination in Budapest – if I begin to read them in the evening I can carry on all night. In fact, I'm not a pure-blooded rat catcher, I know a bit about the garden fly as well… should be reading more on that…"

"Flies… is that interesting?"

"Of course! I collected material for my Ph.D. And it worked out well: I got invited to summer cottages… well-off people, nice food. And then I happened to get involved with rats. I was reading nineteenth-century stuff for days on end then. I came across the notebooks of Count Mokrousov – a notorious man! He's a namesake of your first town-planner. He distinguished himself in the Decembrist Insurrection – or maybe he achieved some kind of victory in Hungary… the fact is that during his retirement he studied rats. And I found out why. It's because of his wife. She was a beauty – there are no portraits, but everybody writes that her skin had a golden tinge. They only wrote about her skin, but it doesn't matter – he loved her. And she died from cholera. In the ice house, rats gnawed away her cheeks and nose. They generally eat soft parts, you know. Like women's breasts. They must have eaten

hers too. He'd been busy suppressing some uprising at the time…
but then he rushed home and saw… Well, he went ballistic. He
left Moscow – he didn't want to bury his wife in a rat-infested city.
He… He buried her in the country. The first Russian rat catcher.
Oldie doesn't attach any scientific significance to him. Mokrousov's
experiments were naive: he'd tie a rat in the middle of the yard for a
hawk to get it, and watch who'd win. Or he'd set a hedgehog on a
rat. He brought an old man from Hungary to catch rats for him…
This old chap had always a chisel by his heel. He'd put a piece of
fat by a burrow and hold his foot above it. The rat would stick out
its snout – and swi-i-ish. No more head. And Mokrousov didn't
give a damn about his health either. He'd build summer houses in
the garden, and make pretty patterns out of rats – little stars, for
example – and in the spaces between the windows he hung stuffed
specimens of the rats' worst enemies: owls, kites, cats. Some rats
he crucified, and wrote an inscription: 'Executed for such and such
offence'. He also made decorations from gilded tails – he would
dry them, polish them, make them stiff, and then gild them."

"And what does he do now?"

"What do you mean 'now'? That was ages ago: he's dead! The
thing is: he couldn't forget his wife. He'd go out into the garden and
shout: where are you? On Olympus? In the Empyrean? In Heaven?
Writers say that he had the misfortune of having a penchant for
drink. He died in a state of complete apathy towards everything."

"But I wanted… is your wife dead?"

"Oh no, no. How shall I put it… we've… separated and don't
see each other. Her relatives can't stand me. I hid her away in the
countryside. They don't understand she's better off there."

"Is she beautiful?"

"Well… how can I put it… To be honest, I've undressed,
well, not more than twenty ladies. All very similar, you know…
Mouths, stomachs, and a few other things – exactly the same.

Especially when they are lying down. It's difficult to compare. But she actually had, believe it or not, three breasts."

"What?"

"Yes, three breasts. Basically, two is the norm. Some have only one – but to have three – that's rare. And that's what she had. Hey, miss, where are you going? I wasn't counting yours! But what a backside you've got... I really love you..."

It was so chilly I went home at a run. I tried to warm my fingers – my breath came out in a cloud. At the gates, the pregnant woman I had found so attractive, with her dyed fringe of hair, was bawling: "Pity for that green garden, that green garden..." She then started all over again, at a higher pitch. I sidled to her side – she had a snub nose and a pretty mouth. I embraced her expanded waist, and it warmed me right away.

"Why is it you only sing one song, uh?"

"It's the one we practise – that's the one we sing."

"You sing really well, all together."

"Ours is the best choir in the region," she replied haughtily.

Her cautious hands got entangled in my sweater and started unbuttoning my shirt – maybe we could do it on the bench?

"Oh oh... what's this?"

"All of our choir is like this. They thought it'd be nice to have pregnant women singing on the veranda... our distinguished guests would be pleased. They asked us..."

"And you..."

"Me? It's OK for me. We've got six unmarried women here, and just as many on a pension already. They had to pretend..."

She fell silent and took out her hands.

"You don't seem to be in the mood today."

I loitered around and went to bed. It was cold. When would they turn the damn heating on?

9

The Pollard Oak

8 Days to D-Day

"Look. That's…"

That's the wind sweeping away the leaves… already brown, and so pliant. The wind is invisible: the treetops start humming and, as the noise dies down, the leaves take off, drift away in a cloud and land like butterflies, rocking and mixing with each other. Another gust of wind, and a new horde is driven away with a dry, whirring sound. Look, over there too. More whispering and rustling. They're falling… all of them.

We were stopped midway through our walk by a stranger, a well-built fellow who showed us a document in his palm with a reassuring gesture:

"Lieutenant Zaborov." Stout as a docker, he waved away the leaves directed to his face and stroked his bald patch. "As a result of the threat, we'll be escorting you with a larger contingent. Klinsky has decided not to involve the police – they've just been deployed to clear up the fallen leaves. Gently now." He got to the gates first. "If anybody's not properly concealed – I'll hold him responsible. Hey, Serdyuk, mate – whose bum's that sticking out from behind the pillar? You carry on talking, don't pay attention to me."

"Thank God," Oldie said. "I slept so badly… I imagined some-body was crawling through the window. These pranks really worry me. Somehow the criminal community here... seems to thrive... They know how to threaten... They kill."

"Oldie, I've got a job on hand..."

"Sure, I'll be OK. How is it going with the little lady? Putting up resistance? Lieutenant, we'll go our separate ways now."

"Going to the bank?" said the big chap. "Run across the square – they're waiting for you there. Don't be scared. If they really want to kill you, they won't give you a warning."

I was so impatient that I started counting the steps in order not to break into a run. But then I ran all the same. The janitors, soldiers, women and older school pupils were combing through the grass, collecting leaves into rubbish bins. A crane was lifting them onto a lorry, and the wind did not abate.

At the bank, the squatting Larionov and Vic jumped up, waving their arms.

"Are they chasing you?"

"I just wanted to have a little run. You got the keys?" I ran my hand on the door – painted wood. Vic was breathing down my neck, and I shoved him away. "I'm going alone. You don't understand? What about a punch in the face? And that'll be your instruction."

You need to know how to enter. You must expect the worst: that the rat has managed to steer clear of the trap and is still alive. You must do everything as if it were alive: no noise, no light. I listened in the darkness – the torch in my hand was getting heavy. Darkness is always secretly alive. But if it conceals a corpse, it takes on its flavour. I turned on my torch. Nothing.

Nothing. Oh well. In general, rats are divided into three categories: the incautious, the cautious and the over-cautious. The first one approaches unknown foods after a week. The last one, never. That's the one I like.

With my light I brushed the dishevelled tresses of the spiders' webs and the reddish walls, throwing small, wave-like splashes of light onto the floor, starting from the dead corners, and then moving around and closer. I approached the burrow and began crawling around it, then thrust the shaft of light into its open mouth, making it flicker. I switched off the torch and, slipping a mitten under my head, I fell powerlessly into a daze. So... nothing.

In fact, she had come out. Not out of curiosity, but to get food. She must be in a bad mood now... not much meat around... she must be angry: that's to my advantage. She had slithered round the traps like a snake, all three rows. There was an equal distance between the tracks in the flour: she had not stopped to think once... I didn't manage to tempt her. The path back was the same. It hurts to see you've been second-guessed.

How could I kill her? A rat is not a flower... nor a human being. I switched on the torch. The earth by the burrow had not increased. Perhaps she'd been digging another hole... I overheard Vic talking to Larionov. I came out as the latter was asking:

"Did it live in the bathroom?"

"Under the bathtub. And it went out during the daytime. None of us ever went in... my parents are also afraid of them. We put down some sort of poison, but we were terrified even to look in to see if it had been eaten or not. We banged a stick on the door, that's all."

"What about a cat?"

"We locked one in there one night... but the cat screamed so much that nobody could sleep. We had to wash in the kitchen and bathe in the bathhouse. Mum couldn't wash any clothes. Now I would... well, damn... but at the time I couldn't even sleep."

"So how'd you manage in the end?"

"We laid out chunks of sausage towards the door. And onto the staircase. We watched from the kitchen. It went out. Eating and moving on. We were afraid it'd have enough halfway along the road. Instead, it went out... crossed the threshold. Dad slammed the door, and the rat fired him a reproachful look. That's how it was with me at the time. And I have been feeling like that since then..."

Larionov asked an inaudible question.

"Yes, I'm grateful to them for teaching me."

I sidled out, scrunched up my eyes in the light and ordered Vic:

"Go to Oldie. Tell him I'll be making a plug. Whatever he gives you, bring it here."

"Don't be so harsh on him," Larionov said, after Vic left. "Don't you see, everybody's leaving the town... but he's come back. He's our future."

"I don't give a damn about your future – I won't be part of it. Go and discharge the traps. There are fifteen traps. I want fifteen pieces of bread in your fist – and not a single crumb on the floor."

No need to go to the bank. Better sit for a while.

In the bank they were painting the window panes. The manager was waiting in the middle of her office. She wore a coloured blouse which came out of her black trousers, and glittering pitch-black boots. I started messing with the lock.

"The key's outside."

I locked us in.

"Why do you keep coming to me like this? You should come with a box of sweets and some nice wine. I could do with a bunch of fresh flowers. Yesterday the Colonel dropped in. He says, 'Alla Ivanovna, you've got the lips of a working girl,' and I go: 'What?'"

I grabbed her hair and gave it a tug – she screwed her eyes in pain, but refused to budge.

"Yes, hurt me... Go on, bite me..." She turned in my arms, panting and shaking. Her hands grew bolder, and she lifted her moist eyes. "You won't respect me any more after this." She folded me in her arms, then tore herself away and blurted out in my face: "Leave me alone... what are you doing to me? Yes, do it. I like it when men do this to me. What are you doing with those chairs?"

I had barred her retreat, leaving only a little corner behind the table. Suddenly she started fumbling among the papers, then leant over and pushed the intercom button:

"Lida, get the policeman on duty to come over – I've locked myself in... can't get out."

She buttoned herself up and gave me a long and elaborate kiss.

"It'll all happen. Now go."

I opened the door, which they had started shaking from outside.

Oldie brought cotton wool and anticoagulants himself. He held up the light, and I pushed large wads of cotton wool into the burrow. The very last ones I soaked in poison and packed in as a solid plug. I placed a strip of plywood on the outside and weighted it down with a brick. There you go.

A determined rat would gnaw its way out. She'd have her fill of the pliable wadding. Then – let's see in the morning. Oldie kept silent.

"What is it you're telling me?"

"You're getting carried away. You could show them any old dead rat... It's a waste of your energies – no one will appreciate it. It's not worth it. But you never listen to me."

"What's been going on in the hotel?"

"No rats fell down during the night. We'll soon be going."

183

Outside, Zaborov wrinkled his worn-out face.

"Still falling…"

The leaves were raining down, stripping the outstretched branches naked. Drizzle fell from the darkening vault of the sky. It was cold and damp… Over the town, a red rocket soared, its sparkling hook latching on a piece of sky. We walked on.

"What a life…" Zaborov muttered. An old man was groping his way along the building, tapping with a stick lifted up high, probably looking for his window, or the archway opening behind him.

Zaborov glanced around, jumped over the fence and rushed across the road to the old chap.

"What're you looking for, old boy?"

Still tapping his stick, the fellow turned towards the voice.

"Wot?" He raised his stick and brought it down precisely and firmly on the lieutenant's head. Zaborov banged against the wall and slid down to the ground, spreading his arms wide in a ridiculous gesture. The old man leapt over him and raced towards us, bolting over the fence. Fanning out on all sides in his assistance, a crew of heavies came pouring out of the archway. They were darting towards us, while we stood like pillars. I jabbed Oldie in the side – "Run for it!"

Pushing aside the bushes, we made a dash towards the square, but the men cleverly drove us away from it. Damn, we should try to break through their ranks. Our legs turned and shot of their own accord to the alleyway behind the bank. In preparation for the big event, there was not a single soldier there! Apart from three women and some kids, the alley was empty. We should have stopped… never do what they want you to do. Oldie outstripped me like a whirlwind. I didn't have time to call out as he ran – in a ridiculous but rather effective fashion – after a bus slowly moving off down the alleyway. With his elbows bent and wheezing under the strain, Oldie was sprinting like a schoolboy. Damn! I too hurled myself after the bus, shrieking madly:

"Hey! Hey!" I couldn't whistle and run at the same time!

Good God, the bus slowed down, and Oldie actually managed to get on, his legs dangling out as he fell inside. He didn't even turn round, the bastard. I raced on in leaps and bounds... the bus didn't brake. I ran for what seemed ages, and finally managed to jump on, crashing down over Oldie, screaming: "Drive faster – faster!" The doors closed, and I noticed that Oldie's hands were tied – but I still shouted instinctively, as the bus speeded up: "To Staff Headquarters!" I was startled when I saw the dirty face of the driver with its shaggy curls around a bald patch.

"Gut lat," he said.

There were four other bearded men in the bus, their heads bobbing up and down because of the potholes. We were now moving fast.

"Ple-ese to sid down."

Just as I made an attempt to smash the window with my elbow, they knocked me down with two blows and tied my wrists with a strap.

"Stop. Let's have a chat."

"You'll have time."

"Are these your goons?" Oldie managed to say. "Are there more?" And his voice broke off.

Now the road became more level and quiet, and the bus screeched to a halt. The bearded men all glanced at the driver.

"We're stopped," he said. "Officer... soltier coming here."

I feel a blade pushing into the back of my head. I narrow my eyes – silence. The doors slam, there's talking outside. Something's happening out there. Still talking. When the driver comes back, it'll be the end. Perhaps Oldie can shout for help, unless he's pinned down like me. The blade's jabbing at my skull – the bastard's nearly piercing me. But they won't kill us.

"Oldie!" I try to call out. The blade jerks away and I feel a sting behind the ear. I forget everything. I bend my head onto the side that's hurting – if I open my mouth, there'll be more pain… if I don't control myself, I'll die. I'm hampered by the floor… the air creeping into my nostrils hurts! I feel needles all over me, splintering inside, a violent pang – I groan. I can only groan using my mouth – and my mouth hurts. Now they are untying my hands – and that hurts too.

"One at a time. With your passports."

"Comrade officer, arrest them!" Oldie shouted. "They've been beating us!"

"I repeat: one at a time. Sidorenko, have you called the guard? Take them…"

"Out!"

"No residence permit? Take your hands away – I'm keeping your passport. You signed that you've been notified about the fourth of September. Sidorenko!"

"Hands up. Against the wall."

"They're kidnappers, don't leave them like that!"

"Shut up! Are they all Caucasians? Except those two lying down? Sidorenko, get them down!"

"Get down, damn you all – heads to the wall."

"Hey, beardie, where's your passport?"

"We left our passports in the sanatorium, where we're staying. We're public health doctors – they kidnapped us."

"So you've got no passports…"

"Out! Empty your pockets! Turn round! Get down, face down, or else…"

He gave me a slap in the face. My heroic left eye opened a chink – I saw a grey, fatigued face under a service cap.

"Why are you so dirty?"

My eye could no longer remain open.

186

"Have you had a drink today? Sidorenko!"

They dragged me out, searched my pockets, but let me lie on my back. My wet collar gave me a chill. I tried to grab the one in charge:

"Inform headquarters... Klinsky."

His boots shifted from one foot to the other.

"Impossible without a passport. You must have a passport."

Some vehicle, hot and stinking of petrol, backed up towards us – its sideboards fell down with a bang.

"Climb up on the left one by one. Where are you sitting, you ass? On the floor! Heads facing that way! Six in a line! Are you six? I'm not gonna count for you. Speak Russian!"

"Can I ask where you're taking us, at least? I am here by pure coincidence – I hope you'll understand..." Oldie's voice was intentionally shaky.

"You were given notice: those without residence permits, with previous convictions, causing public offence, and any suspicious characters... must be out by the fourth. But you've been stubborn. Now you'll be picking potatoes in Kaluga for a couple of weeks."

"I'm not getting in! You'll be in trouble! Don't you dare!"

I unglued my eye again.

"Sidorenko!"

A stocky little soldier trundled up to Oldie and knocked him straight in the chest with the butt end of his rifle.

"Get in, damn you!"

I raised myself on my elbow, whispering:

"Oldie, who are you talking to?"

"You two, come and lift him up."

They dragged me over to the lorry, but after a few steps I was already walking by myself. I was hoisted onto the lorry, and the sideboards went up. Oldie propped up my head, and below I saw a man with a black overcoat – the blind chap – and another one with a yellow sweater – the thug who'd hit me in the sanatorium.

The blind man grinned with his smashed-up face. A soldier pushed him forwards – another lorry was backing up towards them.

Oldie lifted me up a bit more. Along the boulevard people and soldiers were standing, lying around, sitting on bundles. From the square a snake of lorries with Kaluga number plates was crawling up, two four-by-fours of the military traffic police went flashing past – everything was in full sway and flow.

"Turn your face!"

Mr Grubby Beard had been waiting just for that.

"My frent, you found it?"

"Shut up."

And off we went. There was a nauseating stink of night-time railway stations and old boots. Sticky blood was chafing my neck. Little by little, nausea was clinging to my ribs and clambering up. After a while, the lorry shook me up, together with the rest. Smoking towards the rear, the soldiers watched our backs as they pulled off the tarpaulin cover.

We slowed down and rolled over something. Then again. Rails. The lorry moved backwards over an embankment. They let down the sideboards, and thrust three planks in.

"Out... Get that wuss out."

They led us past a man wearing some sort of service cap. I perked up:

"We're not going anywhere."

"Wha'?"

"You heard me! We're not going. We don't want to!" And I ordered: "Let us go!"

"Sidorenko, what's this racket? Put them in the train, quick!"

"You can say what you like: we're not going." I dug my heels in. "We're not going."

In the carriage, people were sitting everywhere. Heads were peering down even from the luggage racks.

"Sit down, my friend – don't drag yourself around."

Oldie let himself down on the floor. I remained by the door.

"You! Go and get yourself some mugs from the conductor."

"We don't need them – we're not going." I could barely see anyone. Oldie pulled my sleeve: just sit down.

A clanging sound rang through the carriage.

"They're coupling the engine."

I began to knock on the door.

"They're smoking on the train platform. Wait till mealtime. Hold on."

The train shuddered, made a grinding sound and set off. At once there was a din of voices, the neighbouring compartments burst into laughter, music blared out from a radio, and someone rushed along the corridor, clanking keys. I knocked again with my fist on the door, which was smudged by the sunset shadows of trees and posts. There was a draught up my back. The train rolled on. People pressed against the window – where were we going?

"And who's doing that building over there, behind the water tower?"

"Refugees – Armenians, I reckon. They bought Vaska Lozovoy's plot of land."

"I give you my officer's word of honour that they'll give you blankets and jerseys, and you'll get to bring some potatoes home."

"You there – if you want them to open, ask the vodka soldier."

"You've got to ask the conductor. What d'you reckon she's got in her water tank?"

"Got a knife?" somebody asked through the wall.

"What do you need a knife for? Have you got something to cut up?"

"We've got bread to slice!"

"Then break it. Or bite from the loaf."

"Stop knocking, man. We're moving!"

"Sit down! Sit him down."

My hands were tired. With a mug I could have knocked louder. But I'd have to ask for one. The wheels groaned as they clung to the rails and came to a standstill.

"Marshalling yard… The next station's Urazovo."

"Hey you, woodpecker! I'll damn well knock you too!"

The door jerked open.

"What now?" the officer yelled. "Will you stop?"

"We're not going."

He fell silent and licked his lips.

"We're getting out. Oldie, let's go."

"Yeah, go to hell."

It was twilight. The soldiers were gathered around the conductor, who was pouring out tea. Others, at the entrance of the carriage, were counting tins of food. The low station platform was made of concrete blocks lying right on the grass and covered with asphalt. Lamps were blazing, and midges flew to them in droves. An old woman was operating a pump, and water was gushing out and foaming down from a bucket. The train started – hands tapped on the windows showing us firm fists: hang in there… good luck! As the train moved away, a level crossing and a car with headlights on came into view. A fellow in a white cap was pacing to and fro in front of it, swinging a red lamp.

Oldie was shivering.

"You reckon we should go there?"

We approached. Lieutenant Zaborov raised his bandaged head, made sure it was us and extinguished the lamp.

"I only just made it."

The road was black, bumpy. Desolate. Every now and then, a milk truck. A girl was hurrying geese along with a twig; they were pressing together on the path, waddling in the grass as if they had no legs. The last ones suddenly spread their taut wings and ran through the air. The girl turned round and scratched beneath her knee, stung by nettles. At the outskirts of the town there were armoured cars. Raindrops were breaking up against the windscreen. People were taking out sacks and old waterproof coats to cover up potatoes piled up in front of their houses.

"Did you get them?" Oldie asked, leaning towards Zaborov.

"How could I find them? There are two thousand people on board. The train can't be delayed. That bastard who knocked me out" – the car went downhill – "dumped his coat, and we've found his filthy spectacles, but how're we going to identify him? There's six carriages of those dark faces." We were now going uphill. "All of a sudden not a single person could speak Russian. Never mind. We've cleared the town – now they're out of the way. Today the password is 'Russia', and the reply is 'God's with us'."

"Russia."

They let us cross the square.

The Governor was striding along to meet us – his raincoat fluttering, his brow pushing against the wind – followed by a group of officers holding their service caps.

"Everything's under control." He firmly shook hands only with us. "I've got a terrible job – really terrible! Now this leaf fall – all the leaves gone in one day!" he said in a snivelling voice. "There's not a single leaf left. And it's only the fourth of September! We were counting on a 'golden autumn with the sun gilding the maple tops'. Why's that? Do you have any idea?" He spread his palms. "These hands have such a burden on them. Ten-sion. Oh yes." His fingers stuck out like wooden sticks. "I'm standing firm, but at what cost? You don't know what it's like."

True enough – the trees were nearly bald: it was frightening. They spread out like a damp black net. We turned our heads around: not a single leaf, anywhere. People were mowing the grass on the lawns, crawling around on all fours in the glaring lights. Tree trunks were being whitewashed. No more leaves.

"Come quick!" said Larionov, from the balcony. "It's raining!"

I left Oldie and turned into the boulevard. Behind the benches, between the trees, people loitered around, painting fences, combing the grass with rakes, rooting up the old grass – bent, headless lumps, crawling like insects. Not a noise could be heard, except the deep breathing, in the dark, of a stout horse with a large mane, harnessed to a cart, its snout lowered. The only chap standing was holding a lamp – it was Klinsky. Leaning with his back on a tree, he was shining the light into the branches above him.

"At bloody last! I didn't expect to see you." He nodded towards the square. "Have you seen that idiot? We're going to greet our guests with a Governor like that!"

"That's an oak, surely?"

"Where? This? Yes, it's an oak."

"And it's lost all its leaves too?"

Klinsky knitted his brows.

"The oak hasn't lost its leaves, mate. The oak's been given a little shave... So as to... not to stress... in short, for the sake of uniformity with all the rest. We've been at it all day long... we've been stoking the boilers – we're burning the leaves." He tapped me on the arm reassuringly. "Smell the smoke? Reminds me of camping. Hello, who's this woman?"

"Comrade Lieutenant Colonel, she's a local... she lives on Mokrousov Street, at number three."

The old woman was dragging a mattress, tied up with bands, and holding a little boy by the hand. I'd seen them before.

"What are you standing there for?" she barked at Klinsky in a severe tone. "To harass old ladies? You stuck up a notice of evacuation. But how? By train? How should I dress the kid?"

Klinsky was dumbstruck.

"They don't even tell you if you have to bring your own mattress! Why aren't you saying anything? He doesn't say anything..." She sized me up. "I borrowed this mattress from my sister – but do I need it? Ah, let's go."

"Granny," her grandson said, "do they have hedgehogs there?"

The heating was on: the radiators were hot, the kitchen windows misted over, and beneath their white coats the nurses wore almost nothing. In the middle of the room the table was creaking under the huge amount of food.

"At last!" Vic leapt up and indicated his shoulder strap: captain. He was tipsy. "They're taking me away from you – so I'll make my goodbyes!"

There were pink slices of rabbit, a fish pie, raising pies, pickled cabbage, compote, crabs, an apple pie, pears and potatoes. Vic's girlfriend, who was wearing a floral skirt reaching to her shoes, cleared a place for me. She was filling my plate, enquiring with her eyes – yes?

Yes please!

"And where have you been transferred to?"

"The Colonel said that for now I'll be a special messenger at headquarters. Lots of things to do there – troops arriving every day – massive contingents! I'll propose a toast. You can raise your teacups. Vladimir Stepanovich said – no drinking till the job's

done. Thanks! I've learnt a lot from you. I can see now why you…
And I'll show…"

"Thanks from us too – the food was very tasty," said Oldie,
interrupting his vigorous chewing, knowing he couldn't count on
me. "And forgive us if we've offended you. We've enjoyed it very
much… so tasty, such big portions…"

"Offended me? You're offending me now… saying you might
have… offended me! Help yourself. Let's go."

His girlfriend prompted him:

"Vic, you also wanted…" She was wetting some wads of
bandaging beneath a tap.

"Yes, I invite you all…" and he stared at me. "There's going to
be a wedding."

"There was something else you wanted…"

"Oh yes! There's a watermelon! In the freezer." He ran off.

"Come, sit down!" She bent my head and put the wet bandages
onto the wound. "Does it hurt?"

I rested my head on her lap, puckering up my face like a child…
peace. A serene sense of excitement and sweetness… She put her hand
on my shoulder – her uneasy hand stroking me from time to time.
Larionov picked up his cup and went over to the corridor, panting
and slurping away. Oldie was crunching away like a meat grinder.

Wind blew from the ventilation window, carrying a smell of
bonfire. The night was peaceful and soundless – no people around.
We'll have a good sleep.

"Does it pinch?"

"Are you bringing that watermelon?" yelled Larionov.

"Another day's gone." The architect joined me on the balcony.
They were clearing away the dishes, and the nurses were changing
the bed sheets. The wind had subsided, as if it had completed its
task.

"The leaves fell down by themselves? Or maybe... to avoid sweeping them every day..."

"Oh, it's not a joke. They've fallen down by themselves, that's the problem. It's a bad omen. It's getting on people's nerves – it's as if some sort of chemical substance had been spread... I rang the weather station: it's the first time in the town's history. Although our history" – he glanced beneath the balcony and finished in a whisper – "is less than nothing. It's a shame, the town is not very pretty as it is... In fact, the man who built it disappeared – Alexei Ivanovich Mokrousov. To be honest, he didn't construct any of it himself!" He paused so that his words would hit home. "But he was talented and even brilliant in his youth! He won a second prize for his design of a Politburo recreation centre. In Moscow he didn't have sufficient leeway or adequate working conditions, so he came here to build, from scratch, a 'communist town'. And what did he get to do here? Not exactly a Palazzo di Montepulciano. A meat-processing plant. A sugar factory. A complex for horned cattle. Still, he drew sketch after sketch – very fine ideas, you know! But in practice they've gone completely wrong. He sketched powerful air draughts beneath the windows which could also give shade, but they were moulded in such a way that instead of an expressive façade we have something that looks like a sponge cake. And for some reason they added a parapet. See those roofs, all these roofs in front of us? They didn't observe any of Mokrousov's projected angles. He wrote: white plaster – and they put grey, or a near black – and the sun doesn't help matters... Just look over there: why have they put in dormer windows? That's Empire style. But who needs Empire style down here?"

"It's no good."

"Every time, they ruined his ideas with some decoration or other. If you're missing something that's required by the plan, just stop. But no, we make it out of whatever's at hand. And not everything can be made out of what's at hand! Obviously his life was getting miserable. He designed all these things himself, but couldn't bear to look at them – those sloping pediments which look like sheds. Those gable roofs over there. An external water outlet. And blind walls. Blind walls. So he gave up designing. He started thinking: how can you be free? To tell you the truth, he didn't know the classics particularly well… didn't read their books… that's why he never went abroad."

"Aha."

"Yes… Only imitators go… but he was their kinsman in spirit, he inherited his talent by right of succession. He thought things out. He used to repeat that military units only become an army thanks to the ideas of their commander. When you enter a town, you have to decide: destroy it or subjugate it? What's the overriding necessity? There's the ideal town built by Hippodamus of Miletus. There's the Roman towns. There's Aristophanes's city of the gods – above the clouds, to separate humans from gods. Mokrousov decided to build underground. I didn't quite understand what he meant. He used to say: if you want to build for eternity, you must be like the people you are building for. If you're building a factory, you should imagine yourself to be a common worker. A policeman, a prisoner. A child, an elderly person. A living person… I thought he was becoming a bit… and wouldn't be able to come back. I didn't quite understand him… Then he vanished."

"They've made the beds," Oldie informed us. And a quarter of an hour later he sighed: "I'm never going to eat so much again before going to bed!"

10

Love and Death in Early Winter

7 Days to D-Day

I slept right through till lunchtime. Oldie lost his patience and went to finish off the hotel on his own. They issued us with pea-green jackets.

A fine icy rain was drizzling down – with each new gust of wind it lashed obliquely and fell at an angle, like snow.

The rat had pushed out the wadding with such force that it had also knocked off the plywood strip blocking the burrow. I flashed light on the cotton wool – she hadn't even tasted it. She must have shoved it with her behind – a strong beast...

I once saw a rat dragging a duck from mound to mound, teeth dug into its neck. The duck was too big for the rat's hole, so the rat approached its burrow from another entrance and pulled the duck from underground. It was Oldie who figured this out. There were many ducks in the nearby swamp. That's how we found the location of a second entrance into the burrow. That rat was strong too. In the village of Khmelevka a rat once stole a fish from a cast-iron pot. The pot was covered with a plank and a stone on it. We weighed the stone – three kilos.

Glass... I stepped on glass.

"Hey, soldier, are you here with me? In the hotel you'll find Larionov – ask him to give me a couple of glassfuls of cement and a trowel. Hang on... I also need some metal shavings..."

In the bank I asked the cleaner for a basin, and took some water.

On the children's playground I shovelled up a certain amount of sand. I smashed a piece of glass to smithereens with a brick. Crudely. There was no time – I had a deadline. I was cornered, I had not much leeway...

I mixed up water, sand and cement – less than one sixth: the solution had to be pliable to the touch. It was still a bit thick, so I added some water, splashing it with my hands. I kneaded the smashed glass and the metal shavings into the mixture. I stuck a piece of cardboard across the hole, a palm deep, and poured the mixture over it bit by bit, stirring slowly with a chip of wood, so that it spread and took firm hold. This would tear apart the rat's insides, jaw, tongue, gums – and kill her. I scraped out the bowl with the chip of wood. I've spent my best years in basements – rheumatism is the inevitable consequence... that's what you get for being an entrepreneur... And can you fall back on a pension? Mmm... not very warm. Where's the hot-water pipe? With the bleak summer we'd had, the rats will be coming back from the summer cottages early.

I'm gonna get you... Had it set? I tried it with my finger. A crumbly, shallow barrier – easier to gnaw out than to burrow round. If she's stubborn like me, she'll try to prove this. If she's a coward and stops when that pungent, stinging feeling kicks in... then she'll be a dead rat walking anyway. She'll lose so much blood that she'll never manage to dig her way out. It's taken a long time. If she surrenders straight away, you just wash your hands and go. If she resists, you'll have to bide your time. Maybe she'll be dead by tomorrow?

Hard to say. Well, it's dry enough. Now let's wash the basin and clean the trowel. Death is hard to pin down...

* * *

"I've been waiting for you! I've put on my make-up, I've made you an apple-and-cranberry tart. Why are you so grumpy?"

"What's there to be happy about, Alla Ivanovna? Does it make any difference to you?"

"The difference is that one woman gives, another teases."

"Do you have a thermometer around? I feel rotten…"

With her bell-shaped skirt, with her delicate snow-white sweater which fitted her plump body without creases and with her perfume, she looked just right – and all of a sudden I felt a strong desire for her, the kind of desire you have at the beginning of winter when you are waiting for a tram by a graveyard, when your heart is pushed up and blocks your throat. Your desire is unbearable, you want any woman. You wade in the muddy snow in despair – frozen feet… a dreadful sky… electric floods and vests in the windows. And now it's these legs in black tights squeezed into leather shoes, these shanks covered with black netting, this ample, tucked-in stomach…

"You're ill?" She sat down close to me, not a bit embarrassed about her body or her clown-like make-up. She placed her hands on her knees – between her knees – like a schoolgirl.

"Yes. Where's that draught coming from?" I slammed the door.

Avoiding her eyes, I stroked her hands: her smooth fingers stirred in response. I drew one hand to me and pressed it to my lips and my cheek. My hand glided over her sweater. She closed her eyes and began to breathe heavily – her mouth quivered and opened. Then she recoiled, swaying, as if she'd dragged herself out of water. I'll undress her now, I thought. But she stretched out on the carpet, losing herself in her skirt.

"I won't get down on my knees in front of a man… Stop it, you hear me? I've got an explosive mixture in my blood… If I push a man, I won't say sorry. I don't apologize to men. I get down on my knees only in front of the dead…" She got hold of my lips, and everything else blurred…

Someone knocked at the door.

"I'm not opening to anybody…" she whispered in between knocks. "Damn!"

Whoever it was, they kept knocking. Alla hissed a vicious curse. I didn't really care, but she was upset. She moved me away from her breast, gazed at the wall as if half-asleep, then slapped me in the face – shut up!

"What's up? Who's there?"

"Open the door…"

"I'm not very well, my dear. Take the invoices to the cashier's office." She pressed herself close to me. "For any queries, go to room number six…" I listened intently… Were they going away? Alla's hands stroked my shoulders.

They weren't leaving. I recognized that voice. It was Vic's girl-friend. We had to open the door.

Her face gave way to an ugly, pouting, lopsided grimace. Her raincoat was unbuttoned. She cast a quick glance behind me.

"I see you are busy… Have you caught it?" She attempted a laugh.

Alla went over to the mirror, heavily swinging the solid lumps of her behind. From the bridge of my nose to the back of my neck, a pain shot through my head.

"I want… For me, for you…" She blinked and touched the door, raising her eyebrows, tightening her lips. "May I have a word with you…"

Outside, I waited while she dried herself off, gulping her tears back and wiping them away.

"You're so flushed. Your ears are blood-red!"

I could tell you a thing or two myself.

"You know, sweetheart, girls are like cats... When one of them rubs against your leg, you wonder if she might have fleas."

She straightened up, buttoned up her coat and ran away, but I followed on her heels, freezing to death. We passed two cordons. I gave the password for both of us.

She stopped, and I embraced her, placing my hands on her back.

"You know I love you, sweetie."

"I love you too."

"I'll give it a go... but not for long... we're going away."

"Do go and see Ivan Trofimovich... come on, let's go."

She only halted at some landing, by a doctor's office.

"Go and talk to the doctor."

There was no one in the room. I skirted a screen: on the couch, in a buttoned-up suit, warrant officer Sviridov was dozing. He started, put on his unlaced shoes, came out and slapped me on the back.

"What's up? Fancy meeting like this... I'm off duty." He gulped down some water and cleared his throat. "I'm covering for the head physician. Hardly any doctors left. Four of them, with no residence permits, were deported. So they transferred me here: if it's not diarrhoea it's scrofula. I'm a doctor too. How are you feeling? You don't swerve to the right when you walk? Stools OK? Swallowing's not painful?"

"How're you doing with the digs?"

"A-ha, you've not forgotten!" He was pleased. "I miss them myself. They summoned me away, but there... well, I won't even begin to tell you: you wouldn't believe a bloody thing, eh? What do you mean, 'no'? They've found a hoard of the Caucasian Tsars! There's thirty-eight kilos of gold alone! Bracelets, signet rings, pendants, coins... and those thingummies that kings wear on their heads... Do you understand? A hoard."

"A hoard."

"You don't understand. You know what it means? A Caucasian royal hoard is something special... they never took it away from their tribe, it's like their banner. It's only ever been found where they lived. If it ended up in Svetloyar as far back as the thirteenth century, it means that those Caucasians wanted to resettle here for ever as a tribe. So... that's what we can deduce from this... It's proof of the tolerance of the Russian people: they were ready to receive anybody, wipe them out and take the treasure into their own safekeeping. Just in time for the visit... and with all this new openness, and the reforms, and the experience of the developed countries... The hoard is of the rarest kind in terms of workmanship... like something... much more modern. And this royal thingummy... it's pretty big. Large enough for your head. Why have you come by the way? Ha-ha-ha... have you... picked up... er... any... animals?"

"How's Ivan Trofimovich?"

"Ivan Trofimovich... Ivan Trofimovich... He's in bed." Sviridov pulled out a document from under the glass tabletop. "A heart attack. That's why they brought him here. Now he's got a cough for some reason, a dry cough. From yesterday... he even threw up. Breathing difficulties... he doesn't even notice it. Weight loss... low energy. You can't make head or tail of these doctors' handwriting! His heart's swollen up... but so what? Reduced respiration – a breath... a breath... and a pause. But why... how? We gave him a foot steam and a dose of sour cream from the dairy. It'd be better to let him go home. At least there's someone there to sort out the bedclothes... to give him water. Do you want to see the old chap?"

"What does he say?"

"He says what everybody else says... all these lunatics." Sviridov gave another sip from the water jug. "He went bonkers when they

saw him off on his retirement. His wife had noticed it before...
you did too. He didn't remain silent, no... 'It's a rat disease,' he
said." He stuck out his lower lip in imitation.

"Not my fault."

"Who says it's your fault? He's dying on his own." He looked
at the clock behind my back. "You're just... well... is it a rat
disease or not? Why are you looking at the floor? Why don't you
say anything? At-ten-shun!" He fumbled with the objects on the
table – a pencil case, a calendar, sheets of paper, keys, a lamp
– then darted behind my back. "Still nothing to say?"

"Well... let me have a word with those treating him."

"It's me who's treating him! You're going mad... I'm going to
treat you as well!"

Outside, the sky was getting overcast as the evening approached.

"Strictly speaking," I said, "I've never come across a proper
description of that disease. Or a detailed reference to it. I don't
believe it exists. There are passing allusions to it as of something
known to people who earn their living in the rat business... You
know, they used to make ladies' gloves from rat skins... and
their beaux would kiss them, swear fidelity on them. Apart from
people in that kind of business, there were also some other dodgy
characters: one profiteer used to sew dog skin round rats and sell
them as dogs of rare breeds... as freaks of nature that could make
domestic pets. One lady wanted to wash her 'lapdog'... the rat
ripped its way out of the skin. The trickster didn't manage to get
away... they arrested him at a coaching inn.

"Few people knew about rats. They were only just starting to
spread... granaries were still not that large... they'd still not laid
pipes underground... people didn't eat in communal canteens...
rail links were few and far between... and you can't spread
many rats on a sledge... There was practically no research on

rats till the Odessa plague, till the nineteenth century. The first book on rats appeared during the Crimean War. Allusions to this rat disease begin from then and continue till 1917, and only in Russian sources. It's always quoted in Russian – *krysinaya bolezn'* – there's no Latin name for it. There's sparse information filtering through... and contradictory versions... All the various accounts agree on the cause of the disease. The word 'infection' is not appropriate. Infection is something you can view through a microscope. But this rat disease begins immediately after a person kills a rat with his own hands.

"As I recall it, it doesn't occur during any disinfestation measures such as poisoned bait, sprinkling the rats' pathways with deadly powder, toxic gases, using trapping glue on paper or various kinds of traps, blocking up their holes with concrete, hunting with burrowing dogs, owls or mongooses, flooding the holes or employing ultrasound devices to scare them away. It only occurs after a face-to-face confrontation. When you kill a rat with a blow. The difference is clear. What is not clear is how it brings about the disease. I've analysed all the mentions... no killing by unprotected hands, no direct contact with the rats. On the other hand, there's lots of opportunities for contact during an extermination campaign, in the form of the unavoidable finishing-off of half-poisoned rats. It only comes about with premeditated killings. No one remembers any instances of the disease coming as a result of non-premeditated killing – for example with a scythe in a meadow, or the destruction of a nest by a plough.

"They used to call it 'sickness' rather than disease. Something stops working in the body. It's similar to the action of an anticoagulant, when the blood stops coagulating. The rat feels that there's something wrong, but just can't understand what. It eats after all the other rats and looks round furtively – how do its companions feel after the meal? Now it drinks a lot and now hardly at all. Then tries not to eat. The rat is surprised. The rat, as you may have heard, is more daring than a wolf... but now it's suddenly confused. It tries to remember: what was it? Keeps going at this to its last. It dies embittered. In crowded settlements, they eat up a rat like this before its end. And it's the same with a man... he feels like a dying rat... he's transformed... he's aware of the rats... he listens in. He's not scared, but he keeps aloof."

"Is it fatal?" asked Sviridov.

"Not at all... why? Not every story mentions death... There are remedies: marriage, good sentiments in general... I mean love for a woman. In modern terms, a strong positive feeling. The disease has got to be nipped in the bud. What are you writing down? There are some funny remedies... You're what – intending to grind up some goat shit?"

"Me? Hmm... if they order me to."

"And mix it with honey and stick it in your eyes? A spoonful of sheep's milk and bear's gall... mix well and drink down. Best of all is the herb called Dog's Tongue."

"Dog's—"

"If you tie it to a dog's neck, it'll twist round and round till the dog dies. It scares off the rats... if you lay it in the corners, there won't be a single one left."

"If I had known that, we'd have stocked this herb in chemists' shops and informed the population over the radio."

Sviridov rose to his feet.

"Well, but no description of this plant remains. What's the matter with you, Sviridov? What are we talking about? He must have beaten some kind of nonsense into his head. We must beat it out again! Take his temperature, and take him to Moscow! Have you got X-rays?"

"Sure... You've been pulling my leg, eh? Well, OK, you go see him. Tomorrow I'll call a doctor who treats alkies... we'll cure him. Injections and all. But hey, rat catcher, how did Ivan Trofimovich get such rubbish into his skull in the first place?"

"Rumours. My granny used to tell me stories like that… she had been in rat disinfestations since 1929. If the presence of rats is long established, people will hand down these rumours from generation to generation. It wasn't me."

Sviridov accompanied me. It was stuffy in the room: the windows had been sealed up.

"Ivan Trofimovich, someone for you." He waved to me: stand here.

I obeyed. His bare shoulders stuck out from beneath the quilt. Without lifting his head, his cheek sunk in the pillow, an unrecognizable Ivan Trofimovich gazed at a phial protruding bottom-up from a narrow transparent pipe that ended with a needle in his arm. He cautiously brought his free hand to his cheek and scratched it. Out of his grey matted hair, pink patches showed through… could he see me? The quilt quivered. He tucked up one foot after the other, as if he were testing the water. His lips, surrounded by bristles, became unstuck, and a wheezing sound bubbled up and died away in his throat. Sviridov urged me to bend down. With a stiff movement, I stooped, breathing through my mouth.

The old man puckered his eyelids, joining the purple creases beneath his brows. There was a rasping sound in his throat.

"So you didn't manage to go away?" He closed his lips tight and stared at me, as if he could not see and speak at the same time.

"I'll leave you," Sviridov announced in a grandiloquent tone, making a wide step to the side and turning round behind the bed on tiptoes.

Ivan Trofimovich licked his lips. He could no longer see me. His hand was now pinching the grey curls of hair on his chest.

I drew up a stool for myself. A couple of sweets lay on the bedside table, and a cut-glass tumbler of fresh water.

"What's it like here, Ivan Trofimovich?"

He screwed up his eyes and tilted his head, as his lips quivered:

"It's... OK. The docs cheer me up." He began to cry, but no tears came. His weeping was interrupted by a coughing fit. He overcame it, but something still crackled and rumbled in his panting chest.

His hand shifted from his breast, crept over his stomach and stole along his body, feeling the sheet. I put my hand out, and he bumped into it, felt it – his hand was dry, colder than mine, and had a sweetish smell – and attempted to squeeze it. The old man kept blinking and jerking up his chin in spasms... he wheezed as his fingers strained, pointing out something... to me. I squeezed his arm in response, gazing round – what? What does he want? Sviridov's on guard, I can see that... but what else?

"Ivan Trofimovich, I'm... Now, now..."

Crumpling his face and drawing his brows together, he managed to tear himself from the pillow – there you go. There was some word that he was unable to articulate: it was pushing inside him in all directions. His fingers quivered in my palm like a bird's feathers... the bedside table? the washbasin? the radiator? his drying trousers? the window?

Suddenly I realized my hand was free... the old man had gone limp, and kept blinking at me with a faltering smile. Yes. The window.

I got up. The window sill was cool. Thin strands of wind oozed through the window panes and got trapped there.

The room temperature: I glanced at the thermometer's scarlet thread and at the blue eyelashes of its marking points. The old man seemed to indicate that I was looking in the right direction, at the town.

"As you were!" barked Sviridov, before banging down the chair and grabbing Ivan Trofimovich by the shoulder. "What do you want? What were you showing him? Can you hear me? I'm talking to you..." he trumpeted in his ear. "What do you want? What were you pointing at, out there? Can't you talk? We'll give you an injection and you'll talk all right."

"Th... than... k you..."

"What for? Tell me!"

"The ward..." he said, sobbing after every word, "with a television... beneath the window... the casualty ward... all the news..." He fell silent. "I learn... the news first... who's done what... yesterday... a husband... knifed... his wife." He gasped for breath a few times and, for a few agonizing moments, silence held sway. Then something seemed to burst inside him, and his chest once again began to shake.

"Oh, I see," said Sviridov, relenting. "He was pointing at the window... there's the casualty ward there... he was being funny. If you don't like it here, old chap, I'll have you transferred to general therapy. From the window there you can see the morgue." And he burst out laughing, his face turning crimson, then gave me a little tug: enough, let's go. I went out in a hurry, breathing through my nose again.

I loitered around the hospital for a long time, gulping down two glasses of sparkling water from a free dispenser near the exit and ending up in the basement, where some people were moving iron canisters, sorting out underwear and chopping up cabbage. I stepped over some broken stretchers and emerged into the light. On the nearest bench, Klinsky was cleaning his shoes with plantain leaves, while Vic's girlfriend was sobbing into her cupped hands. Between them lay flowers wrapped in a newspaper. It was my fault.

"Sorry, sweetie, for being rude to you." I gestured to Klinsky: get the hell out of here! "But you know what… Oldie and I – we're the best of the bunch."

"Why's that?" Klinsky perked up at the end of the bench.

"We're bringing order… if you just ignore the small details."

"But I don't have the right to let one single detail pass!" Klinsky exclaimed. "In Russia details are the main thing. Don't cry. What can you do? Here they all come already. Let's go. Come on."

And true enough, cars were drawing in. The Governor climbed out, then Colonel Gontar, Baranov in full-dress uniform, officials and military people. They greeted each other and straightened their jackets. Klinsky waved his arm. They saw us and headed towards us, stretching out along the path. They all tried to console Vic's girlfriend, and patted her on the shoulder. Vic embraced her and then left with her.

I shrugged and followed them for a while, then noticed a straggling crowd around a small one-storey building made of white blocks. Larionov came to me and pulled me along with him.

"Me too?" I said. "I haven't eaten yet."

"If you don't mind… You knew him, didn't you?…"

"Who?"

"Ivan Trofimovich. He's dead." Then he added, in a constrained voice: "We're burying him."

Stupefied, I moved along with him. What – so quickly? I'd only just… People were scattered around in little groups and went through the doors of the little building. I looked in: there was a coffin strewn with flowers and, beyond it, another room with a smoking orderly and an empty trolley. As many others pushed through the entrance, my sweater got caught on the splintery door.

Nothing much could be seen other than a pale patch, barely distinguishable from the creased upholstery of the coffin inside.

The Governor said something… someone else said something… the ex-Mayor's wife was sobbing, and her children appeared to be holding up her elbows.

Klinsky turned round from the nearest row and, with a firm hand, shoved me into his place. Now I too could see… his face was totally white, his forehead seemed to have been sculpted, his mouth had sagged… his face hardly surfaced from the waves of flowers ready to close over it, like a mask. Larionov stroked the hand of Vic's girlfriend, who was panting and sobbing.

"Look," he muttered, "Ivan Trofimovich is just as he was. See how serene he is." He screwed his eyes, holding back his tears.

"Who's in charge here? Tell them the hearse has arrived."

People rushed back towards the entrance, in a crush. I remained behind. Vic touched my elbow.

"Hey. Can you help? There are so many people, but no one to carry it out and set it up…"

We got there within half an hour. People straggled along, waiting for the last practicalities. There was no orchestra, no decorations. Yellow vans kept bringing coffins and reversing to the gates, opening up the back hatchway in good time. A stocky woman, similar to the barmaid at the café – blue blouse, brooch at throat level – was putting on lipstick.

"Are you from the management? Let's go. I'll wheel out the trolley." She opened the doors and turned on the light. "Don't stand on the mat." She put dead flowers in some vases and rewound a tape recorder on a chair. All around, stone walls, light bulbs and a smell… some sort of smell. The trolley jutted headfirst over a rubber pathway – the kind of conveyor belt they use in restaurants to carry dirty dishes to the sink.

"Close it and lift it up, feet first."

The trolley was wheeled out behind me.

"Close it. Lift it up, feet first," I said to Vic. We lugged the coffin onto our shoulders. A driver leant out of his window: "You sure you're taking the right one?"

There was music now, and we were in full view. Every step was an effort. People formed a horseshoe around. The woman moved her lips and Vic took the lid off. She turned down the volume of the music and cried out:

"Please say some words of farewell."

One of the veterans spoke, then another. There was a long silence. No more weeping – just looking. They closed up the coffin and placed it on the conveyor belt. The woman signalled: a bit straighter! She pressed a switch, and the belt moved along, carrying its burden, then the gates clanged shut.

People streamed out, letting the relatives go first.

"Not a very attractive-looking building, is it?" said Larionov, next to me. "But then, from your point of view, it's clean... nothing left to gnaw on..." He didn't dare to lay a hand on my shoulder. "Don't get depressed. You mustn't think that... It was cancer that killed him."

"Stepan Ivanych, what are you mumbling about?"

"OK, everything's fine then. It seemed to me that you... But it's fine. And good that we've stayed behind. From now on we won't have a chance to talk. From tomorrow we are in a state of emergency... the army's coming in. They'll be forbidding any contact. I'd like to take this opportunity... Just listen. You're a stranger here – you understand everything about us, of course... but we're not all like that. Everybody suddenly wants a better life – you can't blame them for that... that's fine. But it's also frightening, because when people want everything at once, a lot gets forgotten. I've got a letter with me..." He touched his jacket. "Not from me alone... from a few colleagues or, more correctly, citizens or inhabitants... generally speaking, various people... I'm sure you'll get a pass for the events, you'll have the opportunity to hand this letter to the general on duty... or even into his very hands... You're brave..."

"Bark."

"I beg your pardon?"

"Bark. Like a dog. Then I'll hand it over."

Larionov flinched and snorted, holding on to the silky red rope that cordoned off the conveyor belt.

"You won't betray us, will you?" he said, choosing his words. "You're an outsider... they won't do anything to you. What do you care! You can read it, if you like. It suggests how to create long-lasting freedom without devastating consequences, and it lists all the essential needs of our townsfolk... and my personal ones: there's a picture of the town... how to rebuild it. A man tries and tries, but it'll turn out right only once... This is our opportunity. You know how much this means to me... I beg you. We don't have a lot of money. Take this letter."

He darted a quick look at me, his pink forehead showing over his glasses, then averted his gaze and compressed his lips. He pulled himself together, raised his head and, pale with determination, crossed his arms behind his back.

"So?"

"It's not my fault. Don't blame me... I ask no questions... I don't owe anything to anyone... That was my offer: bark."

We went out to the sound of the music. The next coffin was being wheeled in. Ivan Trofimovich's wife was inviting everybody to the funeral banquet, including Larionov — but she didn't recognize me. The architect burst into tears. They stood next to each other and wiped their eyes as people came up to them. Vic's girlfriend had probably already driven away with that prick. And I was left wondering if Oldie had left me any food or not...

11

We'll Send the Rats back to Europe!

6 Days to D-Day

When I woke up the next morning, I couldn't believe that Ivan Trofimovich was dead, or that he had ever lived. They brought us some millet porridge, tea, raisin bread and chocolate biscuits. I made a hole in the porridge and poured in some blackcurrant jam.

Ice had glazed over the puddles. It crunched under our feet. Hoarfrost spread over the square like a rash, the wind made your cheeks go numb. There was nothing to do in the hotel – no more corpses falling down. Oldie had put some cats on the suspended ceiling. They were yammering away, so the guard couldn't sleep. Was it all over?

"Let's have a look at your rat now…"

Dressed in a tall fur hat and dolled up like a Christmas tree, Alla was opening the blinds and keeping an eye on us as we unlocked the basement.

Oldie stooped over a lamp. If he lowered his head, it would mean she was dead. Why was I nervous that he might see her?

"Finished?"

I knew already – no. She was alive. She must have a real crush on me…

"Amazing that she's not leaving." Oldie handed over the lamp to me. "I'm not in the way?"

She had chomped her way out... the clever little thing hadn't touched the lethal putty, and with all her strength had gnawed right through the wall, one and a half bricks thick, leaving fragments of brick and mortar around. Sure, the bricks weren't very good, but all the same... all night long, using only her teeth... a hole so wide that a woman's hand could squeeze through without a watch or bracelet...

"I didn't know you were so serious about it... I'd have dug up the burrow..." said Oldie. "It'll take you two days, but it's effective."

"Don't get cross. Ask the health unit to bring some bacto-coumarin."

"Well... All right, have it your own way. As you wish," Oldie said, scowling. "But you know what I think of preparations containing salmonella. It's just not on. This is a basement... there's people coming in and out, people working up there... anything can happen. God forbid someone gets killed..." He was getting more and more incensed. "You told the two ladies off for this bactocoumarin... threatened them with jail. That's dishonest... you understand? That's not playing by the rules."

"Oldie!"

"It's your decision. I'll tell them, but... I never taught you to act like this."

We stood for a while. He tried to turn away, then he said, more warmly:

"Is it really absolutely necessary for you?..."

"Yes, and by tomorrow. There's no time left."

"Look, this is your area... but if you don't do things by the rules, then anything becomes permissible..."

"Get lost!"

An hour later the bactocoumarin arrived, in a jar formerly containing black rowanberry jam. Bactocoumarin must be applied wet. I put on gloves, stirred it with a wooden chip and coated the outside of the rat's hole with it: she'd step into it and carry the substance off with her.

I poured the rest into a corner, smashed the jar and heaped debris over the fragments, then picked up some earth and spattered it over them too. Finally, I hammered the wooden chip into the ground.

On the basement door I stuck a notice: "Treated with a poisonous substance. Entry only by permission of the military authorities!"

Alla was still at the window... had she been waiting all this time?

I made sure there were no young or old people around, and indicated by gestures what was awaiting her shortly. She seized her belly and rocked with laughter, then wiped her nose and stood with her hands akimbo, sticking out her tongue.

I had to get rid of the gloves. So many people around...

The main road was blocked by lorries and dumper trucks with the driver's cabin at the rear. Soldiers stood in rows along the buildings. Alsatians were barking and straining on leashes, a helicopter's propeller clattered, and people – so many people – were teeming at each building, dressed up in warm clothes, belted up, in winter hats and coats, grey and white shawls and headscarves, with flushed faces, chatting, laughing, swearing. Kids reached out for their friends and were held back... People crowded around placards with the street name and house number, watching the officers who were nailing boards across the entrances and sticking blue-printed papers onto the door handles. A sentry sat on the fire escape... someone was stomping on the roof... buses approached. The number of officers increased... wads of papers were fluttering in their hands. It was the same wherever you looked. Then there was a crackling sound... the wheezing of a radio... the right channel was found, and music was unleashed... a march! Straight away, crows cheerfully flew off in different directions. People pressed forwards, helping old women through the narrow doors of the buses. The invalids were carried to the main road, where ambulances were lining up.

Some soldiers raced off somewhere, on the trail of a clanking noise: someone's galoshes... whose? The officers kept whispering and listening into their walkie-talkies. Nails were thrust into the wood, as a hammer pounded away – bang... bang. I was getting excited myself... a feeling of joy was growing in me, and I ran along in time with the march. Everybody sensed that a festival was near at hand... people were rapidly wriggling into buses, urging each other on, laughing... Suitcases with white labels were loaded onto the lorries... names were ticked off the lists... a small flag in the national colours fluttered on the leading bus... red armbands flashed... no outsiders... the happiness of being necessary... the happiness of being with your own people, united and carefree. A colonel was sorting out cartridges for a flare gun... he took off his wristwatch so that he could fire into the clear sky: people were being taken away... the space was clear...

That reminded me of Moscow in the old days... the Young Pioneer parades... the youthful foolishness of my postgrad days... madcap intoxication. It was time to get out. A horse dragged a wagon on car wheels, and I ran after it. At first I followed it absent-mindedly, then I realized I was drawn on by its sounds: the creaks, the sing-song of the wooden boards and the unsealed shutters... that also reminded me of something close to my heart.

I walked behind the wagon as if under a spell. It was accompanied by four soldiers, like the funeral carriage of a hero. A support patrol allowed us to move into the section of the main road that had been cleared of inhabitants, which was fenced off by barbed wire on light wooden trestles. We turned into a courtyard, the thudding sound of marching persisting behind the buildings... and all of a sudden I could hear rats! Yes – from the wagon. They were transporting rats. I didn't know these soldiers, but they must be from the "Rat King" co-op! They entered a building, and I said to the driver, smiling:

"Can I have a look?"

The chap nodded and leapt down to stretch his legs.

Yes. For the whole length of the wagon, inside glass jars packed between layers of straw, there were dozens of rats... alive, jumping up on their hind paws, their vibrissae touching the plastic lids riddled with ventilation holes... squealing, sniffing, hissing at their neighbours, pressing their snouts against the glass, at times leaving bloody marks. Out of habit, I tried to keep an eye on all of them – but the driver pushed me aside and pulled back some sackcloth, straightening out the corners. The sackcloth quivered... a screeching noise... unbearable.

"Are you taking them from every building?"

"From the basements." He climbed back up.

His colleagues emerged from the entrance, carrying traps and a shaking sack. They threw a shrieking rat into a new jar, marked the lid, and the wagon drove further... the squeal was no longer so audible... not audible at all... or was it? No. But why live rats? I found a dustbin and threw my gloves into it.

I skirted the square along some side streets, cracking the still-unbroken ice. There was nobody around, apart from some soldiers who were lighting bonfires of rubbish on children's playgrounds. I was pleased to see a cat coming my way. The buildings were empty, but each side street came to life when I walked towards a crossing, and then died down. Someone following me. I hastened my pace, and so did Vic's girlfriend, who was wearing an open, reddish fur coat and holding a light package.

"Can I give you a hug?" she said.

I thrust my hands beneath her coat, and for a minute we stood still, my lips touching her cool soft cheek, her hands weightlessly resting on my shoulders. Words piled up in my head – absurd, genuine, hurried words – and then melted away when I realized that for us – for her too – this joy was painful, bittersweet.

"I'm glad I ran into you," she said, moving away with a sad, stony expression on her face, and buttoning up her coat. "Let's say goodbye now." Gravely she gave me her hand. I held it for a while, pressed it tight, then let it go. "Keep well," she said.

"Can I help you?"

"It's not heavy – it's a wedding dress. They wanted to put it off because of the funeral, but… guests will be coming from afar, so… it's OK…"

"At least tell me… what's your name?"

"My married name will be Gubina… Olga Gubina… my maiden name is Kostogryzko."

"Wow… If I had a surname like that, I'd get out of here straight away…"

"My father's from a Cossack village on the Don: half of their village are called Kostogryzko and the other half Motnya. So it could have been worse."

When I could no longer hear her steps, I plonked myself down on a stone, bending over from agonizing pain.

To wait for her or not to wait… how long would I remember her? How long would this pain last? "Keep well" – but we weren't going away tomorrow… so why? What an idiot. I was shaking. Never mind. I'd sleep till morning… we'd see what the new day would bring. "Can I give you a hug?" – damn! Couldn't even do it like normal people would.

I waited. My arse nearly froze over.

I headed off to see Oldie, but realized I was walking in the direction of the sanatorium, so I turned back again.

"Password?"

I mixed with the crowd and reached a building on the corner. There, they were boarding three buses at the same time. Pushing and shoving, I fought my way through towards the cordon, but the crowd swayed and I was carried off towards the building, against an axe-scarred block for chopping meat, while one of the buses kept honking through the march. A soldier carrying out luggage said something to me.

"What's that? Can't hear you!"

I followed him into the entrance... there were rucksacks, suitcases...

"What's this all about?"

"There's some commotion upstairs."

A dog was barking with a hoarse wheeze, women were yowling and, louder still, a child was squealing: "It bit me!" I rushed upstairs, bellowing at them:

"Stand back!" I pushed someone out of the way. The kid sank in my arms.

"Where is it?"

"Behind the pipe!"

A white mongrel, its snout stuck to the pipe, was busy trying to get at the rat with its paw. The pipe climbed upwards, about twenty centimetres across... a corner behind it... should I push the dog out of the way? And what if it leapt at me? Had the rat been poisoned? The dog...

"He thought his puppy had hidden in there! We were just about to leave!"

The kid was dressed to go out.

"Doggie! Doggie!"

And more barking.

I pushed the dog aside and placed my knees each side of the pipe... what if it crawled on me? I saw a grey lump... was it getting stiff? I stirred my leg... no, it was alive, turning its snout. It was clinging firmly right in the middle, and had chosen a very good spot: the dog couldn't reach it there. The dog was pushing against my leg and the women were cackling, while the kid was skittering about – well, then?

"Get that bloody dog out, for Christ's sake! Whose is it, anyway?"

"We haven't a clue, it just ran in."

"Step back! And stop moaning! Fetch me something... like a mop."

"They've sealed up the flats, sir, taken all the keys..." Two men grabbed the dog by the torso and by the neck and dragged it away.

"Bring one in from outside! I'm not going to stand here like this for a year!" Is it still there? It is... what a fool... They've reached the second floor, and keep spreading. I wish I had a sack... I'd press it with a stick and grab the rat by the tail with my hand... What? Idiots, they've brought a stainless-steel spade... What the hell do I need this bloody spade for? It's no good, they've gone away... let's see if it fits... the handle is too thick, obviously... it wouldn't reach behind the pipe. Stinging drops fell from my brows... my clothes were chafing. A sack! It was still there. You raised your head to look at me? You're shielding yourself with your paws? How can I get hold of you? Perhaps I'll try with the blade. But it might slip through... I'd have to stick it in blindly, damn. Where's the bloody sack? I shoved the blade in and pressed hard... the dog released itself and stuck its snout beneath my knee... the handle went off, and suddenly the rat gave out a shriek of pain... I must have hit it! Really? Or was it trying to scare me away? The women raised such a hullabaloo that it seemed as if the walls were coming down. The rat's repulsive screech was as loud as a human's. I couldn't bear it... I had to cut it short. A crack was heard between the blade and the tiled floor. Surprisingly easy. There. A moth quivered on the window like a flame up a cord.

"Where's the kid? Let's have a look at him. Don't be scared. Where did the rat bite you?"

He kept silent and looked tearfully at the dog, which was scratching at the pipe. He was shedding belated tears in response to his granny's whispers.

"Let's have a look at your hands. Was he wearing mittens? Take them off. Was he dressed like this? Jacket and boots? One pair of trousers?"

"Two… and also underpants. Give the nice gent your hand and show him…"

He showed me his palms, his fingers, his wrists. He screwed up his face when I pinched his skin.

"Where does it hurt? And where did it hurt before? Don't cry. Did it just run past and you got scared?"

He sank into his grandmother, who quickly covered his head with her withered hand, his cap topped with a fluffy pompon, his mittens hanging down from his sleeves on a white elastic band. From downstairs they shouted to come out quickly. We went down. I shooed the dog away and threw my catch into the rubbish chute, then opened the front door. Litter seemed to be flying over the street… I only understood when the boy repeated after his grandmother: "Snow!"

The boy's grandmother bent down to put on his mittens. The local residents had already been driven away. Behind us they were nailing the entrance shut and sealing it. The soldiers formed in rows of four, ready to march away.

"Granny, you from flat twenty-six?" said the officer, shielding the list from the snow with his palm. "Two people? Go along to the bank… the yellow bus… your gear's all there! Where are you going? They won't let you through over there... go across the square!"

The old woman quickened her step across the square. Her grandson didn't want to go, and she had to drag him along the slippery road. The dog followed them, darting to one side and the other, sniffing the snow. The officer turned the list over.

"Sidorenko! That white dog there... Where are you looking?"

Two soldiers slunk after the dog with a rope, whistling and trying to lure it. They walked round it, and the dog glanced about, barked and ran away – and they all disappeared in the snowfall. The officer set off behind the formed ranks, imprinting even rows of black tracks in the white and leaving me there, sitting on a wooden log, alone. The smell of snow made it difficult to breathe.

Oldie was rooting around in the hotel. Having little to do apart from gazing at the snow, he phoned his wife.

"We're earning money... lots of it... talk to you later... Kisses to everybody, Lara. All the best... Just look at the weather! It's winter..."

"Let's go to HQ now – I've got something that will amuse you."

Kids were throwing snowballs in the schoolyard, and I moulded one too. Oldie cast a worried look around – what if I threw it at him? By the entrance, two ice-cream sellers in sheepskin coats wouldn't let us in.

"Which department are you in, mate? And who do you want to see?"

"Gubin."

"Victor Alexeich?" One of them began to talk into his sleeve, frowning. The snow was stabbing at his face. "Reception? The two chaps from Moscow. Asking for Gubin. Yes, they're here now. Got it. Got it. OK, up you go mate, into the gym. Hey – leave that snowball behind. Put it down on the steps... I'll keep an eye on it, make sure no one takes it... unless you want to throw it now..."

The gym's changing room was full of telephones and teeming with people handing out mattresses and pea-green jackets. Vic's girlfriend was painting her nails on a window sill, a fur coat thrown over her shoulders.

"You don't want to take your coats off?" said the warrant officer, softly. "No?... well then, I'll ask for him."

There were no desks in the room, apart from two on the far side, covered with documents. Over there, Vic was busy listening to two officers. He gestured to us – one minute – signed some documents and grabbed a telephone.

"Comrade Colonel, sorry to disturb you... They are here. Yes, sir." He got up... so he was a major now. He stretched out, tired. He looked out of the window.

"It's snowing... as if we didn't have enough problems already... makes your head spin." He stared at me with a cheerful, questioning look.

"Oldie, I'd like to introduce this man to you. Vic's surname is Gubin... from the 'Rat King' Co-op... We've been wanting to meet him so badly."

Vic lowered his eyes. He couldn't find any words.

From another door entered Colonel Gontar, followed by more officers. I recognized Sviridov, and he winked at me.

"How's it going with the hotel?" Gontar said. "Are you making progress? Fine. You'll be properly rewarded."

They crowded round us, as the snow blanketed the windows. Sviridov turned on a yellow light.

"As far as I remember, your..." Oldie started in a calm tone, "you intend, in one night, to disinfest something like twelve square kilometres. Could you please explain to me in detail," his voice hardened, "how you propose to achieve this?"

"Well, I don't think... I'm obliged to—" Vic flared up.

"Victor, relax," Gontar interrupted him, gently. "Come on... you're colleagues, you and them."

But Oldie stepped forwards, hammering out his words from his bristling beard:

"I believe it's us that are carrying out... that are responsible for the epidemiological situation. I bear the responsibility! And I demand that your intended plan of action and the rationale behind it be made available to me this very minute! So you lied to us, Victor?"

"Comrades, colleagues..." Gontar raised his arms, smiling every which way. "Let's carry on amicably. It's no good acting like this. I understand your concern... Vic here resorted to local means... but why make a fuss, why make a fuss? It's easy to criticize. We've done some tests, and the benefits are obvious... and it was cheap... so let's not get het up. OK, you didn't know about Major Gubin... so what... don't think about it... we didn't want you to get het up. At this point in time, it makes sense to share the information, so let's carry on..." He offered his hand to Oldie and Vic. "Only one person speaks at a time – everyone else listens."

Vic crossed his hands behind his backside.

"We'll remove the rats from the basements. From a large number of basements. In one night. Just using folk remedies. No science, no poisons – all clean. We'll drive the rats away using a strategy of sudden terror. Fire fills rats with terror. Especially if it's brought by one of the pack. And each rat will know where to bring it. The rat is treated with some inflammable substance, catches fire, and is released. Pain increases its strength tenfold... it runs into the pack, spreads terror by its screams, smell and look – and the entire pack run away. We've captured one specimen from each basement. We'll release them all at the same time, on fire… and over one night we'll force all the rodents out of the required area. They'll all be overwhelmed by panic. We won't allow resettlement in the cleared areas… we'll turn on lights and make noise in the courtyards. To make it easier for the rats to cross the main road, we'll lay down pathways of rubbish and piping, although tests undertaken on Mokrousov Street have demonstrated that rats will cross the road even when there's traffic. There's one difficulty though: we didn't have time to test all the various combustible compounds… which one will burn the longest with the least penetration… so that the rodent has time to run for dear life through all the burrows before losing its ability to move. Perhaps some kind of grease would be most suitable? But how can grease be applied so that the rat's locomotor system keeps working as long as possible? Could you please advise us? Thanks."

"You've expressed your interest and received the desired information," Gontar concluded. "Are you prepared to cooperate?"

"Well, this is what I'm bloody going to tell you," Oldie cut straight in. "You must promise straight away that you'll stop this vile undertaking, or I'll immediately send a telegram to the Ministry of Health and summon the State Health Inspectors… With the mess you've already created, I'm sure they'll take legal proceedings against you!…"

"All right then, we've exchanged opinions," Gontar interrupted. "Dis-missed!"

"Where can I find your Governor? I'm going to see your Governor!" Oldie repeated, as the other men turned their backs. "Let the rodents go!"

Vic folded up his papers, while Sviridov put out the light. I sat down on some netting containing basketballs… all the others had gone.

"Ignorant fools!" Oldie moaned. "How could you… what kind of people are you? Don't you have hearts? You're not worried? I swear I'll set the wheel of the law in motion! But even if you managed to keep it secret, you've got it all wrong… nothing's ever going to come out of it."

"Why is that?"

"Don't you understand? Things don't happen the way you like. Even the grass grows according to a law. Things only happen if certain rules are followed. Setting animals on fire is barbaric."

Gubin tilted his head.

"Who says that?"

"Well there's the Stockholm Agreements, restricting the cruelty of any disinfestation measures."

"It's forbidden to employ sticky paper. There's not a word about fire."

"They wrote the agreements for mentally sound people."

"Do rats suffer less pain when their blood stops coagulating? When calcium blocks up their veins? When traps break their necks?"

"Don't you dare make comparisons!" Oldie made a step towards him, fuming with rage. "We're totally different. We clean people's houses! What you're doing is a scam… You're driving rats into residential buildings, nurseries, hospitals, restaurants – you can't even imagine how much they'll increase in a month! How dare you make comparisons?"

"We can argue till we're blue in the face: either we do this 'scam', or Moscow forces us to…" Gubin responded quietly. "What does this town mean to you? But we've got nowhere else to live. And we depend on any old idiot from the presidential and governmental retinue. The President will declare Svetloyar a National Treasure. Instead of barracks, we'll put up new houses, nurseries, so that there's enough for everyone. And at least one swimming pool... and a cancer ward at the hospital. That's more important to our people than rats."

"For God's sake, I'll repeat it again and again: we won't let you do it! And you won't succeed anyway... but we won't let you even try!"

"Here everything's under our jurisdiction," Vic said more feebly. "Let's not meet any more."

"Vic, Vic... don't you understand?" Oldie said, lingering at the entrance. "The laws which we have the honour to represent here will remain in force even in our absence."

On the landing, I tried to get some sense out of Sviridov.

"But in actual fact... what are you going to do?"

"I don't know exactly," the warrant officer confessed. "Personally, I think we'll first clean the centre, then the whole town, then the region – and push the rats towards the borders... we'll send the rats back to Europe using fire! The rat will make amends for Peter the Great! This young man will become a general... Well, my friends, you know how much I care for you... But as far as rats are concerned, for God's sake, you're wrong... and you're in it up to your eyeballs!"

The wind brought a chill with it. We were sheltering behind the glass partition of a bus stop. The road ahead led into the darkness; the road behind us dissolved into darkness. Sviridov stuck the vampire fang of a cigarette into his teeth, waved his hand, and with a bang a small chunk of the night sky blossomed above him... an umbrella. I'd already frozen stiff.

12

Gubin: a Fighter Trained for Victory

5 Days to D-Day

"You're coughing."

I woke up. Oldie was pulling on his boots. What did he say?

"I'm off to see the Governor. I stayed awake half the night thinking about it. Either they reverse their decision, or we are leaving straight away, and then... Go and have some breakfast."

I tucked myself up to protect against the cold and lay there shivering for half an hour until I remembered: I needed a stick. In the basement, I pointed the lamp into the rat's hole and sat there half-dozing as if by a bonfire, as fluffy specks of dust darted towards the lamp. I plunged a hand into the light and closed my fingers, squashing two black specks in my palm. I brought it closer... just as I thought: dead midges. I leant towards the hole and snorted – what a putrid smell.

Everything would begin to smell like that today, including bread and water. I broke off a stout stick from a shrub and snapped off its twigs, leaving the last one, which I shortened to make a kind of a hook.

I didn't really need such a long one: she had died near the entrance to the hole and could be reached by hand. She had died of vomiting, dehydration, spasms, stomach ache.

I knocked at the bank window. Alla looked out. I waved the stick with its catch, like a flag, and she clapped her hands.

* * *

Oldie was back. He'd kitted himself out in a fresh shirt and was emptying his bedside table.

"You get ready too. There's no Governor any more. It turns out he was dismissed at the garrison meeting. They put Gontar in his place. There's no one for us to talk to now. I said we were leaving. So that they'd bring us the money."

I packed my razor, soap, toothbrush and mug, and fetched my drying socks from the radiator.

"Just in time. Thought I'd miss you..." Klinsky muttered, recovering his breath and closing the door behind him. "It's been a pleasure... you don't often meet people with such experience, mmm... After this kind of encounter, I feel like getting down to work. I wish we could carry on working with you. Shall we sit down for a bit before we hit the road?"

We sat round the table.

"I'm staying," Klinsky drawled out in a sad tone. "During the night I went round the collective farms, billeting people and troops... distributing mattresses, medicines. We had our first casualties: two old women collapsed. There's so much tension... I can't sleep. We've got new people in charge, officers everywhere – I'm worried that they may overdo things. We had more barmy letters."

"What are they writing now?"

"Again about the President's assassination: the money will be left in a blue Niva... they'll leave the town without any problems along the road to Lyubovka. The traffic-police post will be empty at about six in the evening. I've checked: strange but true, they'll be all deployed in town. And the railway station is near... every hour there are fast trains to and from Moscow – that criminal den full of toxic industrial emissions... you leave a car unlocked...

THE RAT CATCHER

it's gone. Once they stole a police car. That's what I'm dealing with…" He waited for my coughing fit to subside and advised me to take some hot milk mixed with honey.

"I don't understand," I said. "How come you're not afraid?…"

Klinsky jabbed with his finger into the blue bags under his eyes.

"Who said I'm not afraid? I wasn't afraid when I was a schoolteacher. What did I know about myself? Now we've learnt to worry about things – what times we live in, my friends… You haven't had a taste of freedom yet… Don't wave your hand at me. You think this is freedom… you can work when you want, you can fix your price… or croak under a water tower. No! Freedom is us! Freedom is like a body in which one part suddenly wants much more… so freedom is like a slut. Freedom is like a region of low pressure. Everywhere else it has benefits: the difference in pressure moves the air, windmills and people's pockets, and puffs out the sails. But in Russia…" – he was speaking almost in a whisper, and we edged towards him instinctively – "…as a result of the harsh continental climate, freedom in Russia, as an area of low pressure, assumes the form of a hole… a hole in which there's no pressure and everything's possible. At first it whirls up, making things livelier and healthier, and it seems we're not worse off than any other people… but then you notice that everything's going down the hole and you've got nothing to fill it with. Then… terror. Sometimes I'd like to find a big enough piece of something to fill this hole. Once I tried to find out where it all began. Before Gontar, it was the former Governor who ran the show, but he was removed because of the leaf fall. Before that, it was Ivan Trofimovich, who died. Our Duma deputy thought this whole thing up, but he's long been sent off as ambassador to Korea or somewhere. And before him Gorbachev, and before

231

him... you won't find anybody. Now I'm faced with the mess... millions have been squandered... problems are piling up... they've brought in armoured vehicles and forty thousand guns... three hundred thousand people have been waiting so eagerly that they'll be disappointed with whoever comes. An enormous force! We could move the town seventy kilometres to the south. But there's nothing that can be done now – we're flying high. I believed in all this at first. Then I hoped it would turn out well for me personally. Then I realized I'd be happy if I came out of it in one piece. Now I know... we'll all crash... and the question is: who will survive? Then a fresh doubt has arisen – are they really coming? But it makes no difference now... We can't cope with all this... and as for you..."

Oldie closed his bag. Was that it? On the table remained a white paper bag for the money. Oldie shrugged.

"All these effusions... you know we're not your confidants... I can see why you've come. We are not going to allow you to set animals on fire. We're leaving today. Just give us the money."

"My only consolation," Klinsky said, hanging his head, "is that we'll all share the same fate. That's the only thing to worry about now. The weather's to blame too. Weak ground. Even a little rarefaction of the air opens up holes. Never mind. At least we'll see where it all goes. One thing's for sure: there'll be no one left to tell."

A slight tickling in my throat made me cough. Lieutenant Zaborov came into the ward with a bandaged head, along with Sviridov and a third person that I didn't recognize at first. No sack. I thought they'd bring the money in a sack. They were dragging in camp beds.

"Why two?" Klinsky said, surprised.

"Comrade Lieutenant Colonel, two of us will be opposite them, and another one will be in the corridor. A third bed won't

232

fit in here anyway." Zaborov measured the distance between the bedsteads.

Klinsky made to leave.

"They'll stay with you till you're allowed to go."

"Hang on a minute! So you're putting us under arrest? Have you got any idea what's going on?" Oldie enquired with a sort of joyful despair, sitting down on his bed. "What next? You're going to kill us? What difference does it make if we leave in a week? So they'll set the rats on fire? You're prepared to end up in jail for that?"

"What if we reduce our fee by half?" I suggested. "Or if we promise to keep quiet about this? Or not take the money at all?"

"You haven't understood anything…" Klinsky said with a sad voice. "There's nothing I can do. We're flying high. Think about it."

Twilight had crept in with a ferocious wind, which hurled the snow against the glossy roof of the hotel. A sense of listless emptiness and futility kept us awake – the building echoed with the noise of distant doors and footsteps on floorboards. Sviridov brought me some cough pills.

"I hear you've done heroics with a spade?" said Oldie, half asleep. "What can we do? We can't fight with them. What do you want to do: forget about the money?"

Sviridov was nowhere to be seen; Zaborov slept on the camp bed which barred the door. I recognized in the third guard the dismissed Governor, who was keeping out of sight, as if he were ashamed.

We fell asleep, and were woken by a horn – a car. I went out onto the balcony. By the gates, a guard was walking back and forth, while another was pouring sand on the path. A milk truck was parked at one corner of the sanatorium. The snack-bar women, in unbuttoned coats, were taking down iron crates full of bottles, and pushed them down the chute into the kitchen. The fire escape ended a metre above the milk truck. It was five-thirty. I moulded a snow ball and waited for the driver.

"You've already got a bad cough..." grumbled Zaborov, without coming out.

The snack-bar women finished unloading, shouted down into the kitchen and went off. Moments later the driver appeared, folding up some papers. He started up the engine; the guard flung the gates open in good time and did not halt the truck. For two minutes the truck had remained unattended.

Oldie had read all the old newspapers right through, including the weather forecasts, and had begun to read the labels on mustard plasters. The deposed Governor relieved Zaborov and gave Oldie a Polish detective novel. Oldie was so engrossed in it that he woke up each time the book fell onto his face. Shestakov and I set about sealing up the windows.

I dipped a bar of soap into water and rubbed it along a paper strip. He carefully stuck it on, tearing off the superfluous bits. No cotton wool, but two layers of paper. Shestakov had had his hair cropped, and in his shortish army tunic, with his timid, shifty eyes, he looked like a quiet drunk. We had finished, but he hadn't noticed: he was standing on the window sill and, for some reason, smiling.

"What are you smiling about?"

"What? Oh yes, sorry. Nothing." He smacked his lips. "The sour cream they bring for the pregnant women is so rich...and fresh too!"

"From a long way away?"

"From the dairy in Lyubovka. I had a bit of it: the woman in the bar gave me almost a whole glass. Ask her... maybe she'll give you some too. But don't say I told you. They bring it here every day."

"Oldie, let's go to the toilet."

Shestakov didn't go with us, but joined the pregnant women watching television. It would be easy to get from the toilet window to the fire escape. The window catches were stuck, though: we'd need something heavy to knock them loose. There was a small dresser. We could lean it against the door.

"What do you want to tell me?"

"Oldie, it's time we got out of here. We'll hang around a couple more days and then shoot off." I set out my idea: the truck, the fire escape, the gates. "We just need to get out of town."

"They'll catch us."

"Surely the troops are not positioned in one solid mass, but around the strategic areas. They can't close off the entire region: and there's the south branch of the Simferopol Highway going through it... they'll be afraid of attracting too much attention. We mustn't do what they want."

"Do you know exactly what they want? You see... It's not the money... Is there any point? One way or the other we won't be able to stop them... they'll burn the rats. Sooner or later they'll let us out, then we can sound the alarm. Although if you want... we can have a go now. But just don't drag your feet."

Sviridov was waiting for us outside.

"Come along. The wedding..."

The summer landscape could hardly be made out in the snowfall. The wind swept over the square like a broad tongue. I picked up a sheet of paper, brown as an old rouble note.

A soldier was rushing around. He stooped down and brushed the snow with his mittens.

"What's that?"

"A sheet of paper, Comrade Warrant Officer. It must have been swept into the square."

Sviridov gestured to me to hand it over.

The soldier stuck the sheet into one of his mittens and headed towards the hotel, summoning his comrades with a whistle. They burst out of the darkness and formed in two columns behind him.

The wedding was celebrated down in the ill-fated basement of the café. There was loud music and rows of tables spread across the room.

From our end neither the groom nor anyone in a white dress could be seen. I sat down opposite Oldie: when we drink, Oldie turns pale while I go red... it would be ridiculous to sit side by side. The wedding rushed to its conclusion. Everyone was drunk, there were no more toasts... it was crowded, hot... people danced. Some dressed-up women cleared the leftovers and brought the food over to us. Larionov was sitting next to us, gorging himself, his Adam's apple rolling greedily.

"What an abject life..." Oldie expressed his compassion for the architect. "They put you here. Constantly checking on you. And you have to stay put."

Larionov, still chewing away, undid the button under his tie with a jerk.

"My friends... eat, drink and be merry. No need to fight," the waiter advised.

And so we did, as we awaited our fate. Our task was over. Oldie hummed a tune, I tapped with my feet. Dancing backsides kept jolting me from behind. The place was really crowded.

"You know..." Oldie leant on the table closer to me, nose to nose, and droned with sleepy sluggishness and bonhomie: "Listen. I don't really want to leave this town just like that."

"That's what I'm thinking too."

"We'll teach them a lesson. A-ha, that son of a bitch's turned up."

Kitted out like a magpie, his jacket open, Victor Gubin made his way towards us among embraces and backslappings. He danced and clinked glasses, then fell on a chair, extending hot and ardent hands.

"My friends! Let's make peace. Don't plot against me!"

"Bastard," retorted Oldie.

"Oh-oh..." Vic noticed our empty glasses and withdrew his hands.

"Vic, why did you call your co-op 'Rat King'?"

Vic folded his napkin from the corner into a square, then into a cylinder, and said:

"She's very kind... She sent me to you... says you should behave properly on a day like this. What the hell do I need you for? Take you for instance..." He grabbed my arm, so that I just about managed to stay on the chair. "You don't know everything! A sailor told me this... On their ship they catch a few rats and lock them in a steel box. They eat each other... only one's left... who's gobbled them all up. He's called the rat king. When they release him, the whole pack leap away from him into the sea."

"Oh, so that's why..."

"See why I got the better of you? I keep a fresh eye! You've been digging your whole life and can't even see what you've found: your sight has grown weak in the basements. But I... I can still see! You're the past. For you, the rat is a temporary drawback of freedom... a consequence of the railways. Not too long ago, we lived without rats... You think that if you make a real effort, so to speak" – he giggled – "all together, you can get rid of them, eh? It just can't be done! I know foreign languages, I've read a lot... any Western textbook on rat extermination begins: 'To fight rats is imperative. To prevail against rats is impossible.' In the West they stopped fighting them ages ago. They keep wealthy homes clear of them. But why kill them for the poor? Killing improves the breed. The strongest survive, and one pair over their lifetime

237

will give rise to three hundred and fifty million rats. Let's leave them alone... they know better how many they should be. A rat won't give birth to more than it can provide for."

"So you've read a lot."

"Shall we make peace?"

"Get lost!" Oldie said, finishing off his drink. "Let's go." He took an unopened bottle from the table. "Congratulations!"

"Wait a minute, Victor Alexeich... you didn't really understand this whole rat-king business. The sailor, when he told you that anecdote, was illustrating a phenomenon which the scientific community calls 'a fighter trained for victory'. And this rat king is a fighter trained for victory... In the nursery, the king is brought up to devour the sick and subordinate. But he can only kill the dregs... he hasn't met any other category of rat. At first the king attacks all the rats, but only until he meets another fighter. Or a suitable female. And then he ends up either dead or settled. That's what they are like. Anyway, we wish you all the best."

13

Delights by the Drained Pond

4 Days to D-Day

Shestakov was guarding our pea-green jackets in the cloakroom.

"Sorry, mate. You didn't bring back any titbits with you? It's OK, no need to go back... it's not for me... I thought you might want something nice for tea tonight..."

Oldie was stepping on my heels and barking at me:

"Lift your feet up!"

A nurse brought warm furacillin for me to gargle in the washroom. I rapped on the window catch with my mug – it gave way easily.

"Let's apply cupping glasses or mustard plasters."

I examined the nurse – grey strands of hair from under her cap – and decided to pass. Better luck with another shift, maybe. I woke up, coughing, to the light of a table lamp... the morning mist traced the limits of our confinement. Zaborov was listening to Oldie over a bottle of vodka.

"I'm a war criminal... an executioner! How many of them I killed with my own hands... Millions! Including pregnant ones! And newborns... You must have heard of the town of Kstovo? That was me. And Volgograd – me too! Budapest, in '72, we were flown in by plane... we spent six months down in the sewer system. The Magyars surrendered to the West... that was me too! My hands..."

I pressed myself into the pillow, coughing. Oldie gave Zaborov a nudge to stop his snoring, then returned to his bed.

"It's tempting to put the rats back onto the ceiling," he said, "so they rain down just as... But there's no time. They'll be inaugurating a fountain. Just imagine, the water will scatter the rats all over the place. We've got to find out about the water mains... the pressure."

I was racked with coughs, which resounded with a shooting pain in my side. Zaborov grunted and gulped. I went to the loo. Oldie raised himself in bed.

"I think about it all the time. It's wrong for us to think how to spoil their festival with rats. We have no power over people. But we can bring in the rats."

"It's hard to say."

I tensed: a female doctor was moving an iron disc over my chest, listening. Looming behind her was Sviridov.

"It's hard to say... coughing is not an illness. It's a symptom of many illnesses. He's got to be under observation. Alkaline inhalations will be good... also potato steam."

"Wake up. Wake up." I woke up. A nurse was pushing a stool with a saucepan on it towards me. "Now I'll open it and you breathe. Cover your head with a blanket. I'm opening..."

I inhaled till I felt nauseous, then I lay down, restraining a rattling coughing fit inside my chest. It has to do some good.

I opened my eyes. Gubin was staggering between the beds, so drunk that his eyes were almost invisible on his face.

"Now... you get it, don't you? Get it... yes?"

"Yes, I get it." I was seized with another coughing fit, but nodded assent.

"Then... just say it!"

"Say what?"

"I kn-knew… kn-knew from the v-very beg-inning… that the whole thing's got nothing to do with rats! But I've demonstrated it to you… And now you tell me… so that I know that you know."

Oldie rolled around in his bed.

"The boy loves intelligent books. My dear friend, this is…" He broke into a shriek: "This is a stupid book… Nothing more… No…"

Vic pulled Oldie to himself.

"W-well?"

"OK. I'll tell you." Oldie hissed. "We don't kill the rats, really. That's just the way it seems."

I'd had a good sleep. Oldie was in a foul mood.

"Your cough is still bad." He stirred his tea while I dressed and went out.

Shestakov came running after me like a dog. We met no one in the street… snow lay everywhere… on the roofs dim shadows moved around, and bonfires wafted smoke to the skies.

From a distance I could see that all the lights in the bank were off. I pushed the door and pulled it. What was going on?

"It's closed."

Shestakov didn't catch what I said: he'd let down the earflaps of his cap, and he turned his sleepy, crumpled face to me.

"Shall we go back?"

I tinkered with the bell, but couldn't hear whether it was ringing inside. Shestakov banged the door with a boot and pressed his face against the front window, forming a cusp to see through with his gloved hands.

"You don't happen to know where the bank manager lives?"

Shestakov squeezed against the glass. Somebody was walking inside. He banged more insistently.

The curtain was drawn back, revealing a cockaded cap.

Shestakov nodded, winked, indicated me behind his back, took one of his gloves off and placed three fingers on an imaginary shoulder strap, most probably meaning Colonel Gontar. Someone opened up.

There was a reek of army boots in the bank hall. On the doors gleamed pieces of stamped white paper.

Alla Ivanovna was locking the cupboards and the safes. Her gingery-red fur coat was soiled below the knees, and she looked tired. She finished locking up, covered her head with a scarf and caught sight of us.

"I need it badly, today. OK?"

"Sure, sure... You must be really sick. Think about what you're saying. Just forget it, you've had your bit of fun." She put out the light and pointed to the exit, firmly restraining a smile.

Shestakov obediently stepped back onto the threshold – she had not recognized him. I didn't move. I was embarrassed to raise my hand to my mouth, so I swallowed my coughs, or turned my lips to one side.

Alla fingered a bunch of keys with her cherry-red nails, then ruffled through a calendar, peering closely at the dates.

"Give me something to eat."

Without stopping, she dipped her hand into a drawer and tossed some chocolate onto the table. I thrust it into Shestakov's hand, and his brows rose like melancholy bridges.

"Thanks a lot. But, well... I'm... I'm not..." I forced him out with the door, and through the last chink he whispered: "I'll wait here on the chair."

Alla closed the calendar and sighed. Behind the door the chocolate foil crackled. Her hands lay flat on the table, like the paws of a stone lion. I stroked her right hand from her gold watch to her nails, drew it to my lips and gave it a timid kiss, until my coughing stopped me.

"You've gone completely barmy, my dear. They've closed the bank. Closed everything. You can't get out without identity papers. There's no bus service. The phone's been cut off. Why have they cut the phone lines? Those soldiers... They said that during the visit we can't go out at all for a whole day. You probably think that life will stop when the guests arrive? What are you thinking of? Well, I know what you're thinking of. Stop fooling around... come on, I've got no time. I'm going to see my father in Palatovka... I'm using the local train... at a quarter to eight. I've still got to pack my bags. I'm on my own... they won't let my husband out of the barracks. Do you have a cold? Do you want a pill? OK?" She tenderly blew onto my forehead. "Let's go, I've got to lock up."

Oldie was lying down, his head raised. A bloke was visiting him. I'd forgotten his name, but it was the one from the meat-processing plant, the one we'd met when we'd gone there for the sausages. Now he was asking for poison.

Oldie pointed to me.

"There's some tablets they've brought for you, and some gargle. They were pissed off because you'd gone out."

"Vladimir Stepanovich, give us some of your Moscow poison. They're gnawing through my boots. They've gone wild... they are swarming in. There's nothing for them to eat... we're not bringing cattle at the moment."

"Why not?"

"Because they stink. They've brought the meat plant to a halt so that it won't smell bad during the festivities. The staff are on leave, and I'm shuffling around on guard duty. I don't go round the factory without a pitchfork."

"Grisha, I think your request can be met. But a convincing argument is needed."

"Just one?" the bloke asked. "What... a half-litre one, yes?" And he disappeared.

"They've brought the milk. The driver was away for ten minutes. He was probably flirting with someone in the box-room." He said thoughtfully: "Must be having it off with some tart." And then he repeated this in a foul language. "You know what? Don't rack your brains... all we need is a can of petrol. We'll plant it into a cluttered basement, then one of their burning rats runs in there and... we've got to choose a building with good air circulation – it'll make a big impression and there'll be no victims. Those blocks are empty. We won't have time to do anything more sophisticated. You're looking at the clock. Are you off somewhere?"

Shestakov pulled a second pair of boot bindings from the radiator, mumbling:

"Still not dry... At this time of night... I'll go and report."

Sviridov handed him a pistol in an old holster.

"Don't be scared. Don't think twice about shooting. We've got people all around."

The chap from the meat factory brought back a bottle of vodka. Oldie cheered up. Our glasses clinked as the table was moved from the window.

"Comrade Lieutenant, just wait a minute," Shestakov said. "I'll go to the bar... maybe we can have some packed food instead of supper. We have time..."

Grisha suddenly grabbed the bottle from the table and pushed it behind the bed.

"What's the matter?"

"Someone's knocking at the door."

"To hell with it... Knock it down! Ah... Grisha, give us the bottle back... It's the wife of some highly placed bastard."

The new bride – wearing a doctor's coat which gave off her scent – made her way straight to the table and lay down a package.

"I've brought some Borzhomi mineral water. If you mix it with hot milk, it will do you good. Warm it up. The doctor should know. Has the doctor seen you?" And she asked more loudly: "Are you any better?"

"Shall we go?" Shestakov looked in – the straps of a holdall were visible on his shoulders. "We've got four tins... well, not much bread... but we'll find some there, I reckon."

I got up.

"You don't mean you're going out?" Vic's wife said. "Where are you going?" She waved her arms. "It doesn't make sense treating your cough if... You should stick to your treatment. Going out... I don't think it's sensible to go out right now. You should keep warm. Take your prescribed medicines..." She started speaking in a staccato voice, and I didn't get some of her words. "I'm going to the doctor on duty... It just... You're adults... medical people yourselves..."

"I'll tell you where you're going to end up... " Oldie intervened. "Don't keep him... Let him go."

Vic's wife raised her shoulders with a jerk, let out a deep sigh and strode off.

We walked through the first carriage. The floor was shaking – the engine must have been on – and the lights shot ahead of us overhead. I pulled open the next door and the following one. A door was stuck, and some fishermen – who'd been smoking in the lobbies between the carriages, sitting on their iron-cornered trunks and wearing hooded tarpaulin capes and railway caps without cockades – pushed it from inside. The carriages were empty, the couplings smelt like a latrine, and a cold draught blew in my ears.

Alla was sitting all alone in the front carriage, in the same fur coat, but now wearing a sweater and casual trousers. She was eating a meat roll. Beside it, in a crumpled pink napkin, lay some bread. She licked away the crumbs from her lower lip.

"I've had no time to eat. There was no one to help me with the bags."

The doors closed, then separated, then came together again, and the train set off. The bags stood on a neighbouring seat, their handles tied with a blue band. I stroked her knees, then my hands glided upwards, on to her solid thighs, which were broadly spread out over the seat, and closed tight. She pulled her coat over her knees and pointed at the window.

"That's the Moscow train there. They're holding it up in the marshalling yard – so that our people can't get onto it or throw letters into the mail carriage." She shook her hand to release her watch from her sleeve and wiped her fingers with the napkin. In the lobbies at both ends of the carriages the fishermen created a kind of wall, pressing against the glass doors but not entering. Shestakov was languishing among them. He squeezed his holdall to his chest and sneaked a look at the time.

"Some Germans came here last year. They wanted these Germans to fix the waterworks here... we're having problems with it. What a way to treat a woman!" She threw the napkin under the seat. "Leave one bag for me."

But I had already grabbed the two heavy bags. At the end of the platform we squeezed through a hole in the fence. The fishermen's tackle clattered as they stepped softly through the bushes in their felt boots. Alla walked in front of me on the path.

"Be careful with that bag... there's glass inside. Those Germans... they talk to you standing up... and bring gifts, as if they owe you something. If you don't accept them, they take offence. They're happy if you agree to go to a restaurant. They talk to you about this and that... Goodness me, I can't see any light in my windows..."

We passed a weir over a pond covered with ice and climbed up a steep slope past a well. A row of sheds stretched out, with heaps of ash scattered at the back.

"That German fellow wouldn't even think of it. He wouldn't understand. He gave me so many presents and only kissed my hand once. He invited me to visit him. I'm sure that if I went he wouldn't dare touch me."

Here the snow was not lying in a solid mass: clods of earth protruded here and there. We went alongside a vegetable garden, rubbing our shoulders against a black fence. We skirted a dunghill behind a latrine with an unglazed window and ended up in front of a locked wicket gate between whitewashed sheds. Alla took an iron bar from the wall, dropped it down behind the gate and pushed the bolt aside. The hens made a racket inside the sheds, banging on a tin rack and rustling with their wings.

"Dad's gone off to bed," she said, stamping her boots on the porch and rattling her keys against the veranda. "Put the bags down. It's cleared up before the night... He must have tidied up, removed the bucket from the well and collapsed. Most likely drunk. Here he is, shuffling to the door. Open up, Dad... how do you mean who... it's Alla, who else?..."

The door opened.

I put the bags on the table, found the stove and pressed my back to it.

"Why didn't you stoke the stove, Dad?... I see. Thank God you made it to your bed!"

"I didn't have time. The radio's off." The old man turned the radio switch in the dark. "There should be a candle here..."

"And no light either?"

"Eh? No, no... What the heck..." He walked with a candle towards me and gave me the once-over, closing one eye.

"Welcome. I'll stoke up right away, you just sit down! Alla!... I was bringing some apples for you..."

The stove divided the house into a kitchen and a front room. In the kitchen there were buckets and iron pots, and a small settee. In the room was a bedstead with gleaming iron rods along the back, a table with a white cloth on top and an icon in the corner.

"And I dropped them all, Alla... near the gate. I was closing it, and the apples all scattered around – big ones, like..." – and he showed us the size. "I wanted to give you a treat, but I've got nothing left... don't be offended."

I went down to the gate and gave up repressing my cough. Let it all come out. I waited for a bit in silence, hardly breathing... would there be any more? I scared a dog away: it dashed to one side, stopped and barked, pressing its springy legs to the snow. I hawked up and spat out. Alla was standing on the porch, her head bare, and looked at me from above, keeping a firm grip on the handrail.

"So?..."

"Nothing," I said in a rude tone. "I get you. Let's gather the apples."

The apples were scattered under the blackcurrant bushes, among frozen patches of strawberries and beneath the fence. The old man was singing... he only seemed to know the first line of each song. I cut some chips from a log. Staggering over the path, the old man was lugging along a bucket of coal, grumbling:

"Three years since they drained the pond, and look: some people have settled there to fish!"

"It's snowing again. Once we have a fire going, I'll put the kettle on... you need a cup of tea."

"Better for me to have a lie-down. And warm up a bit."

She gathered up an armful of apples in the dark and led me onto the porch.

"In the garret it's warmer… it's warmed by the pipe… the house will be frozen by morning… unless we get up at night and stoke up. There's some straw over there. And here's Dad's overcoat to put underneath. Cover yourself with this. And put this under your head. Try to shake it off. Would you like a meatball?"

I heaped up some straw next to the pipe. Garrets are better than basements. There was a smell of chicken droppings and dried herbs, and in the dormer window a few stars pierced the night. I sat listening to each sound, every now and then turning over the straw. The pipe was warming up… a door opened… water was poured out… someone went to the shed and tried the lock… the steps stopped. I got down on all fours.

"How are you doing? Have you settled in?"

I climbed down and took her hand.

"You see, he's drunk, but he's locked up the chickens. Tomorrow we'll walk over to the shop. I must go, or he'll get poisoned by charcoal fumes."

"Come now." I embraced her and tried to pull her up the stairs. She was completely nonplussed.

"What are you doing, you idiot? Are you out of your mind?"

"No." I kept pulling her up. She steadied herself with her foot against a step and whispered:

"What are you doing? You must be joking… Where are you taking me? Stop hurting me. Do I have to fight? You'll make me fall down… You don't care? Come to your senses." She slapped my forehead. "Dad won't lie down without me… what shall I tell him? Just wait, stop pulling! Just calm down! Have you calmed down now? Then listen to me: who gave you the impression… who do you think I am?" We'd reached the ladder – she was now snorting, now sobbing. Once we were up in the garret I closed the door. "How dare you? What's the matter with you? I don't understand what you want. Why did you bring me here? Look at me, open your eyes!" She landed me a more painful blow, but couldn't keep her balance and slumped down on the straw, recoiling. "How could you, in my dad's house? My husband... You've been working with him... you'll see him... Dad may come in. Stop it. What shall I say to him? Just think of me, and calm down! How dare you!" I struggled with the various hooks and tight elastics. "You say I'm good. But you'll be laughing at me later. You won't even look at me." She burst into tears, which then mingled with whimpers... she gave me a kiss and pushed me back. "No!" There were a few more sobs and then a muffled laugh...

I listened. I listened for a sound, with my eyes open. And my eyes wouldn't close... I couldn't hear the wind... I couldn't hear the wind shaking the door... I couldn't hear the fire... Alla was soon asleep, after checking how I was feeling.

"Winter will soon be here. I hate winter!" she had said.

"In winter at least you can see footprints."

I knew my cough would not let me sleep. After a while, it was uncomfortable for me on either side. Better not get nervous, not think at all... Dreams are birds that build nests overnight. When you suddenly wake up, you can see a shadow gliding away, feel the flutter of their departing wings on your eyes, find a blade of grass in your hair... Where are the open fields?

I found myself again with my eyes open, staring at the dormer window: no stars were visible... when would the sky begin to lighten up? I was freezing, as if I'd just had a swim and couldn't get warm. I crouched and wrapped myself up. Had I had any sleep at all? I sat up... I couldn't sleep. Suddenly something fell down on the straw. I looked for it – what was it? From above, Shestakov whispered hoarsely:

"Comrade Lieutenant, I just dropped the milk can. No need to look for it, it's almost empty."

I pressed close to the pipe and covered my face with my hat, but a cold draught blew through the garret. Suddenly I was aware that I was shivering, and raised myself.

"Comrade Lieutenant, why doesn't that old bastard light the stove? Look, my gloves are sticking to the pipe!"

14

Visions of the Kryukov Forest

3 Days to D-Day

We reached the birch trees. Shestakov explained: that's where the Kryukov Forest begins. There were still leaves on the trees, and a firm path covered with snow blown by the wind. We strode on swiftly, going round the fir trees and looking where best to cross the gully which stretched on our right-hand side with steep slopes and a flat bottom flooded with black water. We were trying to find a boardwalk when we heard a rumble of cars on the other side of the gully. We thought we'd better go on foot... it was quicker than by train.

The sky lightened up, and it seemed to warm up a bit. I was exhausted... drenched in sweat. Shestakov found a pine tree that had fallen across the gully. We could cross by holding on to its branches. Whenever I breathed out, I felt a pang in my right side, deep down inside. I pressed the spot with my elbow and coughed, straining myself, spitting and breathing hoarsely in between coughing fits. Shestakov looked at me with pity. I felt sleepy. If only it were warmer...

When we reached the other side, we started walking uphill. No more sounds of cars could be heard, only a din of human voices, like people bathing in a river. Shestakov drew me away from the path and led me straight towards those voices. I looked around for a suitable tree stump. As soon as we stopped, I plonked myself down on a fallen birch tree... that was good. The sun came out, and the snow started melting on the wet birches and dripping down. There was nothing to lean my back on.

About seven feet ahead of us, the ground had been dug out down to the clay layer, and smoothed out by bulldozer caterpillars. It looked like the open quarry of a brick factory. It was surrounded by a military cordon speckled with red shoulder straps. Below, I saw a platform made of new wooden boards. Beyond the platform, some fire engines were spread out. With their backs to us, soldiers with black shoulder straps stretched out in loose ranks, the ones at the back squatting and smoking.

Shestakov cast an annoyed glance at me as I coughed. Some officers appeared on the platform, all holding their hands over their stomachs in the same way, with microphones set in front of them. Shestakov pointed upwards... there, on the other side of the hollow, people with video cameras were positioned on raised platforms.

"Comrade soldiers... Can you hear me? Split the ranks!" This was followed by hoarse obscenities. "Belts off... remove the cockades from your caps... Empty your pockets – watches, pens, combs, razor blades, knives... if you're carrying any – everything out. Put them next to your belts at the back of your ranks. Commanders – check them out! Now space out and stand like ordinary people. So's your hands can move freely. Check out that their hands can move freely. What? Glasses, badges... off as well. Ready? Commanding officers – conceal yourselves! What did I just say? Stand like ordinary people! A-a-t ea-se! Caps up from your brows... coats unbuttoned."

I heard a rhythmic clanking of iron: down the paths descended lines of people in police-type jerseys, flak jackets and visored helmets, among a rattling of identical man-sized shields. The policemen assembled behind the fire engines, opposite the crowd of soldiers, and opposite us. The red-strapped officers detached from the cordon and headed towards the forest. We got up to go, but a hefty chap with colourless brows, who was standing close to us, barked:

"Sid-down."

Shestakov was bewitched: every word from the platform seemed to hit him under the belt... he jumped, copied their movements and smiled entranced, his fists clenched tight against his chest.

"Now listen again for a sec. If anybody can't follow... help them out. This is a drill. You are the people... like townsfolk gathered together. A crowd. Showing discontent... aggressive... threatening to destroy the public order. Throwing a few stones. You've been given cardboard tubes, like the one I'm holding... they've brought them from the mill... they wind fibres on them. You can put clay inside the tubes to give them weight... it's better for throwing... you can do it with clay or a brick... not an entire one... the size of a fist. When I give the order to disperse, you start throwing and insulting the authorities. When I give you the signal, we'll practise how to repel the attacks. Don't just stand there like you've shit your pants, but push and grab one another... After we finish, we'll have some food. Is that all clear?"

The black-strapped officers swayed, jumped, hurled insults and pushed with their shoulders, casting amused, if slightly alarmed glances at the closed ranks of shields behind the fire engines. The policemen holding the shields bunched up and held their breath.

"Let's start! You are people."

They stamped their feet, ooh-ed and jostled about. After a while the commander leapt onto the platform.

"I just... don't understand. What did I tell you to do? Just get on with it, and we'll have lunch. Otherwise I'll make you grovel with your snouts in the snow. Show some spirit... remember who you are. Commanders, forwards to your troops!"

A puny captain came racing up to the nearest formation with a fir-tree branch, and exclaimed in an extremely rude tone:

"Do as you're told! Are you deaf?" He lashed the soldiers' backs with the branch till it broke, and then pounded whoever he could reach with his fist on the head, yanking at their straps. "Pla-toon! Fire!" And he concluded more softly: "Aim at those with the red straps. Whoever hits the Colonel will get forty-eight hours' extra leave."

The first missiles hit their targets on the platform – the commanders leapt down from it every which way, picking up their caps knocked off by the firing. No sooner had they dived behind the shields than a new volley hit the shields… When a cunningly lobbed clod of clay hacked down a helmet which was poking out for the purpose of observation, the black-strapped officers cheered. Then things continued in a merry fashion… not every soldier was throwing things now, but only the most skilful ones, who'd step forwards and hurl their missiles with a sweeping gesture – the rest filled the tubes and prised bits of brick out from the snow. The shield-bearers held firm: occasionally one shield or another was raised to encounter a stone aiming straight at the forehead.

From among the shields a voice reminiscent of warrant officer Sviridov provoked the soldiers with the black straps:

"Hey, you, morons! Blockheads!"

"Citizens! Don't give way to the devious intrigues of some agitators. This is Nikolai Gontar, the Governor of Svetloyar, addressing you. Cease this stone-throwing!"

The black-strapped soldiers all calmed down at once. Just as I had guessed, in leaps and bounds warrant officer Sviridov was brought forwards. He climbed up, took off his cap and made the sign of the cross.

"Comrades! It's my fault that you're here. This public demonstration is understandable. Your problems with the water…

all the criminal activities... the unhealthy conditions... the majority of the housing blocks looking like army barracks... but I'm convinced that in Svetloyar, in the whole of Russia, there's no other path to renewal than respect for the law, peace and faith... everything for which the great Russian people have been extolled since ancient times! The visit of the President of Russia... shows faith in our efforts to put things right. It's disgraceful that we should respond in such a way to this faith. We are working towards it! The former Governor Shestakov has been arrested. Criminal proceedings have been initiated against the town architect Larionov for accepting bribes during the allotment of land plots. Special committees are investigating the police and the security services. Their conclusions – very serious – will soon be announced! I trust that you will not allow the firebrands to lead you into public disorder! If you deny me your trust, I'll resign – though I would very much like to see the fruits of the work I've begun, and will be accountable for them. It's been suggested to me that I should use force, but this is my answer: I won't wage war against my own native people. I have trust... faith in my people! I won't go against my conscience... the conscience of an officer, of a colonel, who for thirty-five years has offered his service to the Motherland... the conscience of a son, husband, father and grandfather. God is with us!" Sviridov put his cap back on his head, stepped aside and returned to the microphone.

"The chairman of the Women's Council will now address you... Exemplary Mother and Veteran of Labour, Praskovya Gavrilova." Sviridov paused for breath. "There's no peace in our town... bread supplies have broken down... the bus service is disrupted... people can't get home from the poultry plant. Ambulances don't get to the sick in time. All the police are here, but what's going on in the outlying districts, where there's no police? Is not such 'democracy' an expensive indulgence? My son died in Afghanistan. I, more than anyone else, know what it is to lose your dear ones. I've been sent by your mothers, wives, children... Go home!"

"Disperse! Clear the road!"

The officers once again rushed to the black-strapped officers.

"Don't yield! Fire! Tell them to go to hell!"

The puny captain squatted and roared for all he was worth: "Don't back off! Liberty for the Russian people! Hurrah! For the Motherland! Forwards!" And he darted into the bushes, like the other officers.

The black-strapped soldiers, swearing away, suddenly advanced with real zest, and new missiles banged against the shields. The hefty red-strapped officer who'd turned out to be our guard spat adroitly and said:

"We'll show you now!"

"Bring the drill to an end! Bring the drill to an end! I am warning you – bring the drill to an end!... Fakel!"

The crowd gasped as the shield-bearers, with a sauntering step, began charging forwards, drawing the fire engines behind them. Their lights started spinning, their engines started up, and hosepipes appeared over the drivers' cabins. The crowd moved back, but those at the rear could not see, so they pressed forwards, pushing the backs of those in front, who floundered about silently in the crush. I gazed on – as if under a spell – as the clean swathe of snow between the people was quickly devoured, trampled under the feet of the evenly striding ranks. Officers hurled themselves and merged, shields rumbled, cudgels flew up simultaneously, gloved hands and elbows went up for protection, everything accelerated, and people whirled as if caught in a river current. They dodged and fell, burst free, staggered forwards, dashed to one side after a blow, groaned... it was like the noisy breathing of the sea: a hubbub, a thundering of shields, without any shouts... The people's crowd yielded in front of the shields like pastry forced out left and right, and at the edges the black-strapped officers, regaining their wits, stopped running, linked their elbows together and took a firm stand, intercepting the cudgels and wresting them from their opponents, kicking the shields with their boots and trying to prevent them from closing in or giving way. At the extremities new waves of fighters were wrung out, allowing the black-strapped officers to surround the shield-bearers more widely. The line of shield-bearers caved in to form a kind of wedge, but then suddenly withdrew, regrouped, and once again formed a straight line.

A patch of muddied snow became visible. Ripped caps and gloves were scattered all over. Soldiers with bloody faces – holding their hands in front of them, groping around, blowing their noses and spitting – were led out of the mêlée. In the forest, others waved at them from tents marked with the red-cross sign.

The shield-bearers calmed down. But among the crowd not one was standing upright: they were digging into the earth, wrenching out bricks and bending and breaking stunted fir trees. They picked up their belts with eager hands and wound them around their fists – brass buckles started flowing up into the air. Soldiers in torn overcoats kept running away in a frenzy into the open space, waving their arms and shouting filthy abuse and threats at the shield-bearers.

All of a sudden, the shield-bearers charged forwards, and the crowd fled from them, almost rolling off their feet. In their attempt to break the chain of people in front of them, they penetrated too deep, and stopped when it was only too late. The "commoners" sensed their confusion and, dashing at their backs, pummelled the flak-jacketed officers with a barrage of blows. The crowd hammered away with such force that those at the front hardly managed to touch the ground with their feet. To the sound of a cheerful groan, the platform was raised with a ponderous scraping, and moved along with a pigeon-toed step: left, right, it staggered forwards and toppled over the shield-bearers, who fled in all directions.

"That's the end," our red-strapped guard announced.

Everybody ran away towards the forest, throwing down the shields and dodging about. The sirens went off and the fire engines started moving – the windscreen of the first one was smashed right away. People were jumping around the wheels like fish, dragging the drivers out of their cabins by their lapels. The fire engines couldn't move forwards, as the crowd rushed towards them pell-mell, yelling all at the same time: "Hurrah! Hurrah!" Suddenly, from one of the fire engines, a hose sputtered and shot out a jet of water, which sprayed all over the snow, soaking the reddish mud and hitting an old pine tree. People broke off in all directions, but the jet went up, squirting impotently into the sky: its new owners, standing on the drivers' cabins, waved and shouted: "They're ours! Hurrah!" A long way off, the commanders, in their tall hats, were running away with heavy steps, occasionally throwing up their hands… were they being fired at? They were chased by three soldiers, one with a spade, which he hurled at them. The first video-camera platform swayed and fell over with a crash. The camera operators dropped everything and leapt away from it. The Alsatians strained and barked furiously around various skirmishes, as shields were thrown at them.

It seemed as if only a minute had passed. The fire engines moved back and forth among the crowd, each swarming with soldiers, who were slinging their caps up to the sky – Hurrah! I observed the shield-bearers' officer as he ran away. He suddenly stopped, as if rooted to the spot, and advanced towards the hunting pack, shouting something passionately and waving his hands. He was surrounded and jostled… they pointed at the red-crossed tent… he swivelled his head trying to respond to all of them... they pushed him so violently that he landed in the snow... then they hit him on his helmet – lie down! In the meantime, as a helicopter roared above, the fire engines were going round in circles, drenching each other... It was complete chaos: anybody who wanted to shouted in the megaphone:

"All hail to Company Number Seven! Hurrah! Give us our demob! For the Soviet Union! Mee-iaow! Pour us a drink! Krasnodar Rovers for ever! Orekhovo-Zuevo United, all together now!"

The helicopter came lower, and the winners aimed the water jet and shook their fists at it. The puny captain chased after his men, screaming with a choking voice: "Stop any resistance! As you were! I command you to surrender! Atten-shun!"

A lump of clay struck his shoulder: he looked round stupefied, and at that very moment he was clipped on the head by a stone. He reached for his knocked-off cap, staggered and slumped down, then he gathered some snow and held it to his head.

One fire engine crashed against another... glass rained down. People were running around it with fire extinguishers... smoke erupted, and everyone dashed to one side. One drunk soldier was gesturing with his hands, then stopped and pissed on a wheel.

Our red-strapped guard stood by in silence, just like us, then suddenly roused himself: the "commoners" were running towards us, their overcoats flapping and, for some reason, still shouting "Hurray!" The guard squatted and fired low over their heads.

"Back! I'll fire, you motherfuckers! Back!" he howled.

Suddenly, as if from underground, some strong arms grabbed him by the coat. He went down head over heels and threw away his gun at once, rolling over onto his stomach, hiding his face and hands, and squealing in a strangely reedy voice:

"Don't kill me! Don't kill me!"

What about us? I was pushed and carried off by the crowd. We broke away through the bushes, but someone shouted "Halt!" and my mouth seemed to fill with hot cotton wool. The chap I was running after grabbed hold of someone. The man's legs gave way, but he raised himself and hurled his pistol away with a demonstrative gesture. I drew back... he blurted out something with a hoarse voice − it was Shestakov! Above the branches, causing a commotion with its blades, crawled the helicopter. I was on a bare slope, visible to all, and ahead was another slope and the forest, with a rivulet shining black in the gully... where should I head? On drunken knees Shestakov shuffled in my tracks, without a cap, his hands dangling as if for balance. My eyes were burning... were we being followed? I had a violent coughing fit, a dry, hoarse rasp which wasn't painful any more, but scorched inside. Shestakov stopped and sank down, pointing with his hands... so it was not my wheezing, it was some dogs barking.

Over our heads, at the top of the slope, red-strapped officers in festive topcoats formed a double chain, with guns at the ready. Shestakov raised his arms; I understood immediately: they'd fire at us. I also sank to my knees and raised my arms, as a grey-chested Alsatian lurched towards us, with someone running behind it...

There wasn't much snow, so we walked off the road. They'd sent a soldier with us, who was helping me to walk. He kept looking back cheerfully to where the sky had darkened from the smoke: they were still firing. Shestakov trudged along in front, wearing someone else's hat. At one point he burst into tears, turning away from me.

"The pistol − they'll rake me over the coals for the pistol!"

In the field some soldiers were taking turns digging a pit with three spades and carrying out the earth. They spread out a coat for me... there was not much snow, and the ground was hard.

"How are you? Don't lie down. Hold him so's he doesn't lie flat. I'll go to the digs to ask for a car... actually, even better, you go, if you know anybody..."

"What are you digging, my friend?"

"The ground! Some chick came to see our bosses yesterday..."

"Why do you say 'some chick'? She's the daughter of the archaeologist woman, the one with a big hat..."

"Sod her. We've still got to make a burial mound for one person... but empty. It'd be good if we found something."

"A stupid head gives your hands no rest! That mechanical digger has remained idle the whole of August."

The railway crossing by the meat-processing plant was blocked by train carriages. It was warm in the car, and my side was aching again. The watchman was chatting with an officer in a railway jacket. The old man didn't recognize me at first, and asked for a cigarette.

"Well, old chap, what time do the rats go out for water now?"

"A-ha, hello... Look who's here! Still spreading poison, are you? They've gone berserk – they go out by day and night. Not straight to the river either, but they run up the hillock and squeal. It can happen that you don't see a single one for a day... there's nothing for them to eat. They fight with the crows – it's weird! Put in a word for me so's they send the army here. There's a regiment stationed at the poultry plant, but me I'm on my own." The old chap peered at Shestakov. "He really looks like our Governor... Have you heard, they've got rid of him... A colonel's taken over. The Governor shot himself. Our women went there... they've laid his coffin, closed, in the House of Culture. They found," he whispered, "horns and claws on him."

The old man looked round to see where I was looking.

"Yes, our architect's come here this morning again. He's standing there by their watering place... he's lost his hope. But he missed them again. You never know now when they'll come out."

"Whistle to him, pal... a bit louder! Shake a fist at him. Don't be scared... he won't do anything to you."

Larionov stopped three steps from the car.

"Well, Stepan Ivanovich... so they've buried the Governor, have they?"

"I really don't know what to say to you," he finally answered.

"No need to keep standing there. It's better to be arrested for taking bribes."

Larionov went completely red.

"Don't get involved. You don't even know what may happen to you... so leave me alone."

They opened the crossing; the architect stepped across the rails, and set off along the road into the town... for as long as I could see him.

The town shone in all its nakedness, wrapped in winter's embrace: the towers, the chimneys and the hotel's statue were all bathed in the beams of searchlights.

"Can you get there by yourself?"

"Yes, I'll manage."

"Tell him to wait. They're bringing a stretcher."

Four people carried me, as lamps glared into my face.

"Get a move on."

"He's crying..."

"Where? That's the snow that's melted."

The lights in the square went out... it grew colder. The lamps were extinguished one by one with a crackle, but a march was still beating away. After it thundered out to its bitter end, a voice boomed in the sky:

"OK. Everybody to their initial positions. Lights... do you hear me? As agreed: two beams on the figure skaters... and follow them with a slight delay! How many times do I have to remind you? There aren't enough young people on the streets..."

The stretcher tilted over and was placed on the floor. In the stagnant cold of the basement, I clutched at the radiators with a groan, but they soon pushed me down with an elbow and tore me off. They carried me over to a trestle bed and lay me down. I instantly sat up. I wouldn't lie down, no way. It was warm. Klinsky had had his hair cropped, and made piping sounds with his puckered lips. Behind a yellow screen, a shadow moved around. Sviridov emerged, all bristled up, and advanced towards me unbuttoning his shirt.

"You feel rotten? What about me? They beat me black and blue! Why the hell have you sat up? Lie down! Here, look: black and blue..." He swung round to Klinsky. "You look too!"

I climbed onto a trolley. I must tell them: I was not going to lie down any more. I coughed.

"Over here. Any unsteadiness in your legs?" From behind the screen Sviridov dragged a tall soldier with a torn black shoulder strap and pushed him down into a chair, his back to me.

"What was the reason? Who gave the orders?"

"It was for liberty... For the people," the soldier answered quickly.

Sviridov gave him a slap on his face. He leant forwards and hissed:

"For what bloody people? For what fucking liberty?" Then he shouted: "Who brought the vodka to the battalion? Drunken bastards! You acted in the heat of the moment, is that it? Who fired at the helicopter?"

"Comrade soldier, this is no time to remain silent," Klinsky informed him. "The whole region is under martial law. You signed papers to this effect. It's a serious matter. Your silence may cost you dear…"

"Were you drunk?" Sviridov bent forwards again. "Just acting the goat? Everybody was banging away so you had a pop at it too?"

"We meant well… So's liberty somehow… together…" the soldier said after a pause and let out a tearful sigh.

"Motherfucker… How can I get it into your thick skull?" Sviridov bellowed. "If you just say, 'I was drunk and did it alone' – you'll get ten days in the cooler. If you say, 'For freedom, and all together' – ten years! And if we find aggravating circumstances, you may get a firing squad!… Damn it all!"

Klinsky glanced at his watch and gently stroked his temples.

"Sod off," Sviridov waved. "You're free. Just wait, just say one last thing. Say it and you can go straight away." And he shouted at full volume: "He was the one who fired at the helicopter! He was the one who gave the orders! Yes?!" He swung the soldier towards me: "Just say it! Yes!" He jabbed at me, and grabbed the soldier's neck with his other arm. "Yes! Just say it! And you can go!"

Drops of blood trickled down from the soldier's nose, which he caught with his lips.

Sviridov opened the door.

"Get lost. I got beaten black and blue and no one's guilty. Hey, put some snow on your nose. Hang on, I'll give you a bandage. It'll get better. What's your name? It'll get better, Mikhail. Are they waiting for you at home? God bless you. Just be off. Was it him? No? Don't be scared. You'll never see him again. We'll give you leave. Was it him?"

The soldier snorted, blew his nose on the bandage, threw back his head and screwed up his eyes.

"Off with you," Sviridov grunted. "Hey, you on duty there… get the X-ray doctor here. Tell him our colleague needs his thorax examined. A suspected case of pneumonia. He likes to go around without a cap, you see… Lie down, don't be scared!"

My sweater slid over my outstretched arms; my shirt was unbuttoned – don't breathe! A protective apron pressed on my stomach – I heard a humming sound.

"Sviridov, what kind of initiative is this?" said Klinsky in an outraged tone. "Under this new Governor you're taking too many liberties. You're not in the same league as him. What do you think you're doing? And why?"

Sviridov jumped up and looked under Klinsky's collar.

"It looks like your shirt's a bit worn out. It's grubby, isn't it? So what? Who'll ever know? No one. Only you and me, and I won't say a word. I'm off. Why do you look so miserable? Let's forget about it. Consider it all a joke."

Klinsky made piping sounds with his lips again and buttoned up his shirt collar. I thought he had started coughing, but he was laughing in fact.

Oldie was rolling a tin of condensed milk round the table.

"Shestakov gave up. They've arrested him. Down at the water canal, someone from the armoured column said that they gave him bribes, and that he accepted them. He confessed it, right in front of me. No wonder… Can you smell it? I'm drunk! All morning I've had to pour water over the square to make a skating rink – I was afraid of catching cold. The milk truck came at the same time. Tomorrow we've got to get out of here. I've put all our things into a bag and thrown some dirty pillowcases on top. The day after tomorrow we'll be in Moscow. Can you hold out that long?"

"I can hardly walk. It's pretty bad."

267

A nurse gave me an injection – a dose of antibiotics. I took vitamins and did a bit of gargling. I didn't have a temperature, but I felt weak. I was given a foot steam with some mustard solution. They showed me the right posture for expectoration. The coughing was less frequent but it erupted with a nagging pain. I was forced to lie on my stomach. My belly ached too. I changed position to find out the source of the pain... to look it in the eyes.

Oldie went out to find a gastroenterologist, and they promised to bring one in the morning. No one's going to come at night. If it was some sort of inflammation, the antibiotics would take care of that as well. Another blanket. Would I be able to get up at all?

Would I resist for two hours? I was bedridden, and that was to our advantage: they wouldn't guard us. It'd take us an hour at most to the station. In the train I could lie down straight away. In fact, everything might be back to normal by morning. Was it food poisoning? What had I eaten? Time to sleep.

The nurse on duty told Oldie that someone was asking for him from the meat factory – Grisha or something.

"He says you know what's it about."

"We can't help him... he must have taken a fancy to us... Tell him we are not allowed any visitors."

"No. Tell him to wait," I said.

"Hey. You're not asleep? Your belly's still aching?"

"Nobody around?"

"Some men watching TV. What do you need this Grisha for?"

"You were right: there's nothing we can do to them. But we can bring the rats in. From the meat factory. Get it? They're desperate... they've got nothing to eat. And if they're cut off from water... they'll go on a rampage..."

"Hold on... are you serious? What are you talking about?"

"Don't get nervous. How many different sections are there? Is there a bone-processing plant?"

"Are you crazy? There must be at least three hundred thousand... How can you—"

"It's an hour to the town on foot. They'll get there in forty-eight hours. Just in time. There are no forks in the road. They're not going to cross the fields, because of the snow. Just show him the right way... They'll remember us. Call him in."

"What nonsense are you talking about?" Oldie exclaimed with passion.

"It makes no difference now."

"All right, all right. But it does make a difference – remember that!"

"Yes, Grisha, yes... there is a way. Siddown. Can you get hold of a tractor with a plough?"

"I've got a mate at the collective farm..."

"I'll draw a sketch for you. There's the fence, if you stand facing it."

"But where's the checkpoint?"

"Here. There's the stream where the rats go to drink. Plough from the corner of the fence along the stream, up to the pipe into which the stream flows, and then further on to the road. But between the furrow and the road leave a passage – three metres wide. Don't step on it, or you'll leave a scent. They won't be able to get to the water, and at night they'll go off by the road if you plough in the evening. But please keep shtum about what we've told you... just do it. When you've done it, stay put behind the gates."

15

The Hitmen Get Arrested

2 Days to D-Day

I couldn't sleep, and Oldie also kept tossing and turning. Fragments of images shot through my mind: my illness... Moscow's walls... the strain of escape... To run away should be fairly easy: they wouldn't stop us by force if we got on the train. How was our friend doing with the plough? From the road it would be imperceptible. And not visible from a car if you didn't know about it. Even if you stood up you wouldn't be able to see it immediately. Only at first would the rats stream through in close formation... towards morning they'd be spreading out. The first impression would not be their number, but their uninterrupted flow. The rule is: where the first ones go, all the others will go to the very last one... even if you batter them with a spade. A migration doesn't swerve... it floods on through any obstacle... You can't compare us to that young chap. God, how many rats he's caught... From every basement... But you have to keep them somewhere... feed them... And he wouldn't know certain details... like what to feed them with before releasing them. I've got no temperature – good. This nurse gives painful injections. Even if I have a relapse, it shouldn't be so bad as to make me bed-ridden. I wonder what the time is.

"Had a good sleep?... Who was snoring all the time then?"

One more injection, the last one... we're leaving! The land

by the meat factory must have been ploughed up by now. The temperature was 37.3. I should have slept with my hat on. I had a drink... delicious water. I glanced at my watch in a festive mood: time was on our side.

I hadn't coughed once, and I was breathing more normally.

Everybody was asleep, and I gave the sign: Oldie brought the bag with our things into the toilet and shoved it under the cupboard. The fire escape was a couple of feet away. The bolts on the windows were now moving freely. I leant on the sink.

"What's wrong with you?"

"Must have bent over too sharply. My head's spinning."

"Go and lie down."

Was it over? Should I get some soap, or not? I needed a wash... I shouldn't give in right away. I drew a toothbrush from a glass and managed to spread out a white thread over the dead bristles at the first try. I'd also get that soap, later...

I stuck the brush into my mouth... it scorched the inside of my lips, and a revolting, lifeless taste spread on my tongue. The brush flew away... paste streamed from the tube... I leant on the wall and... threw up.

With my back to the wall I had no chance... it was all over my trousers. What a brilliant way to begin the day. I felt weak... the lights dimmed... my lips quivered... an unusual pain coursed through my innards... people rushed in from the corridor, jostling each other. I was choking on spittle... my lips were spread hideously apart. Oldie tried to clean up the mess, moving around on all fours, fighting off other people's hands: "Let me do it myself!" – what if anybody saw our bag, I thought – "Take him away, just wait..." He wet his hand and rubbed my face with tepid water. And then a new fit, a new spasm and a thick mass ran from my mouth – that's it. Sal ammoniac... like a winter wind. I tried to avoid it.

"The temperature's 37.8."

I whispered without moving my lips… half an hour had gone by. A voice alongside me continued: should be on a diet… furred tongue… mmm, yes, give him pills… has it happened before? He was probably drinking? Gastric lavage would be good… or shall we wait a bit? High temperature… but maybe it's not linked.

By the window Sviridov was shaking a black X-ray plate… my lungs appeared like two loaves of white bread. There was some sort of formation there…

"Perhaps he's been going around with a chest infection? Have you taken a blood test? The lab's closed… This is a mad-house!"

"Well, Oldie, are you waiting till everybody's gone? They don't know about us… call her." He didn't seem to be catching what I was saying.

"When did he last move his bowels?… The usual colour?… You never pay attention?… What did he eat?… Who accompanied him on his outing?… Go and interrogate Shestakov in the cooler: ask what they ate… Spasms again: get him a basin!… What, is it so hard to find a basin?… Change his pillow – it's all wet."

"What's he showing to you? Oldie, you should understand."

"Where does it hurt, pal?" Oldie asked in the general silence. "Your stomach? It'll pass… must be some food poisoning… just rest in bed… there's nothing in your lungs." He was trying to divert their attention.

"I need her…"

"What's he asking for? What's he asking for?" Sviridov cackled. "Silence! What did he tell you?"

"What is it?" Oldie asked, in a submissive yet eager tone.

"You know. I cannot live without her… Why did she die?"

"Without whom?" Sviridov enquired, breathing avidly.

"Never mind…" Oldie smirked and winced, squeezing my

273

shoulder and looking down at his feet. "That's enough! Too many people here! Let him rest in bed, will you!"

"Everybody out! Irina Borisovna, put somebody on round-the-clock watch in the ward, and call another nurse… Just a minute… Shall I give you a car to go and fetch her?"

"No need for a watch," Oldie said. "I'll do everything myself. Give us some peace."

"No puking, eh?" said Sviridov, rushing in. "He's doing it again! Needs to get his stomach pumped. I could ring of course, but it's not very convenient! Probably, after her wedding, she won't have time for you… Everybody keep quiet about this… Is it her he wants?"

"Maybe…"

"Her, eh? Look, whatever he fancies… just can't promise anything! Suppose she's not at home?"

Oldie covered his eyes with his palms. We listened.

"Number six here. Major Gubin's number, please. Who?… Hello, Yelena Fyodorovna. This is Sviridov speaking. Is Victor there? I see… the incineration is at night. In fact I'm trying to get hold of your daughter. Olga's not around? And when… I see…"

"Why, why did you let it get you down?" Oldie whispered in rapid tones. "Tell them you don't need her. And they're putting this nurse here! Hold out until the truck arrives. Good Lord, why do you think it's all over?"

"No, nothing like that, nothing military," continued Sviridov. "It's all to do with the people from Moscow I'm responsible for… one's been throwing up. No, no diarrhoea. He's asking for Olga. What can I do? Not sure they really understand… They think, since they're from Moscow… I'll be around till six and then off to HQ. Sorry, my friend, she's not there. She's at the dentist's. Have you called in the duty nurse?"

"Sviridov… ring the dentist's."

"That's enough of that!" Oldie chipped in abruptly. "Be reasonable!"

"Am I not welcome here?" Sviridov said in a piqued tone.

"As long as you're here, he'll keep asking. That's the state he's in. He'll have a rest in bed and get over it... I know about these things. Don't put anybody in here."

They brought a table, and an elderly duty nurse made notes, asked questions, read the newspaper, yawned continually and fell asleep.

I raised my head, just to make sure that I still could. Time was light-footed. I could sense sleep coming, but couldn't bring myself to give in to it. My forehead was cold... my insides weren't aching but... it felt as if they were burning... I gulped for air... they brought some cool water... There was no coughing, but the burning sensation did not subside... maybe that's what it's like when it's healing? The temperature's 38.2. Oldie looked at his watch.

"Eleven thirty. So far so good."

"Go and get her."

"Why did you take this into your head, you idiot? And stop drinking... you should know that water won't make you less thirsty... the pills will soon begin to work. Ah, doctor, come in."

The doctor's hands probed my stomach... Have you eaten anything disagreeable? I couldn't think of anything disagreeable I'd eaten. The doctor was at a loss.

"What's wrong with him..."

"Must be the usual food poisoning," Oldie said through clenched teeth.

"What do you suggest?"

"The simplest thing: two fingers down the throat. Or wash his stomach with soda water. Or with a manganese solution."

"Maybe he should really put two fingers in his throat. Or the manganese solution. I'll come back at six."

"Don't worry. I'll be here... his progress is encouraging. He was much paler when he woke up. Come in the morning."

"Ask her to come?..." Then he turned to me: "You're scaring me... Just tell me in so many words that you've gone mad and decided to stay here, and I'll give up... Who's there?"

It was Sviridov.

"Hey... we've tracked her down over the phone and asked her to come... explained the situation... but she can't come today. She can come tomorrow. And that's thanks to me. Tomorrow, before lunch. Or by evening."

"Comrade warrant officer, can I have a word with her?" Oldie went to the phone.

The nurse woke up – what's going on?

"Go away. You're in the way. Get out of here! You're making me sick."

She carried her chair into the corner. I went on abusing her in vain: she was deaf.

"No, today's impossible..." Oldie said. "And she doesn't want to, either. That's that. Have some tea and toast... you need energy. Does it hurt? Yes, and you also feel weak... Don't think about it."

"It's for tomorrow, then..." Sviridov added. "They're taking her for some treatment today, somewhere nearby... maybe she'll drop in? But don't get your hopes up."

It was snowing. I was alarmed... what would the road be like? No, it was just dropping from the roof. It'd be good to get some sleep before lunch...

"Please go and ask her personally... She won't say no to you."

"No."

"Then call Sviridov."

"Why?"

"I'll ask for a car to take me to her."

"Why don't you calm down? Relax. We are planning to escape. You wanted it even more than me, no? Do you still want to? Only if you go and see her? Are you laying down conditions to me? You need it? We must immediately go to Moscow! To a hospital! And have your insides checked!"

"No, we don't need anything... siddown... It's just something to do with work... memories of childhood... I know what he needs right now... right! Just sit down."

"Sorry – it's not your fault."

"But what will I say to her? What do you need her for? Another fifteen minutes and we'll be gone... and all of this will be left behind. They must have done the ploughing... we've set things in motion. They must've set out in the morning, three kilometres a day... they'll arrive tomorrow! It will be clear who's done it! They'll ask us to do something to stop them. They don't know that it's impossible. We have to go away today. That's about it."

"Just tell her I want to see her one more time."

"So we're not going today? We're not going? When are we going then? Tomorrow? Are we going or not?"

To kill the time, I thought of taking a nap. Oldie went away, swearing clumsily, by fits and starts. I came to in the middle of some activity... but then tumbled out of it and found myself lying in bed half-asleep... what was I doing? Oldie was holding my hands. He released them and soaked my lips with a wet rag. I tried to get at it with my lips... I was thirsty... but he took it away. More emptiness and coldness followed in the room... a nurse ran in with a mop... she started scrubbing by the bedstead, then raised her eyes in alarm.

"So... it happened again?"

"Yes, some kind of convulsions..." replied Oldie. "And now nausea? Give it here... 38.6. Oh."

What was new in the room? There were different sounds in each ear, rubbing against each other in the middle of my head like paper. I stretched my jaws around… would the crackling in my ears cease? Would my ears unblock? I held a watch to my left ear. Then to the right. Both equally clear. Five minutes to five. Oldie was dressed up warm, coming straight from the street.

"No. Didn't find her," he said. "No one knows. Tomorrow." Then, louder: "Drink some hot tea." My jacket, my hat and warm socks had appeared on the bed. "It's draughty. Get dressed. It's so quiet outside. They're getting ready to set them on fire. At the house entrances, they've got these boxes with rats, jars, paraffin, rags… they're twisting some sort of torches out of wire. The basements are wide open. There are logs across the main road: that's what they call 'pathways of rubbish'… barricades! Hah, it's so empty you wouldn't mind seeing a drunk or getting insulted by someone… Put on another pair of socks! You know…" Oldie waited for the nurse to leave – he was gloomy, depressed. "Perhaps I should tell them that you're dying… get them to release at least one person for treatment. We've been imagining God knows what about them, but maybe, if we ask them nicely, they'll let us go?"

"I doubt it. I'm not seriously ill, am I?"

The nurse returned, dried her hands, flung an eloquent glance at us and sat down.

"Get dressed, then."

We're going then. It had all become simple. I felt refreshed, and could sit up without help. I pulled the jacket on and took the hat – should I ask for water? Oldie looked out into the corridor and nodded. He checked the bedside table: anything we might need? I leant on the window sill. Beyond it, in the misty darkness, the silhouettes of the buildings loomed bare. It was summer when we arrived.

I tried to see if I could stand upright. In the corridor, a group of orderlies and pregnant women were sitting round the television. On a couch across the exit to the staircase Zaborov was sleeping, his head covered with a jacket, and squatting next to him dozed another soldier. The cleaning woman was sweeping bits of paper towards the toilet. What if she lingered there?

"How you feeling? Don't drink anything."

"I can't keep my eyes open. I've got a temperature, but my head's fine."

"What about your stomach?"

"Not so good." The burning feeling had subsided, but I could sense a cold rubbery lump swelling inside, weighing down heavily. We'd make it.

Despite all our preparations, at the arrival of the truck we froze. Oldie glanced out and said in an unusually slow tone of voice:

"What's that? They've brought the milk. Sit down, what's wrong?"

Now the fever seized me again, nipping and nagging at me from head to toe... the air forced out painfully from inside. I was torn apart by a fit of coughing and, without taking my eyes off Oldie, clutched firmly at my hat so as not to leave it behind and catch a cold where we were going.

Oldie stuck his head out into the corridor and immediately came back, panting. He cast an avid look out of the window. He waited for the right moment, then approached the nurse, who was slouching in her chair sleepily.

"Are you gonna sit here for twenty-four hours? There's a long night ahead. We'll need your assistance mainly at night... when I... as you'll understand... will be sleeping. We don't need you now." He was breathing spasmodically. The nurse didn't understand him, but got up all the same.

* * *

The milk truck backed up to the basement window – the women from the bar waddled out from the porch towards it. On the road, right up to the gates, there wasn't a soul: only the guard was pounding down a snowdrift with a shovel.

"Go and have a rest... gather your strength."

"I'm used to it," said the nurse. "I've been doing this for forty years..." She kept standing there.

The truck suddenly slowed down on the ice. It wouldn't get under the fire escape.

"What decent men you are," the old nurse said, laughing and slapping Oldie's shoulder gratefully. "Some of our patients... we have to tie them up."

The driver was wearing a sheepskin coat and dog-skin hat. He looked under the back wheels: ice. That was it. The women called out to him: get it closer! Try again! Swearing. And what if this wasn't the same driver... what if he wouldn't go inside or wouldn't leave the truck today – what could we use to threaten him?... He started the engine. Oldie feebly grinned at the nurse and went out.

"No need for you to stand by the window. Look at him, he doesn't say anything... I'll go and complain to your people."

Skidding further to the left, the truck trawled right under the fire escape. I returned to bed and gestured to the old nurse: calm down, it's nothing... Oldie must have opened the window in the lavatory, because there was a draught... The nurse muffled herself up.

Oldie returned at a run and stared outside. His eyes were shining: the corridor must be clear. There was a rumble of iron crates... they were unloading. Oldie's gaze was glued to the window, as if he were watching a river. Finally his fingers crept along the window sill, indicating: the driver's going in, slowly.

"Could you be so kind as to bring an enema?"

The nurse went off.

"Six crates left… let's go!"

The corridor looked different: the television had been switched off and was now surrounded by two rows of abandoned chairs and benches. There was another chair where the duty nurse was supposed to be – and a lamp beating down brightly. And the empty couch where Zaborov had been sleeping. A mop leant against the wall, and a pail with a washrag. Over the exit yawned the red duty light.

Winter wafted in from the open toilet window. The door into the ward slammed, and we found ourselves in the dark. The iron crates were still thundering somewhere close by. The last ones resounded, then the silence of the snow followed. The door, blackened by shade, slid off heavily: from the canteen, the nurse shuffled out and gazed at us blindly.

"Where are you going? Just went off for a snack… to get some sour cream." She tugged at the lab door. "I'm going to the ground floor. Can you manage till I'm back?"

She trudged away at an excruciatingly slow pace… she adjusted the chairs, answered the phone, lifted the receiver and got no reply. Suddenly it was all quiet… they must have finished unloading. Oldie was beckoning me.

"Two still standing there. They're locking up the basement. They're talking. I'll be on the stairs… you hand me the bag. They're going! Now they're by the corner. Gone!" With a whining squeak, the window swung completely open. Oldie groped for the staircase and put one foot out. He was completely outside now. He looked down and said with a hoarse voice:

"The bag! Well? What are you listening for? Well?"

"Someone's coming."

"Wh-what?!"

A clicking of heels was heard along the corridor.

"Get back," I said to Oldie. "Nothing doing... later."

He shouted, shuddering on the fire escape.

I staggered outside.

"We're here. Hello."

"A-ha, there you are... we've distracted you from some important business, eh? Where's the damn light?"

The lights were switched on. Sviridov put his arm round me and jabbed a finger under my ribs. Well? Are you pleased? He jerked his eyebrows: it wasn't easy but I managed to bring her!

"Look at him: he's made it to the toilet by himself... and we were going to bury him in the morning... It's because you've come."

Her mother was also there, wearing her thick glasses and anxious to leave, with a hostile expression on her face. Vic's wife stood behind their backs, ashen-faced. She turned away, her hair shining into my eyes... was she nervous?

"Damn," Oldie barked, "Oh, God!" and slumped onto the couch, hammering in words like nails: "It's curtains, curtains!"

"So? Well! So?"

Her mother was in a hurry, they had to rush. One of her daughter's teeth had been pulled out so ineptly that there was an abscess... yes, that's the kind of dentists they had now. A huge abscess... they touched it, and a stream of pus had come out! Lots of pus! God knows what poured out of there... they must have squeezed out a glassful for sure... they had stuffed her mouth full of cotton wool. She was only a few steps away... she bowed slightly: hello... I gave a little nod, shaking. The old nurse tossed a snake-like enema onto Oldie's lap.

"Want some Vaseline? Say something. You've managed without already? Shall I bring it?"

"Yeah," howled Oldie, "yeah, yeah... and be off."

"They're giving you treatment... Maybe we should be off? It's late. Goodbye then…" she was saying, a bit closer to me but still outside my reach. "Goodbye. Get well."

Sviridov ummed and erred, then said: "So it was all for nothing? Surely you wanted…"

"Yes I did. Could I have a word with you, one minute? Over here."

"Where's that 'over here'?"

"It's their ward, Yelena Fyodorovna, it's OK."

"Let them go in. We'll discuss the excavations here."

"But she's got a temperature, she's barely alive! Be quick, you hear. Olga? Is that necessary?"

"Please."

Speak up. The door's firmly closed. Sit down. No, talk like that. Talk now.

"I wanted… I want… it so happens… there's no time…" I stretched out my hand to her. The nurse brought the enema.

"I'll put it here."

She tried to withdraw her hand – what's going on? Why? Just start speaking, or I'll leave. Yes. She recoiled and dropped her bag. She didn't run away, but persistently pushed my hands away in silence, until she fell on the bed. She tried to get up, but we both slid down to the floor. She didn't strike me: she just resisted as I tried to touch her. My hat fell on her face, and she tore herself away from me, shuddering as if at the touch of some loathsome hairy beast. She let out a shrill shriek, and everything went dark. I rolled back… I couldn't call her back with my cough, could I… I just sat up while I still could. How vulgar… I wish I'd cut off my hands… At the other end of the room, she was silently holding her aching jaw, weeping with an offended air, her hair loose and swaying.

* * *

283

"Where she is?... They've taken her away," Oldie muttered, his hand still holding the watch.

We were dressed to go out. My hands still remembered her body, the fabric of her dress. I stroked the quilt... a different sensation entirely. On the quilt remained a clot of cotton wool – from her mouth. I sniffed my fingers, expecting a special scent... yes, it seemed so. And soon – no more. I wish she'd come again. No more time. As for the rats – they'd be here soon. They run faster over the snow. Then I remembered:

"Oldie, the truck! Why are we wasting our time here?"

"It's still waiting!" Oldie exploded. "Still waiting for you!" He banged his hand on the table. "A whole day lost! Idiot! Idiot!" He pushed the chair away and ran to the window. "It's there... you hear me? Oh my! Never mind – the driver's going back now. There's no point. We won't make it." We darted out into the corridor – it was empty. If anyone called out – no turning back! Quick! It'd take the driver some time to start the engine. I looked out of the window: the blue back of that car was so close that it would be possible to jump on it.

"Go, go, Oldie, the bag!" He pulled the bag from under the cupboard and threw out the dirty pillowcases from it. He was wheezing away, shivering in joyful anticipation.

"It's heavy... what did you put in it?" I lifted it. "Iron?..." He drew out of the bag a varnished yellow board.

I'll check out later... I stepped onto the fire escape.

"Damn..." he continued rummaging inside the bag, and I realized that it was the butt of a gun. Oldie got up in a daze and pulled from the bag a rifle folded in two with a distinctive glass sight. Also the cartridge...

"Chuck it away! Quick!"

He stared with perplexity at the blue Niva under the fire escape without letting go of the gun.

Where in the toilet? Not there. Who'd done it? He kicked the door – no one. No sound. Through the window – no one.

"We must immediately hand it over ourselves!"

We ran into the corridor, expecting a peremptory "Who's there!" The lights were still on... nobody was back yet. Oldie was carrying an armful – don't stop! I sent the chairs flying, I banged on the doors: "Hoy! Whose junk is this?" In the canteen, there were bowls of porridge and black bread ready to be dispensed. On the staircase I called out: "Anyone here?" On the ground floor, the television was on. Overcoats and army coats were hanging on racks, and glasses of sour cream lay on the table. "Hoy, ladies!" Something was smoking in a metal bin, a cigarette most likely... but there wasn't anybody on watch. I dashed towards the women's toilet, I broke into a run and threw myself at the closing door... Sviridov!

He was spitting.

"Oh damn, it's you... What a joker... you... You only just begged us... And why don't we have anyone on guard? Whose car is that?" He fiddled with a telephone. "No sound from this phone. Why are you without a nurse? Where's Zaborov?"

"We've found weapons. In a bag. In the toilet."

Dumbfounded, Sviridov gazed around him.

"These fighting cocks... they don't give a damn where they leave their weapons... I'll have them drawn and quartered... but where is everybody? There must at least be... Who's on your floor?"

"No one."

"What? But what about the women? And where are the guards?" He thumped on a door. "Hey, in there, for fuck's sake!"

He looked into all the rooms, shrugged his shoulders, tried the phone again, spat, and we all went out onto the porch, into the silence, into the dark, into the cold. Oldie pressed the rifle close to him, like broken skis.

Sviridov ran around, flinching at every stride. He glanced beneath the black fir trees, banged on a snowdrift – which responded with a wooden sound – and shouted something about the devil's mother. He looked gloomily along the pathway. By the gates, a sentry was walking back and forth.

"The alarm!" Sviridov bellowed. "Quick, here! What on earth…"

Through the lifeless windows, no outlines of heads, no movements of white coats and no voices could be discerned. All that could be seen were skeletons of trees and a roof evenly covered with unbroken snow. The sentry continued to walk back and forth.

Sviridov couldn't bear it any longer: he advanced with huge strides up to the gates and blurted out with fury:

"Comrade soldier!"

The sentry stood still, took off his cap and listened attentively, then slid through the gate and ran for all he was worth across the square, bending against the wind.

Sviridov stood as if petrified, then touched his belt.

"My flare pistol… I've been gone for just an hour and look what's happened. But whose car is this? Who let it in? Does it have a permit?"

The silence was unbearable, it was closing in. We ran after Sviridov, fearing he'd disappear too.

"Comrade warrant officer, forget about the car…"

"How did they manage to get in?" Sviridov was stubbornly heading towards the Niva car. "It's not locked. Where's the pass…"

"Comrade warrant officer…"

"Well then?" he climbed in and pressed the horn. "Take that!" He signalled again. "I'll show them." And again.

"This is not a game," I shouted, screwing my eyes. "Get out."

And I stumbled over my own black shadow... lights were glaring down on us...

The honking turned into a continuous howl, and I looked away from the floodlight. Sviridov doubled up on the seat, clutching at the steering wheel. A pair of black hands grabbed him by the neck and yanked him out. Oldie sank to his knees, raising his shaking fingers, and screamed at the first touch. In a daze, I tried to move towards Oldie, but some kind of tentacles were already grabbing me from behind... that was not for long, only a couple of yards... my feet were frozen... I pushed my neck forwards, trying to cover my eyes and nearly falling down, but they kept their grip on me and dragged me away, my feet scraping the snow. They lifted my feet, and I closed my eyes... so they wouldn't know that I saw what was going on.

16

The Rat Catcher's Departure

1 Day to D-Day

Whatever time was left to me, I wished to spend lying down. Was it cold? I couldn't say, but there was a draught over my face. And this heat in my head. I shouldn't fall asleep: how could I lose sight of all this? Sleep consists of three parts: dropping off, relaxing and waking up... better not to begin if you're not sure there's time for everything. I've drunk so much water today. I wasn't thirsty, but my throat burned, and no quantities of liquid could quench the fire. Despair. The number one cause for despair is darkness. A person can't see anything: he lies there alone and is forced to... But there's a loophole: you can pretend you're not alone, but only a young person can do this. You fall into despair only once, and the other times are just a memory of how that first despair tastes. As a young man, I thought I'd fall into despair at the first death of a close one, or if I were to get an incurable disease. Instead, it happened in the city of Kazan. We were exterminating rats at the local circus... the stables, the cages... the bars. We were hired by a private company selling pies and sweets: private firms had just been allowed, and they were still a bit fearful. The basement... the rubbish heap... Oldie had gone home and I had to sit it out till the end of the contract, to watch over any bad after-effects. But in fact I waited for the conclusions of the health lab on the dead rats in my hotel, the Dustyk. Or was it the Duslyk? I'd walk to the circus along the river… it was early December. From the twelfth row I'd watch female artistes with half-bare bottoms, and rosy cows performing to an orchestra. In the hotel shower room I bumped into the same artistes – injured women athletes most probably – with totally flat bodies and not much taller than a young girl, or middle-aged aunties with colossal husbands and colossal assistants. It was the sort of town where, if you stopped lost in thought, a queue would form behind you. I'd forget what I was doing, wake up and wonder: why?

One night I had an earache. It was all set for my departure to Moscow that day, but at four or five in the morning this earache started. I waited for the light, lying flat, with the pillow clasped to my ear, trying to keep as warm as possible, with no medicines and nobody to call – who needed me there? I remember flat cakes of melting snow with mud, rivulets of sludge rather than water, balconies propped up with rusty pipes, toothless front yards. What's the point of keeping warm? It might make things even worse… You have a fitful sleep, and then you're aware of being awake, and no one cares… I-t hur-ts. My mother used to pour some drops in my ear and put in a wad of cotton wool. And then in Kazan this pain, not too dreadful, conjured up so many unbearable recollections… I'd made my goodbyes, and suddenly there was this intolerable feeling that I'd never return to those simple treasures: warm hands, a bountiful house, immediate help at your slightest groan, your all-seeing mother, the wad of cotton wool in your ear… Despair and pain are not the same thing… Coffins are put out of sight, but decrepitude imperceptibly eats your dearest ones alive. We are left to live… what are we saved for? For despair? That time, in Kazan, it was despair… but its subsequent reoccurrence annoyed me without reaching the heart, however much I felt like howling.

In this prison, instead of the usual wooden platforms there

were bunks, raised during the day and latched to the wall. They had put a mattress under me, and I lay on my belly, head over the edge. When I threw up – when that ticklish filth, lightly touching my tongue, surged loose and burst my throat open, forcing through an acid-tasting convulsion with a short splash, or just empty dribble – then I'd bring my head to the edge so as not to stain the mattress, and in a moment of tearful gulping I saw the barred door and sized up the situation.

Should I lie on my side and keep sight of the door? Then I'd make a mess of the mattress – how to sleep then? Should I roll over to the side with these handcuffs locking my hands at the back? There are some people here. Count them up, quick: when they start their interrogations, my head must be busy with something else. Behind that door there are some steps up. The worst thing is that we are below street level.

Somebody came down the steps. The door sounded as if it was made of iron. Was it a door to the street? Probably not. An internal yard more likely. More convulsions, but the retching had now turned into a kind of yawning... the utterance of an unarticulated word. They pushed me down, dumped me onto my back and dried my face with a towel... a frowning young man wearing a jacket, a tie, a white shirt. He thrust a thermometer under my arm.

"What's the time?"

"Don't start asking questions. Just be quiet."

Supposing it's still night... the rats must have been on the move for the second day now. What's the distance? We'd gone by car, not on foot... and since conversation shortens the distance... it must be at least five or six kilometres. The guard won't tell me in what part of town this prison is. Is it a low-lying area? If it's attached to a police station, there must be cages with dogs in the yard. Fine. Another twelve hours left of this shit... then the rats will be running along the road. And they'll scatter around when they reach the buildings. Who'll be able to see them in the evening? There won't be any panic by the evening – there have always been lots of rats around, and their scattering could be explained by the fact that they're setting rats on fire. If they are running at full speed, we'd better quit the town by evening. Tomorrow at the very latest, before the reveille. Before the arrival of the guests. It's going to be horrible... the migrant rats will start flooding the outskirts and then form an even more compact torrent. The remaining stragglers will press on to enter town for at least six hours in a row. Until they've settled. To make things worse, this is a small town, with lots of barrack-like buildings... which means shabby basements... previous rat infestation... and then all the festivities... the noise... And the local rats, scorched by the fire, will go absolutely berserk – those will be more dangerous. The migrant rats... they'll be hungry, crushed, oblivious to danger... they'll seek refuge underground wherever they can. I need to come up with something – considering that I won't be able to escape – during the next six hours, while I'm here with my hands tied up or in a room upstairs. When it all begins, no one will have time for anything... Someone's crying. Let's see what I could do.

First I sat up and then I stood up, without any problems. The guard had not left his stool. The other prisoner had not stopped weeping.

"Konstantin." I recognized our driver. "Stop that! Cheer up! Does your wife know?"

"She went off to see her dad the day before yesterday. To hell with her. She's given me something." And he touched his trousers. "An infection. A wart. It's sharp-pointed."

"A candiloma?"

"That's it. I call it... candelabra. Every day they're cauterizing it with ammonia... it makes me cry, you see." And he blew his nose in a long blast.

No windows... brick walls... mmm... a blind wall onto the street? Wooden floors... that's no good. Shabby skirting boards... and the heating... two pipes, the lower one in bad repair. But no windows. There's a door, though. A barred door. With a hole above the lower hinge. Free access. The most immediate threat is rat holes.

"Get away from the door. Siddown!"

OK, bastard. I'll have a look at the corridor when you take me to the toilet... unless they bring a commode in here.

The guard checks my temperature – how high is it? – he remains silent. My guts ache. There's a soldier in the corridor. Wearing an overcoat. Is the street near? Four... five. Five paces and he turns back. Let's hope he's got to a corner, not to a dead end. I need that corridor to be long... Why didn't they take me for interrogation, while I was still... It's painful. When they summon me, I'll have a chat with them... everything will be resolved. The nurse who's given me the injection... she's wearing a coat over her uniform. Konstantin is asleep. The guard slaps me in the face.

"I want to be summoned, immediately..."

"Where to?"

"Since it appears I'm arrested, I want to know what I'm accused of!" Suddenly I didn't see him any more, and continued in the darkness: "I want to be interrogated! Otherwise let me go... Take off the cuffs! Call Klinsky."

The handcuffs were snapped off. I spread my arms with a sense of bliss, and was able to lift myself up into the light. I screwed my eyes. The guard called out a sentry, produced some keys and then whispered to me:

"Why don't you sleep... Who's this Klinsky?" He ran upstairs. The door must be outside... Why am I not summoned... there's something wrong... but what... think... I can't understand what they have against us... I must convince them to let me go... but they're the masters of making people change their minds... A cold draught touches my skin... How can they be dissuaded?... I must get away... the fever is keeping my drowsiness at bay... in any case, they'll wake me up. When they open the door, I won't get up myself. Behave correctly. As if you own the place... they need us. Konstantin stirred.

"Can I give you anything? Forget it. They'll keep us here till those guys leave. Been gone long?"

How long? An hour?... Two at least. I raised myself up, and all went black... must be the fever... I clutched at the bars... let them notice me. How long? I started to lose my grip of the bars, as if I was hanging down. Better lie flat... but I was afraid to let go of the bars. They shouted for the guard, and made me sit – I felt the chill from the iron on my hands. The guard shuffled in.

"What d'you want?" he said, bleary-eyed, wearing no belt.

"I want to be interrogated," I said hoarsely.

"They'll call you in due course. Everybody's unwell. Everybody's case is important."

"Just report it," said Konstantin, putting my wish into words.

"What, aren't they asleep too?" mumbled the guard, then shouted to one side: "Shall I call them with a mug or a brick?" With a brick he banged on the pipe going into the ceiling. "See? They're quiet. Must be sleeping, the bastards!" And he carried on banging.

I've forgotten the rest... everything was swimming around... The guard puffed and panted as we went up – hey, hold on, you!... I groped for the banisters... the staircase was protected with iron netting... I shouldn't forget that. When we crossed the road, I threw up, and the sentry leapt away.

"Bloody hell! Are you finished? Wipe yourself!"

My head seemed to be full to bursting with hot sand, painfully trying to force its way into the back of my head…

"May I come in? Please! Where's a chair? Can't see one! How can we talk without a chair?"

"Please sit on the sofa."

There were butterflies in glazed boxes… not my beloved garden fly, too small… If they came close they'd see how my hands and knees were shaking… A comrade with a round face and small mouth sat next to me. From a cheap sports suit protruded a tie, like a wine glass, and a white collar. There was also a hastily made-up camp bed.

"It's such a hassle, you know… we'll have to do without formalities. The building's just not suitable for this. Did you see the iron netting around the staircase? It's a former nursery, you see… What're you so anxious about?"

"Just who… am I talking to?"

"I'm acting as Head of the Svetloyar Branch of the Ministry of National Security for the Tambov Region."

"And what about Klinsky, then?"

"Lieutenant-Colonel Klinsky… you see, he has another job now." Then the man added: "Can I take you back?"

"What? Don't you want to…" No no no, this is a wrong start. "I want to know why we've been detained! What are you trying to prove? I want a lawyer. I'll go on a hunger strike. I'll complain to the Procurator-General. You won't succeed… this is arbitrary rule!"

The man raised his hands imploringly.

"Please forgive me, this is my first day in this job. Somehow I can't recollect your case… so many things to do… One minute… let me refresh my memory."

He dug out from under the sofa a bunch of keys and opened a safe. "Uh-oh, there's a whole pile here… You wouldn't know under which letter of the alphabet... Or are they sorted by charges?... No, I don't think we'll find them. Unless... Where are you registered? In Moscow? Is that where you live? And why are you here? Here you are: Moscow... two of you... that was lucky – right on top of the pile... That's right. There's your file."

He laid some tied-up sheets of paper on my knees. "I'm going to wash my hands, so's not to be in your way. When you go, give the keys to the guard. See that the sheets are still properly tied up, so's it doesn't fall apart... we have strict rules on that. Sorry I was a bit slow off the mark... everyone's responsible for his own department here..."

The letters blended into each other in a treacly stream... the sheets seemed stuck together... I couldn't turn over the pages.

"Can't make it out."

"No? Then let me do that for you. What's this here? Yes, yes..." he riffled through the pages. "Oh, there's so much... I won't look at all of them... it'd take too much time... we've already kept you here half the night... A-ha, there it is, at the end... the gist of the matter. A-ha, a-ha. I'd better rephrase it in simple terms... the way our people write, you wouldn't make head or tail out of it. You've planned the assassination of the President of Russia during his visit to our town." He raised his eyes to the calendar on the wall. "That's tomorrow. Apprehended with firearms while getting into a car. The car was stolen from the village of Palatovka. Ever been to that village? And there's evidence. Two sniper's rifles... for some reason the make of the rifles is not specified... two boxes of cartridges, a map of the town, binoculars, torches, your finger-prints... "

"Money?"

"Nothing here about money. Was there money? You should have immediately declared it when you were arrested. We'll find it. In your shirt you had a sketch of the assassination... Mm,

296

yes, it is difficult to make sense of it... some little crosses. The rifles have been stolen from the garrison warehouse... there's the document: stolen by warrant officer Sviridov. And here's a list of those arrested. Is that all? No, the list continues on a second page... Is that enough... what I have read?"

"I don't understand."

"Some question marks are noted down here. How deeply involved in your plot was Colonel Gontar? Ah... now I understand why Lieutenant-Colonel Klinsky had to take charge of the town administration and I've ended up here. What was the role of the former Mayor? Did he select you? Ivan Trofimovich is dead, isn't he? If so, we won't be able to carry out a proper investigation. But the gist is... an assassination attempt."

"Don't you find this ludicrous yourself? What are you hoping to do? Let's go while it's not too late." I decided I must go on the offensive. "You've gone a bit too far... but those times are over, you know? How stupid... Your Klinsky will end up in jail... but just think about yourself – are you with him?"

The man looked down and suddenly patted my shoulder.

"Listen, please, don't leave me in the lurch... You see, I don't even know how to take notes, how to conduct an interrogation... I wasn't a lawyer in my previous job, you know, and here everything's so complex... and right on my first day! And no secretary... they've evicted all unwanted people. You see where I'm working: I don't even have a clean sheet of paper... I'm treating you decently, and I hope you will too... This case is not ours any longer, anyway... We tracked it down, we made the arrests, but cases at this level are investigated in Moscow. This evening an advance delegation will be arriving on two separate planes... three hundred people. We'll finish the festivities... see them off... and then they'll deal with you. Us down here, we just can't cope... I'm amazed how all the arrests could be made without injuries... very lucky!" Then he added, hanging his head: "We don't even have a proper place to keep you... should we keep you handcuffed? Shoot you on attempted escape? Leave you alive? We have no experience of this... and thank God for that." He crossed himself. "So, then, it's five o'clock." He drew the curtain and looked out.

Light. Maybe some lamps had been lit? The wind bent the flame sideways and stretched it out lengthways. On the other side of the street, a chap was holding up a lamp, and the flame seemed reflected in a series of windows... no, it was no reflection: they were other lamps, raised in the same way... and beneath our windows, illuminated in the same way, shadows crossed in the gleaming snow. There were lights around the buildings, intersecting like the threads of a tightly spun spider's web. The sky seemed to blink and turn pale... a rocket soared up, its lights obediently painting a short arc.

"Beautiful, eh?" the man said. "Cheap too. We can do it, if we have to. It's a pity nobody saw it. The Germans would turn this into a regular tradition. They'd have guests, frankfurters, beer on every corner... They'd advertise it, get investments... orchestras, girls with garlands, citizens of honour holding torches... The burgomaster would be setting the first rat on fire... And they'd time it for the end of the harvesting season... make a spectacle out of it. See them flying up? Ever been to Europe? No? Me neither, never had the chance. What for... we know how things are there."

He went off to have a wash, and changed into a suit. He took out a pair of shoes from a shoebox, threaded in some laces and put them on. He walked up and down the room and took them off.

I felt lousy. It was almost morning. Some soldiers hauled me away. Beneath the threshold there was a crack. Would they come today? Yes. I'd lost track. They gave me an injection, measured my blood pressure, examined my tongue and took my temperature. I didn't ask, and they didn't say anything, but brought me something to eat. I drank some tea, warmed up a bit and fell asleep. Our former driver, Konstantin, was scrubbing the floor. I was desperate: the day was passing, and the rats could have easily penetrated through the door. And the townspeople were not prepared.

While Konstantin was scrubbing, I asked him to tell me what was in each corner. From what he said, I gathered that there were three holes – two close by each other, evidently the branching-off of a passageway. I asked him to chalk a cross over each of them. I didn't try to get up... needed to save my strength for later. Thank God for the table. The table was on my side. Everything else was against: the boulevard in front of the building, the entrance to the basement from the street and the spacious yard. But the table was of the right kind: square... unpainted round iron legs... slippery. I wish I knew what Oldie was up to. When it all began, would they be persuaded to open up the rooms? But who? They would all run away.

It was afternoon. Konstantin had had his lunch. I had tried to eat some dry bread, and for fifteen minutes my guts seemed to turn inside out. I sensed an aftertaste of blood in my mouth. The scratches on my wrists had dried up and darkened. I said that I wanted to make a confession. Oldie couldn't have thought up anything better.

But they didn't want to call anybody. And couldn't find anyone.

Later on they did find someone, but I could no longer walk. The chap from before brought me some toast – his wife had sent some. I declared: we admit that we were instructed to carry out an assassination; we are prepared to confess everything if, for the sake of our safety, we are transferred from here to Moscow. Just let them know: we'll tell them whatever is requested. He didn't even hear me out: they called him to have tea. Besides, I was speaking too weakly. I tried to speak louder, but he just said that all that was probably important, and ordered the handcuffs back on. What a blunder I'd made. I realized that he wouldn't be coming back. The time left to me might just as well be over now.

In the beginning they'd cry out in alarm, for sure. Although soldiers are heedless. There would be a dry rustling, an approaching whistle and then... lightning. Let's just hope that it'll be later in the evening! Perhaps someone will come before that? What an idle thought. When you sense them, your legs do all the thinking. Even if you see them, you can't outrun them.

It's hard for me to imagine... we're used to working on rat settlements with fixed boundaries: a building... a forge... a basement. They are already settled there when we arrive. Here, four million or more will be coming in... the local ones will be expelled from their holes... over an enormous expanse everything will be seething, there won't be anywhere for us to go.

We only ever killed rats. It never occurred to us to let them migrate and observe what would happen. It's like after an earthquake. Pallas saw them in the Urals... they leave death and destruction behind. Whole packs roamed round Lower Saxony. I've seen the articles, though I can't read German, but the numbers there cannot be compared.

I know everything about rats – about any individual one: how it runs and sleeps... I just track it and put it down. If the rats are settled, my knowledge of one rat is enough for me to understand completely the whole pack, and the way they inhabit a basement, a rubbish heap, a meat-packing plant, and even a town or a region. But when they get on the move, having lost their home, when they carry out the greatest move of their generation, their numbers are just mind-blowing. One rat is easy enough: a pack on the run is complex. Even if we were to tag rats with radio transmitters on collars. And if they are on the run over a whole area or an entire country... Perhaps only from a plane... The thing is... we are in their way. This kind of thing happens in the wilderness... and here it's like the wilderness...

I remember the farms in a Moscow suburb. Oldie showed me some reports, from his youth... his exploits during his state service. In '72 or '73, the last pig farms in that region went under... Moscow swallowed them up. They were replaced with new residential districts. When the pig farms were there, there had been four rats to every square metre. From every pipe there's dripping water... there's grain, fodder, warmth... the rats would warm themselves on pigs' backs, eat up their placentae... and they particularly love pigs' ears... They'd nibble off the piglets' legs... and dung-beetle larvae are a real delicacy for them. In Moldova we gathered up twenty-six thousand from one farm, even though the locals didn't let us check out all the floors. We were photographed at the top of a mountain of corpses, as a keepsake.

After the pig farms closed down, the rats streamed into the basements of the new buildings. People just laughed at first. On New Year's Eve, there was a sudden thaw, and the basements were flooded. The insulation, of course, was poor, so the rats slithered upwards along pipes, rubbish chutes and cracks, and gnawed away at the plaster, the door frames and the floors. People didn't hear them – the TVs were blaring out. When it was time to dance, the rats emerged under people's feet and poured into the light to the sound of marches... People leapt onto the tables, lashing out with whatever was at hand... but so many rats came popping up that the floors were shaking... underneath the sofas, under the beds... We live without thinking about the degree of rat penetration in our buildings, and the comparative strength of the rats' incisors against building materials. Those people, those revellers, understood that their life, and their entire peace, could be easily invaded... What's the point of calling the police? What could the police do against synanthropic rodents? The staff from the health service was on holiday. It was only on the third of January that Oldie arrived. He was then a head doctor. They spent six weeks cleaning out three storeys – but the sheer number of them... And they will stop only of their own accord, when they reach their own clear, definite limit... It's no use opposing them: you have to live through it, to bide your time. It's impossible to fathom their soul... What will they decide to do with the two mammals trapped in here?

We'll sit on the table. And avoid touching any of them. They might scratch at our trousers... well, let them. They might bite... well, never mind: they're in a state of panic, so it's in their right. But it's essential not to incite them with our blood: we should wrap a rag around our hands, ankles, face, ears, and try not to knock them off: at the first scream they'll all hurl themselves at us.

Konstantin... Konstantin! Sit closer, while I'm talking, and don't ask questions. We still have time... but first of all: don't be scared. Secondly: let down the ear flaps on your hat, raise your collar, draw your hands into your sleeves, cover your face, sit on the table... If they bite you, first: don't get scared, don't let them taste blood! Pull your legs up. I'll explain it again. But he knows nothing yet... he's not turning round... Maybe I didn't call him... I must have carried on sleeping. Call him, quick, with any strength left.... so that he'll know what to do when they begin to bite... biting is still not eating, don't let them get to your flesh! Konstantin was looking around... what was he looking at?! At me... My legs were shaking: I couldn't do anything... they were drawing up by themselves, tearing loose from scratching creatures crawling up them.

"Are you cold? Wanna ask for an overcoat?" he enquired.

How could I calm him down if I myself... that's nothing... just a chill. They'd bite, yes... it would be painful, but it wouldn't heal soon... just listen!

Konstantin disappeared, and Klinsky appeared in his place. He gave me some water... warm, smelling of kettle scale... and I saw a glossy black sleeve, gold buttons inlaid with coat-of-arms, the snow-white edge of a shirt: he was clean and groomed. After drinking, I took a look at him with relaxed, sleep-gummed eyes.

"What time is it?"

"Can't sleep?" He solemnly waved a dog-eared newspaper. "The visit! It's begun!" And he shook his head. "I can hardly believe it! There've been many negotiations... a speech at the Supreme Soviet... The guests' agenda includes a visit to the archaeological digs of the ancient Russian town of Svetloyar, and their participation in the opening of the monument at the source of the river Don. The authentic Russia is rising again."

"That's what they've written?"

"Yes!" He drew a finger over some marked-out lines. "To-morrow... Tomorrow... The first plane by the evening... two of them in total... that's it... it'll all be steaming ahead. And we are absolutely ready. We can still smell a bit of the burning," he said with a smirk, "but we'll let some air in! I've not come on any business... just to see you. The scope of my concerns, you'll understand, is quite different now... a different level of power." He brought his hand under my nose. "Tomorrow they'll shake this hand. It's the height of my career... I've heard in passing that you wanted to confess, eh? Good for you. These days the Russians are divided between patriots and non-patriots. You and I are patriots!"

"You won't make it."

"I will," Klinsky whispered gently, squeezing on my shoulder. "My dear friend... there are witnesses... fingerprints... evidence... and the capture... was caught on video. And now the confession. The people who are coming down here aren't like us. They don't talk much. You see, they've got their own problems... very serious ones... they think nobody sees through them, and we'll convince them that they can see through us perfectly well. They'll be fascinated... you'll see how their mouths will water. We're nothing compared to them. We stumbled into all this by accident. A stroke of luck! But they'll dig up loads of stuff, and make a whole palace out of it! When I was in Moscow for a brush-up course, they showed us a memory-aid tool. They help people to remember. Even if it's not you personally but someone else who's describing a plan in a pub, at a neighbouring table, it'll stick to your memory... they'll help you remember it! And all the details will coincide exactly!... So, there you go!... They'll gnaw away at you... and you'll squeal! Gnaw!... Squeal!... You'll be left in shreds!" He impatiently leafed through the newspaper.

"But they'll ask: why?"

"How d'you mean?"

"What reason shall we give for our..."

"Huh! How should I know? That's what the investigation is for. They'll sort it out! Maybe Ivan Trofimovich refused to accept the democratization process... Maybe you didn't agree at first, but Sviridov started threatening you... so you decided to yield... It's all in your hands. Show them here... I'll take off the cuffs. Damn... I could never learn how to do this... As a sign of trust.... I'm taking a risk... very little is known about your case... Maybe your documents are forged... maybe you've been trained abroad... I'll give this a bit more thought. OK, quiet... Stand up!... No, I was only joking. Just wanted to check. But why are you shaking? Are you cold?" He gave a few orders, and

Konstantin was led out. They wiped my chin, the bunk and the floor with a cloth… I threw up again.

"You'd better sleep. Tea and toast. Are they coming to give you injections?… Your colleague's flown off the handle. By the way, he's also willing to help the investigation. So that may cause a little bit of competition between you. No no, don't be ashamed… That's not so easy… The court will examine everything. And will take into account who's more cooperative and sincere. Your friend's demanding that you're sent for treatment… he's got quite out of hand. They gave him an injection, now he's asleep. The doctors think there's nothing wrong with you… just some intestinal disorder and the resulting weakness. I've got it too. But it affects me in the opposite way… We'll get the temperature down. Can you see me dis-tinct-ly? Why are you so nervous?"

"I'll tell everything. Whatever is requested."

"Not 'whatever is requested'," Klinsky said in a loathing tone. "What does 'whatever is requested' mean? The truth! Why are you turning red? Why are you sweating?"

"Send us… to Moscow… I'll confess…"

"So, what will you confess?"

"The truth."

"Well, the truth… truth. What is the truth?" Then he furiously bellowed: "What are you proposing to confess?! Do you hear me? The name of the person you were going to assassinate tomorrow?… The fact that you bought weapons and organized a conspiracy?"

"Him."

"Who's 'Him'?" he said, in a barely audible voice. "Say it in so many words: the legitimate President of Russia." He listened attentively, as if the words were echoing around him. He wiped his hands and drew closer to me. "So you really wanted to kill him?"

"Yes."

"Yes." He repeated in a different tone. "Yes... well, this is driving me mad... An assassination attempt. When we figured out your plans and began to work out... from the very beginning I... You're really driving me mad... My friend, you see, there are some actions that don't translate into Russian... They make sense in English... and every word seems to have a perfect correspondent... but if you put the words together... it's gibberish, gibberish! Nonsense. Lies. A cock-and-bull story. Kill the president! On what planet do you live? My friend," his voice became almost inaudible, "do you want me to believe you that you consider him..." he whispered into my ear, "still alive? Oh no... don't think I'm one of those old-guard communists... one of those haranguers who act on hearsay. I've read... studied. Been around. And any progressive ideas that were put into print have reached us here. I've got my notebooks... I can show them to you. I copied whole passages. I admit it's an important matter. People – including us – are used to having something up there. But to contemplate murder... The masses never think at all. A train chops off a kid's legs or a cripple is born... and people apply for support – housing support for example – and when they're writing they believe there's someone there. But there are more daring people. Like me. I always doubted. I need evidence." He raised a finger. "Who's seen him? They show him on TV? Well, they show lots of stuff on TV. It's easy for them... There's a lighted window in the Kremlin? Oh yeah... They leave a light on even in latrines! Sure, you'll say, but what about all those things people have seen? Do you know these people by any chance? I don't either. Those who see too much always disappear somewhere... they're taken away to Moscow... He can make an appearance, yes, but how can you kill him? And how did it come into your head? This is a cross-examination – answer!"

"For the money they promised us."

Klinsky bent over and put his hand to his mouth, holding back laughter. "I can't see through you, can't figure you out. Well... So what next? You'll run away?" He sagged and burst out with raucous laughter, because I'd nodded my head.

"To another country."

"Which one?" And he rolled off into hysterical laughter again. He just couldn't hold it back. "Just don't tell me that... just don't tell me..." He waved me away, then snapped ferociously: "What moron would believe you? Who are you trying to cheat?"

"So you are not letting us go?"

"Eventually... dunno. Hope so. You disgust me... it's a real shame... that I have to deal with such scum... I despise those who are not prepared to endure for someone else's idea."

"I'll be able to convince them."

"No. You're not the sort. Those you could have convinced are no longer with us. Well... what?"

"Well then... release us."

"That's typical Moscow stupidity. I told you: the fist cannot unclench. You think I can just tell them and they'll release you? Huh. I'd be locked up with you straight away. Let this take its own course. I'm off."

Klinsky rolled up his paper and waved it as a sign of farewell. He got up in his leather shoes and glanced at his watch as if down a well.

"I'm going. Yes?"

"Just wanted to ask. In the car... wasn't there any money?"

"Money for what? Comrade soldier, let me out. Thanks. Stand over there." He pushed his head between the bars: "Well then? You know, incredible escapes do take place... particularly with our provincial lack of discipline. But there's no way to stop this now... on the other hand, nothing's been established yet... Speak

307

up: I can't come running to you for every word. Louder! So, is that a yes? Or you'll think about it? Well... there's no time for you to think it over... No? And tomorrow... Moscow, the hospital... the cemetery. I'm joking. Yes? OK then."

"I didn't say anything."

"You don't love Russia."

Had he said all that a long time ago? I collapsed into the past: only the events of the morning, of the day, kept me going... If we didn't shoot, they would... someone would... but they'd arrest us all the same. Perhaps Grisha had not been able to find a tractor... The rats... this will teach you a lesson – it's payback time. No. I should try to protect myself while I still have my wits about me... and I do! This is not the time to lie down.

The guard brought a pink blanket with a couple of white stripes, and threw it onto the neighbouring bunk. He wanted to cover me at first, but I made a gesture – not now, later. When the guard reached the corner and became inaudible, I stretched my arm and slowly rolled up the blanket, leaving my hand on it so that it wouldn't unfurl.

I woke up lying down, and looked at my hand: it was still holding the blanket. As I tried to sit up and lowered my legs, a stream of liquid immediately gushed from my mouth onto the stone floor. With one hand I supported my burning forehead, with the other the rolled-up blanket. I strained my mouth, trying to let out the same sound... for what seemed ages.

I heard a ringing noise – was it the telephone, an alarm... or the doorbell? Was it throughout the entire basement? It was punctuated by some shouts... WAS THAT IT? I grabbed the blanket under my arm and, pressing my shoulders against the wall, started to make my way towards the table. Some people ran along the corridor calling to each other. I looked at my feet each time I managed to open my eyes... nothing.

Clutching at the table – the floor was clear – I rested a bit. Upstairs a door was thrown open, and a mild winter wind blew evenly down the corridors. I turned round and climbed the table backwards. I struggled to draw my legs up but finally my back touched the wall and my knees touched the chin. I raised my collar and checked the buttons up to my throat. There were shouts all the time. I stopped opening my eyes at each shout – I was trying to save my energies. They'd see my feet if they were to get at me. I spread the blanket over my knees and tucked the lower edge under my feet. I took off my hat: I'd decided in advance to cover my face with it, the most vital part. I tried to untie the laces on the hat, but couldn't manage the knot... I tried to loosen it with my teeth, but then, with a shudder, I turned to the wall and poured out a dribble of vomit. I sat there like that for a long time, but I knew I had to hurry. When I managed to turn round again, I didn't bother with the hat... I just pulled it down... but the hat covered only one ear, slantwise. I pulled my hands into my sleeves and unrolled the blanket up to my chin... There were noises – someone was running along the corridor... they still hadn't understood. I had done everything: it only remained to hide my hands and cover my face with the hat.

The scratches on my wrists had not healed. It was evening, and the festivities were about to begin. Some people were approaching at a run. It wasn't too frightening. Actually, it was. I was tired of listening and looking... I would only look. Soundlessly, as if underwater, a bunch of people in overcoats crowded in the door frame, carrying sticks on their shoulders. The door let them all in, and not one of them looked under his feet. Had they come to my rescue? From the sticks hung a green tarpaulin, and they unfurled a stretcher. Outside the door, the officer in charge was fussing more than the others: he was the only one waving his arms. They'd screwed up everything – they wouldn't be able to carry me when… I opened my eyes again: Vic was now saying something to me, parting his lips at a measured pace, his mouth flicking before my nose, sliding over the moist accumulation of his teeth… don't touch me… he was prodding my shoulder in time with his words. I must save my hat, they'll drop me on the floor when… Leave me alone… First they tore my hands away from my aching stomach, then they loaded me in a sitting position, like a living god, onto the stretcher. They asked me to lie down… forced me to… and down I lay, clutching at my belly again, now that they allowed it. I still had my hat with me.

They carried me across the snow. Was it evening? Vic was hurrying the others, striding on with a dry rustling noise. I felt better… I was in good hands. The soldiers had broken into a run… good… I'd be saved. We crossed one cordon after another, with soldiers at every step, calling out the password in advance… riding a train would have been just as good, but a bit warmer, and the carriage attendant would have a medicine cabinet. My pain had frozen.

We must have reached some people. They slowed down and lowered me onto the floor – how could they put me down! With a slow, laborious movement, I moved my hat over my face and put my hands into my pockets, but they whipped my hat away and put someone's overcoat under my head.

Boots, boots and boots everywhere – quite a lot of footwear… What if they leave me here?

"Lift!"

I raised myself on my elbows: it turned out we were on the square not far from the sanatorium… there's the road climbing up the hill. There were a couple of dozen officers and civilians, with stern faces… locals… I'd seen many of them before. They were all gazing at one particular spot in the snow… the wind unfurled the frozen banners, and they fluttered overhead, scattering snow dust which seemed to pour down with the sound of a sprinting mouse... would they leave me there? They are coming... lie back.

Someone was being dragged along at a run – it was Oldie... he was utterly exhausted and made hawking noises as he spat and held on to one side. I was so happy... we were together again! He hardly glanced at me in response... his face seemed to be black and blue, and he kept rubbing one eye. He was standing up awkwardly, touching himself in various places. Klinsky came darting out of nowhere in a wide-open fur coat. He was shouting and waving a watch – not in a particularly threatening manner – and explaining something in haste... maybe where they should go? He dragged Oldie in front of his retinue and pointed at the spot in the snow that everybody was staring at. Oldie stood stock still, looked for a long time, his face expressionless as if he was gazing at a wall, then he touched his eye again and examined his hand. He sank on his knees and leant on his hands, almost touching the snow with his beard.

They suddenly lifted and turned round my stretcher, and as they did so I saw the massive column of the hotel, and recalled what seemed now a distant past and everything that was associated with it. Soon they put down the stretcher again... I looked round for Oldie, but he had been pushed back.

Squatting opposite me was Klinsky, with a crazed look on his face and a heavy collar like a yoke round his neck; behind him were Vic, Baranov and other shoulder-strapped and capped officers.

"Just look!" Klinsky was shouting, "This is some kind of provocation! What's all this about?! What's going on?!" He jabbed and jabbed into the snow with his gloved hand.

Ah, they'd brought me to the place where they'd led Oldie. They wanted me to look too? Should I also get on my knees?

311

"Look at this, please," Vic said, stooping over. "As a scientist. By way of consultation. We'll pay you a separate fee. What does it mean when there are so many worms?"

Right alongside the stretcher crawled thin white worms, interweaving with one another like currents of water and rising in waves as they slithered on top of one another... a huge number, a pathway about seven foot wide. If I hadn't known it was worms, I'd have thought the snow was streaming. The worms were swarming alongside black footmarks... that meant somebody had tried to stamp on them... it was a *taxis,* a very powerful... a massive *taxis.* I stretched out my hand to pick one up, but my hand froze into a contorted lump and I couldn't latch on to a single one.

"What do you want?" Klinsky was whispering animatedly. "Get a move on, if you can!"

I pointed my arm at the *taxis* and detached one finger from the rest... one. Klinsky prodded into the maggots with revulsion and tossed one into my hand squeamishly, as if handling snot. I cupped my hand and looked at what was tickling my palm – yes, I thought so... fly larvae. A large mass of larvae was spawning somewhere. I emptied my hand. Fine. Is that all? But for some reason they were still holding me up and not allowing me to lie down.

"What's all this? We're supposed to meet the guests – where are all these maggots from?"

"That's a *taxis.*"

"A *taxis?*"

"The other one also said *taxis,*" Vic whispered to Klinsky, who'd fallen silent in perplexity. "What does that mean? Where are so many maggots coming from? And what can we do?"

I screwed up my eyes so as not to let out any vomit and drew my knees up towards myself.

312

"Let him lie down... he wants to lie down! Damn! Bring the other one here, quick! And get a doctor for this one, for Heaven's sake. Ah, there you are. Vladimir Stepanovich. Nice to see you again. I'm Governor Klinsky... yes, I started two days ago, and look at all this mess. Who's done this to you? Did they beat you? O Lord, you've got to look after everything... I'll find out who's done it. They must have got carried away... but even so, that's no good. Vladimir Stepanovich, I understand your situation, you're under investigation and so on, but – if only by way of advice – these strange worms, in such quantities... there's never been anything like this before. And this coincides exactly with the big event... it looks like sabotage. Where are they from? What do you think?"

"I told you... it's a *taxis*."

"Sure. And your colleague said the same. But... we just don't know what it is..."

"Give me a scarf."

"Rudenko, give him your scarf!... Here it is."

"Cover my colleague's respiratory tracts."

A shaggy cloth fell on my face... I'd have preferred my hat.

"I'd advise all of you to screen your noses and mouths. And don't stay here too long... they can affect the mucous membranes. You may lose your sight..."

"What's this all about?"

"Let's get going, get the stretcher, I'll tell you on the way." And they carried me off. "This *taxis* is a powerful spawning of a certain kind of pathogenic worms. They are used as a biological weapon for infecting a targeted region. It can happen that they spread over a comparatively large area by themselves, most often in Central Asia, under poor epidemiological conditions, where there are abandoned houses, animal corpses, including rodents, or an area that's been infected in the past. But where did you get them from? This is only the second time in my life that I've seen such a thing. The first time was in Tajikistan. What else… I think that's all."

"Vladimir Stepanovich, my friend, what can we do now?"

"Nothing. In fact, there's a latent period before they spawn… then you can still do something… but now, just see how many of them there are… a million, perhaps!"

They were silent for a minute, then Oldie added with a cracking voice:

"They're already on the move. They've already issued their poison… they've got together and are now heading to the place of pupation. The worms themselves are no longer harmful. But the area's been poisoned, around the square… Well, perhaps the nearest houses too… you can't say for sure.

They stopped and put the stretcher down on the snow. The scarf fell from my face. They were all gathered around Oldie, sticking their noses into gloves, handkerchiefs and collars.

Oldie approached and sat down on the edge of the stretcher. I reached out for my hat, but he pushed my hand away. He kneaded some snow in his hands and inspected it.

"Never heard of these maggots," Klinsky said with a smirk, looking at his people for support.

"It's only the second time I've seen them myself. Your health service should know. Phone Moscow, the Institute of Parasitology. Is that all? Can we go inside?"

"What have we got to do?" asked Vic.

"Major Gubin," Klinsky interrupted him, "allow me to take care of it myself somehow. Do you mean all this stuff here… is something dangerous? Yes?"

"Not really, because this poison has a short period of decay. It'll be clear after a week… you should just keep the people away and sprinkle the area within a mile radius once a day. I'm telling you all this off the top of my head... but it's all in the civil-defence manual." Oldie squeezed my wrist painfully. "Fancy seeing a *taxis* in this place..."

Klinsky growled an inaudible oath as he paced back and forth, stooping as if his coat was crushing him.

"How much time do we have?"

"In half an hour they'll be taking off," replied a soldier who was listening to his walkie-talkie.

"And if we don't do all of this?"

"Well, that's up to you." Oldie shrugged. "Not our problem. Nothing terrible will happen. Within two weeks the poison will evaporate. You can wash it out simply with water."

"And what'll happen to the people?" Vic enquired, as the other officers thronged behind his back.

"Mild indisposition, headache, fainting fits... fainting more than anything else. The victims will be one in a hundred, roughly speaking. But not necessarily... in Tajikistan, I remember, there were twenty-six deaths every thousand people. True, the weather's drier over there, and they'd already begun an evacuation. Nobody can say exactly... Just let them take us away. It'll be better for him to get inside. Look, we are losing him fast – quick!"

Klinsky was running up and down, like a dog on a chain, waving his hands as he turned. He shoved Oldie in the shoulder.

"You know, of course, how to help us... But you're not going to help us for nothing, eh?" And he burst into a malevolent cackle. "Who should we believe? Who should we listen to? Shall we carry on with everything as before? Silence! To your positions, attend to my orders. Look at him! He's dictating his terms! These people are murderers... they'll go to any length now. Yes? Can you help? Stand up!"

Oldie raised his eyes to him and said in a trembling voice:

"I can. But I won't help you, you bastard. If you get it in the neck, we'll be only too glad. I'm sorry for the people, though. But it's your fault."

"Comrade Lieutenant-Colonel," Vic implored, "Let me talk to them!"

"Silence! Take them away. It's all clear now. Let's move on. How can we stop? How can we call things off?" Klinsky screeched, almost leaping up in the air. "To your positions!"

Vic took two long strides towards the stretcher.

"Vladimir Stepanovich, I implore you. I really respect your expertise... forgive me, forgive us... You, you're not the kind of person you want to appear... I know what you really are. You know our situation inside out now... how important this is for Svetloyar, for the country. The first plane is taking off. Tomorrow on this square there will be... tens of thousands... So much has been done... Don't do it for me. You probably detest me... that's the way it's turned out... we've fallen out... But do it for the people. Don't take it away from us... We have wronged you, but we can put things right..."

"Major Gubin!" roared Klinsky. "I'm warning you!"

"Just tell us: is there any way... that in time... We've got the manpower, but we lack the knowledge..."

"Look at the density of the shell." Oldie showed a crushed maggot in his palm. "It's been an hour since it emptied itself, what with the snow and the damp..."

"I forbid any negotiations with criminals! Take them away! Major Gubin, do you hear me?"

"Is it impossible, then?"

"In theory there's still half an hour. If you sprinkle everything right away. It requires a special solution. But you have to be real quick, Vic."

"What do we need?"

Klinsky grabbed a walkie-talkie from the nearby chap.

"Car and convoy." As he waited for the distant sound of a wailing motor, he thrust his hands into his pockets and held his mouth open, before saying: "Well then, Victor... Comrades, we all know the services Major Gubin has rendered... they have been, certainly... but I, unfortunately, must... During the course of our investigation, during the course of our interrogation of certain army officers detained by us and known to you... for example we cross-examined Sviridov... some information emerged incriminating even Major Gubin..."

Biting his lips, Vic cast a wan gaze at the soldiers leaping out of the approaching jeep. Their commanding officer swivelled his head enquiringly and, having spotted Klinsky, raised his hand to his cap.

"I'm never inclined... and it's not in my code of behaviour... to give credence to the first... Far from it. But the situation requires reliability. Firmness, comrades. Yes: by the power invested in me, Major Gubin is suspended from service and, pending investigation, will spend... Captain!" Klinsky jerked his lacquered head towards Vic. "And I'd say it's time, for us, to get off to the airport. To the airfield."

The captain barked his orders, of which not a word could be made out. But the soldiers seemed to understand and surrounded Vic, taking their sub-machine guns from their shoulders.

"We'll let you go when it's over. In a week," he promised Oldie from behind the row of red-shoulder-strapped officers.

"No!" Oldie rasped out, squeezing my hand. "By the very next train. And our fee must be paid in full. We won't say anything to anyone."

"The next train is tomorrow at noon. You'll keep quiet?"

"Sure. But... the money in full."

"Captain, what's the matter?"

"Is it a deal then?"

"Give me your word you won't deceive us."

Vic pondered for a moment as the soldiers took him under his arms, then knitted his brows and gave an awkward nod.

"I promise."

"Everybody here must promise that we'll leave by the first train, with the money we've earned. And we'll keep quiet."

Vic faltered as if he'd bumped chest first into some wire. The soldiers wrung his arms back. He turned to them and hissed:

"That's enough!"

"That's enough, Captain," one of the commanding officers echoed.

The captain staggered, as if stunned, and as he barked new orders just as loudly and incomprehensibly as before, the soldiers released their hands. Vic picked up his cap and lifted it into its proper place, glanced at his watch and, with some hesitation, stepped over to Klinsky. Klinsky shook his head and smirked, baring his teeth in a malevolent grin. He assumed a dignified air and straightened up, his fur coat adding to his stature.

"You? What? What? And?…" he mumbled.

"Comrade Lieutenant-Colonel. The situation has changed… and we're obliged… we are now obliged… we can't remain indifferent. It is my duty to inform you… that a provisional body has been set up to conduct the festivities. Its command has been entrusted to me. I'm placing you under arrest. For the poor health conditions…"

"Be reasonable," Klinsky said under his breath, trying to persuade him, so that not everyone could hear. "You, you're not a vital pawn in all this…"

"Captain. You know what to do, under the circumstances." Vic waved his arm feebly.

The officers, who were already in formation, filed towards Oldie and, taking off their caps as they approached, said solemnly with a slight bow:

"I promise."

"I promise."

"I promise."

Oldie nodded as if to say "Yes, fine, thanks", without getting up from the stretcher or releasing the grip of his hand. With each promise he raised his head less, and in the end he didn't raise it at all.

"They'll swallow you up too," said Klinsky, rustling up to Vic. "Be reasonable." And he fell in the soldiers' clutches. "Tell them to leave me alone! Get away! Obey my orders! Let me speak! Just look over here!" They dragged him to the jeep and, after an especially violent push, he fell silent, although he continued to stare at Vic without tearing his gaze away once. Vic turned to Oldie with a lumbering movement, as if he were carrying a burden.

"Two cisterns of hot water… One barrel of chloric acid…" Oldie began, and after each direction an officer ran off to one side. "Two sacks of table salt… Eight packets of washing powder… A water sprinkler." Oldie was choosing what to allocate to whom. "Two litres of spirit… Eight men… An ambulance." When Vic alone was left, Oldie concluded: "That's it."

"Now… do you think we'll manage? Do we have time? The main thing is… all should be done in a simple, reliable way." Gubin looked around in confusion as the officers ran off on their errands, cars drove up to them and shadows dashed about in the crackling light of the lamps.

In the meantime, I remained flat with my legs drawn up, slightly inclined to one side, where the snow had still not absorbed the stains of my vomit. Oldie raised his collar and muttered furtively, glancing around with bruised, resentful eyes:

"D'you want to have a laugh? Do you know where the worms are spawning from? From the flowerbed. I just remembered: that's where we buried that piece of ham with the rat they'd sent us... It's teeming with worms there now. I thought some dog had been buried there. It's usually caused by a dog... We were lucky. Anyway... we've outplayed them." Oldie scooped a handful of snow, covered his swollen eyelid with it and sat like that for a while. Holding the lump of snow in one hand, with the other he continued to press my hands.

As he stood up to see where some new cars were coming from, Oldie staggered against the stretcher and involuntarily bent down. He touched my shoulder with the tips of his fingers, and immediately drew them back. He froze over the stretcher, his arms hanging down, blinking painfully with his swollen eye, then he took the hat from under the edge of the stretcher, spread it over his fist and covered my face with it.

17

D-Day

There was total silence between the buildings; above each entrance a lamp was blazing. The trampled-down pathway led to a black, snowless patch, where hot-water pipes were concealed beneath the earth and the mud had a scent of spring. The pathway continued on the other side.

A crate was burning on an iron plate, and soldiers were warming themselves, one playing an accordion with the apathetic face of a blind man. The accordion seemed to fold and unfold by itself in his hands. He was playing without any continuity, trying various tunes from the middle and then giving up. His fingers would roam in vain over the keyboard as he tried to remember the tune, but he'd soon lose patience. I looked at the burning boards, which seemed covered with scarlet scales. The warm air reached out to me too. Sleep crept over me.

The player gave up trying any more songs.

"I didn't recognize you," he said, becoming animated.

And I didn't recognize Sviridov either, kitted out as he was in a new police sheepskin coat, his face illuminated by the bonfire. The bridge of his nose and his eyes were linked by a swollen bruise with crimson rims; one of his cheeks displayed a round lump the size of a walnut; there were some scratches by the corner of his lips, and from there red stripes ran down to his neck.

"It's nothing. It's all for the sake of our Motherland… We were called to duty and conducted ourselves with honour. It'll all be reckoned."

We were trying to get into the school building. Headquarters was there, on the two upper floors, curtained off in black. But the school was wrapped in waves of barbed wire. Before the gates they'd put up two concrete slabs as a shelter, with a few soldiers walking along the fence. They wouldn't answer when we tried to ask questions. Sviridov didn't find anybody he knew: he suspected Gubin was guarded by regional police cadets dressed up as soldiers.

On inspecting our documents they admitted us only into the lobby, crammed with three-tiered bunks, and there Sviridov managed to obtain two bowls of millet soup. Then he noticed Baranov heading upstairs, and persuaded the chap on duty that he knew Baranov and needed to see him on some business. This was reported to Baranov; he acknowledged us and took us with him through three checkpoints. When we reached the final one, on a staircase, I noticed a machine gun.

In front of the iron-cased door leading inside, we were sounded out by some special kind of machine, which reminded me of a telephone receiver. They took Baranov's keys, walkie-talkie and pistol, and from Sviridov two spoons and a lighter. Then two men searched us by hand and ordered us to wait.

We waited on a brown bench. Nobody else came up the stairs. From down below a jingling noise reached us, then voices… they were reading out the names of the guard replacements, repeating one surname three times with a different accent. From beyond the iron door not a single sound came.

After a while the door opened. There was no light in the corridor. On every other window sill there were gun slots, made out of sandbags. Underneath each one, head tucked up in an overcoat, a man was sleeping. We went along on tiptoe.

The entrance into the reception room was barred by another iron door. They placed us in front of a spy hole, and the escort shone a lamp on each of us. The door swung open and then back to its place after us, with a grating of bolts.

A barefoot chap in an unbuttoned shirt, who had evidently just woken up, shook a finger at us – quiet! For a long time, he kept his ear strained to hear any sound coming from the studded office door and, the instant he picked something up, he waved frantically to indicate "Get in now!", as if the door was not under his control, and it was important to catch the moment.

Vic was sitting in a corner, barricaded in by safes. Dressed in a white shirt with a loosened tie, he was scrutinizing a white telephone that had been moved forwards from the rest.

There were no black curtains on the windows here, but thick glass screens, against which leant the massive puppets used by the fighters for their training. One of the puppets was wearing a general's cap with golden leaves. Two more puppets were sitting on the floor, behind Gubin's back, which on closer inspection turned out to be two motionless guards.

"So much light," Sviridov said, screwing up his eyes, as we sat down.

Vic's gaze was fixed on the state emblem on the telephone dial. He kept picking at it from time to time with his nail.

"Sorry to keep you waiting, Baranov. I had visitors."

I thought: we've not seen a single soul.

"Victor Alexeich," Baranov began, with a rich fruity voice, which was immediately lowered down, "the troops are concentrated in one area. The regional command have kindly earmarked two more battalions... they're approaching. In about an hour's time we'll deploy all those who are meant to greet the dignitaries: people on the streets, on the balconies, accidental passers-by, those celebrating the opening of the monument, visitors to the archaeological digs... there, I would have thought, three thousand will be more than enough. The rest will be attending the ceremony at the hotel."

"What about now?"

"We'll get everybody dressed up and ready to repeat their words. We'll give them bouquets and take them to their positions. The troops have received their orders. The untrained population is under surveillance – we're arranging a live television broadcast for them."

"Have you got enough women?"

"We're dressing everybody in winter clothes and... they look all the same from outside, Victor Alexeich, especially from a distance. We'll dole out headkerchiefs to our soldiers... that'll be OK. Victor Alexeich..."

"What?"

"Has the plane landed?"

"The second one's landed as well. And the TV crew... another three hundred men." Vic sent the guards away: "Go and stretch your legs." He gave up scratching at the telephone and smiled at Baranov. "So, you're saying I've got too many guards?"

"I didn't say anything. Nonsense. I said nothing like that to you... I've been on your side since..."

"But did it occur to you?"

"Course not! I swear on my mother's heart! Who's been telling you this?"

"Well then... Would you like to... to sit in my place?" Vic roared with laughter, his eyes gawping. "Not quite yet... get a move on, all right?"

"Victor Alexeich!"

"That's what you're saying..."

"Oh come on!" Baranov said, almost in tears. "I've been on your side from the very beginning. Why are you saying this?"

"He's not coming." Vic yawned and moved the white phone back with the others… "Change of programme. It's already in the Moscow evening papers. What shall we do now…" Gubin's face gave way to a crooked grin. "Try to think… but quick."

"But the planes?" asked Baranov, stupefied. "Have they gone back?"

"Have you seen them? What planes?"

There was a long pause, as Vic scrutinized Baranov's face. Sviridov covered his ears with his hands.

"Well well… that's enough," Vic finally said, knitting his brows. "What shall we tell the people?"

"But what *can* we say to the people?" Sviridov had taken his hands off his head.

"What? What do you mean 'what'? The truth, of course, right?"

"The truth. Right. Of course."

"Well, with the right kind of speech…" Baranov suggested, but Sviridov retorted with a snort:

"Why, where have you heard the wrong kind of speeches?"

Gubin burst into laughter, jumped up and started pacing back and forth inside the space formed by the safes.

"Who told you I'm not joking?" he said, seizing Baranov's shoulders. "Maybe I just wanted to see how you reacted…"

Baranov hurled himself at the exit and jerked at the door, while Vic was roaring with laughter.

"Open up!… Bastard!…"

"Siddown, man…" Vic said, in a cheerful tone. "It *is* a joke, in fact… He really isn't coming. It's purely and simply… a ridiculous thing now. But I wouldn't know how to explain this properly. Some ridiculous things are so ridiculous that they're hard to describe. I sit here and think: OK, I'll make an announcement… but they won't believe anything like that… How can I prove it?

The newspaper? They print papers down here as well... They'll think I'm putting them to the test. You see how ridiculous this is? First I thought: to hell with it – tomorrow they'll see he's not coming. And then I realized: no, they won't believe it. They'll think he really has come... and that for some reason I had to show he hasn't. There's nothing I can do... I mean, there's only one thing left... We already have a good track record at this kind of thing. Believe you me: he is really not coming."

Baranov let the door go, found the nearest chair with his behind and closed his eyes.

"I asked them to send us someone... even if it's just the Minister of Culture. But he's in Germany. The minute they changed their mind about coming, I can't get anyone on the phone. So, what shall we do now?"

"Say nothing to anyone," Baranov said. "Jam the radio. But it really is awful. You can take offence or even dismiss me, if you want, but in a situation like this, if I were in your shoes, I'd release all our people. What's the point of holding them now? We should regroup and do some more thinking..."

"And what about Ivan Trofimovich?" chipped in Sviridov. Everybody gazed at him in amazement. "I'm actually glad. Something like this was bound to happen in the end... Once we've set off to battle, they'll try and tempt us to the end. And in the end, we'll have a clear vision that it has all ended in disaster. Our holy duty is to overcome all this with one last exploit. I take the responsibility on myself... And I am granting a pardon: release all detained people. Secondly, and most importantly: you don't know what to do with the people." Sviridov winked. "But I know the Russian people! You need to break their mood, and they'll forget everything..."

"How?"

"Assemble everybody... a Thanksgiving Service on the square... and announce that next Tuesday is the Day of Happiness."

"But what's meant to happen on Tuesday?" Baranov said, taken aback.

"First, there's still time before Tuesday." Sviridov swept his gaze over everyone. "And secondly, on Tuesday we will introduce Happiness. You see, if it wasn't all lies," he whispered slyly, "it'd be precisely what was in our original plan... so why should we be ashamed of it?"

"Thank you," Vic grunted, casting an eloquent glance at Baranov. "Sviridov, off you go on sick leave. Ten days at the digs. And make yourself scarce, or I'll dismiss you without a pension..." Then he bellowed: "Just get the hell out of here!..."

That very night we drove out to the digs. They'd given us a lorry, which was also carrying bread and water to the archaeologists.

"Look!" Sviridov growled. "They still haven't raised the mast!"

"Comrade warrant officer," gasped a bloke I had seen the last time I was there. "We thought that..."

"Prokhorov, it'll soon be dawn... where's the mast?"

"We're still drilling."

"What do you mean 'still drilling'? You haven't finished yet? Where's the mast? What shall we fix the tent on? What if it gets warm or starts raining?"

Down below, the drill's engine fell silent. Workmen and guards had gathered round the drill – had they been working through the entire night? Sviridov went down, skirted the pond of healing water, now covered with ice, and climbed onto a box.

"By morning the mast must be standing! And the tent must be set up... it's already been painted. Otherwise... you've dug up all these treasures and won't be able to preserve them. What will the guests think? Is Yelena Fyodorovna there? OK. What?"

"They've been trying."

"What do you mean 'been trying"… it's five-forty! They've been trying for three days and the mast's not up?"

"We couldn't bore deeper."

"What? You couldn't bore five metres?" Sviridov spat in a fit of temper.

"It's all stone down there. We couldn't find a good place. We tried boring over the entire area… nothing but granite. Here," Prokhorov kicked a light-coloured stone trough, green with moss. "We bore and bump… we pull it out… it's got an inscription. It's like that everywhere. We're afraid to drill… what if we wreck the whole thing?"

"What granite? What do you mean 'everywhere'?" Sviridov threw his arms wide. "Bring the light here."

The trough was reminiscent of a coffin. I could see straight away that it had been carved by hand: along the edges of its flat surface were straight, even grooves, knotting together at the corners to form a tresslike pattern. There was a hole where the drill had made contact, but the coffin itself had not been cracked.

"Yelena Fyodorovna…" said Sviridov as the archaeologist approached. "What's all this here?… What's this?"

"Move away from the light… I can't see… Mmm… 'Year 7115, February the twenty-third… to the memory of the Most Holy Martyr St Polikarp Zmirsky, and the prince of the capital city, Yury Meshchera, who perished in the service of his state and was buried on the twenty-seventh day of the same month… and to the memory of the Most Holy Confessor Prokofy…'"

"Are there any more of these?" Sviridov asked.

"Right the way through," Prokhorov said. "Wherever we tried, we dug one up."

Sviridov gloomily fixed his eyes on the stone coffins, bigger and smaller ones, scattered around in various positions all over the digs, then took a deep breath and said feebly:

"Well, just read this one…"

"'In the year 6814 perished God's servant prince and monk Isaiah Petrov…'"

"And what's written here?"

"'Anastasia Bakhteryarova, daughter of…'"

"Damn. What about there? And there?"

"'Scrivener Barnyshlev who departed this life… Avram Gregorevich Ogin-Pleshcheyev.' And this one… can't make it out. 'Prince Kleshnin. Monk Andrey. Nun Yelena, née Potemkina, passed away from this world in peace. Yelizaveta Zubacheva. Zasyokin. Bishop Pafnuty Krutitsky. Monk Grigory. If God be with us, who can be against us…'"

"Well then, Prokhorov, you've dug them all out… do you reckon there are more of them?"

"There seems to be no earth at all beneath our feet… The clay's only a few inches deep. Directly underneath, there's these stones wherever you drill. We take them out and there's another one below. In one place we decided to keep taking them all out till we got to the end, but we removed six of them and there were still more. It's hard work to take them out by hand… you'd need to dig round… you'd need a crane. And they're so tightly packed… There's just a few bones between them." Prokhorov pointed to a heap behind him. "I've given orders to gather up this stuff, just in case. Now you find a coin, now a buckle, now a cross…"

"Well, guys," Sviridov blurted out, "I suggest we bury the damn coffins back again. Bring the clay over and smooth it down flat… it'll be for another time!"

"But the bones?"

"Smash them to pieces and scatter them over an open field. Prokhorov, issue the orders! Yelena Fyodorovna, by eleven there'll be folk dancers, singers…. they'll be busing in the locals. Our main concern is with the rostrum, the scaffolding and the lamps, in case they get to us late after the celebrations in town. Well? What is it, Kostromin?"

"Shouldn't we, just for the sake of history, copy out the epitaphs and leave some bones... over there there's also some clothes and rags."

"For history?" Sviridov said, his face twisted in a grimace. "Oh shut up. I know what kind of history we need around here. Look." He pointed his finger to the sky. "It's going to rain soon. Go and bury everything. Take some crowbars: you won't be able to lift them by hand. It's raining! It's raining!"

As the rain began to pelt down, a team of workers hooked the crowbars under the coffins and rolled them down towards the pits. The bars kept sticking in the mud, so they brought birch blocks to be wedged under the coffins.

A separate team was putting skulls and bones into buckets and passing them upwards in a line, holding on to a stretched-out rope, as Sviridov issued loud commands.

After a while, the warrant officer gave the order to crack the ice on the pool and poke the bottom with a stick: it was soft. They thrust a pointed stake into the water and rammed it in with a sledgehammer... here it goes!... no stones?... it gives in!

From the pool they dug narrow channels and pushed the water along with their shovels, throwing out bluish slivers of ice. Then the drill was manoeuvred down to the drained bottom, its supports were spread out and its engine tested.

Above the digs, the sky was darkening and the rain dropped heavily, getting stronger and brisker at every blast. People wanted to wait it out, but Sviridov shouted that there was no time, and pressed down a lever with a red ball on top. The drill plunged with ease into the mud, and with a hollow sound it moved shakily into the depths. Then the lever was turned upwards to clear out the hole, and the drill jerked back, leaping out with a slurping noise and hurling around the dark mud that had stuck around it.

With a roar, the drill plunged again into the pit without any trouble, finally reaching the soil deep down. The pulleys started creaking, and the mast was slowly hoisted down. The rest of the workers surrounded the drill and waited, leaning on their shovels.

Sviridov raised the drill two more times and cleaned it, while the others measured how much deeper it had to go. They showed him: half a yard. The drill sprang out again victoriously, and people rejoiced and stretched out their hands: on the very tip was a lump of rich black earth. No more clay! The workers broke it off and tossed it across to Sviridov, raising their thumbs: "Hurray!"

Then there was a sudden gurgling noise, as if a bathtub was being drained, and I froze: the drill appeared to be sinking... only its tip protruded above the earth. The people around were covered up to their necks, and were floundering around, while from above the others were screeching like birds, uninterruptedly. As the rain started to thin out, I wobbled to the stairs to offer some help, and I noticed a swirl in the water... The drill wasn't sinking: it was being submerged... it was the water that was rising!

The stairway groaned and swung loose. Some muddy bundles were crawling towards me, trying to clutch at something with their pink claws as a howling noise resounded all around. They seemed to be kicking the water away with their feet, but the water pursued them, engulfing the tents, the boards, the slabs, the boxes – everything. From below Sviridov shouted:

"Ba-a-ack! Rescue! Make rafts!"

And he immediately started kicking his feet and pulling off his clothes. The turbid water seemed to be motionless, but if you glanced at its edges you'd notice that it was rising with a slow and regular sway, spreading wider and wider. Everyone found refuge at the top: the opposite side of the digs was now the opposite shore.

The water's upsurge began to slow. The rain had stopped, and the sky was lightening. All around us, the open field came into view, with its flattened grass, similar to brown seaweed. There was a spring smell of pine needles, and the sparrows fluttered among the wet bushes and the black trees. I approached Sviridov as he was putting on a dry change of clothes.

"That's all thanks to your digging," I said.

He staggered among the silent people crowding around the fires, pausing to look back at the bubbles springing out of the depths.

"Everybody all right? Yes? Or is someone missing? Thank God... we are all alive. No one's missing, eh? Fetch some firewood and form a queue... count each other... who's not here? Everyone here?" And he raised his voice: "It's nothing, boys, we'll rise again! We'll learn from the Americans. The Americans learnt a long time ago how to raise things up! We were unlucky... subterranean water, excessive pressure. They'll believe us!"

Sviridov covered his face with both hands as black cars sped along the road. The cars halted one by one in a herring-bone formation, and doors fluttered open. The last vehicle to arrive was a Ukrainian-made coach.

"Already here? God, they're good at their work..." His chin shook pitifully. "I'll answer for everything. Don't follow me!" And with a faltering step he walked towards the people who were advancing from the cars. I didn't lag behind. Sviridov mumbled something under his breath, wiping his brows with his hand, then he began to speak in a soft sing-song voice, gathering breath for each line with a heavy sigh. When he reached the spot he'd set for himself, he stopped and sank to his knees, spreading his arms like a yoke and wailing aloud.

"Comrade Warrant Officer! Stand up!" I said, jabbing at his shoulder.

"Serves me right! It's up to them now! Nine regional museums..."

"Sviridov – a-a-s you we-ere! Sta-and!" said Gubin, who was the first one to arrive. "What's all this melodrama about? The entire personnel is looking." Vic signalled to his own people to stop. "Don't come here!"

"I was thinking... this lake... for the people. To have a wash... do their laundry. We could have a rest here..." Sviridov dropped his arms and lunged to hug Gubin's knees. "Forgive me!"

"What? Sviridov, please! What on earth are you... Stand up, at attention! It's simply impossible to deal with you in a civilized manner... Look, we're in a hurry... listen to me carefully. We're on our way to meet the President. The town's waiting. We'll carry on with the festivities. It wouldn't be good to call things off. All the more so as everything's ready... We just need to fill in an empty place." Gubin gave me a little shake. "Not many people have seen you in this town. You're similar in size. We'll dress you up. Give you a haircut. And your absence, Comrade Warrant Officer, won't be noticed. You only need to put a little bit of make-up on. Shut up! You'll do it... I'm asking you. I can't just entrust anybody with such a task. All you need to do is to come out onto the porch and look at them. They'll look at you, take a few snapshots... a little drive through the town... we'll shorten the route. And you, all you've got to do is wave your hand. I've thought it all out. Only one other person knows. And now you. I'll be close by. The whole time I'll be close by. Nobody'll come near. And nobody's seen them from close range... That'll be all, word of honour..." Gubin gave me another shake. "I'm not reneging on my promise...

at midday you'll be at the train station. We'll be on time. Let's go, quick, over there, onto that coach: it's got blinds."

An old lady kept looking back at a picture that was invisible to me. I squinted my eyes: another woman was rubbing black powder onto the warrant officer's cheeks. He was sitting without stirring, probably asleep.

What would she pick up now? She crumpled two flat wads of cotton wool and applied them to my cheeks, to make sure they were the right size. She cut out two round patches from a white sheet and soaked their edges with a white liquid smelling of spirit. She attached one of the cotton wads to my cheek and covered it with a patch – its sticky smeared edges came down to the skin. She smoothed the outside of the patch and stuck it down. And then got down to work on the other cheek.

"Dry off a bit. In the meantime, I'll dress you up."

She deftly removed my clothes – I simply raised myself a bit and leant forwards, lifting my legs in turn to thrust them into new trousers – and laced up my boots.

"Not too tight? I'll put the shirt on later so we don't smear it… Smile. Blow your cheeks out. Close your eyes… unclose. That's good… Not too bad. Look in the mirror."

The old lady dabbed my face with some kind of ointment and rubbed the spots around evenly… my skin took on an off-white colour. She smeared my cheekbones with rouge and from here spread it out over my cheeks, to the lower eyelids, to the ears and to the chin. She didn't rouge the pasted cheeks all over, but left on each side a white spot the size of a small coin. The cheeks looked plump and drooping.

With a little bristle brush the woman painted my brows grey, slightly altering their size. With another brush she accentuated my nose with a brown outline, highlighting the nostrils.

334

"Now the lips. Let him smile, OK?"

"Your chap's all right…" said the other woman, who was still putting make-up on Sviridov. "With mine, you won't be able to see anything anyway. Do you think I should whiten his teeth?"

With ticklish touches, her brush extended the lines of my upper and lower lips, raising them slightly to make a smiling mouth. The skin at the corners was crimson red.

"Like new." The old woman burst out laughing. "A bit stiff… Now let's put some age on…"

She dipped a bit of velvet paste into a little jar containing ashy powder and applied it over my face, lingering especially over the temples, the eye sockets and the cupped eyelids… my skin took on an earthy hue.

A bus halted outside. The old women looked at their watches in unison.

"Finished?" asked a closed-cropped soldier, in whom I recognized Klinsky.

From outside people were tapping on the glass with iron rods. I managed to catch sight of a plane heading for the airfield.

"Let's hope it doesn't rain."

Gubin appeared through the doors. He was wearing a fragrant lilac-coloured general's uniform, and holding a service cap in his hand.

"The plane's landed. Run to the guard house. Ladies, thanks a lot, you stay here… there's something in this bag for you to eat. For the time being, stay here." He gazed at me, at my white face, in perplexity. "The car… there it is. In the back door, please… You haven't got a hat? It's a bit cold. Is that how we're meeting him?… all wrong. This way."

The car – massive and sparkling – was waiting right next to the bus. I was hurried in and made to sit opposite the black man, a thickset sweaty man with bulging lips, wearing a light-coloured suit. He was touching everything with his dark hands: the table, the ashtrays, the television, the switches for lowering the windows... There was a noise overhead, and a draught blew on us. The black man wiped the sweat off his brow and examined his hand with some apprehension.

Klinsky closed the bus doors, as Gubin hollered into the distance:

"Let the driver go!" He rammed his cap on his head and gingerly got into the car: "All nice and cosy? Right... off we go now. I thought: better with no escort, no flashing lights... we'll get there and... All right? Sorry about this." He was avoiding my eyes, with a constrained smile. "We'll have to wait a bit. A minute or so. Shall we turn the radio on?"

"This man here," the black man enquired, "is he going with us?"

"Which one do you mean? Oh, the one with crew-cut hair? To be honest, that's the way I wanted it, yes... Although you're right: he's not really an official... But, basically, he's an experienced comrade, and he can help us, eh? Do you have a problem with that? Why are you asking?"

"I suggest we leave him behind."

"Really? To be honest... not that I myself... I think that..." The car stirred, and Gubin pressed his face to the intercom.

"You there? Go to the hotel, via the boulevard... the projection-room entrance... you know it? Off you go!" And he locked the door.

Klinsky turned back adroitly and gazed at the car as it moved off, without budging from the spot.

"You're not cold? You neither? We'll have a little celebration on the spot... we've prepared what we could... you'll see it yourself, I won't tell you anything beforehand... The whole thing can be better watched from the porch... We've decided not to set up a rostrum… but don't worry, you'll be visible to everybody… Pay attention now, please: on that side you can see the poultry factory and the workers' housing… the factory itself is scattered all over the place… there are several production sites. It's the largest in the region. We've signed a contract with the Germans to supply feathers… but growth's been held back by some problems with the standards of quality…" Gubin pressed his lips with his fingers. "Excuse me, can you close… Thank you. Well… we've been waiting so long… And now… I can hardly believe it."

The black man's eyelids had become blood red. He dropped his broad squashed nose and smacked his lips.

"We are approaching," Gubin bent forwards and cleared his throat. "We're ap-proach-ing!… This is our town… just look how beautiful it is…"

The black man shifted in his seat nervously, clenching and unclenching his fists, sniffing like a dog… it was hot, and he was afraid to start sweating. We should have asked for water.

Gubin groped for the intercom.

"Get to the projection room… right to the door. Show them your pass. Get out and knock – they'll open. Then walk to the square. Later you'll take the other man to the station."

"I'm off!"

"But just tell us, please tell us," the black man began to mumble, flaring up and jerking his head around, "I've heard that you have significant archaeological digs here. Would you care to show them to us?"

Gubin was surprised, but after an awkward pause confirmed in a slow and confident tone:

"That is correct. There are indeed some precious deposits," he said, turning to me for some reason. "An entire town. But it's not here. It's further away. On the shore of a lake. A beautiful spot. It's a shame you can't stay here a bit longer. Although… you're very welcome to stay." He strived to smile. "It'll be our pleasure. We can sort something out."

Outside, he dealt with the situation swiftly.

"Dismiss the guards! Take them all away... all away!"

What was that?! A clap of thunder: ponderous, terrifying marches... the hot breath of a multitude of bodies... it was the TV, which the black man had thoughtlessly turned on. As if bewitched, we fixed our eyes on the screen: the square was unrecognizable... covered with caps and shoulders, studded with banners... the square seemed to sway around the iridescent mass of the brass bands, which were thundering away like a heart, sending off sound waves. There was a crackling sound from the TV, and a perfectly ordinary voice close by announced:

"At the Hotel Don, the local authorities and the regional administration have almost completed their presentation to the President of Russia and the Secretary-General of the United Nations. At the moment, the guests are escorted by the Governor Victor Alexeyevich Gubin, on whom, by the President's edict, the rank of Major-General has been just conferred. They will now all emerge onto the front steps of the hotel, and will participate in the celebrations to mark the unveiling of the monument dedicated to the 'Source of the Don'."

At the hardly perceptible wave of a tiny baton, the marches stopped. The players gathered breath, and the national anthem boomed out with an all-encompassing power.

"Quick! Time to go!" Gubin bawled, opening the door. "Please!" He switched off the television, but the anthem thundered even louder from outside, shaking the ground as we ran through the doorway, to the projection room and beyond. We emerged into a spotlessly scrubbed aisle leading up to double glass doors – in the distance glittered the gold of round doorknobs. The upper section of the glass admitted the sky; lower down, clustered buildings, and at the bottom the teeming human mass. I was gasping for breath in the armour plating of my padded jacket... the black man tried to control his shaking hands.

Gubin leant against the wall, panting – his pale, contorted face thrown back, as if he were in pain. He pulled himself together, pushed his cap down resolutely on his head and, as soon as the anthem ended, threw the doors open and crossed the porch with an assured stride before the eyes of the roaring crowd. For a long time he held up one arm to silence them, while with the other he fumbled for a piece of paper in his pocket.

"This day... for many centuries..."

I didn't understand very much. He was reading short, re-sounding words. Whenever he made a pause, the square burst with applause.

"The history of our great country..."

My shirt was now soaking wet... the hot perspiration dulled my vision, hindered my breathing. I was afraid I'd collapse. I expected each time they clapped their hands it would be our turn to speak. But he read on...

"Achievements... now on the way..."

When the wind opened the doors slightly, a cold draught brought some relief to me. It seemed the whole thing would pass off all right...

Gubin wobbled his way back through the doors, waving his cap over his sweating face. There was not a sound in the square. As the black man headed towards the glass doors, Gubin darted after him with a raised hand, baying like a dog: "Hey-hey-hey."

He dragged the black man back to me, and my elbow offered itself to Gubin. He pushed us forwards, through the doors, onto the raised porch... and high into the sky flew the tousled pathways of fireworks... intersecting, swelling with flashes and outbursts, swelling with light, then turning into flowers and disappearing without a trace.

"Hurray! Hurray!" reverberated below.

Gubin spoke softly into the microphone, and the square went dead.

"Dear friends! We have all been waiting so long for this day! And we've done so much to make it happen. I'll give the honour of unveiling the monument... the Source of the Don... to the President... of the Russian Federation!" Gubin clapped his hands with vigour, and everyone followed his example. He smiled at me encouragingly and shook his head like a horse – there you go! I stepped to the microphone.

"W-we..." The roaring from the square didn't abate... my voice was not amplified. Gubin waved his cap as if to say "no need" and, striking his hands together and making an imploring face, he raised his right elbow. Like a mirror image, I raised my arm, as if wishing to put my hair straight.

"Hurray! Hurray!" echoed around, the sound turning into a low rumble and gathering afresh. "Hurray!"

The cord slipped from the block, and the veil fell down in chunks, like a sheet from a wet body, revealing the stone bulk of the monument on which all the lights were now trained. Immediately after, the snowy tendrils of the fountain rocketed upwards. I suppose it was my arm that had done that.

"Hur-ray! Hur-ray!" rose up and died away, as the banners whirled around and white doves soared high in the sky, growing darker. Gubin took three strides to the step below us and stopped right in front of us. He put his hand behind his back and wagged it... I raised my hand and wagged it in the same manner, as if wiping an invisible glass.

At that, the ranks of people merged and launched into a folk dance, squatting in waves and unleashing their foamy skirt hems, while some parachutists formed a star in the sky. Gubin was clapping his hands more and more, and the nearby officer did the same. I couldn't see a single face... I didn't even feel the wind... I wanted to step down... what if I stumbled into the glass? In the surrounding screeching and whistling, the black man – as if he'd been cranked up – began to beat his palms together and to repeat some words. He was weeping, his padded lips coming off piteously, while black tears dribbled down into his shirt and collar.

And then a united shout of delight rose over the square: they had seen us, they had understood our message! The dances merged, people waved to us and shouted. The black man, his face still wrinkled up from crying, struck me even more firmly on the shoulder and squeezed my arm, raising his black fist. I clapped and clapped, connecting my palms with difficulty. I was breathing... I was alive... I was about to go away... everything was coming to an end... I easily tore my gaze from the people and looked at the surrounding buildings, but there were more people in the way, waving, letting off rockets from every window, scattering armfuls of flowers. I raised my eyes to the roofs, but there people in white capes were forming themselves into letters of the alphabet as they lifted on their shoulders gymnasts and dancers. I raised my gaze to the smokestacks etched against the sky, and the town stumbled away and finally let me go. The black man grabbed a microphone for support and rubbed it in his hands like an apple. He nudged me towards the microphone, and I submitted like a puppet. He suddenly pointed at me and bellowed with all his might:

"Turn it on! I call on you to speak..."

I saw Gubin swinging backwards, almost falling flat on his back, but before he could utter a word the black man had already struck the microphone's head with his finger, and a drumbeat was now echoing round the whole square... it was on! Everyone fell dead silent. The black man raised his left hand, and with the right gave me a nudge.

"Tell them!" His eyebrowless face crumpled up with greasy folds of plasticine, supplicating: "You tell them! Yes? No?" He released my shoulder. "No." He touched his hair and swept his gaze around the square, from one end to the other.

"People," he continued. "He," and he indicated me, "knows the truth. How things really are here... he knows. No more of this! That's what we are here for," and the black man peered round searchingly, as if he'd brought something and put it down somewhere. "Here! Here!" he pointed at Gubin, who stood as if petrified, chewing his lips in a frenzy. "Come here, you!... Officers, take him away to stand trial... for his lies to the people!"

There was a commotion in the crowd. Gubin was seized and borne away, as if by a wave. In front of us stood four officers at attention, hands held to their caps. I couldn't make out what they were saying, but the black man heard.

"What? Aren't you ashamed? It's not me you should serve! It's the people! Them!" He invited everyone, including me, downstairs. "Let's go among the people!" And down we went. "There, go among them!" We had to follow him at a run. "There, go among them!" The black man was galloping ahead at full speed, arms held in front. The commanding officers and the policemen in black uniforms, hysterically sticking their faces to their walkie-talkies or blowing their whistles – and everyone else around – were also racing down. From a roof a helicopter took off, and a voice resounded from the sky:

"Remain in your places! Carry on with the welcoming ceremony!"

But the crowd was retreating... people were fleeing from the square. Many turned their backs and tried to make their way out, and from the heart of the crowd some children in Russian costume, with bunches of white flowers, were pushed towards us. At the sight of the black man, the children faltered and huddled close to each other, then turned back, throwing the flowers aside and weeping wildly. People were running away on all sides, bursting into the streets, streaming off into the alleyways, cramming into the entrances of the buildings.

"What? Where are they going?" the black man wailed. "What, isn't there anybody left?" The commanding officers shouted "Back!" and ran around in pursuit like shepherd dogs.

"Assemble the pursuers! Let's get the people back! Quick! Get in!"

A long open car, the kind used for the inspection of military ranks, with a soldier sitting woodenly at the wheel, drew up and stopped. The black man jumped in and gave directions. "There!" He laughed and jabbed his finger into my side. "Don't worry, we'll get them! Everyone will be coming back!"

Along the kerbs the remaining people were scattering, jumping over fences, hiding behind the boulevard benches, sneaking into the bushes, slamming windows and balcony doors, in a swift, businesslike fashion. Behind us formed a chain of black polished cars, lorries, jeeps and armoured cars with flashing lights on their roofs. Now we could see the whole length of the street, and the dark mass running away. In the heat of pursuit, the black man opened his mouth and wheezed, "We'll overtake them," raising his hand to let those at the back know. We must have been going very fast, because it seemed that the people were actually running up to meet us. The soldier slammed the brakes on.

"What?" barked the black man.

"They're running back."

The black man drew himself erect. "A-ha... They are, aren't they? Halt!" he stood on the seat, assumed a dignified air and pronounced "Well, then? Now you see!"

People were tearing towards us, their exhausted mouths wide open, their faces red, their hair tousled, their legs weakening and stumbling... they were running in broad strides, disappearing into the nearest dark courtyards. There was an indistinct cry, repeated over and over... I shuddered... Look... don't close your eyes now. Without stopping, they tore past as if they didn't see us, as if through an empty space, down an abyss. There were screams behind our backs: someone was trying to stop the crowd. People were leaning on our car, which started rocking. The only thing I could see was hands: hands... hands... hands. The black man was twirling around as if in a frying pan.

"Stop! Listen to me! What are they shouting?" He tugged at the soldier. "Do you understand their vernacular?"

People were streaming around us... it turned out there weren't too many of them, and they went past very quickly. The street was empty again, but in the distance another solid, silent shadow was bearing down on us. A few stragglers went by, stumbling in cast-off gloves and scarves, and all shouting the same word, which it was now possible to make out:

"Rats!... Rats!..."

"R-rats?" the black man repeated incredulously. I gave the driver's shoulders a violent shove.

"Turn round! Turn round!" I mustn't look, no!

With an unbearably slow manoeuvre the car jerked forwards, then back... It was not easy on that narrow street, and the other vehicles struggled to turn round too. The car, honking away, rolled onto soft ground and grass, mounting the stone border of the kerb.

"Faster!"

"Back!"

But we couldn't go back: there were people running away everywhere, blocking the way. We skidded right, and the black man caught sight of something.

344

"Rats!" He thumped the driver. "Get moving! Quicker." The car tore off, and from a by-street on the left-hand side a fire engine moved into the road.

It was warming up, and through the snow the bluish ground was showing.

At the railway station they opened the windows. Sparrows were hopping around Oldie's feet: he was eating sunflower seeds.

Larionov was carrying the bags along the platform.

"Let's go. The train's due any moment now. I've got something for you for the journey… you can have it with your tea… Here." He paused, then added softly: "I've put the money underneath. Do you want to count it? Fine. The local train will take you as far as Yeletz, then they'll attach it to a fast train. Well then… I wish I could see you off there."

"That's fine. Thanks for this."

"All our people send greetings to you. They wanted to see you off, but they're all busy…"

From behind the shunting sheds, from under the bridge, a locomotive was pushing forwards. A workman holding a small yellow flag stuck out from the front.

"Vladimir Stepanovich," the architect said, without releasing Oldie's hands. "Well, basically, you… please forgive us that it's all turned out like this."

Oldie stooped and picked up the bags, then carried them into the carriage. They had attached three carriages: one for passengers, and the others for post and luggage. Parcels and sacks sealed with wax were loaded there. Oldie wiped the glass, covered with two layers of dust. He turned on the radio, but music was carried over from the town. He got down onto the platform and sat on a bronze-painted bin, listening.

345

* * *

Where were we going? We were returning to Moscow. Ahead of us winter was leaving feet first, flowing away into the drains. At Ozherelye it was still summer. Oldie left the train, had some beer in a refreshment room by the bridge, and sank down beneath a lilac bush by a broad-headed water tower: its lowest third was made of uneven white stone with hoops and columns, the middle of pre-revolutionary blood-red bricks, and the highest section was of Soviet carrot-coloured bricks; beneath the roof was the date – 1949. He began to wait for the suburban train to Moscow.

I crossed the bridge, looking into the open goods wagons: there were logs, ballast, coal, pipes. Since the last time they'd dug out some pits and extended some walls. Passing through the construction site I went out onto a field, which was enclosed by fences and dotted with rusting telephone booths and shells of vehicles. I crossed a brook over a log... beyond the next gully a village straggled to the right and downwards. I climbed to the left over a broad, even slope, where people went around looking for something in the smooth grass.

Hello again... hello. I wasn't planning to visit today. You're always saying the same thing: drunk again, wearing rags again.

I put only one stone with your name on it. It'd be silly to have a photo on it. I weeded out all the shoots when I visited... I didn't want a tree to grow there... We've been just passing, that's why I'm here. Yes, on our way from work. And Oldie too, he's at the station. It's true I don't come often enough. It's a bit far... you're not coming very often, either... Although – you must have noticed – it's become more difficult to be together. You've been so scatterbrained of late. It's difficult to talk seriously with you. I keep forgetting to tell you... you don't even know how much we've earned. Over two weeks. But you said I could never earn a living. Now we'll expand… hire people. I'll rent a house here. This winter. Then I can come more often. And complete my thesis… it only needs to be retyped and checked for sources… a lot of hassle, of course, but I have to polish it properly… lock myself up for two months. I'll be working only at home. Once a week in the library. I'll write a paper on baiting methods. How I live… you know it yourself… You see how I manage without you… I'm ashamed. But you didn't leave anything for me. Once, in the summer, I was cleaning my teeth… it was dark… I used to come home late, so I was cleaning my teeth and suddenly realized that the greater part of my life will be spent without you. I knew that already, but it had suddenly sunk in… I only hope that the time between my visits passes quickly for you… it's painful for me to think you're thinking about me all the time. Perhaps you do have something else to think about. Perhaps you go elsewhere sometimes. There's lots of space here, it's far away from any houses. Here, it's the birds that eat biscuits and dry bread. And there's no water. It's not like that in the city. Water's the most important thing for them, but here it's dry. All the same, I look under my feet when I walk here… don't be scared. I wanted to tell you that I haven't forgotten you. Where I live, there's a nursery next door… there's a girl there with the same name as you… she's running away all the time, a real little livewire. I often hear someone calling her… the boys run after her like idiots, shouting your name. I'll come again. And often now. Will you come with me? Wouldn't you like to? But why? I'm only joking. I know all about it. Shall I come to you then? Yes? I don't know myself what I should do. I myself… don't know what I should do. What? I can't hear you – and you know, I don't see you so well now. I'm forgetting your features… no, I remember everything, but it's disappearing almost by itself. All right. No… now I have so much time… but I don't want to cry here.

Acknowledgements

The publisher wishes to thank the invaluable assistance of Natasha Perova from GLAS, a Russian publisher devoted to the promotion of true literary talent. Without all her efforts and her painstaking editorial work, this book would not have been possible.

Alexander Terekhov graduated from Moscow University's Department of Journalism and won acclaim as a writer of short stories. His work has since been translated into French, German and English. He spent his childhood in a small industrial town in central Russia, which still preserved "the spirit of the early builders of communism", and his resulting disillusionment underlies both the complex structure and the atmospheric milieu of *The Rat Catcher*.